BLACK LANTERN
BOOK ONE

Between the Lines

S. P. GIBSON

This book is for all the girls who made it out alive, you are stronger than you give yourself credit for.

Content Warnings

Between the lines is a contemporary romance book that deals with some serious topics. Each character struggles with their own issues and problems that are delved into in different details. If you want to avoid spoilers, feel free to skip past this page and continue onto reading Stella and Luke's love story. The content warnings include:

- Sexually explicit content
- Sexual assault and abusive relationships (not on page, but heavily referenced)
- Toxic parental and familial relationships
- Anxiety, depression (loose mention) and on page panic attacks
- Chronic illness struggles

Playlist

Can We Dance - The Vamps
Wild Heart - The Vamps
Dress - Taylor Swift
The Bolter - Taylor Swift
The Prophecy - Taylor Swift
No Control - One Direction
Boyfriend - Ariana Grande and Social House
Someone To You - Banners
July - Noah Cyrus
Clean - Taylor Swift
Favorite Crime - Olivia Rodrigo
Paradise - Bazzi
Seven - Taylor Swift
You've Got The Love - Florence + The Machine
Poison & Wine - The Civil Wars
Bed Chem - Sabrina Carpenter
Friends - Chase Atlantic
They Don't Know - One Direction

If I Can't Have You - Shawn Mendes
Brother - Kodaline
Treat you Better - Shawn Mendes
Mess It Up - Gracie Abrams
Stranger - Olivia Rodrigo

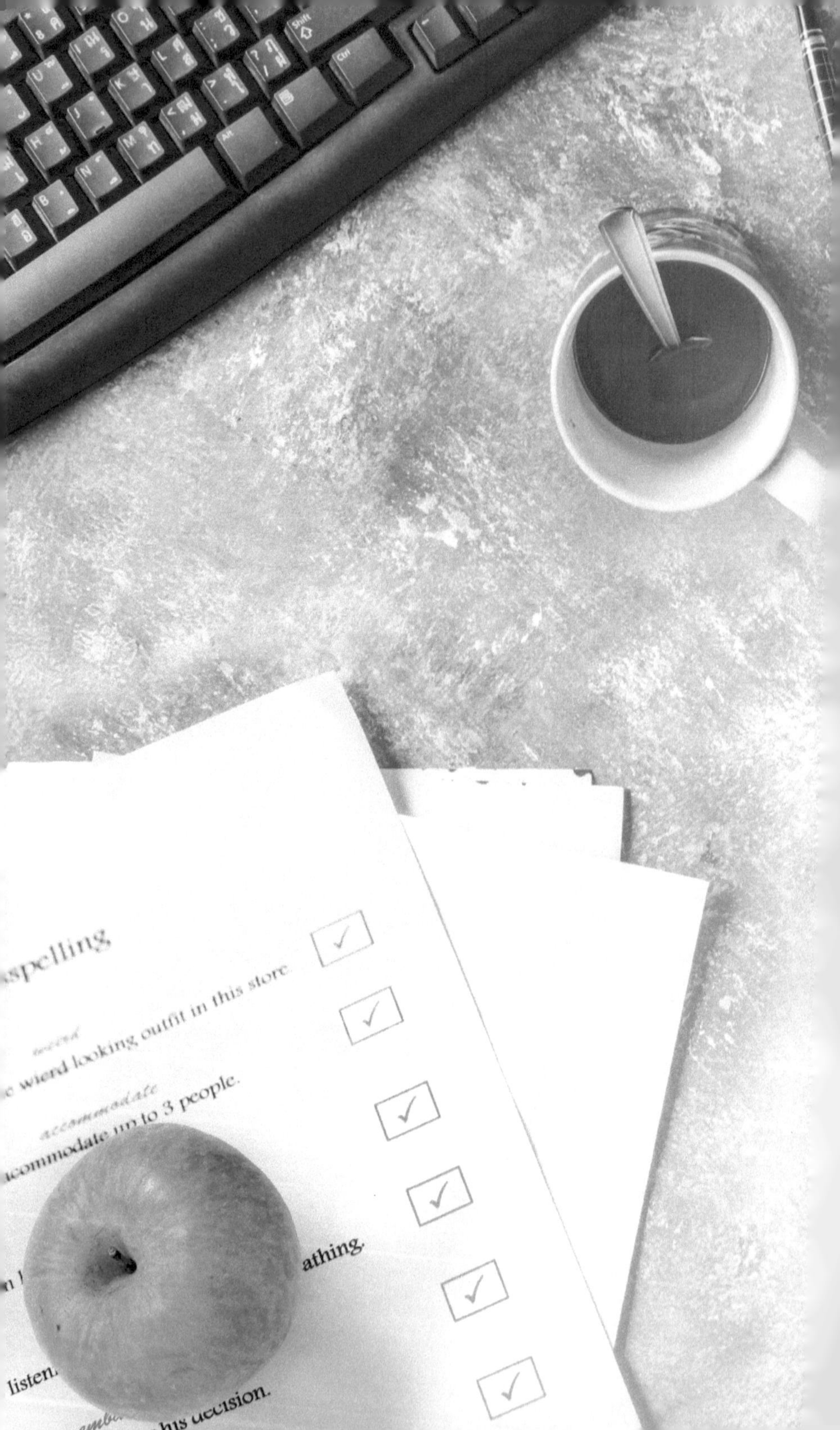
spelling
wierd
e wierd looking outfit in this store.
accommodate
ccommodate up to 3 people.
athing.
listen.
his decision.

Chapter One

STELLA

LOOK, I TOTALLY AGREE WITH WHAT NELSON Mandela said about education being the most powerful weapon, but at this moment – standing in a dimly lit bathroom – I have to convince myself not to strangle a group of seven-year-olds. If dodging surprise attacks and surviving blacklight paint ambushes at the hand of children is part of the job, I definitely missed that section in the teaching handbook. In this moment – standing in the bathroom watching the patches of paint get larger as I scrub instead of smaller – I have to convince myself not to quit.

My roommate, Keets, warned me that this lesson plan for my first class may not translate or come across well with a group of year ones last night at dinner. I immediately called her out on her lack of support as a best friend, and insisted it would be a hit. And inevitably it was – on me. Especially considering my choice to wear a white dress on this fine Monday.

Ever since I got my teaching assistant diploma over the summer, the school has been asking a lot more out of me.

Which I guess makes sense, since I am now actually qualified to assist with the students in a closer way than before. No more standing in the corner, silently begging to do something. It's good in a way. I like being helpful, and I like the job – but I'm exhausted.

It's not anyone's fault, it's just what happens when you have an understaffed school. Hillside Primary is the only primary school in Brookstone and the surrounding towns. Brookstone is known for our public university, the one I go to, and it's pretty renowned because of the academic standard it holds. However, because of its reputation, the local council pours every resource into keeping it well-known. Claiming it's more important to have people coming through Brookstone than to upkeep it for the people who live here. That means that anything unimportant to tourists or the university gets put on the back burner - the primary school included. I honestly don't know if they will be able to make it through one more budget cut.

"Stella?" I hear Ms. Graystone call from outside the bathroom. "You okay in there, hon?"

I quickly throw the wads of paper towels in the trash and straighten out my dress. "Yup! One Second!" I call out, taking a deep breath. I unlock the door and step out, seeing Ms. Graystone waiting for me.

Her gaze falls down to my dress, seeing the patchy splotches that have stained nearly every inch.

"I'm so sorry about that! You are more than welcome to take off early to change, or just to avoid a homicide." She smiles sweetly. This is one of the things I love about the staff here; they all have a sense of humour. Most of my colleagues are at least ten years older than I, but it doesn't feel like it.

I laugh, shaking my head. "Don't worry about me. Just part of the job." I move to walk back into the classroom.

"Very true." She jokes, following behind me. Walking into the classroom, all feelings of anger evaporate immediately. The three boys who were ringleaders in the brutal attack I faced are standing in front of me, holding a card they've painted with neon paint. It has 'we're sorry' written across the front with smiley faces and rainbows surrounding the empty space. Looking down at their earnest faces, paint still drying in splotches on their cheeks, I can't help but smile. Moments like this are what make the chaos worth it.

"We're sorry, Ms. Faraday," Jackson says, stepping forward with the card, as Erik and Milo echo the apology. I reach out to grab the card from them.

"It's okay, let's just keep the paint to ourselves next time."

The three of them nod eagerly before turning back to look at Lily, whom I just noticed standing behind them. Her arms are crossed as she stares at them intently. If she wasn't wearing a sparkly unicorn dress, I'd think she was the teacher here.

"Is that okay?" Milo says, his voice wavering. I struggle to stop myself from laughing when I realise how scared of her they clearly are.

She gives them a once-over before nodding, causing them to sprint outside where the majority of the class has moved on to a new experiment.

Once they're gone, her serious demeanour drops and she runs up to me. "I would give you a hug, but I like my dress too much to ruin it with…" She gestures to the now dry paint on my dress. "That."

I nod in understanding, squatting down so that I'm at

the same height as her. "Did you make them apologise, Lilybug?"

She nods quickly, proud. "They were wrong. My mum says you always have to apologise when you are wrong. They got a little mad at me, though." She pulls at the edge of her dress, suddenly unsure. "Was that okay?"

My smile grows. Lily is one of the sweetest kids I've ever met. She is kind to every single person she meets, but also has an iron fist she isn't frightened to wield. Exhibit A with the boys. I adore how unapologetic she is. She's my favourite girl in the class, and if I'm being honest, probably my favourite overall.

"You weren't mean to them?"

She shakes her head, "Not meaner than they were to you."

I laugh slightly. "Then, of course, it's okay."

The look of stress disappears from her face, and her sweet smile comes back. She's got auburn hair that she wears differently every single day. I always thought the red hair suited her fiery personality. There isn't a single other colour that would fit.

"We should probably go back to the class, huh?" She asks, turning her head towards the group outside. I think they are doing elephant's toothpaste. Remembering the lesson plan – there wasn't any teaching with this one. Just that it was a cool experiment that could be used as a break for the kids.

"Maybe," I say. She perks up slightly, sensing the mischievous tone in my voice. "Or we could skip the rest of the demonstration, and you could show me how you do that criss-cross jump rope trick?"

Her eyes light up, the excitement obvious. "You mean

it?" She asks, shifting on her feet. I grab her hand, standing up.

"Lead the way, Lilybug," I say, quickly sending a text to Graystone letting her know that Lil needed a small break. Lily starts running ahead of me, her fiery hair bouncing with every step. Her energy is contagious. Today I think the rules can bend just a little bit.

The second the bell rang I was out of there. For the first time in weeks, we didn't have any after-school activities that needed extra assistance – meaning I had a free evening. Once I stepped out of the door, I relished the cold breeze, making the tip of my nose freeze slightly. I've always loved spring and summer, but there's something so lovely about a sunny winter day.... I really need to start dressing more weather-appropriate, though. Shockingly, skirts and thin stockings aren't known for being great in the dead of winter. Brookstone is a small university town a few hours from Sydney by train. We are close enough that in summer, the beach is right there, but far enough away that autumn and winter have that perfect small town feel.

Wrapping my scarf around my neck, I start the walk back towards my apartment. The school is on the other side of town from the university, but I don't mind the walk. It's the perfect time to listen to depressing music and contemplate every conversation I've ever had in my entire life.

It's the little things, you know?

As I go to put in my earbuds, I hear a vibrating sound from my pocket. Taking it out, I see it's my mother, likely seeing that it's past 3:00 pm and knowing I would be free. I pick up after the first ring.

"Hey mum," I say, my hands freezing slightly, holding the phone up to my ear.

"Hey, chicken. How was your day?"

She asks cheerfully. One of the many things I love about my mother is how happy she always is. Keets reminds me a lot of her.

"It was good. Long, but good in the end. Excited to go relax for a bit though." The cold air nips my tongue as I talk, making me shiver slightly.

"That's good! Hey, I was meaning to ask – are you spending Christmas with me or your dad this year? I'm just trying to organise my entire life on this lovely winter afternoon."

My mum and dad have been divorced practically since I was born. They weren't a love match by any means – I was the product of a drunken one-night stand that resulted in an elopement because they thought that's what they should do. Pretty soon, they realised that getting married to someone you've known for 24 hours rarely works out. That being said, they are really good friends and have both remarried people whom they love. I have one half-sibling on my dad's side, a little brother. I'm not crazy close with him because of the age difference – but I still love him to death. We started splitting up the holidays once I was old enough to travel. It honestly was just easier than the passive-aggressive argument each year about who would travel where. It works for them and it works for me.

"Dads," I said, stepping around some uneven pavement. "I'm gonna be with you in January if that's still okay?"

"Of course! I can't wait to have you!" She takes a breath. Her tell-tale sign for asking a completely invasive and 'motherly' question.

"Are you going to bring anyone home for the holidays this year?"

I rub my forehead, fighting the urge to sigh. "Mum, it's July. I'm seeing you in January."

"I know." She says, an edge in her voice giving away her plot. "I just would love to see you with someone. I want to see you happy."

I roll my eyes, stopping in the path. Personally, I feel like being 21 and single is a completely normal life choice – but my mother seems to disagree. The thing is, it's not like I'm not interacting with the other sex. I am a lot. Just not in the way that you can tell your 50-year-old mother over the phone.

"I am happy, Mum. I promise. I'd be happier if we changed the conversation, though." I hear her sigh on the other end, resigning to the fact that once again her daughter would be solo for the holidays.

"Okay, okay, I'll drop it."

"How's book club going?" I ask, knowing she recently started reading again after going part-time in her job. She starts talking about the girls in her book club, giving me time to connect my earbuds and look through my notifications. I've pretty much come to terms with the fact that my thought-inducing walk was not going to happen.

When I'm at Hillside, I turn all my notifications off. It's really important to me to give 100% of my attention to the kids. I don't want them to ever feel like they are pulling me away from something. Plus, seeing the influx of messages at the end of the day always gives my ego a little bit of a boost. Two messages catch my eye. The first is from my classmate Rory asking about our study session for tomorrow. I thumbs up the message before moving onto the second one. It's from Keets, my roommate.

Keets: So I am feeling a getting wine drunk and watching reality TV type of night. You down?

I type out the easiest response I've ever written.

Me: Do you even need to ask?

She likes the message, and I put my phone back in my pocket, fully tuning back into the conversation with my mum, trying to pretend like I'm thinking about anything else but that bottle of Moscato that's waiting for me at home.

you were trying to escape. There's a stage at the end of the room that's only slightly raised, with a singular mic stand reserved for karaoke night. Along the windows, there are booths that are always just a little bit sticky with dark red seats that match the bar stools. The walls are covered with vintage band posters and neon signs.

I think I'm obsessed with whoever decorated it.

From the moment Keets and I walk inside, I notice a couple of guys looking in our direction. I pull at my blue top, showing a bit more of the white bra that matches my skirt perfectly. I know I look good tonight, and I'm not ashamed to admit it.

I notice a couple of guys I think are cute, but decide to leave them hanging for a bit. I want to spend some time with Keets first, and I need a bit more of a buzz before talking to anyone.

"He's here." She tugs at my arm, causing me to look towards the bar. Lo and behold, Rory is there serving a group of guys. It's odd though. He's the only one there. Usually, on a night this busy, they'd have at least two, if not three, bartenders to keep up with everyone.

"You mean the love of your life?" I feel Keet's hand clamp over my mouth, and I start laughing. Just when I'm about to lick her hand to get it off, I notice some of our other friends heading towards us.

"Keets!! Stella!! Oh my god, hi!" Imogen runs up to us with Emily following behind. We all lived on the same floor in the first year and have stuck together since. We've grown apart in the last year as we've all started focusing more on university, but we still like to see each other whenever we can.

"Hi!" We walk up and give each of them a hug.

"Okay, so here's what I'm thinking." Emily moves, so we are huddled around each other. Anyone looking on would think we were having a pow wow. "Group of rugby guys over by the bar. There are four of them, so one for each of us."

"Great plan," Keets interjects. "However, it's hard to agree to any game plan without a drink in my hand." She turns to me and grabs my hand. "Shall we?" Keets leads me towards the bar.

We are walking off when I hear Imogen dragging Emily to the dance floor, struggling to get her to leave behind her rugby team.

As we get up to the bar, Keets starts to order her drink with Rory. She's making some joke about the guys he just served, and he seems interested. Didn't notice I was there. I step back and walk to the other end of the bar, giving them some space. I'm content to just wait, but the universe clearly has other plans for me when I hear a deep voice clear his throat.

"What can I get for you, Goldie?"

Jesus Christ. Lucas is staring directly at me. He's wearing a white t-shirt that shows his tattoos on his left arm, and it is just tight enough to see his biceps strain slightly at the edge of the sleeve. He has a cap on backwards and a dishcloth over his shoulder. I guess I can see the James Dean comment.

"Didn't your mother teach you it's not polite to stare?" He pulls me out of my trance, and I lock eyes with him.

"My bad. I was trying to come up with reasons to excuse myself as quickly as possible." I smile, not moving a muscle.

"You don't like me."

"Wow, he can actually understand basic human emotions. Shocking."

"You don't know me." He states, matter-of-factly.

"I know you," I respond.

"Please share, Goldie."

"You are nice to everyone, you smile, you laugh, you joke. You make everyone love you. But it's all part of the act. The whole 'nice guy' thing? It's a performance, and every person who falls for it is just another round of applause."

"Ouch." He says, but there's still the hint of a smile on his face. "You know what I think?"

"Enlighten me."

"I think you actually do like me, but for some reason you're trying to convince yourself you don't." He leans on the bar, moving close to me. "How warm am I?"

I lean in closer to him.

"You've never been colder. Oh, and by the way-" I go up on the tips of my toes and move my mouth right beside his ear. I grab the collar of his shirt to pull him a bit closer to me – I feel his breath hitch. One of the straps of my shirt falls as I do, but I leave it. "Your breath stinks."

He lets out a chest laugh and pulls his head back just slightly. Still just a tad closer than he should be. His eyes trail down my shirt, stopping on my now bare shoulder. His fingers are cold as he goes to pull up my strap, a shiver passing through my body as he does.

"I know I don't know you, but I'm pretty good at reading people. Let me prove it to you." My eyes narrow slightly, but I nod, unsure of what he's about to do.

He moves away from the bar and turns around to grab a couple of bottles. He methodically pours different liquids into a shaker. He adds some ice into the shaker and starts to mix it. I watch as he moves so naturally, smiling and chatting to people. His wrist flexes slightly as he keeps shaking the drink.

Lucas pulls out a strainer and pours the drink into a glass over a big ice cube and adds a mint leaf on top, examining the glass for a second before placing it in front of me.

I don't do anything. Neither does he.

"Are you going to drink it?" I shrug my shoulders, enjoying the look of anger growing on his face. Teasing Lucas is fun. He leans down, pushing the glass closer towards me.

"Goldie, drink it." There's authority in his voice.

I reluctantly pick up the glass and have a sip. Damn it, it's good. I've never had a cocktail like it. It's the perfect mix between alcohol and mixer, and there's a freshness I wasn't expecting.

"There's mint in it."

He nods slightly. "Saw your cup in the library, so thought it was a fair bet." He pauses, "Also good to help with the allergies." I take another sip, glaring at his growing grin. "You're not going to say anything else?"

I see Keets walking towards us out of the corner of my eye. I quickly down the drink, enjoying the feeling of the burn as it goes down my throat.

"Don't think you need any increase to your ego." He smirks before I grab Keets' hand. She smiles at Lucas, and he nods back.

"I want to dance!" I say as Keets nods eagerly, leading me towards the dance floor. "See you later, Lucas."

"It's Luke."

I'm looking away from him and say over my shoulder.

"Thought calling each other the wrong name was our thing."

Just as I am engulfed by the dance floor, I swear I see the slightest hint of a blush on his face.

Chapter Six

LUKE

SHE KNOWS MY NAME. I DON'T KNOW IF I EVER told her my name, but she knows it. People make jokes about my ego, but I don't think it's egotistical to know your standing. Most people know who I am and like to think they know me. And I don't mean that in a condescending asshole way. It's just that I'm one of the main bartenders at the favourite spot. People think that knowing the bartender's name will somehow get them a discount or free drink. And don't get me started on the number of people who have a fantasy of going home with one of us. Beck and Rory definitely indulge in that side of the job more than I do. Hats off to them, but casual hookups just aren't my thing.

Unfortunately, I am the type of person who develops feelings quickly. Or at least I do when I let myself. I've had casual arrangements that have gone well, and casual arrangements that have made me feel like pulling my hair out piece by piece. I'm a romantic, what can I say? There's also the part where I want to open a bar the second I graduate. I don't have time to give my all to that and to another person at the same time. Staying single is easier.

I'm still surprised that she admitted she knew my name. Stella seems like the type of person who'd rather hang herself than admit that she knows anything about me. It's not hard to spot her in the crowd, dancing with the girl she was with right in the middle. It feels like the crowd has parted just enough that I can watch the way her hips move with the music. She moves her hands up her body, lifting the bottom edge of her shirt just slightly. The little sliver of skin I'm left with makes my mouth go dry.

Stella looks around her, shooting flirty smiles at the guys looking at her. She knows exactly what she's doing and the impact it has.

And fuck if I don't like that.

She turns her head back towards the bar and sees me looking at her. I lean on the bar, staring unapologetically. Her smile is off to the side slightly as she wraps her arms around her friend and keeps swaying. What I would do to be that girl right now.

"Who are you looking at?" Rory interrupts my thoughts.

"No one, just making sure everyone is good on the dance floor." I turn to face him, expecting to see him looking at me. Instead, I catch him staring off, looking in the same direction I was previously.

Now it's my turn to ask.

"Who are you looking at?"

He quickly whips his head back to look at me.

"Just doing my job."

We both look at each other. It's pretty clear we are both talking out of our asses, but neither of us wants to admit it. Someone calls my name for a drink, saving me from continuing whatever this is. I nod at him before making my way down the bar to actually work.

Fucking hell. I forgot how busy it gets on Thursdays. It doesn't help that Beck bailed on us last minute, claiming he had to go fix something. Usually these nights are my favourite, the three of us fucking around for hours on end. But tonight, I feel overwhelmed. There's a massive group of girls down by Rory who seem more interested in asking him about his life story than actually ordering. And the couple sitting in front of me are making me feel more confident in my single status.

"I don't always take over things. How dare you say that to me!"

"You do. You literally just tried to order for me. How is that not taking over everything I do?"

"You're being dramatic." The girl rolls her eyes, seemingly used to this.

"Are you on your period or something?"

Ouch. Not the right thing to say. Even I know that. I can see the rage flash across her face and decide to step in before we have to deal with a crime scene.

"Folks, I'm so sorry to interrupt but it's really busy tonight. Could we try this whole ordering thing again?"

I'm met with two sets of eyes glaring at me. Guess not then.

I let my eyes wander back to the dance floor as the couple goes back to fighting. I try to look for Stella, but she's not in the same place anymore. The blonde girl she was dancing with is still there with some other girls, but Stella is nowhere to be found. I look through the crowd, before spotting her standing against a wall with a guy standing in front of her. He has his arm on the wall next to her, and he's not doing a very good job at keeping eye contact.

I can't fully tell in the dark, but it looks like one of the rugby guys Rory was serving earlier. He's got short, dirty blonde hair and is just slightly taller than her. Didn't think that was her type. I see Stella twirl her fingers around her hair and look up at him. She's laughing at something he said, and her other hand goes to lightly smack him on the shoulder. Whatever she says next makes his mouth turn up, excitement flashing across his features.

It doesn't take long before she stands taller to move closer to his face. She says something quietly and pulls back to look at his face. He smiles, nodding before pulling her towards the bathrooms. The whole interaction lasted maybe five minutes. There's a twinge of something in my chest that I can't place, but honestly, the main thing I'm feeling right now is impressed. I've never been that good at picking girls up – might need her to teach me a thing or two.

She comes out of the bathroom twenty minutes later, giggling uncontrollably, and finds her way back to her friends. Her hair is still styled perfectly and her lipstick freshly applied. The clothes she's wearing don't look even remotely different than when she left. I don't dwell on why that information makes me smile.

Or on the fact that I'm watching her the rest of the night until she leaves right before closing, nodding at me as she walks out.

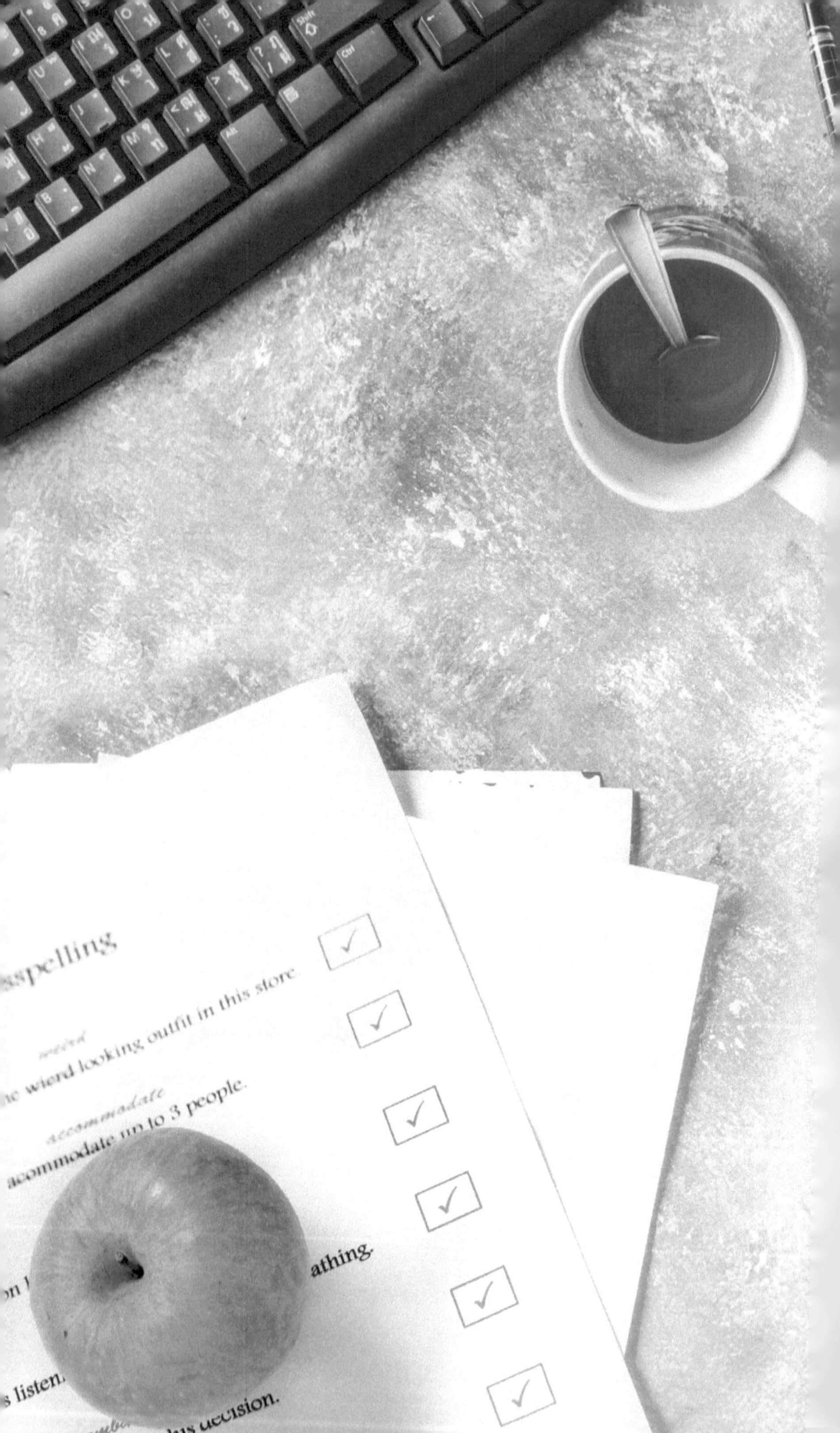
spelling
wierd
he wierd looking outfit in this store.
acommodate
acommodate up to 3 people.
athing
s listen.
his decision.

Chapter Seven

STELLA

WE GOT HOME AROUND 3 LAST NIGHT, BUT WHEN Imogen and Emily decided to stay, I knew we were going to be up until sunrise, debriefing about the night before. Keets makes us some popcorn, as I pull all the blankets and pillows onto the floor. It's not long before we are all seated, talking about the people we saw.

That's my favorite part of a night out – the way it feels to laugh with your friends about all the stupid stuff you each did throughout the night. It took them all of five minutes to ask about what happened with the rugby player.

"See, guys, this is why we listen to Emily's game plans. So at least one of us gets action." She points towards me, and I dip my head in fake shame.

"What can I say? I don't kiss and tell." Popcorn is thrown at my face, from all directions – including from Keets, who is lying in my lap.

"Yeah, bullshit. When have you never not given us all the dirty details?" I see Imogen's attempt at wiggling her eyebrows – or at least that's what I think she's doing.

They're right. I stand by that the second-best part of hooking up with someone is getting to tell your girls everything ten minutes later. Best part if you don't reach the big O. Tonight, it's the best.

My friends are pretty used to this debrief, and I'm usually the one giving it. All my friends enjoy their nights out, but none quite as frequently as I. I used to feel like I should be ashamed or something for hooking up with guys. Like the fact that my body count is in the double digits is something I should hide. Then I realised that was my internalised misogyny talking and that it was complete bullshit to think a girl couldn't enjoy sex as much as a guy could.

I didn't use to be so casual about hooking up. I made a big deal out of my first time and needed somewhat of an emotional connection before I'd even think about kissing them. But things happen, and the way you look at pleasure within yourself changes. I'm happy, so I don't see why I wouldn't keep doing it.

"Soooo? Tell us, was it incredible?" Emily looks at me expectantly.

"I hate to break it to you, but we just made out nothing more. He tried to do more, but it's hard to get turned on when it felt like he was eating my face." I hear laughing. "No seriously, it felt like a fish was sucking my lips."

Emily squeals at the same time Imogen and Keets say, "ew."

"I know, disappointment all around. Aren't sports players meant to be sex gods or something?"

Keets pipes up from my lap, "That's what the books say, at least."

I sigh. "Wait, the guy from tonight. Was it Charlie or Theo?" Imogen asks.

"Honestly, I have no idea. His name didn't come up. Not to mention, I was wasted – wasn't really tempted to try and find out more."

Imogen and Emily both gasp, before I hear Emily jokingly cough under her breath, "slut."

I throw a pillow at her, and she catches it before it hits her face. None of us can control our laughter. Silence from beneath me causes me to look down at Keets. I meet her eyes, but she just shakes her head and starts talking about a dress she saw tonight that she loved.

Clearly, something I said made her react like that, but I'm not sure what it was specifically. I know her, though, and if she thinks it's worth it, she'll bring it up tomorrow. I brush it off and tune back into the conversation.

"Hey, Stel, what about that tattooed bartender? Luke, right?"

Imogen scoots up, seconding what Emily just said, "Oh, yeah, we saw you talking to him. You two got very close." She raises her eyebrows suggestively.

I burst out laughing. I'm not going to deny that I find him attractive, but the idea of us ever going past whatever this banter is makes me giggle.

"There's nothing about him. Something about him pisses me off. And he's not hot enough to put up with that." I look down slightly, knowing that he is, in fact, hot enough. But if I say that, I'd never hear the end of it. And the end product is the same - nothing's going to happen.

"Stella, you barely know him."

Keets chimes in with, "This is like in those enemies-to-lovers books, where the two characters hate each other for absolutely no reason when it's so clear they just need to jump each other's bones."

"He's not my enemy," I say, struggling not to laugh

slightly at Keets' reference. "But it's the principle of him. I've met guys time and time again who are exactly like him, and they are never what they seem. I just don't like it when people aren't genuine, okay?"

Keets sighs, giving up and settling back down. I know I'm probably being ridiculous, but I don't see why I have to interact with someone I don't want to. Flirting with him is fun; there doesn't have to be anything else to it.

"Hmm," Emily says, "so there isn't anything there?"

"Nope, not at all, and there won't be."

"Damn shame. He is fine as hell." She starts talking about him and the other bartenders working that night.

I had almost forgotten about our interaction at the bar. The way he had remembered that I liked mint, the feeling of his hand on my shoulder as he pulled my strap up, the way he watched as I danced.

It's hard to quiet my mind, to stop it from drifting back to those moments.

I was right in assuming we wouldn't get to bed until sunrise. By the time Imogen and Emily were asleep on the couch, it was well past 8 am. I barely made it into my bed, genuinely debating whether sleeping on the floor was really that bad.

I probably would have just slept through until tomorrow, but a loud banging on my door jolts me out of my sleep.

"Stella Faraday, get your ass out of bed. We are going to dinner." Keets shouts from the other side of my door.

"Fuck off, it's only like two pm. Let me sleep."

"It's 7, dipshit. Immy and Emily left hours ago. You

have ten minutes before I come and drag you to the diner by your hair."

Remember how I said she's psychotic under all that sweetness? Case and point.

I groan and throw my covers off, looking at myself in the mirror. The best part about staying up late after getting back from the bar is taking off your makeup and slipping into comfy clothes that I can wear today. Keets and I don't even need to speak to know where we are going. There's a diner just outside campus that serves the best burgers known to humankind. I think it's fair to say it's the best hangover cure I've found.

The walk to the diner is quieter than usual, the silence heavy. I'm not only making most of the conversation, but I'm actually feeling the need too, something that doesn't usually happen.

"So last night." I mosey, rocking back and forth a bit as I talk. I look at Keets, but she just nods and lets out a dry laugh. "Everything good there?" She nods again, really bringing some beautiful commentary to the conversation. "You know, I read this book last week that was about a fork that turns into a human, and they fall in love." She stops looking at me, still not speaking. "Crazy stuff." She giggles a little bit, but starts walking. I don't know what the fuck is going on.

The first time we came here was the night after our parents had left and we were alone in university for the first time. I thought we should go grab some food together to help the bonding process. Except we got completely lost and couldn't find a single dining hall near us. We ended up stumbling across this place, and since we were starving, we just decided to cough up the money for a meal. Keets immediately chose a booth in the corner, and the awkward silence settled fast. It wasn't because we didn't get along or anything; it was just that we were both so tired and anxious about university starting, we didn't know what to say. Keets looked around us and pointed to an elderly couple sitting in a booth on the other side of the diner.

"I bet you a million dollars she's telling him about the torrid affair she's had with her grandson's friend, ending their 20-year marriage." She turned her head back towards me. "He's 18, by the way. Her husband is appalled that they've been married longer than her boyfriend has been alive."

I let out a snort, but my laughter slowed as Keets stared at me with a look of complete sincerity. It was clearly my turn. I picked out two girls who were sitting across from us.

"I bet that they are secretly siblings, but their parents separated them at birth." She raised her eyebrows, waiting for me to do better.

"But no, not for any reason you and I can comprehend. But because together, they possess a secret ability that could end the world as we know it." I mimicked an explosion signal with my hands and made the sound effect to go along with it.

Keets leaned in towards me and whispered, "I guess this is as good a place as any to be blown to bits." I laughed and we didn't stop talking the rest of the night.

It's unspoken between us now that whenever we are tired or just need a girls' night, we come here and people watch for hours. It's one of my favourite traditions. I'm too focused on whatever is going on with Keets tonight, though, to even think about the other people here.

"I need to talk to you about something." Keets blurts, her face completely flat.

"Okay?" I slowly close my menu. "What's up?" I see her

fidgeting with her napkin, clearly not sure how to say what she's thinking. "Keets, it's okay, it's us. No matter what you have to say, I'm not going anywhere." She takes a deep breath.

"I'm worried about you."

"Worried about me?"

"That guy last night is the fifth person you've gotten with whom you haven't been able to tell us their name. Their name, Stel. That's like the first piece of information you tell someone."

I tilt my head to the side slightly. "Well, to be fair, the first thing you told me about was that I'd have to deal with you listening to your wake-up Taylor playlist every day."

She shakes her head, getting frustrated.

"Stella, that's not what I mean, and you know it. And you were so drunk last night. When you went into the bathroom, you were so out of it. Who knows what could have happened."

"Wow, way to call me an alcoholic." I joke, unsure of what else to say, hoping she'll start smiling again.

"Stella." My smile dissipates. "I mean, come on, are we ever going to talk about Par-? "

"Don't say his name." I cut her off, coming off a bit harsher than I intended. She retreats slightly.

"Okay, I'm sorry. I just don't understand why you can't just try to be in a relationship again.

They aren't all like him. You like hooking up, great. In a relationship, you get a built-in fuck buddy."

I go to say something, but she cuts me off.

"And don't tell me there aren't guys who are interested, because I know for a fact at least half of them leave our apartment the next morning asking to see you again. The walls aren't that thick."

I sit there, not saying anything.

"Okay, and even if you don't want a relationship, what about a friend with benefits or something? Just something more stable where you are being smart and aren't getting hurt."

I raise my eyebrows suggestively. "You offering something, Keets?"

"Stel." I close my mouth. She's serious. I need to stop joking around. "And I'm only saying this because I am worried about you. I just– I know you, maybe better than I know myself. But when it comes to this stuff, I can't read you. I don't know what's going on in your head. I just want you to be happy and be safe because you know there are those girls who end up on the side of the road de-"

"Keets, breathe." I grab her hand on the table, waiting for her to take a breath. "I'm not mad. How long have you been worried about me?"

She chews her bottom lip. "A while, and I think Immy and Emily have been too. But I didn't want to bring it up, because I don't want to be that person who controls what their best friend does."

I nod in understanding, having experienced a friend or two like that in my time.

"I'm sorry you've been stressed, but I promise I'm okay. You can't read my mind about this because there's nothing to read. I'm just enjoying being 21."

"Okay," she nods a couple of times before grabbing her menu. I can tell there's more she wants to say, but I know my answers won't satisfy her. There isn't some deep psychological reason why I don't want to be in a relationship. Yes, maybe I've had a particularly nasty experience, but I'm not ready to get into that with her or anyone else.

So, I leave it at that.

She pipes up quietly, "So, are we okay?"

My eyes soften and I squeeze her hand, "Of course we are, my love. I love you so much for caring about me. I could never, ever be mad at you for that."

She straightens up, and that smile I love so much returns.

"Okay, good, because I've been dying to tell you about this. Well, bitch, I say in the most feminist way possible, in my tutorial."

The next hour flies by, and everything is back to normal. We eat our food and talk about things as we normally do. If I said I had fully stopped thinking about her words from earlier, it'd be a lie. Sure, I've been enjoying myself a little more than I used to, but isn't that what university is for? I feel like being an idiot is just part of the process. But, I didn't realise I was stressing her out so much. That's the last thing I'd ever want to do. She's my rock. And she mentioned Immy and Emily. Have they talked about this? How long exactly have they been worried about me?

Keets' phone buzzes.

"Oh shit." She picks up her bag. "I am so sorry, Stel. I have to go. The same girl I was just telling you about, somehow, she's managed to fuck up our lab."

"Don't worry, you're so good. You'll get me next time. Give em' hell."

"You know I will, love you, Stel." She bends over and places a kiss on my head, before rushing out. Leaving me to spiral about everything she said.

Luke

I watch as the blonde girl from the bar, Keets, I guess, walks out the door of the diner. I know it's bad manners to eavesdrop, but it's not my fault they were talking loud enough for me to hear. I was kind of surprised when Stella didn't acknowledge me as she walked in. I'm sitting in a booth right next to theirs. Granted, I was sitting with my back facing their table, but I would have thought at least one insult would have been thrown my way.

I like this place a lot because it's close to campus, but not a lot of students come here. I got no sleep because Beck had the just incredible idea of going into the city to a club after our shifts. And because I apparently don't know how to say no, I agreed. I don't even know what time it was when we finally got back to our flat, but I do know the sun was up and blazing. The burger sitting in front of me is the first meal and quiet time I've gotten all day.

I shoot a quick peek over my shoulder and see that Stella is still sitting there. She's staring at her lap, her hand messing with the straw in her iced chocolate. Her eyes look glazed over, and she's biting her lip slightly, as if she's stuck in her thoughts. That lunch seemed brutal for her. I mean Beck fucks people like crazy, and I've never thought of sitting him down for a talk about that or his life choices. If anything, I'm impressed with him, and definitely impressed with Stella. The girls got some moves that Beck could only dream of having.

The worst part was that Stella sounded genuinely worried. Her voice was shaking as she questioned Keets. Every word she said was taken to heart. I know it. And the way she cut off Keets when she tried to bring up that guy. I've never heard her be that stark before. I don't know if I've heard anyone be that stark before. Dude must have really fucked up to be on the other side of Stella's blade.

It kind of sucks to see her this down. She looks like she's lost some of the fire that I've grown fond of. Before I know it, I'm sliding out of my booth and sitting straight down in the spot Keets just was. The sound of me scooting into the seat makes her look up quickly.

"Long time no see, Goldie. Are you stalking me or something?" I see the smallest hint of a smile, which makes me glad I came over. But there's hesitation when she goes to lift her head.

"Considering you're the one who came to me, I don't think I'm the stalker."

"There has to be a dirty joke in there somewhere."

She lets out a short breath, which feels like the closest I'll get to a laugh right now, so I count it as a victory.

"You are four years old, an actual child."

"Trust me, Goldie." I pause for a second before saying, "There's nothing boyish about me. All man." I flash her one of my signature grins, feeling pretty proud of myself for that one.

She shakes her head, laughing out loud. Score, although I wasn't really trying with that one.

"Is there something you wanted, Lucas?" I wonder when I'll earn the right to be called by my actual name.

"So, listen." I sit up slightly. "I may have overheard your conversation earlier with your friend."

"Seriously?!" Never mind, maybe she sounds angry often.

"Yeah," I say, starting to regret risking my life here. "And I may have thought it sounded like it kind of sucked, so I'm here."

"You're here to check if I'm okay?"

"You make it sound like I'm a monster or something." When she doesn't deny it, I cut in. "C'mon, could a monster look this good?" I wink at her, causing her to choke on what she's drinking.

She coughs, "Clearly you haven't read many

paranormal romances." I don't think I want to ask about that one. Especially not if monsters are involved.

We are both quiet for a minute before I hear her, just above a whisper. "You do know that it isn't your job to make sure every human on the planet is happy, right?"

"Wow, really? Guess I'll just leave you to your misery then." I go to stand up, stopping before I properly move. Even if she sat here in silence for the next hour, I still wouldn't leave. I don't know who she has to support her right now, whether or not she has people. I am painfully aware of what that's like, and I'm not going to be the dick who leaves her alone.

She clearly notices that she's not going to get rid of me that easily. "I'm fine. I just didn't think what I was doing was impacting her. And I don't really know if they have a right to be worried necessarily, but I know it's just because they love me. I don't know, I guess I'm just trying to figure out how I can stop them from worrying without me having to change who I am."

My brows furrow slightly. That sounds familiar as hell. "Bit of a dilemma, huh?" She lets out a dry laugh.

I don't really know what to say to that. Normally, I'd say I'm pretty good at talking out of my ass in situations. But considering I'm in a similar situation as her right now, it's hard to give advice when I don't know what I'm going to do.

It's kind of funny that this girl and I, who for some reason would rather be anywhere else than with me, are in the same position. It really fucking sucks trying to live your life for other people. I think back to talking to Beck and Rory after that dinner. Rory gave me absolutely no advice, seeming as stuck as I was. And Beck? Oh yeah, he suggested I hire someone to be my date. Sometimes I question if he was dropped on the head as a baby. Hire someone. Crazy. Or maybe?

"What if I had a solution?" She perks up slightly. My brain is running a million miles an hour trying to stop me from speaking, but clearly my mouth moves faster. "What if you find someone to date, but who knows that it's not real. That it's just a cover."

"Fake dating someone?"

"Is that what the kids call it these days?" I joke. The deadpan look on her face tells me it didn't land.

"Oh sure, or what if I get kidnapped by aliens and move to Mars to repopulate Earth."

Huh?

I tilt my head, confused. "I thought we were listing things that would never happen in real life."

She goes to grab her bag and stands up. I quickly scramble, lightly holding onto her arm.

"No wait, hear me out. You need someone to be your boyfriend in front of your friends. That way, when you are out all night or when you just want to blow off steam, they think you're with him, not out doing something dangerous or whatever. But, because he'll know it's fake, you're free to do whatever the hell you want without feeling guilty about anyone worrying about you."

She sits back down, chewing her lip in thought. "Okay, if in theory I didn't think that was the worst idea in the entire world, what idiot would do that? For free, might I add, I'm not exactly making a killing."

I tilt my head forward a bit, looking at her, trying to convey that 'the idiot' she's referring to is sitting right in front of her.

"Yeah, nope. Not happening. Nope." She stands up properly this time, so I stand with her.

"Why not? I'm perfect. Your friends have seen us interact over the past couple of weeks. It's clear the tension is there. Also, I'm hot, you're hot. We'd make an attractive couple. What's the problem?"

"No problem, I'm just not doing it." She stops for a second, before looking directly at my eyes, squinting. "Why would you even want to do it?"

"Let's just say I have my reasons for needing a cover, too."

"And those reasons are?"

"Something I'm not sharing unless we have a deal." I put my hand out, ready to shake and feel the sense of victory that would come with securing this incredible plan. Stella goes to grab my hand, but instead of shaking it, she pulls me closer to her.

Our faces are just inches apart as she speaks. "Never happening." She lets go of me and starts to walk out of the diner.

Cupping my hands around my mouth, I shout, purposefully loud. "Think about it and get back to me, Goldie. You know you want to."

I can practically see the massive eye roll from the back of her head. She may think it's insane, but I think it's perfect. It would solve both of our problems with one swell swoop.

She'd come around.

Eventually.

Not to mention.

I don't give up that easily.

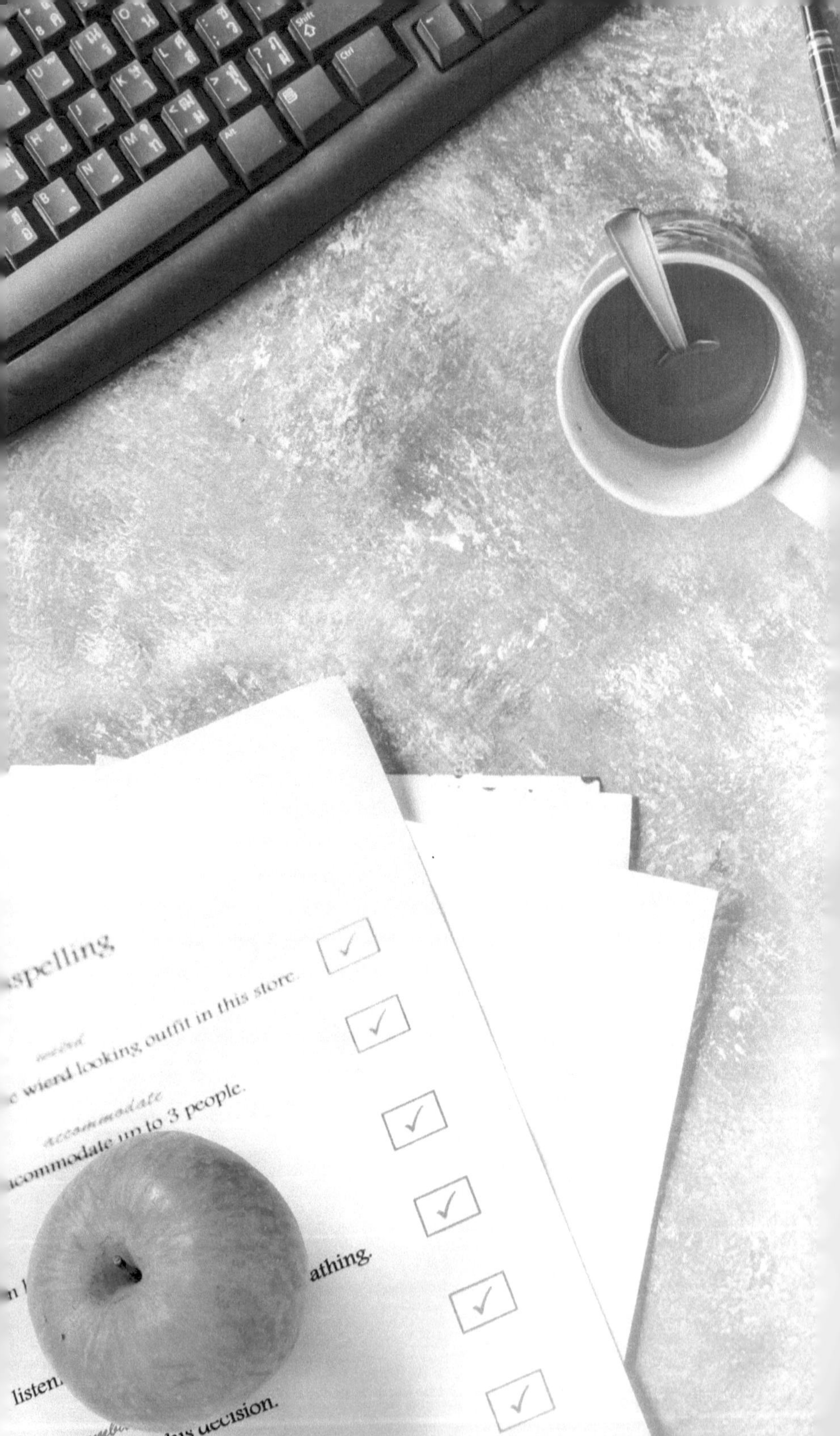
spelling
e wierd looking outfit in this store.
accommodate
commodate up to 3 people.
athing.
listen
his decision.

Chapter Eight

STELLA

I WALK INTO THE LIVING ROOM OF RORY'S PLACE only to be greeted by a massive shirtless man with a buzz cut with smiley faces dotted around his head. I think his name is Beck. He's one of the bartenders at the Black Lantern. What he's doing here, though, I could not tell you. I look down at my phone, double-checking Rory's message.

Yup, he definitely said to come in. Shirtless man is just staring at me, seemingly unbothered by a random girl in his living space.

"Hi, sorry, I'm here to see Rory?" I say, expecting some sort of direction on where his friend might be. Instead, he just nods and walks into the kitchen.

"Want something to drink? Coffee? Tea? A shot of tequila?" It's 10 in the morning, but I keep that thought to myself. Judging Rory's possible roommate is probably not a great first impression.

"Um, coffee would be good, thanks." I move and sit on the stools at the kitchen counter. I shoot a quick text to Rory.

> Me: Hey, I think I'm downstairs with your roommate?

I place my phone back down on the counter, just in time to grab the mug that is slid across to me.

"Thanks," I murmur, taking a sip of the surprisingly good coffee.

"So are you and Rory like…" He makes a movement with his hands that could only be described as some sort of signal for fucking.

I laugh into my cup, "No, nope. Just study buddies."

Beck nods, "O'connor, I assume?"

I nod, feeling more and more confident I'm in the right house.

"Hey, if anything changes, my main man Rory is a great lay."

I raise my eyebrows at him. His face drops and he stutters as he back pedals, "No wait, not like because I've slept with him or anything. Just like he's cute, and I assume with that blue hair, he has to have something else going for him. Not that there's anything wrong with guys sleeping together, I love it."

I can't stop laughing. Luckily for him, there's a sound of someone running down the stairs.

"Saved by the bell," I say, seeing Beck audibly let out a sigh.

"Beck, please tell me you didn't creep out Stella. I actually like this one." Rory says, walking into the living room. Beck holds his hands up in defence, making me laugh.

"Don't worry, Ror, I am thoroughly untraumatised. Just entertained."

He nods, unconvinced. "Promise." I gesture up the stairs, "Shall we?"

Rory nods, and he leads me down the hallway past the two doors, which I assume lead to a bathroom and Beck's room. Rory lets me into his room. He has a desk that has his insanely impressive PC setup. I couldn't actually tell you a single thing about the specs or whatever, but I can say it has cool rainbow lights. That has to attest for something, right?

"You can just sit on the bed if you want? I thought we could go over some flashcards." I nod, kicking off my shoes and getting comfortable. Considering the amount of pillows on his bed, it's not hard.

"Jesus Christ, Rory, do you think there are any pillows left in the entire country?"

Rory rolls his eyes and picks up a pillow on the floor. I must have accidentally kicked it off the bed. "Shut up and read the flashcards, Stella."

I pick up the deck on his bed. "Aww Rory, the amount of love I feel right now is out of this world." He turns and stares at me, 100% his way of saying he loves me too. I know it.

"Okay, so," I grab the first flashcard, internally groaning, reading the question. "Why is a fictional persona used to explain Woolf's thoughts on fiction and women in A Room of One's Own?"

"I can't do this anymore. Who the hell made these flashcards?" Rory grumbles, shoving a pillow in his face. He moves to lie next to me on the bed, clearly regretting the hundred flashcards he made for our course.

"Hate to break it to you, nerd, but you did." He grabs

the first pillow he finds and throws it at me. I catch it in the air and return the throw, eliciting a groan out of him. I laugh before stretching to see the time on my phone: 2:00pm. Jesus, we've been at this for four hours.

"Okay." I jump up and grab his hand, sitting him up. "We've been at this too long. It's time for lunch."

He scrambles to his feet.

"Oh, I am so down for that. You are so smart, Stella." He walks past me, rubbing my head as if I am a dog who just did a trick. I scowl at him. "I'll go start some pasta. Come down whenever. There's a bathroom in there if you want to fix…" He points towards my perfect hair, which he's just ruffled up. "That."

I run towards him to hit him, but he's too fast and is out the door before I get a chance. Bastard.

I walk into his pristinely clean bathroom and see that my hair has become a frizzy mess. Damn it. I love the whole embracing your natural hair thing, but at least twice a day, I think about taking a razor and shaving the whole thing off. Quickly, I put my hair into two plaits before I actually go searching for Rory's shaver. The smell of the pasta sauce Rory is making seeps into his room, making me immediately run to go downstairs.

I swing the door open and face plant into a wall.My hand moves to touch what's in front of me, and I very quickly realise it's not a wall, but rather a person.

Another roommate? How many are there, Beck, Rory, and…

Oh, please don't be who I think it is.

"Nice to see you too, Goldie."

Fuck my life.

I step back quickly and eye Lucas standing in front of me. He's wearing a loose singlet and shorts, clearly having just come back from the gym. I can hear Bruce Springsteen playing from the headphones around his neck. His hair is swept back, leaving his amused eyes and shit eating grin on full display.

"Lucas. I was just going anywhere but here." I go to walk around him, but he shifts, blocking me.

Fucker.

"Rory told me to tell you lunch was almost ready." He is trapping me in; every sense is heightened because all I can feel is him. I place my hands on his chest, pushing him back. He moves without any effort.

"Thank you, Captain Obvious." I walk downstairs, disappointed by the footsteps following behind me.

"Hey Ror, did you make enough for me too?" Oh fuck no. I turn and stare at Rory, trying to convey that I'd rather die than stay here, but he is either stupid or ignores it.

"Yeah, man, of course. For all four of us." I just noticed Beck standing in the kitchen, as undressed as before, but this time wearing a bright blue apron. Rory's wearing a green one, a neon green one.

What the hell?

"Beck bought us Powerpuff Girl aprons. He's Bubbles, Rory's Buttercup, and I am Blossom." Lucas says as if it's the most obvious thing in the world. Clearly, Rory's blue hair wasn't enough to convince Beck to let go of bubbles. "Checks out if you ask me." He walks past me into the kitchen, setting up the table, and the rest of them sit down.

What happened in my life to put me in this exact moment right now?

"You comin', Goldie?" Lucas calls from the table. Moving, I sit down, wedged in between Rory and Beck.

"So, how's the studying going?" Lucas asks, looking at me and Rory. I stay silent as Rory speaks up.

"Fine, we're almost done for today, I think. I can't seem to grasp the whole lack of description around the narrator written in the body."

I nod, but honestly, it's my favourite part of the book. The ambiguity in it is how it's completely up to the reader to decide what that means to them.

"Yeah sure, I totally know what that means." Ror smiles at him, before Beck turns his body to face me. "So Stella, got a boyfriend?"

"Sorry?" I nearly choked on my food.

"Jesus, Beck, can we not kill my friend, please?" Rory interjects.

"It's an innocent question, Rory," Lucas says, looking me dead in the eyes. "Do you have a boyfriend, Stella?"

I stare back at Lucas with the same intensity with which he's looking at me. "Nah, not really into the whole boyfriend thing. Although based on what I'm seeing now, I can say pretty confidently I get more action than the three of you combined." I smile sweetly, picking up a piece of pasta and taking a bite.

Lucas's grin drops slightly as Beck pats me on the shoulder. "Yeah, I like this one."

It's 4pm when I finally start to head out of Rory's place. We probably still have like three days of hardcore studying before we are even remotely ready for our exam, but it's a good start. I said goodbye to Rory in the room, stopping him from walking me out. I don't need an escort to walk me five metres out of the house. Rounding the corner, I open the front door, but it doesn't budge. It's locked. When I try to turn it, it still doesn't move. Shit.

"Need some help there?" A low voice asks from behind me. A voice that very clearly belongs to Lucas. Of course, he's here right now. I know that my feelings towards him are a bit intense for the little interaction we've had, but that interaction just reminded me of someone I don't want to be reminded of. So, he makes my guard go up. I don't see how that's a bad thing.

"I am perfectly capable of figuring this out on my own. Thank you very much." He raises his shoulders in a shrug, as I keep fumbling with the lock, trying to get it to move. It won't.

Fuck me.

"Fine, I guess you could help me if you want." I move out of the way, letting him go to the door. He reaches out to the door and then stops.

"What the hell, Lucas?" He turns around, his body fully covering the door.

"Agree to fake date me and I'll let you out." Jesus Christ, he's resorted to kidnapping me.

"Are you joking?" I ask, shockingly unsurprised with his actions.

"Nope. What do you say, girlfriend?" He asks, his hands still nowhere near the lock.

Yeah, no, I think not.

I turn and walk through the living room and open the back door. Looking around the garden, it's surprisingly well looked after, the grass having just been mowed. I can see over the top of the back fence, and it looks like some sort of alleyway. Before I can think twice about it, I gracefully climb over the fence, landing in a street between their house and the back of someone else's. Smiling to myself, I start to walk down the street.

Luke shouts behind me, "Well played, Goldie."

I smirk, point Stella.

Chapter Nine

LUKE

"BECK, WHAT THE FUCK IS THAT?" RORY SHOUTS louder than I thought was possible. I turn around, dropping the rag I am currently using to clean the booths, seeing Rory and Beck behind the bar together. Ror is holding a cocktail glass filled with some liquid that is the exact same colour as a piece of kryptonite.

Beck frowns, "That's not a very supportive reaction, Ror." He looks down at the glass, trying to play some sad puppy eyes shit. "And to answer your question, it's going to be called the lucky lantern – hence the green. Get it?" He raises the glass up to try to show me.

"What that is, is an abomination to the cocktail world. Sorry, Beck." Rory turns to me; they both do. Jesus, I'm not in the mood to puke tonight.

"Alright, hand it over. Surely, it's not that bad." Beck runs over and hands me the glass, excitedly waiting for me to try it. Smelling the glass, I immediately realise what a mistake I've made. But because I am a good friend, I take a sip and choke it down. Swallowing saliva to try and stop the imminent gagging.

"Yeah, I'm sorry, dude, that's horrid." I put the glass down on the bar, patting him on the shoulder.

"Nope." He shakes his head, taking a sip of his drink and very clearly attempting not to gag. "That is genius. It's going on the menu next week. I've decided." Both Ror and Ror go to speak, but are cut off. "I said it's been decided. And when I sell millions of the Lucky Lantern, you will reap this day, gentlemen."

"Millions?" Ror asks.

"Yes, millions." He nods and walks out from the bar towards our back room. Probably to throw up. Rory is chuckling as I return to my current task, but I am interrupted by my phone buzzing.

Incoming Call: Mum.

I take a deep breath before picking up.

"Hey Mum." I see Rory's head stick up. As well as Becks, who's now returned from the 'mysterious' location he was just in.

"Hello Luke. Is now an okay time to speak?" I don't even get a chance to respond before she starts speaking again. "Good. I wanted to call you to ask about what you were thinking of wearing to the reunion."

"What? I don't know, it's months away." I hear a heavy sigh on the other side.

"Luke, New Year's Eve will come before you know it. You have to make sure you've thought these things out." I raise my hand up to my head, rubbing my temple with my fingers. Is it possible to get a headache in under five minutes?

"Okay, mum, I'll take a look at my closet and call you back." I see Beck's mouth 'closet.' Clearly confused. I shake my head, brushing him off.

"Okay, fine, I guess. Just make sure every bit of those scribbles is covered." A slight edge was clear in her voice.

"Yup, of course. Wouldn't want to send the wrong image." I say, heavy on the sarcasm. She either doesn't register that or is just choosing to ignore my lack of sincerity.

"Okay." She hangs up.

Goodbye, mother. Love you too. Isn't that how most people end a call with one of their parents?

I close my eyes for a second, taking a deep breath, going back to cleaning the booths.

"What'd she want?" Beck asks. I turn back to see them both looking at me, eyebrows furrowed. Worried. They don't need to be. I've dealt with my parents my whole life, and I am more than able to do it on my own.

"Just something about wearing the right suit to the family thing on New Year's Eve." They both nod, the silence lingering in the air. I quickly turn around, unable to look either of them in the eyes. My parents have the uncanny ability to usurp any feeling of joy, leaving me completely and utterly alone. It's not a new feeling, but that doesn't mean it doesn't hurt all the same.

I'm curious if my brother is treated to the same formality. No scratch that, they'd never hang up a call with golden boy without telling him how loved and perfect he is. Wonder how that feels.

I feel a hand creep up on my shoulder to see Rory standing behind me. I don't turn around, but I can hear his voice barely above a whisper. "We're here for you, man."

I force my head to nod, but I can't bring myself to speak.

Not when I still can't convince myself to believe they mean it.

When I finally finish the job I was doing, I tune back into Rory and Beck's conversation.

"I'm not even kidding, O'connor sucks ass. It's like no matter how many essays I write, it's still not good enough." Beck nods. We've both heard complaints about this professor a couple of times.

"How's it going studying with that girl from your class? Didn't you say she had cracked the code or something?" My interest peaks at this.

"Stella? She's been helping. She's also just nice to hang out with. It's made the class a whole lot more interesting having a friend in it."

So, she does know how to be nice, just not to me.

I would find it funny if I wasn't just so damn confused.

"What's up with her?" I speak up, causing both Beck and Ror to turn and look at me. Right, I hadn't made my presence known again.

"Stel? No deal, she's doing a Bachelor of Arts and is still kinda figuring out what she wants to do with it. She's chill, I guess."

"Huh." I wonder why she was so defensive with me when we first met. I genuinely didn't mean to offend her. Since then, it seems that she's warmed up slightly, but not as much as I want. Especially not enough to get her to agree to my plan.

"Huh?" Beck asks.

"Oh, you don't know? Luke has some weird obsession with Stella. It's really cute."

"Aww, Luke, do you need some help with it? I know it's been a while since you've touched a girl."

"Fuck off." I turn to Rory. "It's not an obsession. I'm just curious why she's so against me, but with you, she's all sunshine and rainbows. The other day she literally climbed over a fence to get away from me."

They both laugh. I've met girls before who disliked me from the get-go because they assume I'm some fuckboy player bartender who treats women like objects. But it's clear it's not that, because she's completely fine with Rory.

"Look, man, I don't know for certain. I do know she was in a shit relationship a couple of years back and that it still sticks with her. Maybe something you said just brought up a bad memory or something."

Shit. That would make sense. Fuck I really hope I didn't hurt her.

Beck laughs, "Okay, so I was only half kidding earlier when I asked if you needed help. However, now."

"Okay, both of you listen to me." They both turn quickly, wearing some dumb, fake focused look on their face. Clearly making fun of me.

These shitheads.

"I do not like her. I just feel bad for offending her. So, get any notion of us walking down the aisle out of your heads." They are both quiet for a second, and I think I've gotten through to them.

"Aww, Ror, did you hear that? He's already thinking about their wedding." Rory pouts, agreeing with Beck's assessment.

"Rory, can you please give me her number?" His brows furrow, debating whether that's the right thing to do. "Please, I just want to apologise."

"Fine." He hands me his phone, "but if she seems like she's going to castrate you, I know nothing."

Castration, Jesus.

I think I just felt my dick crawl back inside of me. Unlocking his phone, I find her contact and send it to myself.

This is going to be fun.

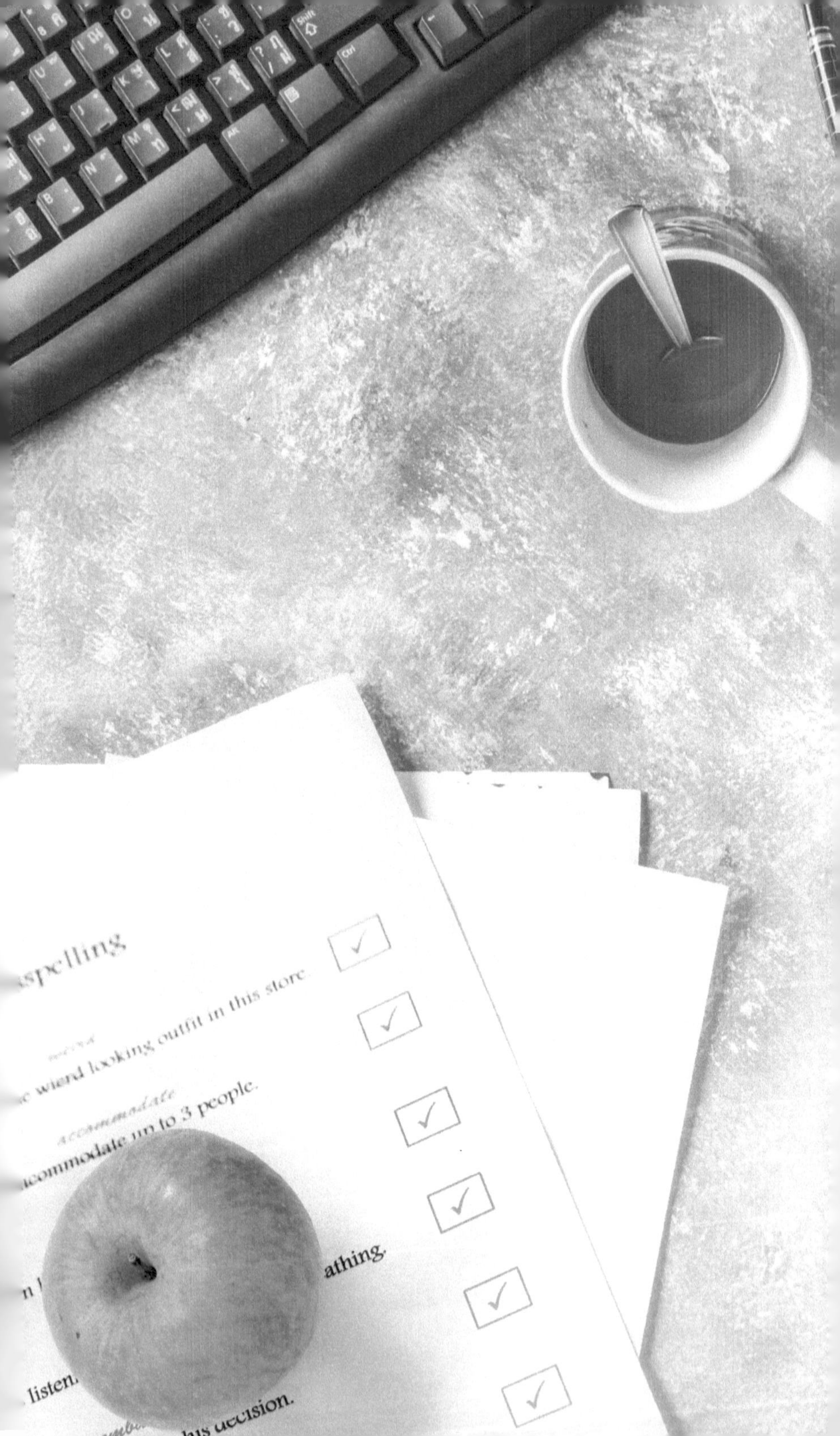
spelling
wierd looking outfit in this store.
accommodate
commodate up to 3 people.
athing.
listen.
decision.

Chapter Ten

STELLA

THE ENTIRE WALK TO HILLSIDE, I'M TRYING TO run through all the reasons why I should not agree to his plan. It's insane that it's still in my head.

There is absolutely no way that Lucas' idea is even remotely smart. I mean it would require us somehow fooling the people who know us the best. Lying to Keets would not end well. I'm sure she'd see through it in ten seconds. She can always tell when something is off about me. Not to mention, he still refuses to tell me why he wants to do this. And how am I meant to get into something without knowing his true motives? He probably just wants to hook up with me, and this is some long-winded attempt because he's bored.

No, it's stupid.

But still, as I'm sitting in my bed, it's all I can think about. I haven't been with anyone since that night at the Black Lantern. Every time someone flirts with me, all I can think is Keets being worried. And I know it's my life, and I shouldn't let it get to me like this. I just can't drop it.

"You are insane," I mutter, alone in the staff room, eyes widening when I realise I'm talking to myself. "And now for more than just Lucas." Before I get to think about it more, Lily comes running into the staff room. She's wearing a yellow dress today that matches the massive bow in her hair.

"Hey Lilybug. Everything okay? You're not meant to be in the staff room, chicken." I glance over at the clock. There's still an hour until class starts. Students are meant to be outside with the staff.

She nods, looking apologetic. "I know, I know, but I had to find you. It's an emergency." I quickly put down the mug of coffee and let her pull me towards our classroom. She is refusing to answer any questions I am asking as she runs with me. Kids are typically not the best at acting rational in stressful situations; that's meant to be the teacher's job. I've been pretty lucky in my time working here, never having to deal with a serious emergency. I'm not meant to work too closely with the students in emergency situations, but with the lack of staffing recently, there's not much else I can do right now. She stops running right in front of her class and turns to look at me. Her eyes are wide, blinking fast.

"You have to promise not to be mad at me, okay?" I smile at her, nodding as calmly as I can. What the hell am I walking into?

She opens the door, and it's dark in the room. Except for the smart screen, which has a list of names written on it in Lily's very messy first-grade handwriting. She must have set it up when she dropped her bag in the class. There's a seat positioned in front of the board with a name tag saying 'Ms. Faraday.' I stop, confused.

"Where's the emergency, Lil?"

She closes the door and confidently walks to the front of the classroom.

"Please take a seat, Ms. Faraday." It finally clicks that there isn't an actual emergency – just a ploy to get me into the classroom. I smile, because despite her nearly giving me a heart attack, this is one of the things I love most about working with these kids. The stupid but hilarious stuff they get up to on a day-to-day basis. Nodding, I walk and sit down on the chair, being as formal as possible.

"It has come to my attention that you do not have a boyfriend or girlfriend, Ms. Faraday." My eyes nearly pop out of my head as she says that. How would that have even come to her attention?

"I'm sorry, what?"

"Yup." She nods very passionately. "All the other teachers with boyfriends or girlfriends talk to them. I see them outside school, and they act all gross or wear ugly rings. But I've never seen you talk to anyone or wear an ugly ring. So, you don't have a boyfriend or girlfriend."

I try to hold my laugh as she explains how she came to this conclusion.

"Okay. And why am I here then?"

"Because I have made a list." She turns and gestures to the board, causing me to truly take a look at what she's written.

Benjamin

Mr. Austin

Ms. Carson

Oh my god. Please don't tell me she did what I think she did.

"These are all the people who also don't have

boyfriends and girlfriends. I thought you could go buy an ugly ring and then be their girlfriend." She's staring at me, waiting for a response. How do you explain to a 7-year-old that one, that list is made up of people both 15 years younger and older than me, so I will not be dating them. And two, I enjoy hooking up with strangers too much. I go for neither.

"Lilybug, what made you think I needed a list?"

She looks at me in confusion. "Because my mummy said that single people are sad, and you look kind of sad. So, I didn't want you to be sad anymore."

She really does mean well, but out of all the days to bring up my lack of relationship status, today is not the day. Opting to avoid any deep conversations about relationships or to break her heart after she clearly worked really hard on this, I respond.

"Thank you for thinking of me, Lilybug, but I promise I'm not sad being single."

She nods, "Okay, Ms. Faraday. But remember this list if you do get sad."

I walk up to the door, opening it to let us out. "I promise I will."

fall back into my bed, landing on the pillows, once I get back to the apartment. I hear my door creak and see Keets stick her head through.

"You good there, girl?"

I let out a deep sigh and sat up. "Somehow, Lucas got my number and has been texting me nonstop." I throw my phone on the carpet. "You'd think he doesn't know how to understand basic human emotions. When someone isn't responding, typically they don't want to talk to you."

She laughs and sits on the edge of my bed.

"Oh, and today, Lily, that first grader in my class, tried to set me up with every eligible bachelor she knows because she thought I was sad being single."

Her eyes bug out before responding. "It's not his fault that he's been caught in the web that is Stella Faraday. It's pretty easy to become obsessed with you. Trust me."

I smile at her.

"And the Lily thing. I'll leave that one alone. It won't help when I just insult you more." She smiles this time as mine drops.

His texting me incessantly is not technically a lie. I got the first text this morning at like 8 am.

> Luke Astor: So, when are you finally gonna agree to this plan?

I picked up my phone and changed his name to Shorty, laughing, thinking about the diaper-wearing cupid from Tangled. Within five minutes, he had sent five more texts, including offering money and wingman services to convince me.

Not a bright one, that Lucas.

"So, I have to be punished because I'm hot and men just can't control themselves around me?" I lay back down. "I say humbly, of course."

Keets stands up and opens my closet. "Sounds like a hard life, truly." I feel a piece of clothing hit my face. My favourite red dress?

"Hey!"

"Get up, we are going to The Lantern."

"You can't make me." She puts a hand on her hips and gives me a look. We both know she could.

"Please no, I don't want to deal with the town idiot tonight."

She lets out a short laugh, shaking her head. "I have it on good authority that he avoids The Lantern every Monday. Something about despising anything to do with karaoke."

"He won't be there."

"No, he will not."

"Fine." I get out of my bed, pulling off my pajamas. She turns to walk out the door, stopping right at the threshold of the room.

"Hey, you are gonna be okay tonight, right?" Her lips quiver slightly, almost as if she's scared to ask. I know she's referring to our conversation earlier.

"Of course I will be. I'm excited." A smile returns to her face. "But only if you go make me a vodka and coke." She leaves my room. "Light on the coke, please!"

"And heavy on the vodka?" I don't even need to respond, knowing Keets' pre-game games are always deadly. They are usually more fun than the night out itself.

Chapter Eleven

LUKE

I REALLY DON'T KNOW WHAT I'M DOING HERE. I'VE made it a pretty clear rule that I don't come into the bar on my off days, especially not on karaoke night. I originally thought it was inspired to bring a microphone to the bar, and that it might attract some more people. What I didn't realise is that it meant listening to at least 20 people screeching for a minimum of 3 minutes each. Don't even get me started on when the theatre kids find out about it. No disrespect to the community, I personally have been known to listen to a Cabinet Battle or two, but no one needs to hear drunken Defying Gravity three times in one night.

I do really like it here though, it'd be a lie to say I don't. When I was in my first year, I stumbled upon this place one night when I was walking home from some party. The silence and pitch-black room didn't seem to deter me from staggering in and asking for a drink. Another student was in the bar and ended up making me something, although he looked as if he felt sorry for me. I hate when people look at me like that, so I made a dumb joke to ease the tension. He laughed. We chatted for a long time, and after the third time, he told me his name I was able to remember that it was Rory. He told me his dad owned the place and that it used to be "the place" in the early 2000s, but business has gone downhill. They were trying to clean it up slowly, but it was hard to get a new place going when there were already so many places for 18-year-olds to get drunk, living in a university town and all.

Me, being absolutely shitfaced, decided I was going to make it my mission to revive this, albeit slightly run-down, bar to its full glory. I made this decision without any request from Rory or Steve, his father. It was clear when I left that Rory didn't expect me to come back the next day, but I did – with a ceramic frog I had found on the side of the road. It was a necessity. And the next, and the next. We decided to rename it to the last Black Lantern – mainly because Steve found it hilarious that I managed to insert myself in this process despite the place being closed when I found it. A couple of months later, Beck came in looking for a job and was hired on the spot. There are a lot more people working for us, but the three of us (four, including Steve) have stuck together. Beck and Ror are like my brothers.

This is home.

"I swear to god, Luke, if you open your mouth one more time to complain, I will smash this glass on your head." He turns to face me, smiling.

"Beck says lovingly," Rory says, taking a sip of his drink.

"Go fuck yourself. We all know how I feel about Open Mic Mondays."

"And yet, you are its one and only creator."

Beck, always the charmer.

In all honesty, the only way they managed to get me out

was because of Stella. Apparently, Keets spoke to Rory earlier about them coming tonight. I haven't been able to stop thinking about the arrangement since I brought it up. It sounded dumb at first, because this isn't a romance book. But the more I think about it, the more it makes sense. She needs someone to cover for her, and I'm the perfect candidate. I've got my own reasons too, but that's not something I'm ready to share with her. Plus, there are worse people for me to fake date.

Looking up from the table, I scan the bar and spot her immediately. She's standing at a table with a group of her friends. Her arms are linked with Keets, and while Keets looks nice, I can't keep my eyes off Stella. She got the top half of her hair in a bun, and the bottom part wavy. A red dress that ties around the neck is covering her body, causing my mouth to go dry. It's impossible to deny that she is beautiful. Romantic interest or not, I'm not blind.

"Hmm, seems like Romeo doesn't regret coming out after all," Beck says, staring at me as if he's caught me drooling over her. Which definitely is not the case.

"Romeo? Jesus Beck, you're spending too much time with Ror."

"Is it really that crazy that I'd read a book on my own?"

"It's crazy that you know how to read."

I cough on my drink, laughing when Ror pipes in with that one. Beck's face is priceless.

I look back up to her table to see that her friends have left and she's there alone. If I'm going to convince her of anything, now's probably the time.

"Well, gentlemen, I'll be taking my leave." I muster up in my best British accent. Sounding more like a character from The Prince than from The Crown.

"Gentlemen? What is this, the eighteen fucking

hundreds?" Beck says as Ror says in an equally bad accent, "Enjoy, good sir."

Stella spots me before I make it to the table, staring me down.

"Hey Goldie, want a picture? You could look at it every night as you fall asleep."

She rolls her eyes. "I'd rather gouge my eyes out than think of you before I go to sleep."

"Aww, why? You scared of the types of dreams you'd have?"

She tries to hold back a laugh. "Any dreams with you in them would be dreams of me killing you, slowly. Violently. And those bring a smile to my face."

Talking with her always keeps me on my toes. I enjoy how she acts like she doesn't like me, even though she could have asked me to leave at any point. And still hasn't. She brushes the strand of hair in front of her face behind her ear and looks up at me.

"Is there a reason you chose to interrupt me, Lucas? Isn't there some other girl you can go bother? Or are you not trying to get laid tonight?"

"So curious about my sex life, Goldie, I'll ask again – interesting dreams?" She rolls her eyes, again. I wonder if there's a world record for how many times someone can roll their eyes in a conversation. And more importantly, if I were to get the world record for being the one to make her do it.

"Yes, I did come over here for a reason. To make you reconsider my offer from earlier."

She laughs but stills as my face stays unchanging. "You were serious about that?"

"Serious as a heart attack, Goldie. I'd never joke about being your fake boyfriend. It would be my fake honour."

"You are crazy if you think I'd ever agree to that." She tries to stare at me like she thinks I'm insane, but her eyes have a hint of understanding behind them, like she's starting to fold. I'm not insane, though. I've thought all this out. Like I said, there hasn't been anything else running through my mind. I step up next to her and grab her shoulders, turning her to face me.

"Sure, I may be crazy, but not for this. Think about it, you want to sleep with a bunch of people without getting shit from your friends. Which, by the way, I totally support – girl power and all that jazz." I say, using my hands to make a cheering motion. "I need it too. It's a win-win and you know it."

I can see the cogs in her head turning as if she's actually thinking this through.

"Plus," I put my fingers under her chin, making her look at me. Her eyes go wide. I like making her look like that. "Surely there are worse people to cover for you. Your street cred would go up immensely."

She looks me dead in the eyes, speaking dryly. "Being a girl with boobs does wonders for my street cred. Thanks for the offer, though."

She steps back, moving to walk away.

I can't let her leave.

"Do you want me to beg, go on my knees and all that shit?"

She whips her head around, staring at me. "You'd beg? Why? Why do you want to do this so bad?"

I'm not really in the mood to dive into my psyche with her right now or explain why I have to fake my life for my family. Neither am I in the mood to explain that I just want to help her. So, I opt for neither.

"Because I have shitty parents who seem to think I can't

look after myself, and not to mention, my life is a tad boring right now. By the way, I was serious about begging. I do like being on my knees."

She just stands there unmoving for what feels like ten minutes. Not saying anything. Her eyes soften a bit, looking at me with pity. I don't do too well with pity. Or extended silences.

"Insert some dumb joke."

Somehow, she stays silent after that one. Don't know how. That one even makes me laugh.

She rests her arms on the table. "My friends would never believe it." She walks back to standing right in front of me. "It wouldn't make sense why I was shitting on you earlier today, and now I'm dating you. And I don't date; they wouldn't believe I'd just change my mind with no warning."

"Fine, Goldie, if convincing your friends is all it takes. I think I can figure something out." That's all I say as I turn and walk towards Ror, who's now operating the computer for karaoke.

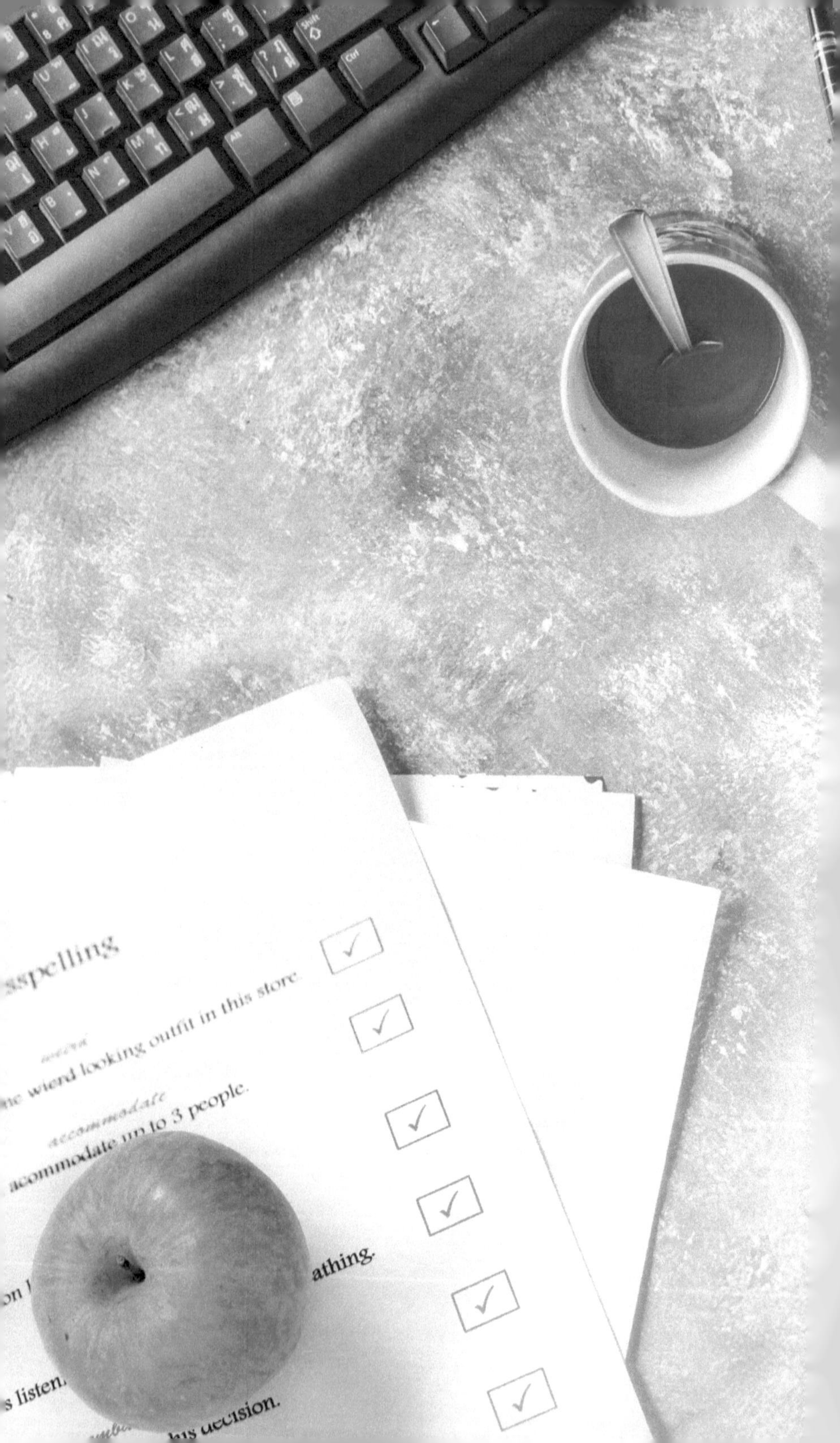
sspelling
ne wierd looking outfit in this store.
accommodate
acommodate up to 3 people.
athing.
s listen.
decision.

Chapter Twelve

STELLA

THERE'S NO FUCKING WAY. THAT'S ALL I CAN THINK OF as I see him walk through the crowd towards the stage. The bar is completely full tonight, with barely room to dance, yet as he walks, people move to the side, letting him through. It pisses me off that he has that effect.

When he reaches the stage, he leans down and whispers something to Rory, who's running the computer for the night. Rory laughs, nodding, and Lucas's face lights up with that smug grin I know too well. I have absolutely no idea what he's up to right now. I've not said a single nice thing about him to Keets, or any of my friends for that matter. There is no way in hell they'd believe me if I tried to explain. Lucas? Of all people? Not a chance.

"Hello, earth to Stella." I turn around to see Keets has come back from the bar, holding two alarmingly bright green drinks in her hand.

"Sorry, just zoned out." She makes a face that I can't quite place. "What the hell is in that cup?"

"It's more fun if you just drink it. Gotta live life on the

edge, Stel." Keets gives me the extra cup she's holding, and I make the horrible mistake of drinking it. It tastes like what would happen if you let a 14-year-old boy who just discovered alcohol make a cocktail. He'd probably also laugh at the word cocktail. The sharing of my disgust is interrupted by the sound of microphone feedback, causing all of us to turn towards the stage.

Is he actually going to sing? Maybe he'll finally suck at something. I can't even find the words to express how much I hope that happens, but deep down, I know better.

"Hey." He's standing right in the center, looking more comfortable than I have ever seen anyone on stage. His outfit looks annoyingly good on him. The button-down shirt he's wearing over his white t-shirt is the exact same shade of brown as his eyes. Those eyes that I absolutely refuse to get lost in right now. And his jeans fit perfectly, all around. He keeps running his hands through his hair – the only sign he may not be as confident as he appears.

"So, there's this girl who's here tonight, a beautiful girl, and despite my best efforts, she seems to not believe me when I say I am interested in her. Seriously interested. So, I thought I'd tell her exactly how I feel in front of all you incredible people. Through song, of course."

The crowd reacts immediately, buzzing with laughter and excitement. I hear Keets' voice somewhere behind me, laughing and chatting with the group of girls who've gathered around her. But I can't focus on that. Not now. I feel a strange wave of unease wash over me as his eyes begin scanning the crowd. I can feel the moment his gaze lands on me, and for a split second, my heart stops. He winks. And the music starts.

Can We Dance by The Vamps?

That's the song he's going with?

He keeps singing, the crowd egging him on – likely due to the excitement of someone singing who doesn't sound like a dying whale. I don't even know why I'm still standing here, rooted to the spot, watching him. He's not bad. In fact, I have to admit, he sounds pretty damn good. He moves from one side of the stage to the other, looking out over the crowd, smiling at everyone who's singing along and dancing. I didn't even know he could sing – or if he could, I certainly didn't expect this. But damn, he looks happy. Genuinely happy. It's kind of messing with my head.

"Stel, let's dance. C'mon!" Keets tries pulling me towards the dance floor, but I stand my ground. I know he's doing this for me. To help create a story of why we are suddenly together, why I am all of a sudden obsessed with… him. However, giving in has never really been my style.

"Go without me. No need to boost his ego any more than it already is."

I can practically feel Keets' eye roll as she drags some other girls to the dance floor with her. She might be getting slightly sick of my, thing with him. But best friends have to listen to you talk about the same situation time and time again without complaining – and if they do, they need to get over it and listen with open ears.

I stay at our table, sipping the green concoction I was given as he approaches the bridge of the song.

Hearing him sing the words of the song makes me laugh, but I stop as I see him step off the stage. Of course, he wants to sing in the middle of the dance floor. Nothing better for him than to be the centre of attention – literally. But he doesn't stop when he reaches the middle of the floor. He keeps walking towards me.

I go completely still, unsure of what he's doing or planning. I don't know how to react to this, to the way he's walking toward me like he's got all the time in the world, like everyone else around us doesn't exist. I try to remember everything I've read in romance novels, every movie scene I've watched, but none of that prepares me for this. For him. For this moment.

He reaches out for my hand, and I grab it lightly.

He leans into my ear, and I can feel the warmth of his breath as he whispers, "Go with it."

My legs buckle slightly as his words tickle my ears. He pulls back and looks at me, searching my eyes to see if I'm okay with this. I nod and he pulls me with him, singing the last chorus. I follow him as he walks backwards until we are in the middle of the dance floor. People are staring, but he keeps his eyes on me and his hand on mine. My brain can't wander off to another thought because all I can see is him.

Lucas pulls me closer, his other hand finding its way to my waist, gripping me in a way that feels almost possessive, and places the microphone between us. Despite the people surrounding us, his eyes are only on me. Staring into my eyes, smirking while singing.

The song finishes, and the crowd erupts into cheers. But we don't move. We stay exactly where we are, locked in place. Lucas's face softens, a smile playing at the corners of his lips as he watches me, eyes crinkling slightly at the edges. I've never noticed the freckles on his nose before, the way his hair falls over his forehead, partly covering his eyebrows. For a moment, he looks so... different. Like he's no longer the guy who's been annoying the hell out of me for the past couple of weeks. He's something else entirely.

My cheeks heat up, betraying me. I hate it when they do that.

Lucas' eyes drop to my cheeks, his smile rising more. He stares for a beat too long, and I blink, breaking eye contact. My Pop would always talk about eyes being the windows of the soul. It makes me uncomfortable thinking about someone seeing me like that.

He clears his throat, putting the mic down by his side. "I think that oughta do it, Goldie."

Oh right. My friends. The whole plan. I had honestly forgotten the reason for this. For a second, it was nice to think that this type of thing would happen to me. I was the girl to get the rom-com moments and the girl to be in a relationship that others stare at, wishing it was their own.

"Yeah, I think you're probably right about that. Nice acting skills, Lucas."

He kisses my cheek and walks off. As he left, he said something about texting me tomorrow so we can talk more about our plan. I don't hear him mainly because all I can hear is my name being shouted by Keets. Time to face the wolves.

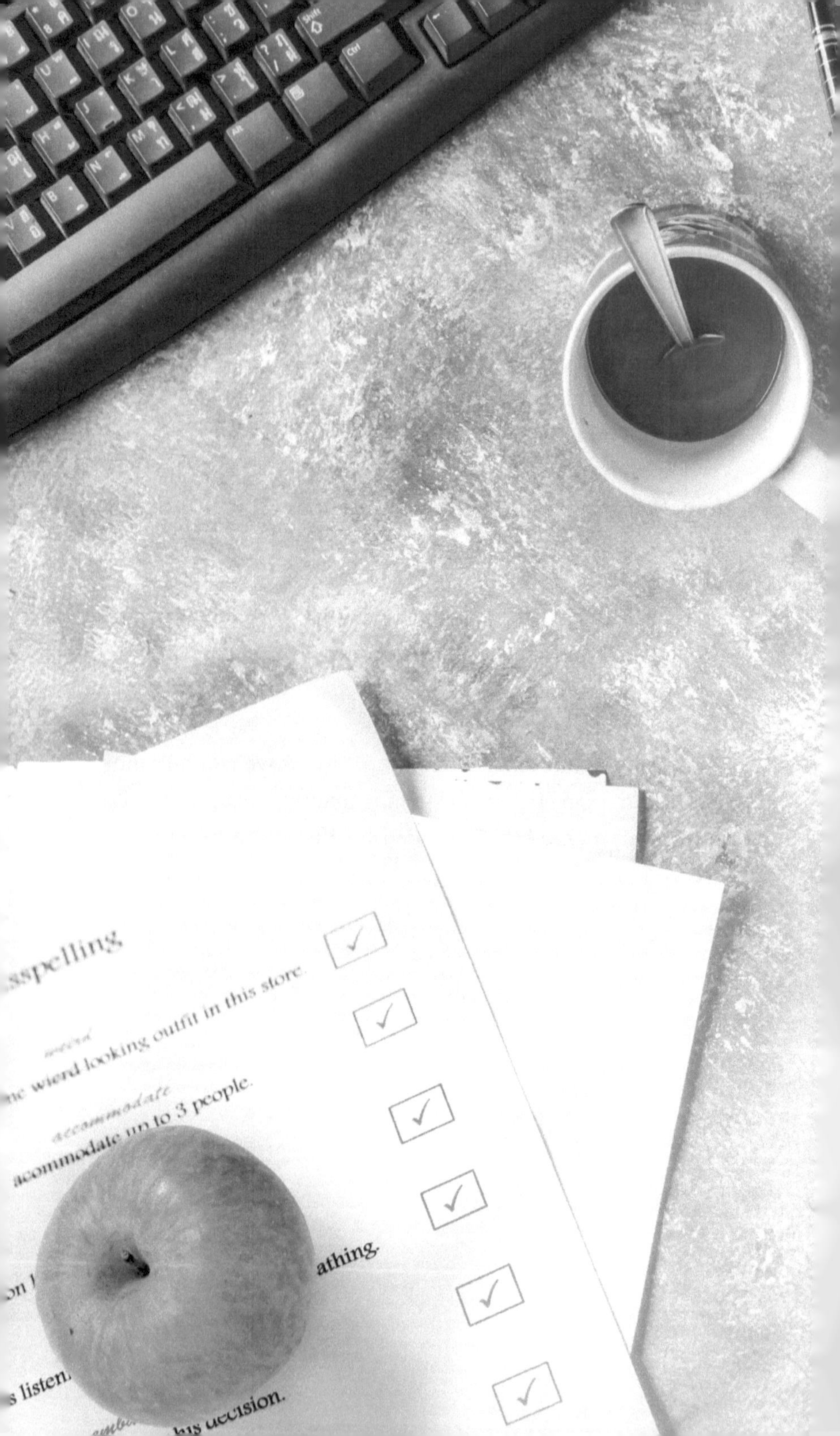
sspelling
weird
ne wierd looking outfit in this store.
accommodate
acommodate up to 3 people.
athing
listen
his decision.

Chapter Thirteen

STELLA

THE POUNDING HEADACHE AND NAUSEA I'M currently feeling is 100% the fault of that cocktail Keets gave me. I didn't even have more than just one glass, and somehow, I'm still dead.

I managed to play the part of a star-struck girl with a crush last night when all my friends came up after Lucas' song. Luckily, a lot of my friends are big talkers, and I didn't need to say much to explain myself. Unfortunately, Keets wasn't as easy. She had a lot of questions, which I ignored by dragging her to dance to someone butchering Defying Gravity. Maybe a slightly off song to dance to, but I didn't know how to explain it to Keets and thought if we got drunk enough, she'd drop it. At least until I figured out what to say.

I very slowly sit up in bed, catching a glimpse of myself in my vanity mirror. My waves are all over the place. I'm still wearing my red dress from last night, but the halter strap has come undone, leaving only the boob tape holding them up.

I drink some water, put on some music, and look at the stack of books on my bedside table, trying to decide which one of the three I'm in the middle of I should read. There is no surprise when my hand just happens to reach for the first book in my favourite book series about three famous sisters, their romance, and the found family they all form. Just when I'm about to open the first page, my door gets slammed open.

"Good morning sunshine!" Keets bounces in – yes, bounces – and jumps on my bed. I fall back with a groan, completely unable to understand how she is so awake.

"Why do you hate me? Screaming so loud, waking your poor best friend up. So mean." I roll over, pouting and shove my face into my pillow, hoping she'll leave. Knowing her, that won't happen.

"You were awake before I came in. I heard your reading playlist." She comes and lies next to me on my bed; her blonde hair nearly suffocates me. "You have some explaining to do, and I'm not leaving until I get some answers. And you know I mean that." She does.

"Ugh, fine." I roll back onto my back, trying to remember what I came up with to say to her last night. "He came up to me at the bar yesterday to try and convince me to let him take me on a date. I said no because he annoys me, and he told me that annoyance was just out of sexual chemistry. I say that last part with air quotes. Keets is just sitting next to me, nodding along. Which makes sense considering she probably agrees that we just need to fuck.

"I told him I wasn't interested in dating anyone, and he asked what would make me change my mind to go out with him." I sat up a bit, trying to really play my part. "I jokingly said to him, 'Go sing something and get people to dance to you and I'll go out on ONE date with you,' and the fucker did it."

"So now you are going out on a date with him?" She asks, staying deadly still, her face contorting slightly. I genuinely can't tell if she believes me.

"Well, he hasn't texted me or anything, so I don't know. But I don't go back on my word, so I guess, yes, I am."

She nods and gets off the bed and walks towards the door without a single word. She opens my door and walks out, half closing it behind her. She's gone for a minute before she comes back holding a piece of paper. She's smiling a little bit too hard.

"Here, read this."

I unfold the paper to see the date written on the top. It's the day I first talked to Lucas in the Library.

On it, she's written,

I, Keets Ellis, solemnly predict that Stella will end up falling madly in love with Lucas. Or at least fuck him more than once (basically the same thing to her)

And she signed it at the bottom.

"You've got to be kidding me. What about me saying he enraged me made you get this vibe?"

She twirls around and heads back for the door, humming a song as she leaves the room. I guess his performance worked. I'm about to return to my book, but my phone dings.

Shorty: Hey, it's your boyfriend. You free today?

Stella: Hmm, odd. I don't remember agreeing to date anyone.

Shorty: Oh, sorry, jumping ahead of myself. Let me try again.

Shorty: Hey, it's the guy you've been drooling over for the last 2 weeks. You free today?

Stella: Your ego never fails to astound me, Lucas. I can meet up with you for dinner. I have plans today.

Shorty: A hot date? Cheating on me already, it's like an arrow to the heart. But sounds good. I'll see you at the restaurant where it all started at 6

Stella: Where did it all start? Who are you, Hemingway?

Stella: Also, no date, just bed rotting with a romance book, thank you very much.

I put my phone down only to hear buzzes going like crazy. I pick up my phone to catch the last message.

Shorty: You are totally one of those girls who read cartoon cover books that are just straight porn, aren't you? It's all making sense.

Chapter Fourteen

LUKE

WHEN I SEE THE READ NOTIFICATION ON THAT last text, I smile at my phone. I didn't expect her to respond to it, but I find it funny she turned on her read notifications. They hadn't been there when I texted her a few days ago.

"Who are you texting?" Beck cuts in. He's standing in the kitchen, only wearing a towel. Beck's not exactly known for being modest, but today, it's like he's purposely trying to make a statement. His eyes flicker over to me as he leans casually against the counter, the towel hanging dangerously low on his hips. I grab the shirt hanging off the chair next to me and chuck it at him.

"For once, can you wear clothes? Rory's sister is coming over soon."

"I forgot that it was this morning." He grabs the shirt and puts it on. "You know, maybe you'd be less grumpy if you just let the boys breathe for a bit. They don't like being all cooped up."

"Can you not refer to your balls as boys, please?" Rory interjects, walking in with his younger sister. She's 16 and goes to high school in Sydney, so he gets to see her a lot. He's really protective of Jessie. It's obvious how much he loves her. It's hard sometimes seeing them interact.

"Hey Jessie." Both Beck and I say in unison.

She walks up and puts her school bag down. "What were you two bickering about?"

"We weren't bickering."

I say at the same time Beck says, "He wouldn't tell me who he was texting."

I turn to him and glare.

Shut up, shut up, shut up.

"And why does it matter who he's texting?"

"It matters because he was smiling like an idiot." He says in a tone that sounds like he's a 12-year-old schoolgirl singing the kissing tree song. Then again, he kind of always sounds like that.

Rory and Jessie both spin to look at me with the exact same widened look on their faces.

"Explain." This time it's coming from Rory. I stand up, pushing my chair back into the kitchen island.

"Okay, it's not that deep. I'm texting a friend who's helping me with that reunion thing I have to go to."

Beck practically jumps with excitement. "Wait, you listened to my advice? Found someone to pretend?" It's kinda sad how excited he is that someone actually took what he said seriously. Then again, the reason we don't is because usually his advice comes in the form of fucking and forgetting or as some long-winded rant that usually loses the original point by the end.

"Don't tell me you actually..." Ror goes to rub his forehead.

"I did. And it's going to work perfectly."

I walk up the stairs to my room. If I'm having this dinner later, I need more than a couple of hours of sleep.

"Can I at least ask who the girl is?"

I turn back to face Rory. "Stella," I say as quietly as humanly possible.

"Sorry? What was that?" Beck adds.

Standing a bit taller, I say, "Stella."

Both their eyes go wide as I nod and walk upstairs, going straight to my room.

I think I hear Jessie ask, "Who's Stella?" Before I slam my door and pass out.

"Here you go, doll." The waitress puts down two iced drinks, vanilla for me and chocolate for her. I was surprisingly nervous about this and got here like fifteen minutes early. So, I thought I'd do the boyfriend-ly thing and order us some drinks.

I'm going to be so good at this.

I thought it made sense for us to meet at the same place where I first suggested the whole fake dating thing. Full circle moment and all. Not to mention that I'll take any excuse to eat a burger and not the slush they call dining hall food.

The bell of the door makes me look up, and I see Stella walk in. She's got her curly hair in a bun at the top of her head, similar to when I first met her in the library. She's wearing a hoodie and shorts. Shorts that are way too short to be wearing when I'm trying to control myself. I try mentally telling my dick to calm down when it twitches at the sight of her.

"Didn't your mum teach you it's not polite to stare,

Lucas?" she says, throwing back the same thing I said to her at the lantern. I laugh, as she puts possibly the biggest bag I've ever seen on the table. It makes a loud thump as she puts it down.

"Okay, Jesus Christ, Goldie. What do you have in that thing?" I say, pointing at the Mary Poppins bag.

"You never know what you might need when you're out. Some gum, lip gloss," her eyes trail off, "mace. You know, just girly things." She smiles extra sweetly, as my eyes bug out.

"You thought you might need mace to come meet me for an early dinner?" I question.

"Well, considering the current company." She drones.

I mock grab my chest, "Goldie, I'm hurt."

She shakes her head, signaling a lack of care. Rude. And then pulls out a notebook and pen.

"Okay, let's do this."

"A notebook and pen? Seriously, you've watched too many romcoms." I reach over and grab the notebook from her. It's not stupid to take notes, but mine will definitely be better. "Just drink your iced chocolate and breathe."

She looks down, seeming to only just notice the iced chocolate I ordered for her. Her face twists in confusion, before reaching forward and grabbing the glass.

"Oh, thanks." She takes a sip.

Jesus Christ, has this girl never experienced a single act of kindness ever?

We sit in silence for a few minutes while we enjoy our iced drinks.

I can see her confidence slowly coming back. "Alright, let's do this before anyone sees me in public with you."

There she is.

"Isn't being seen in public together the whole point of this?"

"Shut up." She takes a thoughtful sip of her drink. "Wait, you still haven't told me exactly what you need me for."

"Other than your dazzling personality?"

She scowls.

"Okay fine, as you know, my parents are dicks. They have this notion that because I have tattoos and work at a bar, I'm somewhat of a devil reincarnation." I don't miss the way her eyes move down my arm, looking at the tattoos. Nor the way my hair stands on its end when she does so. "It doesn't help that after I graduate, I want to own a bar."

She nods, "Yeah, I can imagine that's very Luciferian actions."

"Exactly. So anyways, there's this family reunion thing coming up and my little brother is bringing his new fiancée in his dazzling sports car that he got as a gift from the perfect law firm he's joining after he graduates."

"I'm sensing some slight tension."

Now it's my turn to scowl.

"I just want my parents off my ass, and showing up with a pretty girl will help. It won't stop them from trying to micromanage me or from comparing me on the daily to him." My voice lowers. Shaking it off, I keep talking. "But it might give me some peace. At least for a little bit."

I look up and see her looking at me with those same soft eyes I got last night. I shift a bit, that look making me regret opening my mouth. She must sense my discomfort.

"You think I'm pretty?"

I ignore her and open the notebook to the first page. Titling it, 'Goldie and Lucas's super-secret contract.'

"What are you doing?"

I look up at her. "Making a contract. I feel like that's always a part of fake dating. I mean, isn't that why you brought the notebook?"

"Well, yes. But let me do it. You are going to ruin it." She goes to reach for the notebook and promptly knocks over her iced chocolate. "Shit."

The waitress comes over with some paper towels to wipe it up. Stella's constant apologies to the waitress reach my ears as blush starts creeping up her neck.

"She'll have another one, thank you."

The waitress nods at me, smiling, and walks off. I turn back to face Stella.

"What was that about me ruining it?" She scoffs but doesn't say anything else.

"Okay, so point one, you will attend the lovely family reunion with me. It comes with a weekend stay at a fancy resort, an open bar, and of course." I gesture to myself, "yours truly."

"Woo, an overnight trip! Exactly what I was hoping for." The words would seem enthusiastic, but the dry look on her face says otherwise.

"Point two, you have to take me on dates that my friends are highly aware of. I suck at lying, and I'm more stressed about it than I'd care to admit, so you gotta help me come up with ways to sell it. Oh, you also have to cover for me on my nightly adventures, let's say."

I start writing, "Lucas must take credit for every slutty action Stella takes part in, including taking blame for hickeys." I'm smiling, looking down, especially as a straw wrapper is thrown at my head.

"Seriously? No one actually enjoys hickeys."

I look up at her. "I think you're getting hickeys from the wrong person." We both stare at each other. My eyes roam down to her neck, wondering what she'd sound like if I were the one doing that to her. How she would say my name, how her body would react. Stella takes a deep breath. We are interrupted by the waitress clearing her throat, placing the iced chocolate down.

Stella also clears her throat. "Put that if, at any point, either of us wants to pull out. Don't." She says prematurely at my snicker. "We can. No hard feelings, no anger. It just stops."

I nod, writing it down. That was a no-brainer to me, but it seems important to her that it's written, so I do.

"Oh, and also."

"Yes, Goldie?"

She fidgets with her shirt again, seemingly nervous to say what she's thinking. "I don't want you to kiss me."

"I'm sorry, what? No one is going to believe that you, I say in the nicest way possible, wouldn't kiss the guy you are with. What do you suck at it or something?"

Her nose scrunches up. Cute. "No, I do not suck at it. I'm a great kisser. Thank you very much. But no kissing. I've forced myself to do stuff I was uncomfortable with before, and I won't do it again." She stares at me. I nod and write it down. She seems dead set on this. What happened to make her so against kissing me for this? I shake the thought off; it's none of my business.

"Goldie, one last thing."

"I swear to God if you say, 'you can't fall in love with me,' I am going to leap over this table and strangle you. Drinks be damned."

I put my hands up in defense. "Woah okay, I'll just shut up then." I thought it'd be funny, but living all of a sudden sounds better. I sign the bottom and pass the sheet to her, watching as she reads over it. This girl has absolutely zero faith in me. She signs it too, before pulling out her phone and taking a photo. She smiles sweetly, a smile I've come to realise means danger.

"Just for safekeeping."

"Of course." I reach my hand across the table, holding it out for her. She tentatively reaches for it, shaking my hand.

"It seems we have a deal, Goldie."

She nods and goes to signal for the bill.

"What are you doing?"

She looks at me, confused. "We made our agreement. Is there something else?"

"Yeah, no way in hell am I leaving without a burger. So, put your hand down and look at the menu."

She quickly pulls her hand down and goes to open her mouth, but I interrupt her.

"Look." I point aggressively at the menu.

She huffs and her face scrunches up, her freckles disappearing into the crevices, but she looks down. Point Lucas.

I have a feeling this is going to be a long, few months.

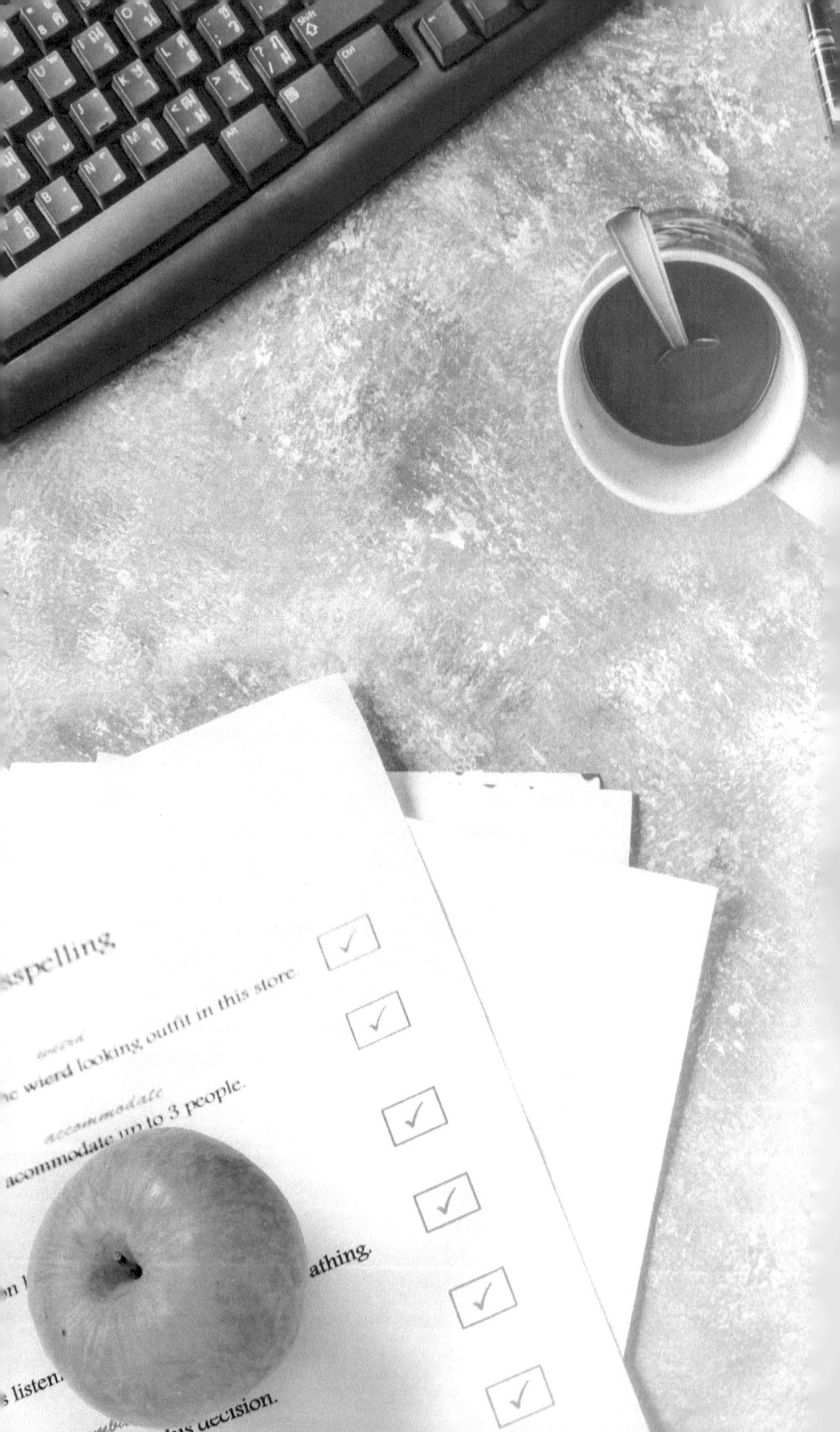
spelling
wierd looking outfit in this store.
accommodate
acommodate up to 3 people.
athing
listen
decision.

Chapter Fifteen

STELLA

ROLLING AROUND IN BED, IT'S IMPOSSIBLE NOT TO think about the shit show I've agreed to be a part of. I was adamant on this being the dumbest idea I've ever heard a few weeks ago, and now? Now I'm jumping every time I get a text, scared it's going to be him making plans for our first date.

Date. Jesus. I haven't been on one of those in years. Although I don't know if I'd call what I used to do with my ex dates, per se. They definitely weren't anything like the pre-planned, thoughtfully chosen dates I see everyone else go on daily. Bitter party of one apparently.

I had a surprisingly good time with Lucas last night, not that I'd ever share that information with him. It's easy to talk to him. He's so upfront about what he's thinking that it's impossible to be embarrassed. I haven't laughed that hard in a while.

Lucas paid for dinner last night. Didn't say anything, just put cash down on the bill and got up to leave. Like it wouldn't even have been a suggestion for me to cover any of the costs. He also kept ordering me iced chocolates when I finished them. When I got back from the bathroom, there was a new one sitting on the table. I thought that I was going crazy because I swore I had finished it before I left, but there it was. The only other person to look out for me like that is Keets. She does limit me to one every meal, saying I'm going to die if I keep drinking them. My phone dings, causing me to jump. I stand up, reaching for my phone on my desk.

Predictable. I pick it up and see Lucas texting me.

Shorty: Are you doing anything tonight?

Me: No plans yet. Why?

Shorty: Is Keets home?

Considering I can hear her pop girlies playlist I'm going to go with yes on that one.

Me: Yeah, Why?

Shorty: Be ready in twenty minutes ;)

Shorty: Shit meant :)*

Me: Sure you did

Me: Answer the question, why?

Shorty: Because it's time for our first date, girlfriend. Go get ready

My breath hitches in my throat. I knew it would happen eventually and that he wasn't just going to forget about our agreement, but I was kind of hoping he would. I don't know what people do on dates. What do I wear? He didn't even tell me what we are doing, so how am I meant to know how to dress? And what if I'm late or he's late or something goes wrong?

Woah.

I grab onto the side of my desk, feeling lightheaded.

Four in, four hold, four out, four hold.

I start repeating the box breathing I found online. It's not working. That's what the website said. It said if I kept breathing like this, it would stop. Why isn't it stopping? Fingers dig into my arm, holding me tight.

My heart feels like it's running a marathon, sprinting away from me. Is this what a heart attack feels like? I'm only 21. I can't be having a heart attack.

Four in.

Fuck.

There's a tingling sensation that starts in my hands. I hold it up trying to massage it. My body drops to the floor, trying to hold onto the desk, but I'm not able to. Four hold. I can hear yelling. Someone is shouting. I can't make out who it is. Crouching up, I hold myself together. Trying to feel my body, trying to feel that I'm okay.

Four out. Stella. Breathe.

There's a knock at my door.

"Stel? You okay? I heard a bang." Keets shouts. I go to respond, but my chest starts getting tight. Date. When was the last time I went on a date? It was probably right before Par– he broke up with me. Was it at his place? In that room?

"Okay, I'm coming in." Keets bursts through the door and sees me hunched over. She quickly comes up to me, crouching just below me and looking up.

"Hey, breathe. Deep breaths. What's happening, Stel?"

I'm gasping for breath. "Lucas. He's- date."

"Okay, he's coming to get you for a date now." I have no idea how she got that so quickly, considering I could barely hear myself talk.

I nod slowly, still counting to four over and over again. I don't know what's happening to me. I've never not been in control of my body like this.

"Okay, that's exciting, right! I'm sure he's got a great plan for you guys, and it's going to be fun. But I need you to keep breathing for me." She's holding my other hand and rubbing it. "In, one, two, three, four." How does she know about the box breathing? I follow her advice, my breathing slowing, listening to her speak. I start to feel myself calm down after a couple of minutes and go to sit on the bed. She comes to sit next to me.

"I'm sorry," I say with my head down. I can feel tears starting to well in my eyes. Nothing seems adequate to say after that.

"You never have to apologise for that ever. What happened?"

"I just started freaking out when he said he was coming to pick me up. I don't know why."

"Yes, you do. And it's okay." She pats me on the back. "You know it's different this time, right?" I nod curtly. "And if it's not, you call me, and I'll cut his dick off and feed it to him."

A hollow laugh escaped me, barely more than a breath. "Ew Keets, morbid."

She shrugs. "There's nothing else you need to tell me about this date, is there? Because you know I'm your best friend and you can tell me anything."

Shit.

"No, I promise. Just normal anxiety." Keets smiles,

seemingly accepting my answer. "Hey, how'd you know about the box breathing?"

"Oh, I read about it online somewhere. After you started getting nightmares, I just wanted to make sure I knew how to help." She turns and smiles at me. Jesus, I'm lucky to have her. I lean my head on her shoulder and close my eyes.

"So, when is he picking you up?"

"Oh god, in like five minutes!" I spring up and start running around like a mad chicken. "What do I wear!?"

Keets stands up and places her hands on either side of my shoulders.

"You go do your hair and makeup, fast." She turns towards my closet. "I'm going to pick out an outfit for you. Hey Google, play my pre-date hype playlist." The song Maneater starts playing on the speaker, causing me to laugh. Especially when I turn and see Keets' very serious expression looking at the closet.

She turns back. "Stella, you're wasting precious getting-ready time. Veet!"

Chapter Sixteen

LUKE

MANEATER BY NELLY FURTADO IS FILLING MY EARS, with the noise of speaking following suit, as I walk towards her front door. I wonder if she knows how little sound protection her door provides. Everyone can probably hear her talking when they walk past. There's no privacy.

She should do something about that.

I got here ten minutes early. Leaving my place way sooner than I needed to because I wanted to get her flowers. I thought it was pretty crucial that I should play the part of the doting boyfriend. Honestly though, I don't know if I'm going overboard on this date. After what Rory told me, I just thought she deserved something nice, even if this was how it happened. She should have hope that this will happen for her one day. And if she really is as against relationships as she says, it's clear someone would need to sweep her off her feet to get her to try it again.

I'm just playing my part.

I thought it would take me ages to pick out some flowers for her. I've never bought a girl flowers, so I don't really know what the protocol is. But I walked into the flower shop and saw the ones I'm holding now. It was a no-brainer. They look like little bird heads, with orange feathers, fiery, unique. It just made me think of Stella.

Before I think twice about it, I knock.

No harm in being early, right? The door swings open, and the sight in front of me is really for sore eyes.

"Why are you here?" A breathless Keets asks me. She's wearing some sort of top hat and fluffy scarf. It looks like she was playing dress up.

"I'm here to take Stella on a date?" I gesture to the suit and the flowers. Keets gives me a look up and down.

"Yeah, no shit." She shifts on her feet. "But you're ten minutes early? Also, why are you wearing a suit?"

"My bad?" I ask, my head slightly twitching. I'm really confused. "And I'm wearing the suit because it's a date. Isn't that like a date protocol?"

I think I hear her curse under her breath.

"Stel, we gotta change our game plan." She shouts over her shoulder. Turning back to me, she says as calmly as she can. "Come in, I guess."

I go to step into their apartment, peeking my head in to look around. It looks a lot like what I'd imagine the inside of a teenager's head looks like. I'm interrupted by Stella's voice coming from what I can only assume is her room.

"Don't let him in! He can wait outside. Punishment for not telling me the dress code."

"Hey! I thought it was common knowledge that 'date' meant dressing up."

Keets pushes me out of the doorway and holds onto the door. "Sorry, pretty boy. See you in ten." She smiles and waves as she slams the door shut. I then hear very loud and quick footsteps as the music is turned up. What the fuck just happened?

Checking my watch for the third time, just to make sure I'm actually on time now, I stand up, brushing off any creases that have formed on my pants. The music has also been turned off, which feels like a good sign. My hand is shaking as I go to knock.

The door swings open, except instead of Keets, Stella is standing there, and the wind is taken out of me. Her hair is down, the waves perfectly styled – except for one piece that's fallen in front of her face. My eyes move downwards, spotting the dress she's currently wearing. It's a dark green silk that falls perfectly on her body. The dress goes up to her neck, but I can see from the way she's standing that her back, and a bit of her side, is completely out. I'm going to have to walk in front of her for the entirety of tonight. She lifts her hand to push her hair out of her face, and I see that she's got rings on nearly every finger and a chain that connects to the bracelets she has on. I feel my hands drop a little, going lax. There is no denying this girl is beautiful.

"Well, greet each other and be cute." I hear Keets say. I just noticed she was there, fluffing her hands around like a mother sending her daughter off to prom.

I let out a small cough. "You clean up nice, Goldie."

Her eyes, which weren't on my face before, snapped up.

"Oh, this? Barely took any effort. I just look like this naturally." She shrugs her shoulders.

"Careful there, you are starting to sound like me."

She makes a fake gagging sound, but stops when I hold up the bouquet.

"I got these for you." She doesn't say anything. Just stares at my hand holding the flowers. Oh shit, did I go too far? I thought she'd like them and it would do well in the whole convincing Keets thing. "If you don't like them, that's okay. I can take them back. Or better yet, throw them in the trash. That's totally fine. No stress." I go to put them down outside her apartment, but her hand stops me.

"No, I'm sorry, they are beautiful." She grabs them from me and places them on the counter in the kitchen. Walking back to me, she smiles apologetically. "No one's ever gotten me flowers, so I was just surprised." Once I hear that, I have this overwhelming urge to buy her flowers every week. But only because Keets is sitting right there, and no boyfriend would hear that and not buy her flowers.

She goes on her toes and kisses me on the cheek. My stomach flips. She's good at this.

"I really do like them, though. I've never seen flowers like them."

"Yeah, -um, they reminded me of you." I stutter like a schoolboy. She smiles, and in that moment, I know I would do anything to see that smile again. I'm not used to this sweet side of Stella. It's nice. I am missing getting bullied, though.

"Okay, you two, go be cute somewhere else. Let's not forget I am incredibly single." Keets says, pulling me out of my daze.

"Of course. Have a good night, Keets. Goldie?" I turn so she can link her arm through mine. "You ready?"

"As I'll ever be," she says, her arm loops through mine.

The door closes behind us, and Stella moves away from me immediately.

"I'm going to pretend to not be offended by that."

She rolls her eyes. "Oh, come on. You can survive without me touching you."

I hope so.

"So are we just gonna go to the diner or something?"

I whip my head around. "Excuse me? Who do you take me for? An amateur?"

"My bad, Jesus."

"Just keep walking. The cars unlocked right outside."

She's walking ahead of me. I see the back of her dress, and yep, fully open. I feel my dick twitch. Not the time. It's hard to look away. The dress dips just low enough that every few steps I see a peak of black lace. The dress is barely covering the sides of her tits. I need to move. I quickly walk ahead of her, opening the front door and the car door, muttering something about being a gentleman. I think I played it off perfectly.

"Get yourself together," I mutter, getting in the driver's side.

"Where are we going?" She asks the second I'm in.

"Can you be patient for, like, two seconds? The drive is literally five minutes."

"Tell me. There's no need to actually do surprises. You know that, right?"

I turn to look at her, staring her dead in the eyes. "Be quiet and let me take you on a date. You said you were anxious about lying, so you are not going to have to lie about what we did."

She stares at me, before huffing and sitting lower in her seat. She's silent for a minute while I get the car started.

But then she speaks, quietly, as if she's being held at gunpoint. "You look alright too, I guess."

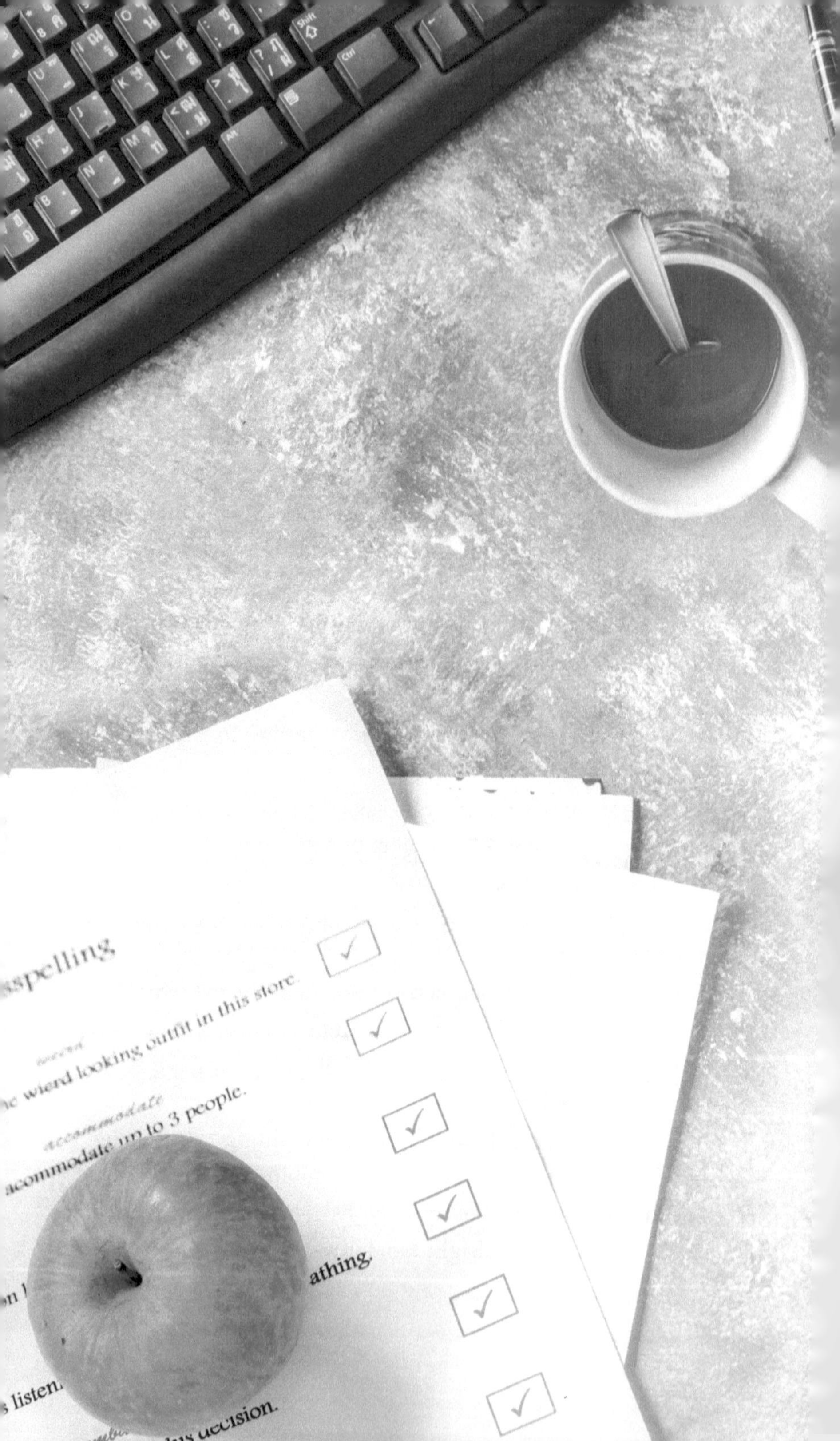
spelling
wierd
he wierd looking outfit in this store.
acommodate
acommodate up to 3 people.
athing.
listen.
his decision.

Chapter Seventeen

STELLA

HE WASN'T KIDDING WHEN HE SAID THE DRIVE WAS only five minutes. Despite the length, he still managed 3 dirty jokes and 2 ego-boosting comments. His own, of course. I can't deny that I was entertained. He makes me laugh more than I'd care to admit out loud. I guess it wouldn't be horrible if we are friends, considering we are stuck with one another at least until the new year. I feel the car come to a slow stop and see Lucas put the car into park.

"Okay, we are here."

He unbuckles his seatbelt, stepping out in front of the local bookstore in Brookstone. It's a tiny place run by a woman named Evangeline. Although when you drop as much money as I do there, you get upgraded to Evie. She's completely incredible. Her voice somehow carries the weight of both the oldest soul you'll ever meet and the cheekiest person at the same time. I don't know anything about her personal life, just that she was the first one to recommend paranormal romances for me.

The building itself looks like it's fallen straight out of a

French mediaeval town. The original cobblestone still decorates the outside, and flowers grow from the vines running up and down the wall. Because of all of this, it's at the end of our street, and it's not uncommon to feel like you are being watched by a vindictive ghost.

All this to say – I love it here.

My car door opens, and Lucas puts out his hand to help me get out. Pushing it away, I pull myself out of the car.

"What are we doing here?" I ask, straightening out my dress. He's staring at me and quickly swallows before responding.

"We're here for our date, Goldie." I feel his fingers intertwine with mine. "Now be a good fake girlfriend and pretend like you aren't repulsed by my touch."

Yeah, pretending that is going to be easier than he might think.

He starts walking ahead, pulling me behind him. I run a little to catch up, silently questioning why I chose to wear heels.

"Lucas, stop!" He comes to a halt, turning and facing me.

"What?" I look up at him. Oh. That's why. The glow from the streetlamp lights him up perfectly, his freshly shaven face and the fact that he towers over me on display. Which most guys don't.

I catch my breath.

"I've been here enough times to know they aren't open to the public at 8:30 pm." He stares at me blankly.

"No shit, Sherlock." Lucas starts walking again, stopping right in front of the closed sign on the door. "That's why we are breaking in." He turns towards the door, blocking my vision of what he's doing.

"Lucas, I don't know your middle name, Astor. What

the hell are you thinking?! Are you serious!?" He pushes open the now unlocked door.

"Jesus, no, Goldie. Evie would castrate me. I don't have a death wish." Evie? The low light causes something to shine in his right hand. "I have a key." Lucas grabs my hand again, pulling me inside, the sound of a soft click behind us. I'm left thoroughly confused about what the hell is going on. "Oh, and by the way, my middle name is Jude."

I don't have time to respond because he starts walking faster through the first row of bookshelves. I can see the faint glow of something at the end.

"Close your eyes."

"I am not closing my eyes." He looks at me and I stare straight at him, clearly not backing down. He rolls his eyes, stepping behind me, capturing both my wrists in a single, unyielding grip. A free hand slides up to cover my eyes, and my breath hitches.

"So stubborn, Goldie." I feel his breath against my ears. "Now, walk."

I walk forward until I hear a stop whispered gently. My hands are released, and I slowly open my eyes, adjusting to the new low glow I am surrounded by.

We are standing in the back area of the bookshop. Fairy lights are strung along the bookshelves, lighting up the room. The big windows that completely cover the far wall are open, letting in a breeze. But what stops me is the scene on the floor. There is a picnic blanket with pillows surrounding the borders, food and drink covering the centre. My throat starts to tighten slightly when I look up and see him staring at me. His brown eyes are soft, and his hands are fidgeting with each other, waiting for me to say something.

"What is all of this?" I ask quietly.

"Our date." He says as if this is the most natural thing in the world. As if any guy would go through this much effort for a girl they like, let alone someone they didn't. "I had to plan something that would make sure your friends would understand why you are all of a sudden dating exclusively. And like I said, you didn't think you'd be very good at lying, so this way, you aren't. Well, about the circumstances, sure, but not about what we did." Breathe. Breathe. I am not going to have a panic attack in front of Lucas Astor. This is fake. You aren't actually dating anyone; it's not like last time. I keep repeating them over and over until I start to feel my heart rate slow down.

Lucas is still standing there, unmoving. I go to sit down, making myself comfortable on the pillows – kicking my heels off.

"Well, c'mon then Lucas, can't let all this food go cold." He lets out a breath I didn't see he was holding.

"Yes, ma'am." He responds by sitting down and opening the food.

"Okay, no, there's no way! I do not believe you!" I shout at Lucas, who's just told me the most outrageous story known to man.

"True story."

"You kidnapped the mascot of Bridgetown?! It's a cat – that's alive." He nods, laughing into his drink.

"Trust me, I know. When we gave the fucker back, Rory and I were left with physical scars, whereas Beck was left with a quote-unquote gaping hole in his heart."

"Beck bonded with the cat?"

"Like you would not believe. It broke my heart slightly

to tear them apart. But as fun as drunken antics are, I was not about to go to jail because of it."

"What a sweetheart you are." Lucas nods, closing his eyes as if he's some tortured soul. I pick up the last blueberry from the charcuterie board and throw it at his face. Hitting him square on his left cheek.

"Hey!" His eyes open, spotting the berry now on the blanket. He picks it up and places it in his mouth. "How dare you waste the last blueberry. They are sacred!"

"You are so gross." Unable to contain my laughter as he nods again, completely okay with that label. I don't know how long we've been sitting here talking, but it's nice to pretend for a while. And for someone as narcissistic as he is, Lucas has been throwing back every question I've asked him. Not only that, but he seems genuinely interested in knowing the answer.

"Okay, I have a question." Lucas pipes up, his face suddenly becoming serious. I sit up slightly, trying to match his new energy.

"Shoot."

"Do you..." He stops for dramatic effect before continuing, "Ever listen to anyone who isn't Taylor Swift?"

A laugh escapes me, "Nope, and proudly." I smile, sticking my head further in the air.

"Really?" He asks, his face contorting in slight judgment.

"Yup, I am one with the pop girlies through and through. With no shame. I love it. Who do you like listening to?"

A small smile creeps across his face. "I like older music, The Beatles, Bruce Springsteen, some Midnight Oil. Think classic Aussie dad bangers."

I groan, rolling my eyes, "Wow, Lucas, you are so not

like other guys. It's crazy. Next thing, you are going to pull out your film camera that you keep in your second-hand leather satchel."

His mouth drops open. "How'd you know?"

I laugh softly, my head tilting in amusement. "Okay, I'm sending you a playlist of Taylor songs. And not the ones you know, I'm talking Illicit Affairs, New Year's Day, maybe some Haunted action."

His eyes are dancing with humour, but he doesn't object. Instead, he nods, accepting his future. The small silence that follows reminds me I still have no idea how we made it in the bookstore.

I look up at him. "Wait, you never told me how you got a key to this place. We aren't actually going to get murdered by Evie, are we?"

He chuckles, "No. Let's just say living with her son gives me a bit of an in."

I think for a second, "Beck?"

"God no. I mean Evie loves him and all, but I think she'd go crazy if they were related. Rory's her son. She runs the bookstore, and her husband, Rory's dad, owns the Black Lantern." All of a sudden, a wave of realisation washes over me. It's almost scary how similar Rory looks to his mum when you think about it.

"How did I not know this?!"

"I don't know. Take it up with my best friend." He's wearing a shit eating grin.

"Evie would be a fun mum, and I guess his dad must be pretty cool to be married to her." I turn to face Lucas.

"Yeah, they are the best. I think I've spent more time with them these last few years than with my parents ever." He lets out a dry laugh, and I notice his eyes darken slightly. Before I have a chance to ask, he quickly goes back to smirking. "It feels good knowing something you didn't." My hand moves to grab something else off the chopping board.

I'm stopped, however, by Lucas grabbing my wrist and saying, "Let's not make hurting Luke a regular appearance, please."

Dropping my hand, I start laughing again.

"You know, despite your best efforts, Goldie, you seem to be enjoying yourself." I shake my head.

"Go fuck yourself."

"Gladly, we are all about sexual positivity in this household." Oh my god, this fucking guy.

"Shut up and eat your cheese, Lucas." He shows a smug smile, grabs some Gouda from the board.

Against my better judgment, I think I could get used to this whole 'friends with Luke' thing.

Chapter Eighteen

LUKE

IT USED TO BE SO WEIRD BEING HERE DURING THE day. Seeing the Lantern filled with light streaming through the windows, over the dim lighting it normally has, was weird. Ror used to joke that it felt like we had an alcohol problem being in a bar this many hours a day.

Now I enjoy all the extra time I get to spend here. Maybe it's me getting sappy in my old age, or maybe it's just the realisation that I only have a year and a half left at Brookstone. Who knows? I'm just a sentimental piece of shit, clearly.

And while I love running the bar and making drinks, days like today are my favourite. Where it's just us.

Today I got the invigorating job of washing all the cups for tonight. You don't ever realise how many drinks you truly sold until you have to do all the dishes the next day.

"Hey, I'm going to take the trash out. Need to throw anything else in?" Daniel asks from the other side of the bar. Daniel is a pretty new hire, but is settling in well. He's

22 and is in his last year of uni. I like him so far. He's a good bartender.

"Nah, I'm good, man. Thanks, though." He nods, walking out of the bar. Acknowledging Beck, Rory, and Steve, who are sitting at a booth discussing the upcoming schedule. I don't know how I got the short end of the stick with the chores that needed to be done today.

Steve sticks his head out slightly, making sure Daniel has left before speaking up. "So, how do we feel about the new hire?"

Both Rory and I nod, saying he's good at the same time that Beck says, "he's hot."

I think it's Beck's personal mission to traumatise Stevo in any way he can. The look on Steve's face every time Beck opens his mouth is hilarious.

"Keep it in your pants, Beck." He holds up his hand in defense, not taking back his previous comment. Rory slides out of the booth and sits down on the bar stool directly across from where I'm standing.

"Aww, Ror, was the booth too far away from me?" I joke, giving him a kissy face.

"You know it." He responds, winking. I chuckle, going back to washing the glass in front of me. There is an orange stain on the bottom that won't budge.

"So," Rory says, dragging out the word, causing me to look back at him. I arch an eyebrow, silently questioning. "You had the first date with Stella, did you not?"

A loud bang causes both of us to look over to the booth where Beck has just fallen out of. He stands up, brushing off his pants, and walks over to the bar. Trying to play off whatever the hell just happened.

"Smooth son," Steve calls out from the booth where he's

still sitting. Rory and I snicker as Beck sits down, flipping both of us off. I turn back to Rory.

"Not sure I'd call it a date, per se. I took her out on the first fake date a couple of nights ago." Trying to place emphasis on 'fake'.

"Okay. And what did you do on this fake date?" Beck asks, placing a similar emphasis on the word fake. I didn't tell them what I had planned beforehand because I knew exactly what they would say. They're all convinced this arrangement is headed for a different ending than I'm expecting – meaning they're analysing every word I say when it comes to Stella.

"Oh, you know, just dinner. Nothing fancy." I lie, brushing them off. If they found out what I actually did, I'd never hear the end of it. Not that I'm ashamed of her or anything, just that I would like to keep their tiny faith that we aren't going to end up head over heels in love with each other.

"Wait, Luke. I thought Evie mentioned you needed access to the bookstore. Wasn't that for the date?" Steve pipes in, sitting in the booth. At first, I think he's genuinely asking, but the second I see the shit eating grin on his face, I know he just wanted to throw me under the bus.

Rory and Beck are both staring at me expectantly. I can practically see the gears turning in their heads.

"You took Stella to the bookstore?" Rory says, his mouth twitching as he holds back a smile.

"Yes, I did. It had to be something big so that her friends would believe what we were doing." I turn to look at Steve, who's desperately trying to contain a laugh. "Thanks for that, Stevo."

"So wait, wait." Beck holds up his hands as he speaks. "What exactly did you do in this bookstore?" I look back down at the sink, not wanting to give them the satisfaction of an answer. They are going to act like it's a big deal. When it really isn't, I like doing that sort of thing. Even for just a friend. And I don't think it's crazy to call Stella a friend.

Rory swivels around on the stool, facing towards Steve.

"Dad?" He asks. Beck swivels around to look at Steve too, presumably making some sort of begging face. Steve's eyes find mine, and the daggers I am sending his way – ones that he doesn't take seriously. That becomes clear as he smirks and coughs, clearing his throat.

"Well, from what Eve told me, there was takeout and candles involved. And, apparently Luke even wore a suit."

"How the hell would you even know that?" I ask, exasperated.

"Security cameras, son. They see everything."

I groan, throwing my head back as Rory and Beck turn back around to me.

"A suit, huh?" Rory asks.

"Don't forget about the candles, Ror," Beck says, fluttering his eyelashes at me. I know they aren't making fun of me for what I did. More than I did all of it, for Stella.

"Okay, calm down, you two. It's not that deep."

"They are totally going to fall in love and be together forever and ever and ever and ever." Beck grins at me.

"How many times do I need to tell you guys? It's fake. She's a bad liar, so I wanted to help her out, okay? If I do well on my end of the bargain, she'll be more inclined to do well on hers."

Both Rory and Beck's heads bobbed, the gesture dripping with sarcasm.

"Wait, bargain?" I hear Steve ask from the booth. I forgot I hadn't told him about all of this yet.

"Yeah. I needed a date to take to my family thing, and

Stella needed a cover with her friends. So, we said we'd fake date. Just to help each other out." He nods as if it isn't completely insane. I point to Beck and Rory, "and these two idiots fully believe we are going to end up together. Which obviously is not going to happen."

I expect Steve to pipe up and tell me that I'm crazy for fake dating someone. Or to pipe up and agree with me. He does neither.

"Well." He says, drawing out the word like how his son spoke earlier. "They have a point."

"Yes, Papa Steve to the rescue," Beck shouts, earning him a light-hearted glare from Stevo.

I groan, "Not you too!"

"All I can say is that I have some specific experience in this area, and I did in fact fall in love with the girl I was meant to be covering for." Both Beck and I gape, shocked at what Steve is saying.

"Sorry, what?" Beck asks, "You fake-dated someone? Why?"

Steve chuckles, "Not just someone, Evie."

I shake my head in disbelief. "True story. I was a really bad student and needed someone to help tutor me. Eve was top of our class. The problem was, she couldn't stand me – thought I wasn't serious enough about anything. She flat-out refused to help, until one day, out of the blue, she made me a deal. She'd tutor me if I taught her how to date. We were seniors, and she'd never even been kissed. I said yes, and the rest. What do the kids say these days?" He pauses for a second, thinking. "Oh yeah – is history."

"That is the best meeting story ever," Beck says, his mouth hanging open. I'm shocked, but trying not to show it. In what world do people actually do this stuff?

Ours apparently.

"Okay, yeah. That's cute and all, but that's not what's happening here. So, let's just drop it." I turn around to pick up the next crate of glasses. I still have like ten to go – I'm never getting out of here.

"What are we dropping?" I struggle to stop myself from letting out a groan as Evie walks in. Now the whole families here – I'm a goner.

"Just Luke's slow-motion car crash of a love life," Beck says. Evie nods as if she understands completely, but is cut off from saying anything by Steve.

The second he saw her, he was out of the booth, walking over to give her a kiss. They are both in their fifties and are still just as in love as the day they met. I've never once experienced the love that is on their faces right now – it looks pure and beautiful. I ache to feel that.

"Hi, Beautiful," Steve says, still holding onto Evie. Whenever they're in the same room, they're always in sync – whether it's a quiet conversation, stolen glances, or the way they gravitate toward each other, almost without thinking. It's like there's an invisible pull between them, a connection that doesn't need words to be understood. Evie smiles back at him, her face lighting up with the kind of joy that's impossible to fake. Her eyes shine as she looks at him like he's the only person in the room. She gives him another kiss before joining the conversation I was desperately hoping was over.

"So I'm going to make the assumption that this is about Stella?"

Rory nods as Evie walks over and gives him a kiss on the head.

"We should start a bet pool or something for how long they are going to take to get together officially."

"Yes!" Beck shouts, standing up, giving Evie a hug. "That is the best idea you've ever had."

I don't even deign to a response, rolling my eyes and walking into the backroom. They are insane for thinking that's going to happen. It is a mutually beneficial relationship – that's it. I just happen to be good at planning dates, so what?

I peek my head out of the back room, causing them all to go silent and stare at me.

"100 bucks says we don't get together." Beck nods, and I return to the room, satisfied that I'm going to win this bet.

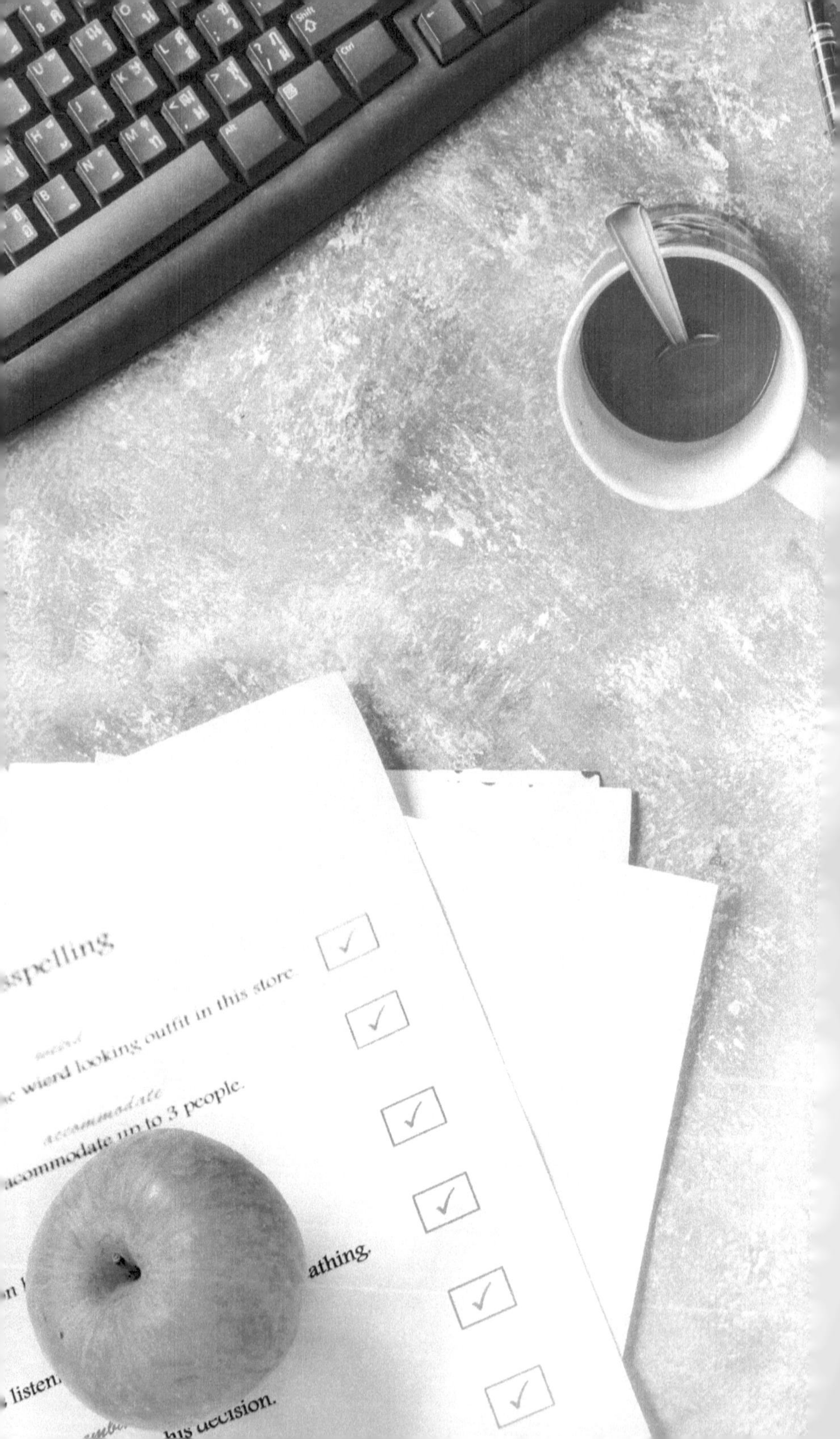
spelling
wierd
he wierd looking outfit in this store.
accommodate
acommodate up to 3 people.
athing
listen.
his decision.

Chapter Nineteen

STELLA

"OH THANK GOD COFFEE." I PRAISE KEETS AS I walk into the kitchen. The smell of her cafe spreading through the air in the kitchen got me up pretty fast.

Keet's hands me a mug. "Why are you so dead today?" She reaches and grabs a bit of my hair. "And you know typically it's good to, you know, look after your appearance."

I slap her hand away. "Firstly, rude. Secondly, the teacher for my pre-k class needed help drafting the lesson plan for next week, so I was up all night."

She nods in understanding.

"Why don't you just go to sleep? Just lean into the whole grandma 6pm bedtime thing."

"Um, I can't." She turns to face me.

"Why not? We have no plans tonight."

I take a sip of my coffee, trying to mask what I'm saying. "I have another date with Lucas."

"Sorry? Come again for Big Fudge."

Lowering my mug, I say more clearly, "I have another date with Lucas tonight."

She says nothing, staring at me – her eyes unblinking.

"Okay."

That's it? I don't think I've ever heard Keets say a one-word sentence in her life. I take it as a blessing.

"Okay." I give her a curt nod and quickly leave the kitchen. Eager to be out of there before she starts asking me more questions.

I'm in my room for barely five seconds before the door gets swung open. Keets runs in and sits on the edge of my bed.

"Yes?" I ask, pulling my hair up into a ponytail. I'm running late again, shit.

"It's just." She looks like she's going to draw blood with how hard she's trying to bite her tongue. "A second date? Like an official second date?"

I nod, "yup."

"Okay, and we are happy about this?" She eyes me wearily. I take a deep breath. I can do this.

"Yes, we are. I'm still nervous as hell about the whole thing, but I'm trying." She nods, and I can see a small smile shadow her lips.

"And you're not seeing anyone else?" I pause the brush that's currently applying my blush. I actually have to lie now.

"Nope. No one else." Her mouth opened slightly, but I cut her off. "No more questions. I'm already stressed about running late again, and I still need to finish my makeup. I love you, but get out."

She falls back on my bed looking like a toddler throwing a tantrum. For a second, I think I'm fucked and she's going to keep asking me questions.

But then she gets up and walks out. "You better tell me everything tomorrow as she closes the door." Okay, that went alright, right? There were no accusations of my lying, and while she did look like she was going to bug out, she seemed convinced. I can totally do this. For a split second, I think this is really a bad idea, but the smile that was forming on her face when she realised I was committed to someone makes me shake that thought off. I'm sure if I told her what I was really doing, she'd say I didn't need to do it and that I was being insane. But her reaction, the peace that settled on her face, is why I'm certain I have to do this.

Even if it's just for a bit.

Throughout our entire friendship, Keets has been nothing but perfect. Anytime I've needed someone, she's been there without a second thought. Her laugh and smile is contagious, and no matter how harsh the world gets, she's always right there beside me. While I'm busy ignoring the little things, she's already three steps ahead, watching out. She's the sun in my life. I don't know how to exist without her. And if I need to fake date Luke for a little to give her a respite from stressing about me, that's what I'm going to do.

No doubt in my mind.

I also had a decent time at the "date" Luke took me on last week. He's a fun person to be around. And even though I haven't used the benefits of this arrangement yet, I'm glad it's there. I did get a message from a guy I used to talk to about hanging, so I think I'll see him after this date. I'm nervous about the logistics of this working, but I'm sure we will figure it out. I'm so scared about lying to Keets, though. Every time a word about Luke spills out of my mouth, my heart stops, thinking that she knows I'm lying. Plus, this plan isn't forever. We'll 'date' for a bit and then break up, which will give me a pass on hookups for a while.

And maybe then I'll feel ready to talk to Keets.

About everything.

I grab my bag and head out into the living room, only to find Luke already standing in our living room. Keets is nowhere to be found; however, I'm assuming she's lurking in the kitchen somewhere. It's one thing to lie to her about the circumstances of our date or to have a two-second interaction as we are leaving, but it's a completely different thing to have to pretend to be head over heels for him while she's right there. The first time we did it, I felt like I was going to pass out. I cannot do it again. I quickly walked up to him.

"Hi Lucas, shall we?" I point towards the door, trying to get him out of the apartment.

"Woah, Goldie, what's the rush?" He grabs my arms and stops me. His eyes are squinted slightly.

"No rush, just excited to go to the carnival, that's all." I smile up at him, hoping he'll get the sign that I want to leave.

"You guys are going to the carnival? Nice, Stel loves it there." Keets pops out of the kitchen holding a glass of water that she hands to Luke. He downs it in one sip.

"Yeah, Goldie seemed like that type. Here." He turns to me and hands me another bouquet. It's got some of the most beautiful flowers I've ever seen. I grab the bouquet from him, examining the flower he's chosen for me tonight. They have a dark purple middle, almost the colour of the amethyst crystal, and white flowers sticking out every which way. "They are called amethyst in snow. I think finding unique flowers for you is becoming our thing." He smiles and pulls me into his side, kissing me on the head. I stiffen slightly. "Oh, and by the way, you look beautiful."

It's sweet of him to say that, but I don't. I threw on the first clothes I could find and barely put myself together. I looked a lot better on our first date. I look up at him, trying my best to show a loving smile, but all I can think about is Keets staring at us.

"Thank you. We should go through." I place the flowers on the coffee table, knowing Keets will replace the now dead flowers from our last date with these ones. "Bye Keets, love you!"

"Love you too, baby." I see Luke laugh at her response.

Are you really best friends if you don't get dating accusations on the daily?

I grab his hand and rush us out of the door, closing it behind us. When I hear the click of the handle in the frame, I finally breathe. Turning around, I see Luke's head tilted, looking at me as if I have three heads. I shrug my shoulders.

"Why don't you want me in your apartment?" I really don't want to have to explain this to him. I shift on my feet, getting slightly annoyed.

"I don't want you in my apartment, Lucas. You are reading into things. I just want to go to the carnival." I go to walk down to the car, but am stopped by the lack of footsteps following me.

"Yeah, no, I don't believe you." He leans against the doorframe and places his hands in his pockets. He's wearing tan baggy pants and a grey knit sweater. I can see the collar of the white t-shirt he's wearing sticking out. He looks good.

"Lucas, I swear to god." He doesn't budge.

"Stella, this only works if we are honest with each

other." I groan. He called me Stella. He's not going to budge. I walk up to him, lowering my voice.

"Fine. I am nervous about faking it in front of her with you there, okay? Keets has this weird tendency to know exactly what I'm thinking, and she will be able to tell this isn't real in two seconds if she sees us properly interact." He looks at me blankly before pulling out his phone and typing out a message. I hear the sound of the message sending before he pockets the phone again. He turns back towards the door.

"Lucas? What are you doing?!" He doesn't respond, knocking on the door. I try to jump to stop him, but he uses his free hand to hold me back easily – it's borderline embarrassing. The door opens, and Keets is left seeing this beautiful scene before her.

"Hello Keets, you mentioned earlier that you didn't have any plans. Correct?" Oh god no. She nods, confused. "Perfect. Would you like to come with us to the carnival? I'd love to get to know Stella's best friend, and my best friends will also be there, so you won't be third wheeling." He lets go of me using his hand to put it up to the side of his mouth, loudly whispering, "I know that sucks."

His friends are going to be there? Since when? She looks back and forth between the two of us, clearly amused. I know that look. That look tells me that Keets is now joining us on our date. Great.

"Let me just get changed quickly." She leaves the door open and goes into her room to get ready. I then hit Lucas on the head with my handbag.

"What the hell!?" I whisper yell, "I literally just told you I don't want to do this in front of her!"

He reaches his hand up, rubbing his head. "My God, woman, what do you have in that? A ten kilo dumbbell?" I roll my eyes. He's being dramatic. It's a cloth purse with a wallet and lip gloss. I'm holding my phone.

"Yeah, I wish, then I could bludgeon you to death with it."

He moves to stand in front of me, blocking my view of Keets' room. "Stella, the whole point of this was for Keets and your other friends to think you have a boyfriend. That can't happen if they never see us." I stare ahead, not looking at him. He's right, but I'm not about to admit that. "And the people I was just texting, Rory and Beck. If they are there, it'll take some of the focus off of us." I stop staring over his shoulders and move to look at his face. He seems sincere.

"Okay." He nods, looking too cocky. "I can still bludgeon you if you piss me off."

He chuckles, "Don't worry, Goldie. I know."

Chapter Twenty

LUKE

THE CAR RIDE OVER HERE WAS THE MOST FUN I'VE had in a while. I spent the entire car ride getting embarrassing stories out of Keets about Stella. All the way from getting too drunk on Halloween and calling everyone in her contacts to getting everyone to call her sparkles for a year when she was 10. The stories were funny, but the best part was seeing Stella turn more and more red. I think if she were a kettle, one more story would have made her boil.

The carnival is a 30-minute drive away, in between the main city and Brookstone. It comes through a few times every year, and while it's fun the first few times, the more you go, the less interesting it becomes. Ror, Beck, and I had the brilliant idea two years ago to come, get wasted, and play as many carnival games as we could. I don't think any of us realised how competitive we got once drunk. Overcompetitive drunk 19 and 20-year-olds versus rigged carnival games never end well. Honestly, I'm surprised we didn't get banned after that particular adventure.

Pulling up, Rory and Beck immediately spot us and head towards my car.

"Ror and Beck are walking over," I say to no one in particular, but I don't miss the blush that starts to take over Keets' cheek. Based on Stella's sly smile, she doesn't either. When we've stopped, Keets gets out incredibly fast, mumbling that we should have some couple time.

"So she knows that everyone knows she has a thing for Ror, right?"

Stella jumps and slams her hand on my mouth. "Oh my god, shut up, Lucas. You don't say that shit out loud. Girlcode man." I laugh, still trapped by her hand. And there is only one valid reaction for this situation.

"Eww!" Stella squeals, "tell me you did not just lick my hand."

I try to hold back a smile. "Okay, I won't."

She screams again and jumps towards me, moving to rub her hand over my face. I quickly dodge her attempts and pin her hands together in front of her chest. She's halfway on my lap at this point, having practically leaped to try and get me out. Her breath became heavier as her eyes jumped around each crevice of my face. I meet Stella's eyes, neither of us speaking. Her eyes are the most intense shade of green I've ever seen. I let my eyes roam down and immediately realised the mistake I'd made. She's wearing baggy jeans, which luckily hide her lower half, but her top doesn't do me that favour. Especially when I'm holding her arms together like this. It's a dark green tank top that she's tied in the back to make it fit her body completely. And unfortunately for me, at this moment it dips low enough for me to see that she's wearing a matching green lacy bra.

Fuck.

No. I am not getting hard while she is practically on my

lap. I look down and see that her ass has slid and is resting on my right thigh. A couple of inches to the left and she'd be right over where I wish she would be. Even if this arrangement didn't exist, I don't think I'd be able to fully control myself around this girl.

No, think of your grandma or something, Luke. Don't be stupid.

Luckily for me, the sound of knocking on the windscreen interrupts us. We both snap our heads around quickly and see Keets standing there, with Beck and Ror, making out in the background.

I lean down and whisper in her ear, "It seems we have an audience, Goldie."

She looks back at me, a deadpan look on her face. "In your dreams, Lucas." She's not entirely wrong.

Then she climbs off me and gets out of the car. I need to cool off before standing up. It's not that I'm into her, I'm not. Genuinely. But Jesus, there is no way to stop thoughts when she looks that good. She knows how to dress and how to move. I've got to get my shit together. Scaring her off with a hard-on before New Year's Eve is not an option.

"Took you long enough. We were just trying to figure out the best route through the carnival." Beck says as I walk up to them. I instinctively go to stand next to Stella, putting my arm around her. Her slight flinch doesn't go unnoticed. I feel her arm snake around my waist.

"I was saying that we should do the big rides first and recover with carnival games and eating." Keets interjects. She's standing next to Rory. He's dead still, almost like he's unsure how to act.

"And I was saying that that is the dumbest plan I've ever heard. We need to do carnival games first to warm up and then eat. Then big rides, because living life on the edge is way more fun." I hear Stella laugh beside me.

"Hey! No laughing at Beck. Not nice, Stella." Beck says that, referring to himself in the third person for some reason.

"I am so sorry, Beck, truly. Your plan is absolutely fantastic." Stella says, dipping her head in apology, her statement dripping with sarcasm.

"So anyways, we all know Stella is automatically gonna agree with Keets." Beck starts. Keets reaches up and high-fives Stella, one that she returns without a second of hesitation. "And Rory will obviously immediately agree with me." He turns to look at Ror, who stares back at Beck. I'm not as confident with Beck's assessment here. "So you are the tiebreaker. What do you say?"

I think for a second, looking between Keets and Beck. Normally, I'd agree with Beck; it's kinda fun to be an idiot at these carnivals. But as Stella's boyfriend, who's meant to be sucking up to her best friend, there's a pretty clear answer.

"Sorry, man, Keets is right. Rides first." Beck groans and throws his head back, as Keets squeals and jumps up. Rory starts walking towards the festival grounds, followed by Beck and Keets, who are calling Beck a loser and making L's with their hand towards him. Stella is still standing next to me, but lets go of her arm that was clinging to my waist.

"I feel like those two are either going to end tonight as best friends, or with one of them crying." She looks in the direction of the rest of our friends. "Maybe both."

I look down at her. "I'd place money on Keets making Beck cry." She laughs, not disagreeing.

"If we were doing Beck's plan, what food would you eat?" I ask out of curiosity.

She looks at me. "In a perfect world, sushi. It's my comfort food. However, at a carnival, probably a corndog." I go to open my mouth, but she moves her hand up. "Don't." I stifle my laugh.

"I can get behind some sushi, although Chinese food is always the best, let's be honest." She turns her head to the side a bit, disagreeing. Everyone else is ahead of us by a couple of minutes now, but she still doesn't move. Stella shifts on her feet, seeming nervous. I grab her hand and start walking towards them.

"Cmon, girlfriend, the circus awaits."

"You are such an idiot, Beck," Rory says, patting Beck on the back as he throws up behind a bush. It seems he decided his plan was still the best and snuck a few churros before going on a ride named the whirlwind. It's just so hard to see how that went wrong.

"Shut up and hold my hair back, Rory." I see Rory shake his head. Only Beck would manage to still joke while throwing up. Rory pats Beck's buzz cut, mouthing "idiot" in my direction. I chuckle and turn my attention back to Keets and Stella in front of me. They are playing a carnival game where they need to knock down a tower of cans with a ball. Seems simple enough, if one ignores the weighed-down cans and way-too-light balls you're given.

"Cmon, babes, put your back into it. We need that frog." Stella says, rubbing Keets' shoulder. Anyone seeing them would think they were getting ready for an MMA match.

"I've got this." Keets stretches her arm and grabs the first ball. She throws and…

"Ouch," I say, seeing the poor panda bear that just got

pegged in the face. Keets try again with the second and third ball, missing badly each time.

She slumps her shoulders, sighing, "This is rigged."

Stella pats her on the shoulders as I say, "You're only just figuring that out?"

They both turn and look at me, eyes narrowed.

"Sorry, let me guess. Stating the obvious is out of girl code." Before either of them has a chance to respond, Beck and Rory show up.

"Hey, Mr Vomitron over here finally stopped and wants something to eat."

"Is that wise?" Stella asks. She steps towards me, closing the already small distance between us.

"Stella, come on, I'm the wisest," Beck says, using his hands to stroke his invisible beard.

"Anyways, we were wondering if any of you wanted to come to get some food?" Rory asks.

"I'll come." Keets says almost too fast, "Being a third wheel with these two might make me hang myself. Oh, also Beck." She pokes him on the nose. "Vomit on me and I'll make your hand wash my clothes and buy me a new outfit." He scoffs, but Keets stares him down – she's not joking. I see him nod softly before they all walk off, leaving Stella and me alone.

"You're getting better at this," I say, turning to face her.

"Huh? Better at what?" She looks up at me, a little disoriented.

"Being my fake girlfriend." Her breath hitches slightly, eyes darting,

"Oh yeah, right. I guess it's just easier with other people here. I'm not overthinking it, you know." I nod in understanding. Looking over her shoulder, I see the carnival game that she and Keets were just playing.

"What were you trying so hard to win?" Stella turns around and points to a frog in the upper corner. It's wearing a monocle and a top hat and has eyes at different levels. "Seriously, that?" Glancing down at her, it's clear she's dead serious.

"Yeah, are you kidding me? He's adorable. He looks exactly like the one you guys have at the bar." I think back to the frog with a top hat sitting on one of the bar shelves. It was the first decoration we put up in the bar after I stumbled in with it. The frog is the unofficial mascot for the Black Lantern. I nod and pull out my wallet to give fifteen dollars to the carnival worker. Fifteen dollars for three balls is such a rip-off. I don't know why I do, but I gotta get that frog – she wants it, so she's going to get it.

"What are you doing?" Stella asks, as I throw a ball and knock down the first can.

"Isn't it obvious?" I throw the second ball, causing the bottom of the cans to move, but not fall. "I'm getting the frog. It's the boyfriendly thing to do."

"Oh my god, no, that is so cheesy." She gags, "The whole being taken to a carnival and the guy shows off his insane manliness by beating every carnival game and getting her ten stuffed animals that probably cost ten cents a piece." She scoffs as I throw the last ball, knocking over the cans.

"Well, it's not my fault. I just have insane manliness." The carnival worker passes me the frog, presumably overhearing our previous conversation. I hold the frog, examining it. It somehow looks more messed up the closer you look. "You know you might be the most unromantic romance reader I've ever met." I joke. She falters slightly, her face dropping. It's an obvious shift in her mood, and she steps back from me. Shit. I quickly lift the frog up in front of her, hoping she'll go to grab it.

She does.

"Ah ah ah, no frog for you, Goldie. You've hurt Reginald's feelings." I use my hand to push Reginald's head down, showing his betrayal.

"Reginald?" She asks, smiling again.

I nod, "It's the only name suitable for such a dignified frog like him." I push him right in front of Stella's face. "Now apologise."

She grabs the frog's hand. "I am sincerely sorry for calling you cheesy, Reginald. I would be most honoured for you to come home with me tonight."

Mustering up the best old-timey British accent I can, I respond as Reginald, "Why yes, good lady, I'd love to go home with a beautiful lass like you. Especially if I get to see all of this." I lift him up slightly, causing his head to look down her shirt. She laughs and smacks my arm out of the way. I'm actually pretty proud of myself with that one.

"You are an idiot."

I shrug and hand Reginald to her. "Maybe, but an idiot you now have a son with." She rolls her eyes, about to speak, but we both are distracted by the sound of someone crying. Turning around, we see it's Beck.

"Keets wouldn't let me buy a third ice cream." He wails. I turn to Stella.

"So did we end up making that bet or not?"

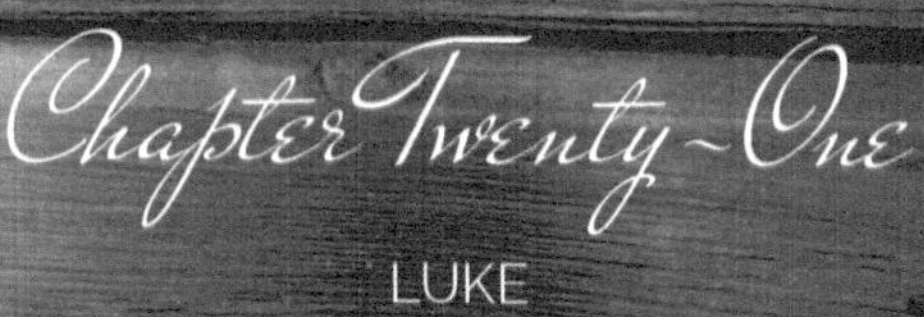

LUKE

Goldie: Beck showed up at our door this morning, stating he wanted to have a romcom marathon, and you guys said no to him.

Goldie: Keets says she's angry at you guys for hurting Beck

Goldie: I think somehow both my predictions at the carnival were correct.

Me: Okay, no, he clearly left out a lot of the story. I'm normally down to watch some Notebook type shit, but Ror has class and I had lunch plans with my brother.

Me: I cannot believe he's playing the victim like this

There's a beat before she responds.

Goldie: He admitted it, and Keets threw a pillow at his face. We are still doing the marathon, though.

Goldie: I will say, I'm slightly frightened to be around these two.

Me: Yeah, try to avoid getting caught in the crossfire.

She likes my message, and I turn my phone off, getting out of the car. Honestly, there is not a single flash of surprise on my face looking at the restaurant Leon chose. He picked a Japanese fusion place that's the top floor of some office building. Stella would probably like it here. It was a challenge finding a parking spot nearby that wouldn't involve valets turning their nose up at my car.

It takes me two seconds to spot Leon when I walk in, sitting in the far corner of the restaurant. He's wearing a polo and khaki pants, an Astor specialty outfit.

"Hello Luke." He says, standing up as he sees me. I shake the hand he's put out.

"Hello." Are all families this formal? I know this isn't how Rory and Jessie talk with each other. But maybe they are just a rare case. I pull my chair out and sit down across from him. I look down in front of me. Why are there so many different types of cutlery at a Japanese restaurant?

"So, how are things?" He asks, pouring me a glass of water. I take a long sip.

"Good." I search for more to tell him. "School's getting busy, but that's the usual for the end of the year."

He laughs, "I get that. Law school is killing me." Took all of two seconds to bring up law school. No shock there.

"I can imagine," I say, biting my tongue. The waiter comes over and takes our order. Leon orders us a pre-chosen menu, stating 'he's got it.' No complaints from me. I desperately want a shot or something right now. It kinda feels like the only way to get through this lunch. I don't know when it got like this. I just know it feels like it will never be like this.

"So, there is a reason I asked you to lunch." He sits up straighter.

"Figured so."

"I wanted to ask if you found someone to take with you to the reunion?" He looks at me, awaiting my answer. There's a part of me that doesn't want to tell him about Stella. I don't want them to ruin it.

But I know I need to.

I give a quick nod. "Her name is Stella. She's my girlfriend."

"Girlfriend?" His eyebrows are raised, but there's a smile on his face. It disappears almost as fast as it came.

"Yeah, we've been friends for a while and it just felt right." The lie slips out easily.

"What is she like?" He asks. It's weird, but it almost seems genuine.

"She's incredible. Stel's a bit closed off, but when you get to know her, she's one of the best people to be around. I don't know. She just makes you want to be better as a person. And she gets me, on a level a lot of others don't. And she's beautiful, she's got the most insane eyes, and her hair is wavy and untamable. It matches her perfectly." I respond, words leaving my mouth with no hesitation. Easier than I was expecting them to. Leon smiles properly this time.

"I'm glad to see you happy, brother." He replies warmly.

The word brother sounds unnatural coming from his mouth.

"What about you? How is Camilla?" Asking about his fiancée is always an easy conversation. He swallows, his smile dropping slightly. It's not gone, but it feels less somehow.

"She's good. Busy with mum planning the wedding. No space for me there." His smile quivers slightly, before he catches himself. "But I am completely okay with that. I'd be bored with all the details. And Camilla loves mum, so it's working out okay. She's excited to become Mrs. Astor." He forces a light laugh, trying to make it sound nonchalant. I want to ask if he's okay, but he's always loved this stuff. Or at least he has in the past...

"That's good. Your wedding will be perfect, I'm sure. Mum and Dad wouldn't let it be anything less." There's a bite as I speak, one that's hard to swallow. Ignoring the fact that they have an incessant need to show off, Leon is their baby. Whatever he wants, he will go. I wonder if he realizes that. He hesitantly dips his head, not wanting to open that can of worms. We are silent as the food comes and while we eat. He keeps looking like he's going to say something, but shuts himself up. I prefer it this way. I get enough attacks from our parents. I just want to eat without getting my entire future questioned.

"How's the bar?" Leon asks quietly, as the waiter clears our plates.

"It's good. Still bartending with my friends. Still planning on buying my own after graduation."

"Rory and Beck, right?" He says, looking at me through his eyebrows.

"Yeah," I say, surprised he knows their names. I'm sure

I've told him about them before. I just never thought he was listening. We fall silent again for the rest of lunch.

Leon pays the check, and we leave the restaurant.

I don't know what to say to him.

"I'm over there," I point towards my truck.

"Ah, I'm that way." He tilts his head in the opposite direction. "I guess I'll see you later." I give him a curt nod and start walking. This feels wrong. Lunches with Leon are normally cold; he talks about his school or Camilla the entire time. Doesn't ask me anything. I try to think back to the last time we did this, but I'm struggling to remember. It must have been last year? Jesus.

"Luke!" I hear someone call out from behind me. I spin to see Leon standing down the street with his hands in his pockets. He almost looks nervous.

"I really hope you get your bar."

"Thank you, Leon," I say, trying to ignore the rising confusion. He's never had any interest in my life before. Why now?

Once I'm in my truck, I pull out my phone to check my messages. A couple from Beck and Rory, and one from Stella. I ignore the ones from the guys and swipe open Stella's message.

> Goldie: I hope lunch with your brother went okay. If you need someone to beat him up, I can call someone.

I laugh to myself. I remember telling her that my family situation wasn't awesome, so she must have assumed that it extended to my brother as well. Before I think too hard about it, I pull up her contact and FaceTime her. She picks up on the first ring.

"Lucas?" She asks, sounding confused. She's got her

hair in a bun and is wearing a hoodie that is drowning her. I look behind her, noticing her fridge that's covered with magnets and coasters from bars around the area. It's sweet.

"So you wouldn't even come yourself? You'd send someone else to do your dirty work for you?" I ask, the shock on my face clear. She giggles.

"I can't ruin my manicure, Lucas. At least I'd do something."

"I guess that's a fair point." She's ridiculous. "How are you?" I ask, settling into my seat.

"Good. We are only one movie into the marathon. Beck has a long list for us to get through." She laughs, shaking her head. I like that she's getting to know the guys.

"Which one did you start with?"

"27 Dresses. Beck got very angry when he found out I hadn't watched it."

My eyebrows raise involuntarily. "Yeah, no shit. Who claims to like romcoms, but hasn't seen 27 Dresses."

Her head hangs low in shame.

"I know, I know – but at least I've seen the error of my ways."

"I'm glad to hear that," I respond, my thoughts scrambling for a follow-up. I don't really want this call to be over. "How was your thing last night?" She went on a date with a guy she's been chatting with for a while. The only reason I know is because I got a text from her saying if Keets asks, I'm with her. I made the deduction about what she was up to, even more so when I got a text saying she was home at like 3 am.

She doesn't miss a beat before responding, "It was actually better than expected."

I'm honestly impressed with how casually she is talking about sex. I respect the hell out of it.

"I'm glad to hear that, Goldie." She nods, clearly happy. I am genuinely glad to hear that the plan is working for her. She deserves to enjoy her 20s without stress. And if this gives her that, it's worth it, even if there is a part of me that wishes it were me.

"Okay, so, how was lunch? No catfights?" Stel asks, changing the topic smoothly.

"It was fine. A bit weird though." I say, thinking back to the lunch. I still can't really place my finger on what was off with it.

"In what way?" Her tone is warm and sincere.

"My brother just seemed off, like he wasn't okay? I can't explain it. Something just felt weird."

She chews her lip in thought. "You could text him, just saying you are there if he needs anything. Doesn't have to be a big thing."

"Yeah, maybe." I probably should; it really feels like something was off.

"Love birds, hang up!! We have a romantic rain scene to watch!!!" I hear someone shout from outside the camera. I can tell immediately that it's Keets. Clearly, Beck isn't the only one invested in this marathon.

"The notebook?" She nods, tucking her lips onto her teeth. "I'll let you go then." She smiles at me. She has a beautiful smile.

"Seriously, think about messaging your brother."

"I will. Bye, Goldie." She whispers bye before hanging up.

I know she's right and I should message him. It feels like the more I think about it, the worse of a brother I realise I am. Before mum and dad got involved, we used to be best friends. Neither of us was alone. Not letting myself overthink it too much, I pull out my phone, finding his contact.

Me: If you need anything, I'm here.

He responds immediately.

Leon: Thanks, man.

And even though he only responded with two words, it feels like a step in the right direction.

Chapter Twenty~Two

LUKE

FOR SOME REASON MY HEART HAS BEEN RACING all day. Seriously, since the moment I woke up this morning. I've hung out with Stella time and time again, but now it feels like it's more. I don't want to dwell on the fact that I am.

I walk into the diner, seeing Stella already sitting in what's become a usual booth for us. I got her text this morning saying we had to meet up and that she had something important to talk about. Because that's always a good sign. There's a part of me that's scared she's going to end this, which would suck. But just because I still need her for New Year's Eve. That's it.

Her leg is bouncing under the table, looking around for me. I slide into the booth effortlessly, trying to hide the anxiety on my face.

"Hey Goldie."

Her body visibly slackens as she notices me, "Lucas."

She smiles slightly before taking a breath. "Okay, I'm just

going to get straight into this, and I'm sorry if I ramble, but I just need to get it out."

I nod, trying to keep my breathing even.

"Keets asked me yesterday about our sex life, and I didn't know what to say. I panicked and told her that we were waiting until the right moment, but the way she looked at me was. I don't know. Like she knew."

I laugh a little. "Yeah, I mean, us not having sex is pretty obvious to some issue here."

"So anyways, now I don't know what to do because if she doesn't believe me, then there's no point doing this, and we might as well call this whole thing off."

I feel my stomach drop at that, at the idea that she might call this off.

"No!" I said a little louder than I was intending. Her eyes bug out slightly – confusion evident. "I mean, no, we don't need to call it off. There must be some other solution."

She shrugs, unsure of what to say. I don't know either. We need to convince Keets that we are having sex, in a way that doesn't include Stella lying. Great.

"If only you were a girl."

I shoot my head up. "What do you mean?"

"Girls are well versed in faking enjoyment in sex." I roll my eyes, but the humour dissipates when I realise that could work.

"Wait, we can just fake it." She stares at me as if I have two heads, a look I'm used to. "No, seriously, we can pretend to have sex. Make the noises, bang the wall, convince Keets it's happening. Then no one needs to lie because she will hear it herself."

"I'm not pretending to fuck you so that my roommate will hear Lucas."

I lean in. "Why? Scared you won't be able to control yourself?"

She leans in to match me, clearly aware of my challenge. "Trust me, I'll be fine." She sits back thinking for a second before adding, "Okay. Tonight, Keets is going to be home, and I can tell her you are coming over to join us for movie night or something."

I nod, picking up the menu, silently cursing for what I just got myself into.

I park the car and walk up to her apartment. I knock once, and the door immediately opens. Stella stands in front of me, looking just as out of breath as I am. I smirk, thinking that she might also be nervous for tonight. She's wearing a white baggy long-sleeved shirt that falls off her shoulder and is long enough to cover her shorts. Her hair is out, a bit wild, but I've come to notice that she always wears her hair exactly as it is. And it looks good.

"Hey!" She says a little bit too loud. Definitely nervous. I raise my eyebrows slightly. "Sorry, hey. I've been running around all day, spending half of my time watching reality TV and the other half cleaning." She gestures for me to come in. "Okay, I guess the watching TV part wasn't really running around."

I step into the apartment and look around for Keets, not spotting her.

"Keets is in the shower if that's who you're looking for. Just you and I."

"Oh, by the way, did you get the package I sent you?" I ordered them a soundproofing kit when I left their place a few weeks ago. I knew it would take a while to come.

"So you were the one to send us that? I thought it was some neighbour trying to passively-aggressively tell us to shut up," I laugh. "But yes, it's all set up." She points at her door, which now has the rubber strips around the edges.

"Good."

"You are a creep for that, you know." Probably, but I don't know her neighbors, and didn't want any actual creeps annoying her.

I hold up the bag I am holding behind me. "I guess none of this for you then?"

She raises her hand to go and grab the bag, but I pull it higher. Despite her being tall, she's not quite tall enough to reach it.

"Lucas, what's in the bag?" She looks at me in a way that makes it clear she'd easily kill me. It's my favourite look of hers.

Giving in, I hand her the bag.

"Oh my god, okay, you can survive through the night." She says, pulling out the boxes of sushi. I didn't know what type she liked, so I kind of just got all of it. I was justifying the purchase by knowing I was feeding three mouths tonight. And I have a feeling if it came to me over the sushi, I wouldn't win that battle.

"Yeah, I remember you mentioning it at the carnival, so I thought I'd supply, as the incredible boyfriend I am." She smiles and puts it down on the coffee table.

"Wait here." She says, dashing into the kitchen. I hear the fridge door open and close before she comes back out holding… blueberries?

"Apparently, we had the same thought." She hands it back to me before taking the sushi into the kitchen to plate it. I look down at the blueberries in my hand, my chest tightening slightly. I can't believe she remembered that.

And that she actually went out and bought a fresh pack for me. It's almost like she doesn't hate my company anymore. I pop a couple of blueberries in my mouth before pulling the fresh bouquet of flowers from my bag.

I went with teddy bear sunflowers today, mainly because after the carnival, I thought a stuffed animal flower was suitable. I toss the old flowers in the bin and replace the water with some in a water bottle on the coffee table. Feeling content with the arrangement, I set it back down on the windowsill and sat down on the couch. I'm not sitting for long when the bathroom door opens and Keets comes out wearing a duck slipper and her hair in a towel. She stops short when she sees me, raising her chin slightly to acknowledge me.

"Hey Luke."

"Hey Keets." I responded, "How are you?"

"Pretty good, starving though." As she says this, Stella walks back into the room with the sushi plated and chopsticks in her free hand.

"Oh, yup, okay, Luke, you are welcome anytime," Keets says, shoving a piece of sashimi in her mouth. I make a mental note that that's what she likes next time I come over. Impressing the best friend is boyfriend 101, no? Stella places the tray down and sits next to me on the couch. Keets takes the bean bag next to the coffee table.

"So Luke, did you and Rory make it up to Beck?"

I laugh, remembering the story he spun, "We did, he made us watch When Harry Met Sally while he explained all the behind-the-scenes facts that we were just dying to know." Sarcasm is heavy as I speak.

She nods, "Naturally." She takes another bite of the food. "Good job. He can be annoying when he's upset." I have a feeling Stella was right. I think those two are going to be the best of friends.

I look to my right. Stella's staring at the windowsill. At the flowers. Keets has turned on the TV, so I lean down to whisper in her ears, "You okay, Goldie?"

She shakes her head quickly, "Yeah, I was just noticing the new flowers."

"Oh yeah." I kept whispering, "I noticed that the other ones were dead. Hope you don't mind." She shakes her head, but still stays quiet. I sit back in my seat, placing my arm around her. Classic movie theatre trick, stretch and settle.

"So what are we watching?" I ask no one in particular.

Keets responds, "Too Hot To Handle, Stella and I are addicted."

"And Too Hot To Handle is?" I ask again, this time pointed at Stella.

"It's a reality TV show. The premise is they drop a bunch of horny twenty-year-olds on an island and tell them they aren't allowed to touch or else they lose money from the prize fund." She smiles, "It's so stupid, but so addicting."

"Do the guests get veto power? That sounds insanely dumb and boring."

Keets laughs and shakes her head, "No veto power. But trust, I felt the same before Stella got me hooked." She presses play on the show, and it starts. I settle into the couch as Stella leans a little bit more into me.

I say, my voice low, "I think if we were in there, I'd blow the entire cash prize in ten minutes, Goldie." I think I see a blush creep up her neck. She turns and looks to see if Keets was paying attention. She was, considering how fast she looked away when Stella made eye contact. Right, I totally said that knowing Keets would overhear.

What is going on with me?

"Oh no! Rob, come on! Don't be an idiot!" I shout at the TV. Anyone who would give up Isla must actually be an idiot. Both Keets and Stella laugh at me. "Both of you shut up. This is emotional for me."

Stella sits up a bit, so she can see my face.

"I thought you said reality TV shows were dumb." I use my hand to cover her mouth, gesturing to Keets to turn the volume up. She pauses the show instead, inciting groans from both Stella and me.

"Okay, calm down." She stands up, "I'm heading to sleep." I notice Stella shift beside me, concern lacing her face. "Stel, breathe. I'm good, just one of those days. My body needs some rest." Stella deflates, settling back down into the couch. I'm clearly missing something, but it doesn't seem like my place. Keets walks to her room, calling out goodnight over her shoulder, leaving Stella and me alone.

She scoots up on the couch. "I can clean this up tomorrow." I nod.

I know I should offer to help, but right now all I can think about is what we are about to do. We stand there in complete silence, both of us waiting for the other to speak. How does one platonically fake fuck someone they are fake-dating? A strained smile takes over her face, but her eyes are much more telling. At least I'm not alone in feeling terrified. I fear we are getting into complicated territory as she stands up and walks to her room.

Despite my instincts screaming at me to stay put, something strong is pulling at me. I follow her.

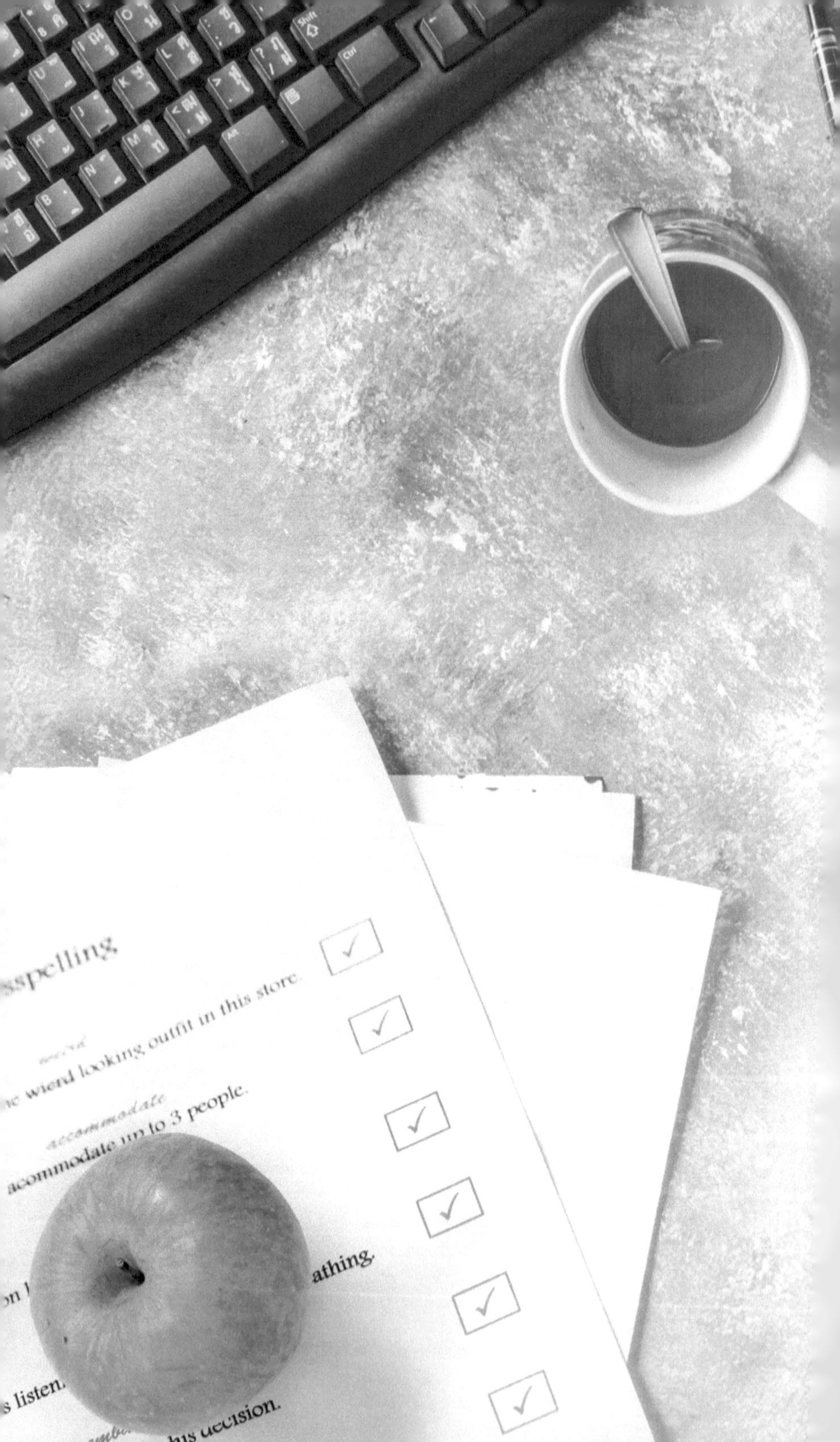
sspelling
wierd
c wierd looking outfit in this store.
accommodate
acommodate up to 3 people.
athing.
s listen
his decision.

Chapter Twenty~Three

STELLA

OKAY, THIS IS TOTALLY FINE. THIS IS TOTALLY FINE. I've just got a 6'3 tattooed bartender in my bedroom, planning on staying the night. Just a typical Wednesday. Except it's not typical. I don't let people stay over. Normally, it's wam bam thank you, ma'am. Wam bam? What am I even saying? But tonight he will be sleeping next to me, in my bed. The only reason I decided that was because I'm not cruel enough to subject him to a night on the floor. Keet's body pillow will be shoved between us.

"So."

"So," he responds, having yet to actually make his way fully into my room.

"You know you can actually step foot past the door threshold, right?" He nods, stepping into the room still barely speaking. Mr. Cocky from before gone. He walks around the room examining every part of it.

I was really excited about getting this room. The entire right wall is filled with windows that allow me to watch the sunset every single night. It fits my vanity, bookshelf, and bed, that is filled to the brim with stuffed. There is not a single part of the wall that is empty; every part is filled with posters and fan art of things I love.

"You think there's any printer ink left in the world?" Luke gestures to my wall.

"What can I say, I like clutter. Makes me feel at peace."

"I think most of the time it's the opposite, Goldie." He lays down on my side of the bed, seeming to be more comfortable than he was earlier. I sit down next to him on the bed.

"Hey son, you still creep the hell out of me, but I love you. Sorry for being a bit of a deadbeat dad." He grabs Reginald from the very sought-after middle of the bed position. I laugh as he kisses the top of his head. I don't know where this notion of Reginald being our child came from, but it's fun. However, I did make it clear to him that I was not sharing custody.

He's mine.

Sitting up, I drop my hands in my lap turning towards him. Luke puts Reginald down and mimics my actions exactly. Rude.

"So, like, what do we do?" I ask, hoping he'll basically talk me through this step by step. He seems like the type of person to talk you through it. Not that I'm thinking about that.

"I guess we just have to be vocal, hopefully, the walls are thin enough. Bang on the wall a bit. Gotta make sure it's a while, though, a guy has a reputation to keep up." The shit eating grin returns. There's a part of me that wants to finish this in two seconds, but again, not that cruel. He stares at me, waiting for me to do something.

"Nope, I am not starting this." He rolls his eyes.

"Seriously, Goldie, typically girls are more vocal than guys."

I stare back at him, "but what if I like vocal guys?"

He swallows.

"Okay then. No laughing." He points at me like a teacher would when scolding a child. Luke takes a deep breath, bringing his hands down in front of him as if he were doing a theatre warm up.

"Oh fuck, you look so good like that, baby." He says in a deep voice. Not quiet by any means, just lower. "Mm, yeah, just like that." I can feel his voice vibrating as he talks. He holds his thigh – almost as if he's steadying himself.

I take a quick breath and move to sit up slightly, sitting on my calves. He opens his eyes and looks at me, gesturing for me to make noise.

"Oh yeah, fuck Lucas. Right there." I say in a breathy moan. I feel ridiculous. I look at him only to see him staring at me, not saying anything.

His face is still. I keep going, "yes, please don't stop."

He's not moving.

I knock him on the knee to remind him he also has to be embarrassing the hell out of himself right now. He seems to knock out of it and gets up on his knees to start banging on the wall a bit. When he puts himself in that position his co-crotch is right in front of me. I try to look away, but I can't. Not when it seems like he's hard.

"You're taking me so well." Luke bangs the wall again; his legs are shaking slightly. "Good girl."

He did not just say that. Fucking hell. I shift on my heels, instinctively trying to find some friction. I blush as I notice what I was doing and go to join him on the wall banging. I also need to get myself out of the eyesight of his dick, especially as I feel my nipples pressing against my top. Fuck, I knew I should have worn a bra.

Once I'm at the same level as him, I notice his eyes drop. Traveling slowly up my body, stopping exactly where I hoped he wouldn't. I keep lightly banging on the wall, hoping he won't say anything. Slowly, I turn my head to look at him and see that he's already looking at my face.

The embarrassment is long gone. He's looking at me with a different look. Hunger. I keep his eye contact as I keep banging the wall.

"You like that, Goldie?" He keeps staring directly at me. "I bet you like how I'm fucking you." I swallowed, trying to steady myself.

Guess he is a talker.

I moan, but I'm not sure how much of it is fake. His facial expression changes causing him to lose some stability. I really fucking hope he didn't hear that last one. I don't have time to overanalyse it, though, because one second I'm up on my knees and the next I'm being crushed by Luke's body. His hands are either side of my head, holding himself up inches away from my face. His eyes drop to my lips and I see his Adam's apple bob. I shift slightly, quickly realising that was a mistake because now all I can feel is him. Exactly where I want him.

He leans down and whispers in my ears, "You doing okay there, Goldie?" I quickly nod, unable to say anything else. Okay no, this is ridiculous, pull yourself together Stella. I roll out from underneath him and sit at the edge of the bed. Taking a deep breath.

"I think that'll probably do it." I hear him shift to sit up as I speak. I turn my head around to see him now sitting on the edge of my bed. With a pillow. On his lap.

"Yup. Definitely convincing, I think."

"Okay well, I'm going to go to the bathroom and get ready for bed. So you can just get comfortable. I'll, um, be back in a second." I dart out of the room, heading to the bathroom. Once the door is closed I let myself panic. What the fuck was that? I mean Jesus. I know he's attractive, but I've never gotten this wet that fast. I need to breathe, I cannot fuck Luke Astor.

I put my hair into a loose plait in the back of my head, careful when braiding it to make sure I don't wake up looking like a zombie.

By the time I'm heading back to the room, I'm determined to have a peaceful, horn-free night. Easy enough.

Not easy.

It's 2 am according to the clock next to my bed, and I have yet to fall asleep. I keep peeking over to Luke to see if he's out, and he hasn't stirred once. How has he just fallen asleep so fast in a stranger's bed? Was he as impacted by what we did as I was? And why am I still thinking about this?

I've never been sexually attracted to someone I see as a friend. I can't just sleep with him and call it a day like I usually would. I don't want to lose him in my life. So I need to get my shit together.

"Get it together, Stella," I whisper out loud.

"Do you sleep talk or are you talking to yourself?" I hear Luke groan as he rolls towards me. Deep-voiced, sleepy Luke.

"Which is worse?" I ask

"Probably sleep talking, I can deal with borderline

craziness. But sleep talking is subconscious." I laugh because, of course, he has logic about that.

"Then I was sleep-talking." I smile even though he can't see it. "Anything to annoy you, Lucas?" I pat him on the head.

"Such a sweetheart you are."

"Go back to sleep, Lucas, it's the middle of the night."

I turn away from him, trying to tell myself the same thing. As I'm closing my eyes, a bright light gets turned on, making me dive under the covers like a vampire.

"Dude?! What the hell?" I squeal from under the covers. Luke pulls the blanket off, forcing me to see him sitting there. He's wearing his shirt, don't most guys sleep without their shirt on.

"What are you staring at?" He asks.

"You are wearing your shirt." Luke looks down at his chest and then back at me.

"Well, yeah, I didn't want to just strip and make you uncomfortable. But if you want to see my chest that badly, all you have to do is ask."

Right, yes, that's the normal, nice boyfriend behavior. Gotta remember that.

"No one truly wants to see that, Lucas. Now, why is the light on? It's two in the morning."

"Because," he says, Reginald in between us, "you woke me up with your ramblings. So now you must entertain me."

"Entertain you? What are you six?"

He tilts his head to the side, "I hope not, considering you had fake sex with me two hours ago." A blush crept up my neck, thinking about the things he said to me. Not the time.

"Fine." I say the first thing that comes to mind, "Why do you call me Goldie?"

He chuckles a bit, "I'm surprised you haven't figured that one out yourself." I squint my eyes, confused. I've thought about it, but it never made sense. I'm not blonde in any way, like almost the polar opposite in fact. "You'd think you've never seen Tangled before."

I look at him, tilting my head. He doesn't say anything else, seeming confident that statement was enough.

And then it clicks.

Rapunzel hair.

Her gold hair.

My favourite film, the one he caught me crying at in the library.

That sneaky fucker.

"You are a shit head."

He lays back in the bed looking very proud of himself, "the lantern scene is the most romantic Disney scene, and I'd die on that hill." I laugh, still a little bit shocked he's seen the movie.

"You like Tangled?" I ask

"I didn't when I was younger, but a recent rewatch has made me a fan." Recent rewatch? I'm about to ask him why he rewatched it, but I'm interrupted.

"Ooh! I think I packed cards. It's time you get crushed in bullshit, Ms. Stella Faraday."

The competitive side in me wakes up pretty damn fast, "You are so on, Mr. Lucas Astor."

Chapter Twenty~Four

LUKE

THE SUN STREAMING THROUGH THE WINDOW IN Stella's room wakes me up. You'd think she'd invest in curtains to prevent this exact thing. I peek at her alarm clock. It's 8:30. Two hours earlier than I would ever consider getting up on a day I have no classes. I go to turn around to fall back asleep, but I finally notice the pressure on my right arm. Stella is lying on my arm. She is, in fact, nestled up right next to me. She looks so peaceful.

Last night, we didn't end up falling asleep until four am. We played two rounds of bullshit, each lasting an hour. I didn't realise how competitive she was until halfway through the first game, when she threw half the deck at my head when she fell for my bluff.

Note to self, never play cards with her if there are weapons around.

When we finally gave up on playing cards, it took me a while to fall asleep. I couldn't stop thinking about last night. The way she was looking at me while we were faking it, her eyes wide. I swear I saw her staring at my dick, but I don't know if that was just in my head. I genuinely think telling her to do this might have been the dumbest thing I've ever done. My body already has some visceral reaction to this girl, but now I know what she sounds like moaning. What her face looks like when she's turned on. There's not much to do to get that out of my head.

All of this to say, I didn't get much sleep. I look back down at Stella. Her hair is loosely braided down her back, most of it having fallen out. I wonder why she does that. Maybe to keep her hair looking the same? Knowing I won't be able to fall back asleep, I reach to grab my phone – being careful not to move her. I have two notifications. One text from Rory,

'Hey, you down to meet up for lunch tomorrow? Beck is craving Pizza.' I respond with a thumbs up, asking what time to meet. The second is a text from my dad.

> Dad: I hear you have a girlfriend you are bringing to New Year's Eve. I hope she is who you make her out to be.

I audibly sigh. Great, just what I needed to wake up to – my dad being a dick. I'm thinking about whether or not I should respond when I hear a whimper from Stella next to me. Her eyes slightly flutter open and she realises that she's resting on my arm. Faster than I've ever seen her move, she sits up, blinking a few times – clearly still adjusting to being in the land of the living.

"You'd think I was made of poison or something." I

joke. It comes out more croaky than I intended, but it is the first time I've spoken.

"Haha," she lets out a short laugh, "Morning. Sorry if I drooled on your arm." She seems very thrown off waking up so close to me. Not in a judgmental way, but I assumed she would have people spending the night a lot more than the average person.

"It's okay, I think I'll somehow survive." I laugh while stretching my arm. It's gone practically dead from her sleeping on it. I'll never understand how guys in the movie make that position look so enjoyable – it kills me every time. Stella reaches and grabs her phone, smiling at the notification she's received.

"Keets said, and I quote, 'Jesus Christ, I am extremely envious of whatever you got last night and am going to hang myself with singleness.' I think she might have bought it." I nod.

"I'd say so." I get out of bed. "Honestly, I'm more surprised she didn't send something about shutting the fuck up while playing cards at two am."

She mock gasps, "Excuse me, I was not that loud."

"Oh, trust me, you were." The double meaning is clear. She shifts on her feet slightly.

"Well, to be fair, you weren't all that quiet either." I stand up and walk towards the desk shc's standing near. Stopping right in front of her, her breath hitches slightly as she looks up at me.

Dropping my voice low, I say, "I thought you liked it when guys weren't quiet." It's hard not to laugh when I see her face. I back up and grab my bag. "I'll leave you to enjoy your day. Thank you for the date, Goldie. It was fun."

She smiles, "Yeah, I'll see you soon."

And even though we don't have a date planned right now, I'm confident it's the truth.

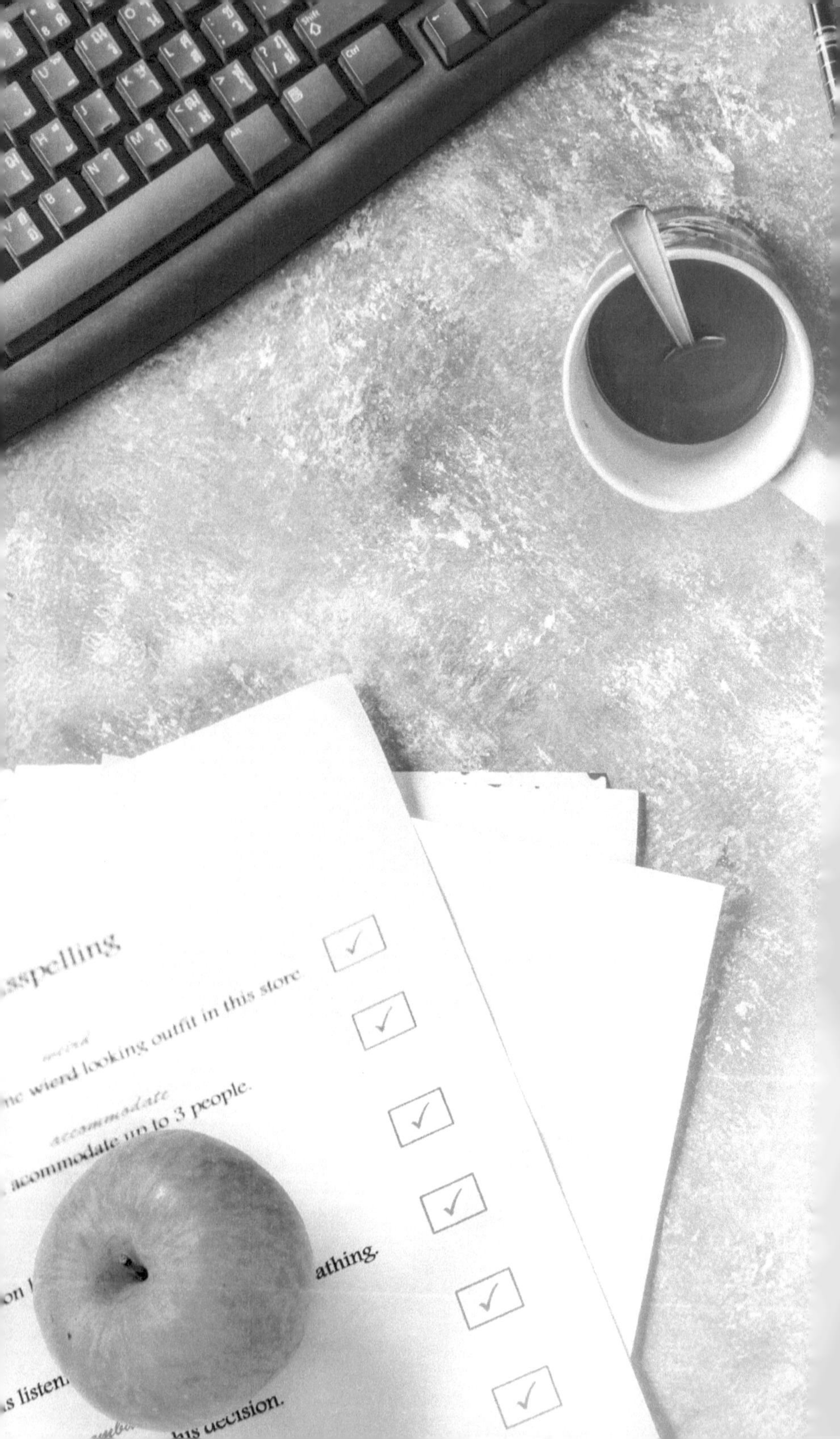
sspelling
wierd
ne wierd looking outfit in this store
accommodate
acommodate up to 3 people.
athing.
s listen.
decision.

Chapter Twenty-Five

STELLA

MY ALARM GOES OFF AT EXACTLY 6:30 AM, BUT I'M already awake. I don't know why, but I didn't get a very good sleep last night. The fact that I have a full day of work today feels like a cruel, cruel joke. And I'm covering a class that often makes me question whether I actually enjoy working at the school.

But honestly, I know that having an occasionally crazy class is part of the job, so I suck it up. Even with a hard class, I still have that feeling of warmth when I'm working with them. Nothing feels better than when you see the look on a kid's face when they've figured something out they were struggling with. I genuinely believe teaching is one of the most rewarding jobs, and I have so much respect for the people I work with who do it full-time. I honestly don't think I'm good enough to do it, but it's nice to dream right now.

"Stella, please tell me you don't have a busy day today." Mr. Austin asks as soon as I walk through the doors of the staff room. I have to hold back a laugh seeing him, thinking back to Lily's list. He's cute, but in a golden bachelor type of way. Okay, maybe that's excessive; he's probably in his 40s. That would be something I'd read about, but participate in – probably not.

"Busy in what way?" I ask, making my way to the food area of the staff room. The school is tiny, but the community helps out way more than the cynical side of me would expect. Every morning, there's breakfast for the teachers and students donated by the parents. We all love it.

"I have a bunch of parent-teacher meetings all day today, and the person I had subbing my class just called in sick." He curses, clearly stressed. I think I can see a new piece of grey hair sprouting on his head. "Anyway, I have to do these meetings, but I can't look after my class at the same time." I peek around his shoulder to look at the schedule on the board. I'm meant to be helping out in the Year Two class today. They are little demons, but with them I'm not on my own. What he's asking is leaving twenty little kids completely in my hands. Scary.

"Umm." I shift on my feet, not really sure how to respond.

"Please! I'd be indebted to you forever, it's just that there is literally nobody else to take over." I nod in understanding. We are so understaffed, it's insane. If one more person calls out sick today, our principal would consider just cancelling their class for the day.

"I'm just nervous about looking after a whole class on my own." I look down, "I've never done it before."

He looks at me, surprised, "Really? I assumed after you got your certification last summer, you'd be a hot commodity. You are good at what you do, Stella. Plus, they are in year five, practically mini teenagers." I smile at him, nodding. Even though the whole mini-teenager part makes me feel like throwing up.

"Okay, okay. But if a kid turns up missing by the end of the day. You didn't ask me anything." He chuckles, walking backwards towards the door.

"I severely doubt that will happen." He's almost out of the room before calling over his shoulder, "Please don't lose anyone."

I laugh, trying to play off my anxieties to him. But inside, I have never felt less confident. How does one wrangle 20 ten-year-olds without losing one's mind?

The answer – you don't. When I walk into the staffroom at lunch, I don't think I've ever been this exhausted in my life. I introduced myself as soon as I walked in, and the look on their faces when they realised a sub was covering today probably should have told me how today would go. The first 20 minutes of class were spent with them trying to convince me that Mr. Austin wanted them to watch movies all day. Their arguments were honestly pretty good, one of the kids pulling up an article on burnout and how students need breaks to remain mentally healthy.

I eventually got them to agree that if they worked all morning, I'd let them watch something after lunch. Compromise right? Mr. Austin had left really in-depth instructions for the substitute who was meant to be there. The sigh I let out seeing that was audible – maths is not my strong suit.

When they finished that work, we moved on to editing the written pieces they had done the day before. The groan that filled the classroom as I told them their task was palpable, but in all honesty, I understood. Not wanting them to go and tell Mr. Austin that I was the worst cover they ever had, I tried to think on my feet about how to make it more fun. In the end, I ended up coming up with a game of bingo with common mistakes kids their age make in writing. It got messy when one of the girls, Angie, decided that we needed glitter paint as the bingo markers.

And that is how, nearly five hours later, I am standing in the staff room covered in glitter paint and pen marks. It worked, though, and we got through all the work he had set for the day in the morning. Sinking down on the couch, I relish a moment of quiet and close my eyes. The fifth graders go to lunch earlier than the rest of the school, meaning I've got about fifteen minutes of alone time in the staff room.

"Hey Stella." Eric, Mr Austin, and Moises entered the room. I open my eyes, sitting up immediately. The last thing I'd want is to be let go for unprofessionalism.

"How were the kids?"

I put on a smile, one that doesn't quite reach my cheeks, "they were good. We did all the work and no one's dead."

He notices the bags under my eyes, "You seem tired."

I let out a humph, "Life of a uni student working basically a full-time job." He nods, going to the fridge. He pulls out his lunch and mine, coming to sit down beside me.

"You know I just went into the lunch area to chat to them, and the kids loved you." He hands me my sandwich. "The glitter bingo was especially a hit."

Laughing, I shake my head. "That one was a very in-the-moment thought."

He turns to me, a sincere look on his face. "It worked. You are good at this, Stella. I don't know what your plans are for your life, but I think it'd be a disservice to not consider teaching." I nod, not really sure of what to say. He smiles and stands up, saying something about needing to work while eating. I'm not really focused on what he's saying, though; all I can do is try to stop the grin that's starting to spread across my cheeks.

"No shit, Stella, you are insanely good at that job. Took them long enough to realise." Keets says on the phone. I called her the second I got the chance to gush about my day on the walk home.

"Thank you, Keets." I smile to myself. I wonder what life is like for people who don't have someone who is unconditionally their person. I hope to never find out. "How are you?"

"Honestly? I've been better."

I sit down outside the school steps, "What's wrong? Who do I need to beat up?"

She lets out a dry laugh, "Nobody, it's just one of those days where the world just feels a bit mean."

"Bad doctor's appointment?" Silence is the answer I need. Keets has struggled with a chronic illness her whole life. It's not technically life-threatening, but it's rare that there's a day that it doesn't impact her somehow. I don't know how she's able to be so positive about it. "You know you can talk to me about anything, right?"

"I know, Stel. I promise I've just had a really long day. The whole happy thing is running a bit low." She responds, swallowing in between each word.

"Okay." I take a breath, "It is okay to not be happy all the time, babes."

"I know," she says quietly.

"If you change your mind and want to talk about anything, I'm there in two seconds. Without any hesitation."

"Forever and Always?" She jokes, referencing one of my favourite Taylor Swift songs.

"Mhm, except I actually mean it. Unlike that dirtbag Taylor was singing about." She laughs, and it makes me feel more hopeful.

"Hey, Stel, I'm gonna go. I just kind of want to wallow and sleep for a bit." Her voice sounds a bit lighter.

"Of course. I love you, Keets."

"I love you too." She pauses for a second, but doesn't hang up. "Thank you, Stella."

"For what?"

"For knowing what I need." I smile and say a small goodbye before hanging up. Keets is the type of person who prefers not to talk about it when something is wrong. Especially when it comes to her illness. She's like me in that sense, except she's even more closed off. It took me a while to realise that when she pushes people away when she's upset, she genuinely needs it. Whereas with me, it's a cry for people to keep pushing. When she's ready to talk, she will, and I'll be here the second she needs me. Even though it sucks not knowing how to help right now, I have to push down my guilt and do what's best for her.

I'm about to start the walk home when I feel my phone buzz again. Picking it up to look at the notification, I nearly dropped the phone in surprise.

> Toby: Hey, I'm passing through Brookstone
> for the night. Was wondering if you wanted
> to grab drinks tonight? Pick up where we
> left off?

The text makes me laugh. Toby and I were friends in high school for almost two years. I was completely infatuated with him – he was the classic sporty, cocky, cool guy who everyone swooned over. Me included. However, he didn't see me as a friend, teetering on little sister vibes. Right as he was about to graduate, he invited me over, and we got plastered. We drunkenly decided it would be a good idea to say fuck it to friendship and hook up. We probably got to 50% of said hookup before both of his parents and his little brother caught us. The awkwardness never really left, and once we had graduated, neither of us was anxious to stay in contact. I open the message and ask where he wants to meet.

The insinuation of his message is obvious, and I've had a long day. Plus, the teenager in me, whose ego was getting boosted by this message, got the better of me.

He sends the address of his hotel and says to meet at the bar at 6. Just enough time for me to shower and get changed. Gotta stick to the rule – always look better than how they remember you.

Chapter Twenty-Six

LUKE

SO MUCH FOR LUNCH, IS ALL I CAN THINK AS I SEE the clock turn to 3 pm. Beck and Rory were at the mechanic getting Beck's truck fixed, and it took longer than I think any of us expected. Honestly, I was completely fine with pushing it later. I was so fucking exhausted trying to play catch-up from that sleepover at Stel's. Once I got home, I was grilled on my whereabouts by Rory, Beck, and Jessie, who decided to crash at ours. It took me an hour to convince them that it was a friendly sleepover purely to convince Keets we were properly together. I just happened to leave out the part where I got harder than I've ever been before, and based on the state of her nipples, Stella wasn't doing too well either. I haven't been able to get anything about that night out of my head. I know I don't get around much, but Jesus, I've never felt like this before.

I groan frustratedly, falling back on the couch. I do not want to be thinking about her right now. Yesterday, when I was trying to do my business assignment, I literally wrote her name on the page, like a fucking middle schooler dreaming about their crush. And I couldn't refocus; the half-finished essay is still sitting on my desk upstairs.

This is exactly why I don't date. Unlike Stella, Beck, and Rory, I develop feelings. I don't do it casually. Once I start falling for someone, it's hard to stop. I know myself, though, and know it's not at that point with Stella, but I also know that all I can think about is fucking her, seeing her fall apart underneath me. Her breath hitching, her body giving into me. I imagine falling asleep with her next to me, the warmth of her body pressed against mine, snuggling in closer as if the world outside doesn't exist.

Maybe with her, my whole no casual thing would be different. It's so unbelievably obvious that a relationship with Stella is like sunlight to a vampire. She'd do anything to avoid it.

My phone buzzes on the couch next to me, and I sit up and stare at the message.

Beck: Hey, man, this is taking way longer than I thought. Do you want to meet for dinner instead? Ror wants tacos.

Rory: Fuck yes, I want tacos. Please say yes – Beck won't let us go out without you.

Beck: Yeah, no shit, Rory, we are a trio? C'mon, keep up.

I quickly respond before they rip each other's heads off.

Me: Yes, tacos sound incredible, meet at 6?

They both thumbs up the message, which means I now have 3 hours to kill. I should finish that assignment. Fuck me.

"Beck, I swear to god, if you throw a straw wrapper at me one more time, I will strangle you." I smiled at him, "said sweetly, of course."

"Ooo, Dad's tense tonight." Beck teases.

"What's got you all worked up?" Rory asks, taking a sip of his horchata.

"It's a stupid business essay. I should have finished it yesterday, but now I still have to do the conclusion and all my referencing. I'm just stressed." They both eye me. "Okay, but not stressed enough to go home and actually do it. So I'm breathing and eating my taco."

Rory nods, accepting my answer.

"So what happened today exactly?" I ask after swallowing my bite.

"I cannot even get into it." Beck swipes his hand across his body as he says, even, for dramatic effect, I'm sure.

"Yeah, they fucked us," Rory adds on.

"Just the way they were, like, 'Sir, we know more about cars than you do. Trust us. After literally trying to scam us out of 200 dollars. 200!"

"Didn't realise your dad's a mechanic, huh?" I ask

Beck shakes his head, "Nope. That's the last time I will go anywhere but to my dad. Stupid vacation."

I laugh, knowing Beck's anger here has more to do with the fact that his dad and his girlfriend took a trip without him over the whole mechanic situation. Rory speaks up, asking Beck something about the Rabbitohs, trying to get him off this topic. My phone buzzes as he speaks. I ignored it at first, not wanting to be that guy who cuts their friends off. But as it rings for the third time, I excuse myself to pick it up.

"Goldie, What's up?" I ask, but am cut off by a very hushed voice,

"Lucas, please come to the address I am about to send you. I need you to save me, I'm begging."

"What the hell are you talking about? Why are you whispering?" I ask, confused as ever.

"Okay, listen, I am on the worst pre-booty call drinks of my life ever. I need you to come and get me out of here. And I'm whispering because I am hiding in a bathroom stall, trying to avoid interacting with this man ever again." I snort, trying to contain my laughter. "Lucas, please."

I swallow my laugh, "I'm on my way." I interrupt her stream of thank yous, "Don't thank me, I'm never letting you live this down."

"Fuck you."

"Mhm, I'll see you in twenty."

I walk back towards the table, amusement clear on my face.

"Everything okay?" Rory asks.

"My incredible fake girlfriend seems to have gotten herself into a date with a guy she desperately needs out of. So now I have to go be all alpha and stake my claim on her or whatever." I grab my coat. "I am so sorry, guys, dinner tomorrow is on me." I stare at them, silently begging that they won't be mad at me for this. I can't leave her alone when she needs me.

"Oh no, it's fine. Go save your girl, Luke." Beck teases. I feel a weight lifted off my chest.

"And for that comment, you are covering my tacos tonight," I call over my shoulder as I run out of the restaurant.

When I pull up to Silver Ridge, I have to double-check that I am at the right address. This hotel was built a couple of years ago and is used for dickhead businessmen who don't want to stay in one of the more local places. So basically, the type of place my parents would stay at. No shit, she needs saving for whoever she's with in there. I park and get out of the car, heading for the bar, she said it's where she was.

Walking into the lobby, I immediately feel out of place. It's all modern black and white decorations. All the employees look like they are silently judging you for every move you make to the people on the other end of their earpieces. I quickly find the sign for the bar and walk towards it, before someone questions what I'm doing there.

I spot Stella right away, despite the bar being almost full. Genuinely, I don't think I've ever seen someone look as bored as she does at this moment. Stella's head snaps up, smiling as soon as she sees me. I give her a glare, trying to get her to stop looking so happy about the fact that she's just been caught cheating.

I think she gets the message because I hear an "Oh, shit" muttered right before I walk up.

"What the hell are you doing with my girlfriend?" I ask the guy, who's facing away from me, mustering up the best angry voice I can at this moment. The guy turns around and looks me up and down before looking back at Stella. Who the fuck is this guy?

"You know him, Stella?" He asks, still not even bothering to look at me.

"I am so sorry, Toby. That's my boyfriend." She tries to look scared, but I can see the laughter behind her eyes. The guy, Toby, takes a long sip of his drink before standing up and looking at me.

"Yeah, dick. She's mine, so fuck off." I say, trying to muster up as much possessiveness as I can. Honestly, if my girlfriend were really grabbing drinks with someone else, I seriously doubt I'd be here doing this. If he were here without her wanting him to be – that's a whole other story.

"Sorry, dude, I don't really care if she's your girlfriend. She came here of her own free will." I gasp, really just having fun now. It's pretty obvious this guy poses absolutely no threat.

"Stella, baby boo, you didn't! I thought we had moved on from this after you slept with the entire bike gang!" I scream. Her face drops for a second, seeing all the people who have turned around to stare at us. I can tell she's debating whether to kick my ass or not. But after a minute, she joins in.

"I'm sorry muffin cake, I can't help it! I swear I'll do better!" Toby is looking between us, extremely confused.

"I don't know, schnookums, how can I trust you? Am I not enough for you?" I swear I see her swallow a gag at the nickname schnookums. Maybe Goldie should be replaced.

"You can, I promise you can." She gives a sly smile, which scares me slightly, "It's just…"

"Just what?" Both Toby and I stare at her, confused.

"I'm pregnant." There's a gasp among the crowd. "And I don't know if it's yours or a member of the biker gangs or.." she gulps, "your dads!"

Toby takes a step back, shaking his head, "What the actual fuck?" He turns to face me, "I am so sorry, dude, she used to be normal in high school, I swear." His face pales, and he backs up. It's comical how fast he runs out of there. The second he's gone, Stella and I both burst into laughter. Eventually, I catch my breath, especially when I see people are still staring at us from around the bar.

Right, we are in a five-star hotel. Everyone probably thinks we came from the circus.

I lean down, voice low, "We should probably get out of here before someone kicks us out." She still hasn't stopped laughing and doesn't even register what I said. Jesus, her night must have sucked if this is her reaction.

"Okay, fine. We are leaving, though." I scoop her up and throw her over my shoulders, walking out of the bar.

"Lucas!" She squeals, "Put me down, you psycho." She's manically hitting my back.

"Nope, this is what you get for fucking my dad and getting pregnant." Her hands stop hitting me, and I feel her body convulse as she starts laughing again. Unable to stop. I see the snobby receptionists staring at us as we walk out, one of them clearly calling for security. I shout out,

"Calm down, we are leaving! Stella remind me to tell the biker gang to never ever come here again!!" After that, I pick up my pace, desperate to get out of there as fast as possible. I carry Stella all the way to my car, opening it and rushing in.

The second we are both sat in the car, we both burst out laughing again. I swear her laugh is one of the sweetest sounds I've ever heard.

"So.." She says once she's managed to calm down. "Maccas drive-through?" I nod.

"You took the words right out of my mouth."

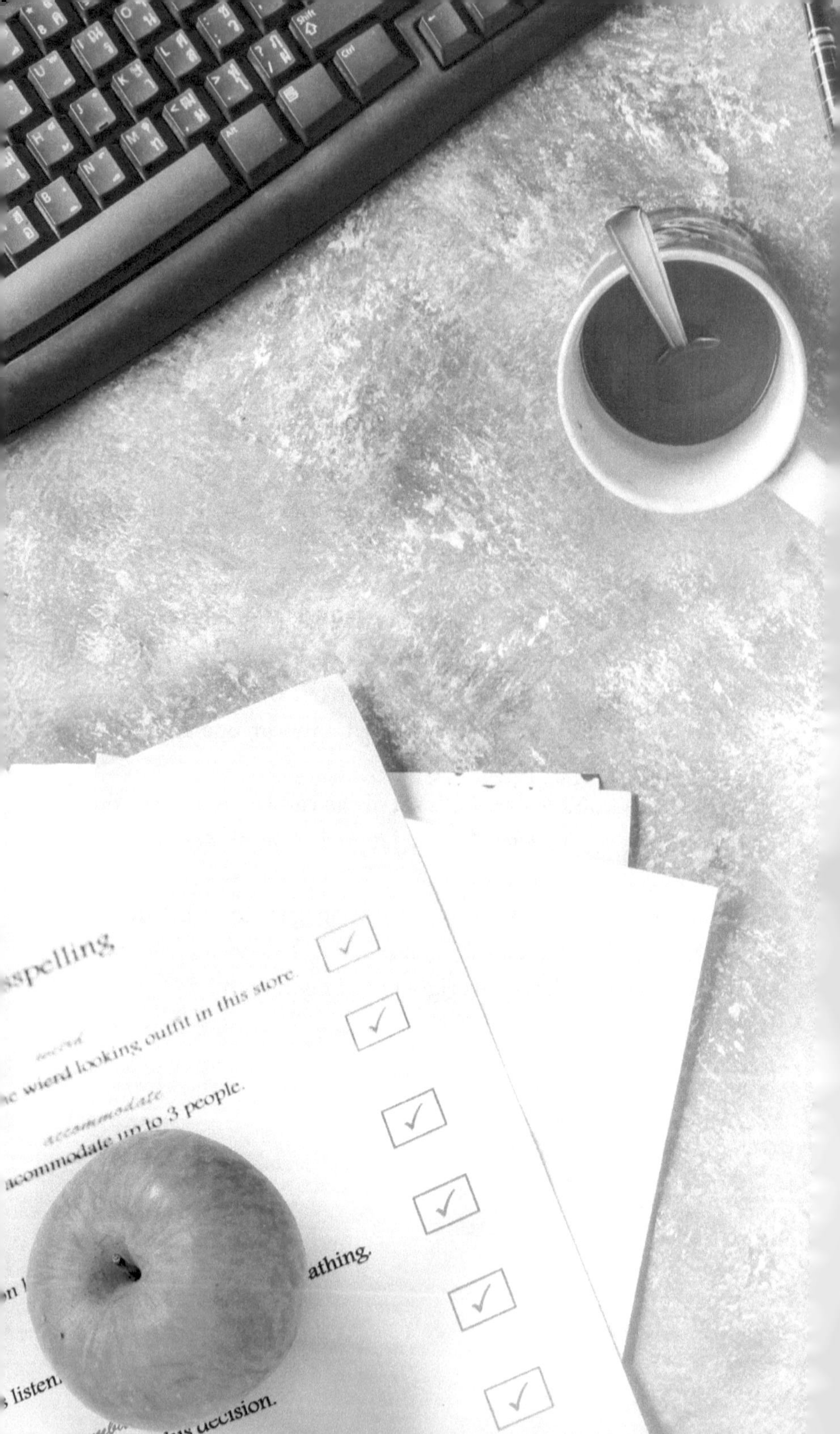
spelling
e wierd looking outfit in this store.
accommodate
acommodate up to 3 people.
athing.
listen.
his decision.

Chapter Twenty-Seven

STELLA

TWENTY MINUTES LATER WE ARE PARKED IN A completely empty parking lot eating burgers. Luke, to the surprise of absolutely no one, got a Happy Meal. He told me there was no point in going to McDonald's unless you were going to get a toy with your nuggies. And no, I am not the one who said nuggies.

"No shit, really?" Luke exclaims, taking a sip of his drink. "A full hour of crypto? Jesus, how did you survive?"

I shove a handful of chips in my mouth, hoping food will help erase the memories of the last couple of hours.

"Clearly, I did not. I mean, he was always, like, full of himself, but in high school it was in a sexy way." Luke raises his eyebrows, seeming unconvinced.

"No, I swear! It wasn't in the 'I'm a finance bro, so I'm better than everyone in the whole world because I know what day trading is.' Like it is now. Ugh." I slam my head on the dashboard.

"Hey!" He says, sounding concerned. For a split second, I think it's concern for me. That second is cut short as he reaches and rubs the dashboard, "no hurting the truck." I throw a fry at him, which he annoyingly catches in his mouth.

Why was that hot?

"So, what I'm hearing is that he was sexy in high school when he was cocky, like I am, and now that he's not like me, not so sexy."

I roll my eyes, "Of course, you find some way to make this about yourself."

He gives a self-satisfied grin. "Was he at least good at hooking up?" Luke asks me, looking at me as if he's searching for some sign that my taste isn't absolutely horrible.

I shrink a bit in my seat, covering my head with my soda cup. I feel a nugget thrown at me.

"C'mon, Goldie, all of this and no orgasm?!" He shakes his head, "I expected better from you."

I quickly sit up, ready to defend myself, "Usually, I am better; the guy I got with last week made me finish twice." I say proudly. As much as I love hooking up, it's embarrassingly rare how little I actually finish. I will say, there is not a single part of me that believes in faking it. If a guy asks me if I've finished and I haven't, I tell him. Lying doesn't do either of us any good – I'm looking out for the future girls over here.

"Twice isn't that impressive, Goldie," Luke says, voice deep. I can't quite place what the look on his face is. I don't know how to respond to that. He does that a lot – leaving me speechless. "Okay, I cannot talk about your borderline depressing sex life anymore, Goldie. Change of topic."

I laugh, he is the only person on the planet to call my sex life depressing. "I like how you just announced that."

He bows his head, proud of himself for the tenth time this hour.

"What did you get up to today?" He asks. I grin when I realise I get to talk about the school again. I tell him all about the class and how I became a teacher today. And all about Mr. Austin and how, for the first time, I actually saw a future for myself.

"So you want to teach?" He asks after I finish talking.

"I think so? I don't know. It's hard, I want to do something that's my passion, that I'm good at. I don't know." I respond, still unsure if I could do it.

He shifts in his seat, facing towards me, feet up in the chair. "Okay, tell me why you want to do it?"

"Right now?" I ask. He nods and then gets comfortable, waiting for me to continue.

"Um, okay. When I was in high school, I wanted to work in biomedicine. It was my plan for university and had been for years. But then I had a horrible biology teacher. Like genuinely bad. She would tell us on a daily basis that she hated her life, her job, and didn't want to teach us." His eyebrow shot up in surprise. "Yeah, crazy. And so I started to dread the class because it was clear she hated us. And then when she started picking on me and other kids in the class, it just solidified my hatred. And quickly it seeped into the subject, and now I'm doing anything but biology. I just saw what a bad teacher can do to a student's passion. That being said, I've also had good teachers who changed my life with their support. I think being a teacher is one of the most important jobs, because you have a chance to make a difference in so many kids' lives. Give them hope and strength that they might not get elsewhere. I want to do that." My brain wanders back to the classroom and the things I get to do. "There's also this girl – Lily. I love all my students, but she's particularly special. She has this ability to make you happy, even on the worst day. Students like her make it feel worth it." I take a breath, my mouth dry, not realising how much I had just talked.

"Goldie, if you think that's not your passion, I think you don't understand the word passion. Why aren't you doing a teaching degree right now?" He asks, his gaze uncertain, as if trying to make sense of it.

"I guess for the same reason I love it. Having such a large part of a kid's life like that is kind of terrifying. I don't want to mess it up, to be the reason they change their life plans."

Luke raises his eyebrows, clearly not believing a word coming out of my mouth. "There's something more. Every choice has risk, but we make it anyway. Why do you think you can't do this?"

My throat tightens slightly as I swallow. He's not wrong.

"Look, someone just told me I couldn't do it. And I know it's dumb to base my life choices on that, but he wasn't wrong about much."

His face becomes more serious, "Stella, if you think for one second that you could mess up those kids, you aren't as intelligent as I thought you were. I've only known you a few months, but it's pretty damn clear you are the exact type of person I'd want looking after my kids."

My throat tightens slightly, caught off guard by the sincerity of his words. Also, by the use of my full name.

"And Goldie? I know what it's like to get your dream thrown around by someone you think knows best – but trust me, if it's what you love, it's not wrong for you."

"Thank you, Lucas." I respond sincerely. Shaking my head, I suddenly feel uncomfortable with how long we've been talking about me. "What about you? What's your big plan with the bar?"

He doesn't skip a beat before responding, "I want to move to Sydney to open it. It'll have different specialty drinks each week and live music performers. I want to work behind the bar, but also sing on the stage. It's going to be a place where people can come to forget about the real world for a bit, to enjoy and dance and just be happy." He has a hint of a smile on his face as he talks about it.

"You want to sing?" I ask, remembering back to his karaoke performance.

"Yeah, I do. I love it. But I'm not a singer – I don't write songs, and I don't want to. I love music, don't get me wrong, but what I really love is telling other people's stories through songs. It's such a beautiful form of communication, how you can share someone else's story and still find solace in it – even if it's just for a few minutes."

I nod, "I completely agree."

He smiles, lost in his thoughts about his future. I'm envious of that – having a plan, knowing exactly what you want to do. I love teaching, but I've loved things before, and they've never stuck. How are you just meant to know what you are meant to do for the rest of your life? I don't understand it.

"What would you call it?"

"The Hidden Alibi." I smile, it's a good name.

"You'd better name a drink after me, Lucas."

He nods, "Oh yeah, you best believe it, Goldie." A comfortable silence falls for a second before he interrupts. "Sorry not to bring up demons of the past, but why exactly did you go on a date with Mr. Corporate Chad?"

I hang my head, feeling embarrassed by myself.

"It was mainly because high school me got a bit excited." He responds with a knowing gesture.

"And the other reason?"

I swallow, not knowing how much I should explain. "Keets had a bad day and was at the apartment. I wanted to give her space, so I thought this would keep me out all night. I told her I was with you."

Concern flashes across his face, "Is she okay?"

"She's got some stuff going on, but she's strong. Plus, I'm not going anywhere."

"We all know how stubborn you are," he remarks

"It's just-"

"Just?" He pushes.

"I don't know, I'm worried. I want to cheer her up so badly, but I don't want to push. All the things I'd normally do don't feel like enough right now. And she won't talk to me because she's not ready, which is totally fair, I just don't know how to help." I stop talking, still looking at my hands. Keets being upset is one of the worst things in the world to me. He sits thoughtfully for a minute before chiming in.

"Text her if she's free on Friday night."

"What?" I cock my head, puzzled by his words.

"Do you trust me?"

"I guess," I respond, realising I really do.

"Then text her." He says, handing me my phone off the console. The light from the street light bounced off his face. "Let Luke fly in and save the day."

"Never refer to yourself in the third person again," I say as I type out a message to Keets.

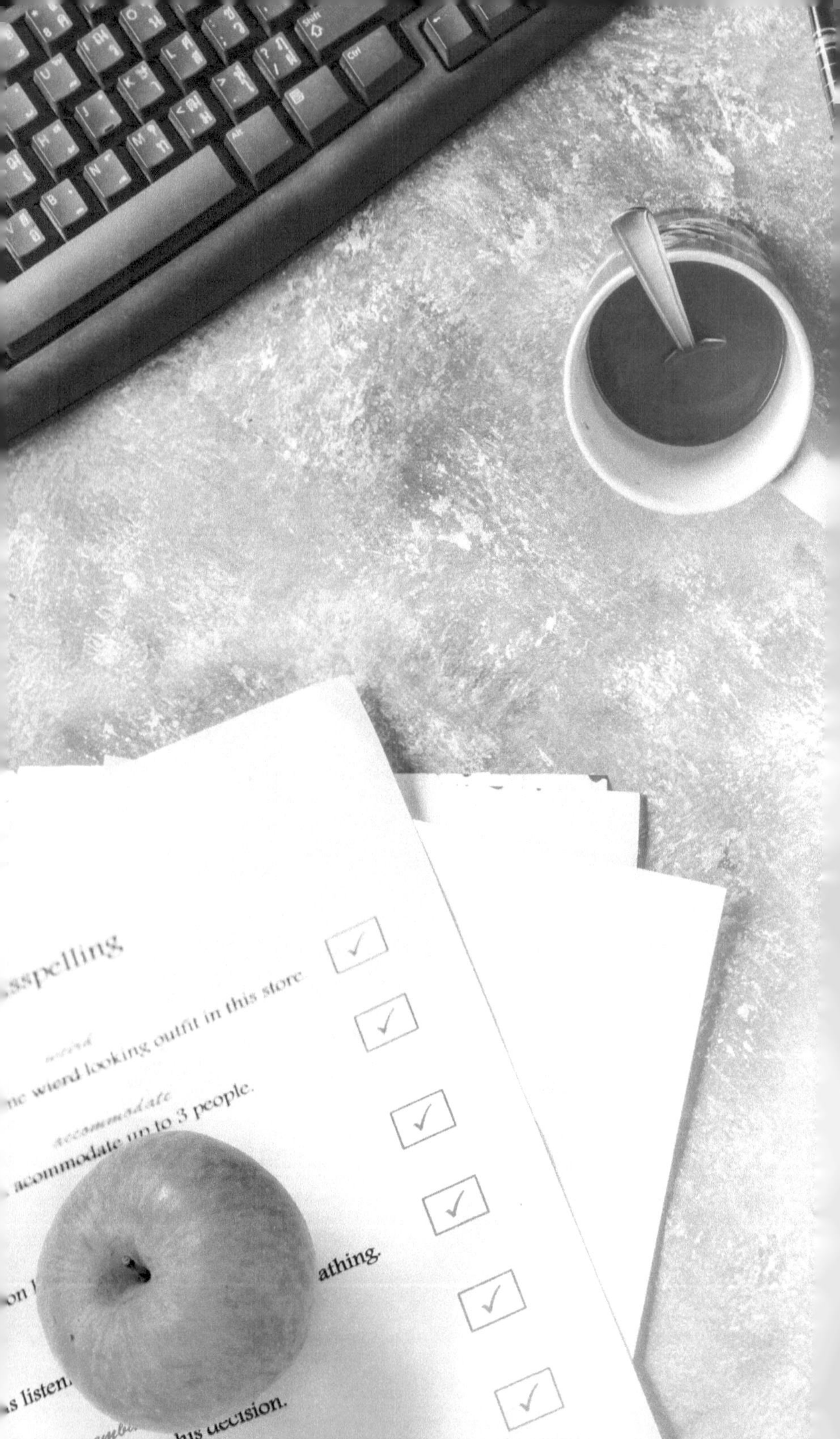
sspelling
wierd
ne wierd looking outfit in this store
accommodate
acommodate up to 3 people.
athing.
s listen
decision.

Chapter Twenty-Eight

STELLA

"SO WAIT, YOU HAVE NO IDEA WHAT WE ARE DOING tonight?" Keets asks me as she picks out a dress from my closet.

"Nope." I respond, lying on my bed holding Reginald, "Lucas just told me to meet them at The Lantern at 8."

She nods, not looking totally convinced, "Okay, so we are going to a, what, dance party?"

"No, I don't think so? He said it wasn't going to be a regular night."

"He's good at this." She lets out, after a beat.

My eyes squint slightly at her, confused, "Good at what?"

She shakes her head quickly, almost as if she's backtracking. "Being your boyfriend, duh." I nod, taking a deep breath. I'm clearly letting my anxieties about this whole situation get the best of me. There's no way she could know. Keets holds up a blue mini dress, one that would make her look alarmingly like Cinderella.

"You know that's my dress, right?"

Her lips curl in a sly smile, "You mean our dress?"

"Oh, okay." I put my hands up in defense, "My bad, my bad." I told her she could pick out our outfits tonight. Partly because I can't be assed, but mainly because she sounded so excited about the prospect of doing something special tonight. I want it to be perfect.

"Okay, Stel, so you are wearing this dress." She points towards the one on the bed, "and I'm wearing the blue one. Now let's go put on some music, do a shot, and then get ready." She goes to walk out the door, "No rush though, it's always more fun to be fashionably late."

I laugh as she goes to pour our drinks, and laugh even harder as I hear 'As Long As You Love Me' by Justin Bieber start blaring through the speakers.

An hour later, we are almost ready, about to head out. Keets is in her bathroom, finishing her hair. Staring at myself in the mirror, I feel my stomach flip. The dress Keets has put me in is nothing short of beautiful. The dress is tight around my chest, but dips right below my waist in the back. The skirt is flowy and moves as I walk, looking almost like liquid. The dark green colour makes me think back to the first date with Luke.

I bought the dress a while ago, but I have never had a reason to wear it. Nothing's felt right for it.

I'm being silly about tonight, but I can't stop thinking about how much effort he's putting into this for Keets. He hasn't told me anything about his plans for tonight, just that we will love it. I don't understand why he cares so much, but for right now I'm just glad he does. It's an understatement to say that I feel grateful for him – his friendship that is.

Keets emerges from the bathroom, hair in a messy ponytail – she looks gorgeous.

"Looking good, baby girl!" Winking at her, trying my best to be seductive. She walks up behind me and gives me a tap on the ass.

"Thanks, sugar." She says, dropping her voice, sounding like a 50-year-old woman who smokes five packs a day. We both giggle for a moment before she cuts in, extending her hand with a playful grin. "Shall we?"

"We shall," I say, grabbing her hand, leading her out the door.

The Black Lantern is living up to its name a little too much right now. As we walk up, it is dead empty inside. I can't even see Luke from the windows outside. Never in the three years at Brookstone has this place been this empty. Not even on a Tuesday night. Keets glances back at me, her expression puzzled, clearly noticing the emptiness inside after peering through the window. I shake my head at her, not having an answer. Pulling out my phone, I shoot a text to Luke.

> Me: Are you sure you meant 8 at the Black Lantern? There is not a single soul inside.

He responds almost immediately.

> Luke: You aren't looking hard enough.
> Come in.

"He says to go in?" Keets cautiously pushes the door

open and walks in. To our surprise, Luke, Beck, and Rory are standing there waiting for us.

"Took you guys long enough," Beck says, leaning against the bar, letting out an exaggerated sigh.

"What is going on?" I ask, thoroughly confused. Luke walks up to us, stopping right in front.

"This is a cocktail class. We are gonna teach you guys to make some drinks, and then we are going to drink the drinks and do whatever the hell we want because the bar is just for us tonight."

"But it's a Friday?" Keets asks. I can't even imagine how much money they'd be losing tonight. Rory walks up and grabs her hand to lead her to the other side of the bar.

"Congratulations, you can read a calendar." I see him smirk, "This is more fun anyway."

Even though I can't see her face, I know she's blushing. Luke moves closer to me, grabbing my waist to pull me towards him.

"Hi." He says, smiling, looking at me.

"Hi." I let out a short laugh, shaking my head. "What is this? What are Beck and Rory doing here?"

He brushes my hair behind my ears, "You said you were worried, so I texted the guys. Operation cheer up Keets. They like you guys and wanted to help out. Plus, Beck boosts everyone's ego because he hits on anything that moves. And Rory, well, I don't think that needs much explanation." I nod, finding it funny that we both see what's going on between them even though they haven't seemed to realise it themselves.

"Well, thank you, this is exactly what Keets needed.

Thank you for doing it for her," I say, still slightly unbelieving that he did this.

"I didn't do it for her, Goldie." I look at him, confused. "I did it for you, idiot." He then bends over, whispering in the ear he just tucked hair behind. Talking quietly, so no one can hear him, he says, "By the way, this is now my favourite colour."

He stands up and leads me behind the bar, where Keets, Rory, and Beck are waiting for us.

"Okay, bartending 101. Starting with a pretty simple drink – mojito."

"Oo yum, I love mojitos," Keets exclaims, as the guys start setting up the stuff we'll need. Luke comes to stand behind me, telling me the instructions while holding onto my waist with his right hand. And for the first time in years, the feeling doesn't make me scared.

"Okay, moving on. Now that you guys have upgraded, it's time to make one of the hardest ones." Rory says. I stare at the lineup of the three cocktails we've made so far proudly. Granted, Beck, Rory, and Luke probably made ¾ of each drink for us, but that fourth was done with my brilliant hands.

"Ramos gin fizz," Beck says, holding up some white drink, with froth at the top. I opt to not say what first comes to mind, trying to seem mature.

My face clearly gives me away because Luke bends down and whispers, "Don't worry, we all thought it."

I move my hand in front of my mouth to try and stop the giggle that arises, trying not to interrupt Rory explaining how to make the drink. Luckily, someone else interrupts him for me.

"No, okay, I have held back this whole time, and I cannot do it anymore," Beck mutters, clearly exasperated.

"You okay, buddy?" Luke asks, seeming concerned.

"No, I am not. I cannot believe I am destined to be a fifth wheel right now. I need a boyfriend or a girlfriend or something. This is embarrassing for me." Keets and I both burst into laughter, especially since Beck sounds like he's eight years old with the tone he used. "Oh yeah, laugh it up, Ms. Goldie and Ms. Rory can't keep their eyes off of me. Life is so hard for both of you, huh?" When we don't stop laughing, he sighs angrily.

"I'm serious! This friendship group will not work if I'm the only single one."

Keets interjects, "Rory and I are both single, Beck." Rory nods, hesitantly.

"Yeah, and also Beck, friendship group?" I ask, "This is the second time we've hung out."

He gasps, "I detest it if you think that this is not our official friendship group, Stella. I've decided it is, so you can't change that." Luke laughs into my shoulder behind me. Honestly, I have no idea how Rory is keeping a straight face.

Rory cuts in, "Okay, Beck, I love you, man, but you have a new person every week. It's not like you're single. You could get someone in two seconds if you wanted to." He thinks this through for a second before settling on agreeing.

"You are so right, Rory." He turns to Keets, "What's up, sunshine?"

Keets doesn't even get a chance to respond before Rory cuts in, "Nope."

"I hate being single."

He sulks down on the bar chair. I detach myself from Luke and grab the glass that Rory was using to demonstrate the drink.

I lean down and whisper in his ear, "Would throwing a drink at all the happy relationship people make you feel better?" He nods, making a puppy face at me. I hand him the drink and step back, enjoying the look of confusion on the others' faces. I gesture for Keets to move, and she does just in time. Beck stands up and throws the drink at the guys.

"Oh, that felt good. I now see why girls throw drinks at me." Beck exclaims, seeming ignorant of the looks on Rory and Luke's faces. Rory grabs a glass, fills it with some liquid, and starts running after Beck. Keets follows behind them, possibly trying to stop a murder. I'm still standing there, clutching onto my stomach laughing, when I see Luke walking up to me – holding a drink hose. I put my hands up in defense.

"Wait, no, Lucas, think about this." He keeps getting closer, "I'm wearing satin."

A devilish grin spreads across his face.

"Should have thought of that before you told Beck to throw a drink at me." He grabs onto my waist, pulling me closer to him, and sprays me with the drink hose. Drenching me with some sort of soda. I squeal and try to get out of his hold, but he doesn't let me. He looks down, laughing, but doesn't stop staring, his soft eyes looking at me like no one else matters. I match his gaze for a second before using the moment to wriggle out of his hold. I run back to the bar, trying to arm myself. As I grab a cup, Keets shows up next to me, looking just as drenched. Her face looks light, her smile reaching up to her eyes. I smile and nod at her as we fill multiple cups, ready to attack.

An hour later, we are all sitting on the floor, soaking wet, laughing. I'm sitting leaned up against Luke's chest across from Beck, Rory, and Keets.

"Okay, but let's all be honest, when Stella found the water guns from the end of summer party last year, we were all goners."

I laugh, dipping my head in a bow as they all applaud. "It's hard being as talented as I am, it's true."

"Hey, I hate to be the one to break this up, but we do have to start cleaning before my dad comes and kills us slowly." Beck and Keets join Ror, but Luke holds me on the floor a bit longer. I look at him, confused, but when he doesn't say anything, I don't look away. The buzz from the alcohol we did manage to drink is settling nicely, and I'm just happy. Based on the lazy look on his face, I'd say he's not sober either.

"Lucas, we should help." I urge. He places his hand under my chin, pulling it up.

"We will, just." He swallows, "Do you want to stay over?"

I sit up a bit straighter, unsure. He sees the movement and corrects himself, "just because that's probably the boyfriend-girlfriend move, right? And I'll sleep on the couch, I don't want you to think I'm trying something."

My lips upturn into a soft smile, trying to reassure him that I don't think that. But I know it's a lie. It was the first place my brain went to when he mentioned sleeping over, but I know if he says he will sleep on the couch, he will. And friends have sleepovers too – that's not like an inherently relationship thing. So no need to have a bad flashback brain. I need to push myself eventually, right?

"Okay." I nod, pulling him up to help clean.

Chapter Twenty-Nine

LUKE

THE EXTREME NAUSEA I FEEL WHEN I WAKE UP makes me severely question who let me drink that much last night. I roll off the couch in my room, checking to see if Stella is still asleep. She's not in the bed, which makes me concerned, but when I go to try the bathroom, I hear her call out.

"Nope, do not come in here. We are not close enough friends for you to see me vomit, Lucas." I laugh. At least we can be in misery together. I fall back onto my bed, looking up at the still-spinning ceiling. There's no way I'm still tipsy from last night, right? I check my phone to see what the time is, only to see it's only 4. We've been asleep for an hour and a half. That would explain that. My brain keeps flashing back to last night, the way that Stella fit so perfectly into the group. Into my life. Like she's meant to be there.

My eyes start to flutter closed, but open quickly when I hear the bathroom door open. Despite the fact that she was just puking in the bathroom, she still looks beautiful.

Especially in the shirt of mine that looks like a dress on her. She sees me on the bed.

"Oh, if you want, I can take the couch. I'm sorry, just while I'm drunk I'd prefer." I cut her off,

"Stella, do not apologise. I thought it was morning, that's the only reason I'm in bed." I stand up and go sit on the couch. "Go back to sleep, Goldie." She lazily nods and climbs back into bed, falling asleep almost immediately. I follow along, dozing off, barely five minutes later.

"No, stop. Get off me." I shoot up off the couch, eyes wide and frantic. What the hell? I turn towards the bed where Stella is practically screaming. "Please, I'm sorry. Please don't."

"Stella?" I ask, still a bit discombobulated.

"No. Stop. Please." She keeps whimpering. Her voice is desperate, pleading with someone. She must be having a nightmare. I get up and walk over to the bed. I take a few steps toward the bed, my body moving before my mind fully catches up. She's thrashing, her limbs moving violently as if she's trying to fight off an invisible attacker. My heart sinks, and my thoughts race. What the hell is going on in her head right now? I rub her shoulder, trying to get her to calm down,

"Stel it's okay. It's just me." She doesn't wake up, but fights my hand off her.

She screams again – louder, more desperate, and something in my snaps. I give up on the gentle approach and start shaking her, trying to wake her up. Her body bolts upright in response, panic flashing in her eyes as her muscles tense, her breath short and erratic. She turns to look at me,

"Lucas?" She asks with tears in her eyes.

"I heard you screaming. Are you okay?" She nods, but

it's weak. She's deep in her thoughts, not fully here yet. I tilt my head to look at the time, 7 am. The sun is just rising.

"I'm sorry, I-" she is choking her words out, tears silently falling down her cheek. I move to sit next to her and wipe the tears off her cheek.

"Hey Goldie, what did we say about that whole apologising thing?" She chokes a short laugh before settling back into bed. I go to stand up to go back to the couch, not entirely sure to help, but I feel her hands grab me.

"Can you stay? I don't want to be alone." I hesitate for a moment, the weight of her vulnerability pressing on me. I nod, trying to keep my own emotions in check, and climb into the bed beside her. She settles into my side, taking deep breaths as she falls back asleep. Despite my best efforts, I can't fall asleep, and my heart won't stop racing. All I can think about is whether she is okay. Last time we spent the night together, that didn't happen. At least I don't think it did. I know what it sounded like, what she was screaming. She's never mentioned anything, but the pieces are starting to fall together. Especially after what Rory said about her ex and the way she's so cautious around me. But then I think about how comfortable she is with the guys she gets with. It doesn't seem like how she'd act if she were attacked, like it seemed from the nightmare.

I watch her all night, making sure she doesn't stir again. I don't know if she's truly okay, and I'm too scared to let her out of my reach.

LUKE

MY PHONE RINGS FOR THE THIRD TIME THIS HOUR. For the eighth time in the last two. And I've lost count of how much over the last day. And like every call after that first one, I hit ignore. The missed calls from my brother, father, and mother fill the screen. It's 7pm, and despite it nearly being summer, the sun has completely set. The only thing lighting up my room right now is the mood and the flashing of my phone. My hand is starting to cramp up from how hard I'm holding onto my pillow.

When my mum called me, I picked up without hesitation, Stella had just left. Because, despite a part of me aching to never talk to them again, I could never do that. I assumed that she was calling me to complain about something because the list of people who came before me was busy. I was wrong. She called to inform me that it was collectively decided that I would not be a part of the wedding party at my little brother's wedding. I asked her if she truly meant just the wedding party or if she meant the wedding too. Her silence after that question is what made me hang up. And that hang-up meant I was subjected to a plethora of phone calls. Likely to yell at me for being such a disrespectful son.

My phone starts buzzing again. Buzz, buzz, buzz. The contact name Mum flashes across my screen at the same time that I receive two messages from my dad. I can't take this anymore. I snatch my phone and hurl it onto the ground, watching it smash. The deafening crash of the screen almost feels satisfying. Hopefully, it meant I wouldn't get any more calls. I sink down on the carpet next to my bed. The phone is lying there, and I can see every little crack in the phone that has formed. I can see how broken it is, but how hard it's still working to turn on. To show me it still works.

My head hangs, feeling crazy for relating to an inanimate object that I just smashed into smithereens. I just feel empty.

Everything my mother said on that call I've heard before. I've built up a steel armour against everything they say to me. Trying so desperately to not let them see the cracks forming. But this. My little brother is getting married. My parents reject me every day, but for him to reject me too. I know we aren't best friends. I know that. I also knew that there was a possibility my parents wouldn't want me there. But I thought at least he'd fight for me. I thought it was getting better.

Then again, it's not like I've ever truly fought for him. Not in the way an older brother should. I was out of the house the second I turned 18. Never called, never checked in unless I was contacted first, nothing. So much for brotherly love. I let out a dry laugh. There's something dripping down my face, cold, wet. I move my hand to touch my cheek, feeling the tears that have drenched my face. I didn't notice.

"Luke?" I turn my head slightly to see Beck standing in my doorway. I didn't hear him get home either. "Are you okay?"

He walks towards me. I can see the way his brow scrunches when he sees the phone on the floor and the vase I seemed to have knocked down when I threw it. I shake my head, not having the energy to lie right now.

"What happ-"

Cutting him off, I say, "I'm sorry I can't talk to you about this. I just can't do it." My head falls again. I'm so tired. "I'll be okay, just please. Go."

I see his feet move slightly as he retreats, but he stops. "I'm going to go out for a few minutes, and then I am going to be outside that door if you need me. Whether you want me to be there or not." He leaves the room and closes the door behind him. That sliver of light is gone as he shuts the door. Leaving me in darkness again.

STELLA
TO: LUKE
11:00 AM

> Me: Studying might actually be the death of me. Want to come over later and watch the new episode of Too Hot to Handle?

1:30 PM

> Me: Please tell me yes, I need something to look forward to.

5:00 PM

> Me: Whoa, a group of shirtless girls just walked into the library asking for the god that is Luke. Crazy!

7:00 PM

> Me: Are you okay?

4 messages and not a single response. Not even about the shirtless girls in the library. Which normally would result in him making some dirty joke and me criticising him on either being childish or sexist.

He is neither, but it's what we do.

Logically, I know he's probably just sleeping or studying, but I have this pit in my stomach. Especially after the nightmare situation last night. I didn't bring it up this morning, hoping he'd just leave it, and he did. But what if he thinks I'm too much now? Too much baggage. I've only known him for a couple of months, but he's become one of my best friends. It's really fucking terrifying to realise that, but right now I don't care. Luke is constant in my life that I'm really scared to lose, and I need to make sure he's okay. Picking up my phone, I pull up his contact to call him, but I'm stopped by Beck walking towards me.

"Hey Stella."

"Beck?" I question, "What's up?" He takes out the seat across from me and sits down. I can see his chest heaving in and out, as if he just ran here.

"It's Luke." My stomach flips. I stay silent, waiting for him to continue. "Something happened with his folks. I don't know what, but he's not doing well. He won't talk to me or Ror because he's an idiot who won't accept that we love him and are here for him. Instead, he assumes we are going to bolt at the first sign of difficulty, which is so insane

– but I can't convince him of that right now. So I need you to come. Now. I already took too long to find you here."

I shake my head. "I don't think I'm the right person." I'm not his real girlfriend, like Beck thinks I am. If Luke isn't talking to his two closest friends, he won't talk to me.

"Yes, you are." He stops for a second, thinking before speaking again, "I know you two aren't really together." My head snaps up at that.

"What?" How the hell?

"So does Rory. Don't worry, we won't say anything. But I'm here hoping that beneath the faking, you see him as your friend." I nod. There's not a single doubt in my mind about that.

"He needs to talk to you. He needs to talk to someone who hasn't been there the whole time, who hasn't seen it at its worst. Someone who is separated from it, who understands. As much as it sucks to admit it, that's not me and Rory. You are that person, Stella."

He stares at me for a beat before getting up. I don't know how to do what Beck is asking me to do.

"I hope I see you at the apartment, Stella. You understand this part of him more than Ror and I do. I don't know what you've been through to get it, but you do. He needs that."

I'm left sitting there alone as he walks away.

Chapter Thirty-One

LUKE

MY PHONE STOPPED TRYING TO LIGHT UP A BIT ago. Don't know if that means it finally crapped out or if that means they've finally left me alone. I don't have it in me to check. I guess I'll have to get a new phone at some point. And a new vase. It's fuzzy trying to remember if I broke it on purpose or not – it's my mother, so maybe subconsciously? Not really in the mood to deep dive into my psyche right now. I should move. Get up, go apologize to Beck for denying his help. I really hope he isn't mad at me. I just needed a second. He'll understand that ri-

"Luke?" My head snaps up immediately. I could recognise that voice anywhere. But the door is still shut. "If you want me to leave, say something; if not, I'm coming in." I stay silent as I hear the door handle turn and her footsteps as she walks in. She closes the door behind her, keeping the room almost pitch black. Stella's eyes roam across the room, adjusting to the darkness. She spots the phone, and I drop my head into my lap, not wanting her to see my face. She silently places herself down next to me.

I feel her hand on my knee, "I'm not going to say anything. I'm just going to sit here with you. If you want to talk, I'm here to listen." And with that, I feel her hand drop and move down next to her body. Looking up, I see her looking directly forward, not peeking at me. Somehow, she knows I don't want to be seen like this.

It's at least twenty minutes later when I finally speak up, "My parents and my little brother don't want me at his wedding. He's getting married and thinks I am going to somehow ruin it." She stays silent. "You know, when we were kids, he'd talk about his wedding all the time. He was so excited to fall in love and always said I'd be up on the altar with him as his best man. We'd always talk about the suits we'd wear and the girls we wished we'd be with." I let out a curt laugh, "Now I won't even be in the chapel. Funny how life changes, huh?"

I glance up to see her already looking at me, at my eyes. Searching almost. She moves closer to me and grabs my hand that's resting on my knee.

"They are idiots if they don't want you in their lives. And I know my saying that won't magically fix all your problems because being betrayed by someone you trusted cuts really fucking deep. But listen to me, you are a good person. Trust me when I say everything feels better, feels easier, with you there. And Luke, it's not just me. Those guys out there, who are totally not pressing their ears against the door listening-" I laugh, especially as I hear footsteps tumbling down the hallway, running away as if they had been caught by their mother. "Are you family. They love you, even if you can't believe it, they do. And they'd never want you gone. None of us do."

I nod, my chest feeling tight. She doesn't say anything else because she doesn't need to.

Before I can think of what to say, my phone lights up again. Not dead. My face drops again, but I go to grab it. Stella doesn't move.

> Leon: Please don't do anything rash with mum and dad. They think it's better if you're not here. It's better for you.

> Leon: Please still come to New Year's. I want you there.

I drop my phone on the bed and sit down next to Stella on the floor again. "My brother still wants me to go to the reunion." I stare straight ahead. "God, why can't I just let them go. It's not about their money as much as I try to say it is. I don't understand why I can't just not... care."

Stella doesn't move as she speaks.

"Because they're your family. Because you see the good in people. Because despite everything, you still care that you are their son and his brother. I get it, I used to be the same."

I turn and look at her; she's still staring ahead.

"Used to? What happened?" I ask. She swallows, scrunching her face slightly.

"My ex-boyfriend." She takes a breath, "Parker. He, um." I see tears start to well up in her eyes. Instinctively, I reach for her hand.

"Hey, you don't have to say anything, Goldie."

"I'm sorry." Her head drops slightly. I cup her face.

"You never have to apologise for not being ready to tell me something. I'm here for you when you are ready and want to talk, but I'm also here for you while you're not." Using my thumb, I brush the tear that's fallen down her cheek. She nods and stares into my eyes. In this moment, I think I truly realise how big a part of my life Stella has become.

She's one of my best friends. I can't lose her.

"I'm tired." She says, resting her head back on my shoulder. I can't tell what tired she's referring to.

"I have peppermint tea downstairs," I say. I bought a pack once she started coming over more. Wanted to make sure she was comfortable here. I hear a groan come out of her. "I also have coffee for when you want to give up on the caffeine-free life."

"Shut up, Lucas." She sits back up as a final tear falls from her eyes. I reach my thumb to her face, brushing it away.

"What a pair of gorgeous, emotionally damaged people we are, huh, Goldie?" She laughs at that, and I chuckle with her. There's a warmth in my stomach seeing her smile.

"Don't they say emotionally damaged people are more interesting?"

"Exactly, we are just unique."

Seeing her smile again at that last one, all I can think is there is no other place I'd rather be. And when Beck calls us down for pizza, her face drops slightly, and for a split second, I think she feels the same.

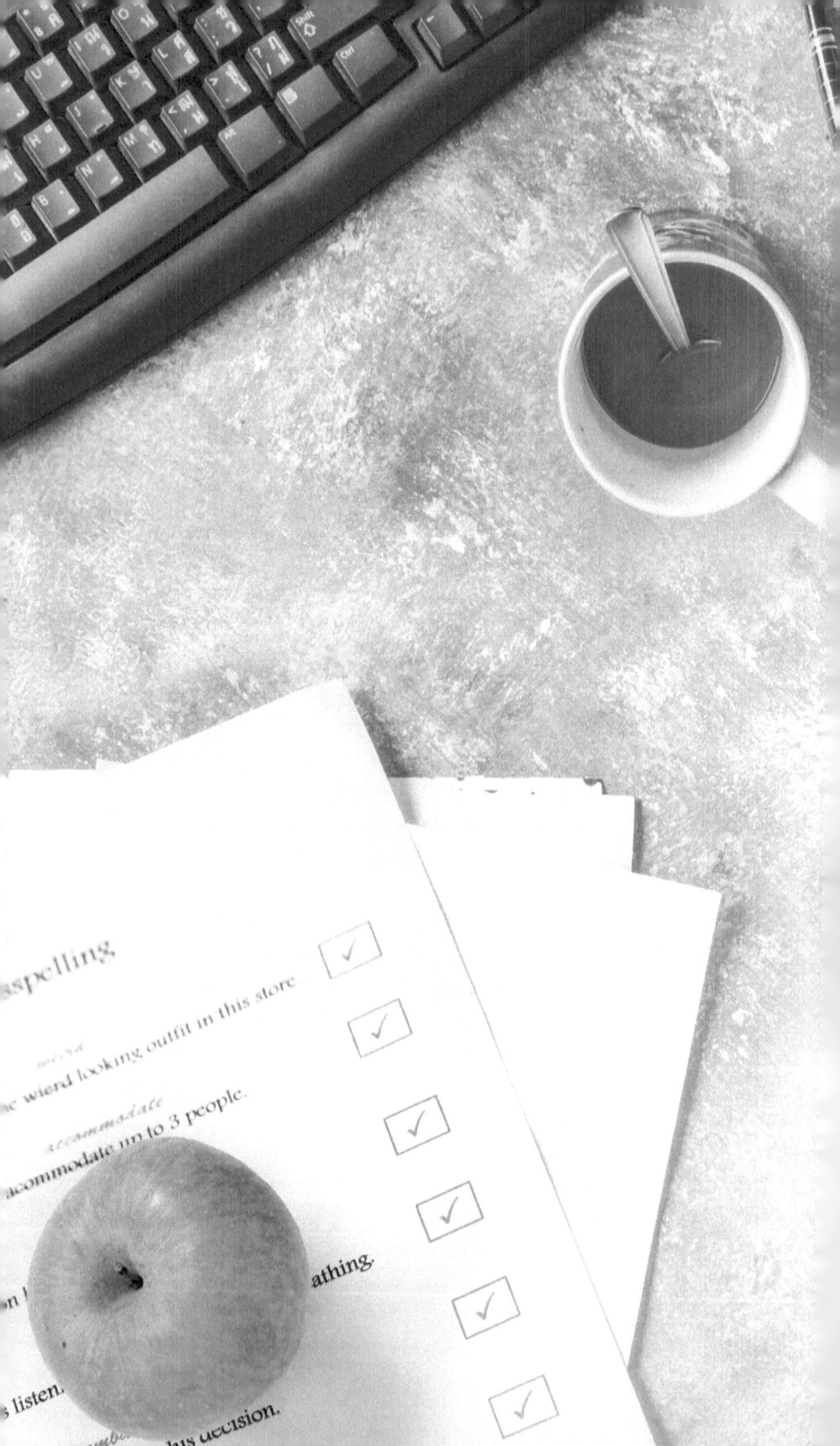
spelling
e wierd looking outfit in this store
acommodate up to 3 people.
athing.
listen.
his decision.

Chapter Thirty-Two

STELLA

ERIC ASKED ME TO COVER THE FIFTH GRADE CLASS for him again today. And just like the last time, I am dead tired, but also have never been happier. The day was just filled with teaching science, which I usually despise – but Keets got me excited about some cool experiments I could teach. There was a very palpable air of disappointment when I denied their request at a movie today. It was stupidly hard to say no to a group of whining kids, but there was too much work. Eric told me that it was a part of teaching – the whole having to get used to 20 kids going from loving you to hating you in the span of ten seconds. Excited for my future.

My future in teaching. Is that really what I want? It's the first time I've actually thought about it properly. I've been thinking about changing my degree since that night with Luke, but I'm still so scared. For some reason, it doesn't matter if 100 people tell me I'm good at this; all I can hear is his voice telling me I'm not.

Groaning, I kick a rock on the side of the path at the part

near uni. I kick it a tad too hard, and it falls right in the middle of a flower patch, killing a few of the flowers. There are usually insects in those areas, many of which I probably just crushed.

Great, now my midlife crisis is murderous.

I'm about to walk over to assess the damage when a guy cuts me off.

"Having a bad day?"

I look back at the guy standing in front of me, and I saw him earlier sitting, reading a book. His black hair is sticking up in every which way, trying to be messy – but I'd be willing to bet millions he styled it like that. He's wearing jeans and a hoodie, dressing completely opposite to the weather we are currently having. I don't know what it is, but something about him is familiar.

He's also looking at me like I'm his next meal.

"Nope, just struggling with the crushing expectations of university." I give him a sweet smile. He laughs at that. Is he flirting with me?

"I feel you. I'm graduating at the end of this year, just finished my honours year, and I have no idea what I'm going to do." So, he's a year older than Luke.

I laugh lightly, "I think it's extremely abnormal to know what you want to do with your life in your 20s. You'll be okay." Luke is definitely abnormal for having his life plan. I twirl my hair around my fingers, laughing way more than necessary. He seems nice and clearly goes to our uni.

"I'd be better if I could take you out tonight." He says, moving into a flirty smile.

Bingo.

"I don't know," I say, shifting. "What if you are a serial killer?"

He raises his eyebrows, nodding. "Good point. Well, my

name is Daniel, I live in room 104 of Fenton Hall, was born in Brisbane, and I am more than happy to send my phone location to someone you know in case I do get some stabbing aspirations and dreams."

"Good response," I reply, my head tilting in approval. He pulls his phone out of his back pocket.

"Good enough for your number mystery girl?" He asks, holding his unlocked phone in front of me. I grab it and put my number in.

"Good enough for now." I hand him back his phone. "Oh, and the name is Stella." He holds out his hand, and I grab it to shake it.

"Nice to meet you, Stella. I'll see you tonight."

"Bye, Daniel," I comment, a flirty smile on my lips, while he walks off, leaving me behind. That was unexpected to say the least. Looking back down at my phone, I see he's already texted me a bar a little bit out of town. Shit, I'll need to find someone to give me a lift or something.

Ten minutes later, I spot Luke in what has become our usual booth. I asked if he wanted to have a snack after I finished work because I knew he was doing some crazy study session all day. Thought it could be a nice break. I'll also do anything for an iced chocolate and some chips.

Recently, Luke and I have been hanging out. After that night a few weeks ago when we both basically broke down to each other, we've been a lot closer. I think we've been together more than we haven't. And it's not just been us two all the time, Keets and I have been over the guy's house all the time. Beck has made it his mission to make us hang out at least twice a week. That naturally means he's been setting up dinners and movie nights. It's sweet, and Keets has been helping out a lot. Every dinner we have has some sort of theme to it, complete with a dress code we have to adhere to. Last week was Bob's Burgers themed, and Beck made Luke and me dress up as Bob and Linda.

There is a slight tension in the air, making a weird dynamic in the group. Everyone knows Luke and I aren't actually together except for Keets. I'm starting to get scared when it comes out, but I don't really want it to be over. Every moment I spend with Luke feels like a breath of fresh air. He's reached out a couple of times to plan our next date, but I keep putting him off. If I see him again, there's only one more time before that's it. And I don't want that to be it.

For the first time since starting uni, I feel like Keets and I have a place, and I don't want to lose it.

"Hey Goldie," Luke says as I slide into the booth across from him.

"Hi, Lucas." I take a sip from the iced chocolate already sitting in front of me. "Thank god for iced chocolates."

He chuckles and settles into the seat more, "You know, there are other beverages to have, right? Like I don't know sodas or milkshakes or anything else." He grumbles, rolling his eyes at the mention of chocolate.

"Seriously, Luke, your weirdness is showing. Who doesn't like chocolate?"

He grins, his smile creeping across his face, "psychopaths obviously." I laugh and call the waitress over to order some cheesy bacon chips for both of us, and Luke orders a vanilla milkshake. I have not been able to think of anything else all day.

"So.." I say, slamming my hands onto the table, "How's studying going?"

He groans, rolling his eyes, "I hate my degree, Stel. It's not even funny, I know I want to own a bar and shit. And I know that will require knowledge in how to run a business, but Jesus fucking Christ." I laugh, having heard this rant a couple of times.

"What are you doing now?"

"Okay, so picture this, we have been told to write a 20-page report on this hypothetical company, right? I'm talking market research, SWOT analysis, operation plan, the whole nine. And the company is called…" His face turns dead serious, "are you ready, Stella?"

I sit up straight, "on the edge of my seat, Lucas."

"Sintra socks: step into the left lane." I lock eyes with him, my confusion apparent.

"What, you don't know what that is?" He asks, and my head shakes. "Shocking. They are socks with mirrored designs to try to make left-handed people feel more included." What the actual-

"I'm sorry, but that's the dumbest thing I've ever heard," I say, genuinely shocked. Who comes up with these things?

"My point exactly. I swear my teacher does some shrooms or something before assigning us our projects."

"Sounds like the two of you would get along." I quip, earning me a slightly angry stare from Luke.

Before he has a chance to respond, I remember I still haven't told him about Daniel.

"Oh, also! Guess who has a hot date tonight?" I ask, raising an eyebrow, bracing for the usual excited interrogation. But instead, I'm greeted with a face of stone, his expression darkening, the corners of his mouth turning down just slightly.

"You?" He mutters, his voice lacking his usual energy.

"Yup, it was so random. He just walked up to me, it was

a real 50s meet-cute." I say, trying to get some sort of reaction out of him.

"Cool." Again, quietly. "You're going?" He asks, finally making eye contact with me again.

I nod, "That's the plan. He's cute. I'm shockingly not hearing wedding bells, but you know, just the usual fun. His name is Daniel, he's a bit shorter than you, and he has kind of spiky black hair."

There's a flash of recognition across his face when I say his name, but that's all he gives me. He's not acting the same. I don't understand what's going on. Usually, we quip about this stuff and joke around. Even when he's feeling down, he still musters up some sort of insult about my taste or brings up 'corporate chad,' as he calls him. He still hasn't said anything.

"Everything okay there, Lucas?" I ask with a playful edge to my voice, making sure it sounds casual. He gives me a curt nod.

"Of course, why would anything be wrong?" Before I get a chance to respond, he picks up his phone as if he got a message. Not that I heard a notification. "Oh shit, Beck needs me for something. I'm so sorry, Stel."

"That's fine." I barely get out, confused as hell. Luke takes some money out of his wallet to pay for our snack and walks out the door. Without saying anything else, he's gone.

What the fuck just happened?

Chapter Thirty-Three

LUKE

SHE'S GETTING DRINKS WITH A GUY. AND NOT JUST any guy – Daniel. Like the guy I've worked with at the bar for the last year. I mean, Jesus, I guess bro code is just out the window. I don't care that he probably has never seen us interact; it still rubs me the wrong way.

I wonder if there is a way I could get him fired. You know, like, being a dick. I'm sure Steve would go for that – I can pull out the puppy dog eyes. Or get Beck to do that for me.

They are going on a date. Like a date that will end in him seeing her naked. Good. That's great. I mean, that's what she wanted. To be able to hang out with whom she wants without stressing her friends out. It's good that she's getting to reap the benefits of this bargain.

Repeatedly.

That's fine. That's good. It's great in fact. Truly, I've never been happier for another human being in my whole life. I'm sure the look that's been plastered on my face for the last few hours would back that up.

I still have yet to go back to my place. The idea of sitting in my room by myself right now, while some dickhead takes Stella out, is enough to make me lose my mind. So instead I'm sitting in the blaring heat, which is way too strong for October.

I don't understand why I can't just leave this. Just do what I usually do. Make fun of her a bit, get some info, and her live location, and then enjoy my night. Usually, the only stress I feel when she's with someone else is the nights when her 'I'm home' texts come later than usual. I genuinely don't understand why I'm so freaked out over this. When she told me, I just felt this sick twisting feeling in my stomach, and my chest clenched. All I could think was that I needed to get out of there.

It was like I was suffocating.

It's been a couple of weeks since she told me about a date she was going on, and I guess I just assumed she wasn't feeling it or something. Did something change in those two weeks for me? I know I want to fuck her, that's not news. But I've wanted to hook up with lots of girls. It's never come with this sort of feeling before. Stella occupies my brain all the time.

All I can think about is her smile. The way her hair is always just a little out of place, but how adorable it looks on her. The way my heart skips a beat when I see her smile, and the way it stops when I know I was the one who made her smile.

Oh.

Oh.

Shit. Shit. Shit. Okay, so maybe I want to do more than just fuck her. It feels like I have a crush. Jesus Christ, I haven't had a crush since I was five years old. What does one do with a crush? Specifically, with a crush on someone who is so against relationships, she fakes dates with someone to avoid it?

I seem to completely hate myself.

I'll figure out the logistics later, but right now she can't go on that date. I stand up, checking my phone. It's only 6, she probably hasn't left yet. So I ran.

And that's how five minutes later I was on her doorstep, trying desperately to make it look like I had just leisurely walked instead of sprinting. I knock on the door. She answers after the first knock with her hair straightened, and I tilt my head. That's different.

Stella looks beautiful, she always does – but I like her natural hair more. It's her.

She's also wearing tiny black pajamas that don't leave anything to the imagination. My eyes drop straight to the little bow right in between her tits.

Fuck my life.

"Luke? What are you doing here? I'm grabbing drinks with Daniel, remember?"

I snap my eyes up. "Yeah, but I felt bad after I left the restaurant earlier. I was just in a bad mood, but it doesn't excuse me for being a dick. I'm sorry." A slow smile crept on her face, making me feel a lot more relaxed. I was a massive dick earlier. "Plus, I wasn't sure if anyone saw me walk off like that. Didn't want anyone getting suspicious, we weren't madly in love, you know?"

"Oh yeah, I guess that's true." She steps to the side and gestures for me to come in. "You gotta just sit there and look pretty though. I'm running so late."

I follow her into her room and plop myself down on her bed, lying on her pillows. I immediately grab Reginald, because who can leave a frog with a monocle sitting on his own? She sits down on her vanity to continue her makeup, and she looks at me in the reflection.

"What?" I ask when she raises her eyebrows

"Nothing, it's just nice that Reginald has such an attentive dad."

I look down at him proudly, "damn right he does." I sit up slightly, trying to figure out how to get her to call off this date. I can't just tell her I have a crush on her; she'd run for the hills. Not to mention, there is still a slight chance it isn't really a crush and is just my dick getting confused with my head. "Tell me about the guy, how'd you guys meet?" She seems to brighten up even more as she tells me about her meet-cute with this douchebag. And about how he's not her usual type, but she's excited to see him tonight. Dickhead.

"Hmm," I say, purposefully ending my response there.

"Hmm?" She asks

"It's just this guy, he seems a bit too smooth. I don't know if he's kind of giving player vibes, you know?" I ask, taking at the end. There isn't a hint of a lie in my voice, because I'm telling the truth. Similar to Rory and Beck, Daniel enjoys the benefits of being a bartender. I see him give out free drinks like he's trading Pokémon cards.

She makes eye contact with me in the mirror, bringing her eyebrows together slightly, "You are very right about that, but that's kind of perfect. If the guy is already casual, when I want to split, there's no harm." Shit, she's got a point there.

"I guess, I don't know." I let out an exaggerated sigh. "How do you know he's not a serial killer or something?"

Stella lets out an adorable laugh, "You know I said that exact same thing to him?" I'm fighting the urge to lock her in this room. She's not taking me seriously.

Stella starts looking around her desk for something.

"Dammit, I left my blush in the bathroom, one sec." She jumps up and walks out of the room. I immediately stand up. Before I think too hard about what I'm doing, I go to her desk and grab a couple of miscellaneous makeup items. I barely make it back to where I was before she sits back down, stuffing the items in her pillowcase. She looks down at her desk again, holding her blush.

"What the hell?" She murmurs.

"Everything okay?" I ask, paying very close attention to her reactions.

"Yeah, I just swore I left my brush and mascara right here and now I can't find them." I force up a laugh.

"Sounds like you are going a bit crazy, Goldie."

She lets out a dry laugh before shaking her head. "Apparently so. Guess we are going for natural makeup tonight." She keeps applying her makeup, which she does have. Okay, I need to try something else.

"Hey, what are you planning on wearing?" I ask, feigning curiosity.

She tilts her head to the bathroom, "It's hanging behind the door."

I get off her bed, quickly grab the makeup I hid in her pillow, and peek behind the door of her bathroom. There is a pale yellow mini dress hanging. It's got flowers in a darker yellow embroidered all over it.

It would look beautiful on her.

Too bad I have to fuck it up. I take the black tube I'm holding and "accidentally" rub a bit on the dress. I back up, making sure I've hit enough of it. I'll pay for the dry cleaning, or better yet, I'll buy her a new dress that she can wear on our date. Once I feel satisfied, I call out.

"Hey, Stel?" My voice was wavering slightly, making an effort to seem distressed. She comes running in a second later, her hair now having small braids scattered through it.

"Yeah?" She asks, concerned. I hold up the dress to show her.

"I don't think that's part of the design."

She grabs it from me, examining the marks, "Oh shit shit shit," she curses, looking closer, "Keets must have accidentally marked it when she was getting ready earlier." Stella groans before walking back to her room. I follow behind her, finally feeling like we are getting somewhere.

"Goldie, I say this in the nicest, most supportive way possible, but it really seems like the universe is against your date." Her eyebrows shoot up, and he places a hand on my chest and starts pushing me out of her room.

"Lucas, you are officially failing at just sitting there and looking pretty. Go wait in the living room. I'll be five minutes."

I sit down on the couch and start looking around her apartment to see if there is anything else I can do. Would a broken TV make her cancel her date? Maybe not, but if I fall over and hit the TV, maybe she'd stay home then. Especially if I hurt myself in the fall, a twisted ankle isn't that painful, right? I'll obviously replace the TV, and then everything will be fixed. Okay, maybe I just need to take a breath.

I'm trying to convince myself this is fine when she walks into the living room. She's wearing baggy jeans that sit right on her hips and make her legs look longer than they should be. She's wearing a top that's tight around her tits, and loose everywhere else. She looks like a goddamn goddess, and that's why she can't go on this date.

"Hey, the taxi should be here in like ten minutes, so you can head off whenever," she tells me as she puts on her earrings.

"Taxi? Nah, I'll drive you." I say standing up.

"Luke, seriously, it's fine. He offered to pay for my cab anyway." Oh, I do not like that.

"Nope, decision made, Goldie. It's just parked at the diner, so I'll be literally faster than the taxi. Sit." I gesture to the spot on the couch I was just sitting on.

"Fine." She sits down on the other end of the couch. I look at her, offended. "Dude, if you think I want to sit where your hot ass just was, you've got another thing coming."

I'm shaking my head, walking out the door, trying to hold back a laugh.

Oh my god, why is it still hot? It's 7:00 pm. I'm staring at my truck that has been parked outside of Stella's for the past three minutes, trying to talk myself into doing this plan. The engine purrs softly, reminding me I need to move my ass at some point.

Fuck it.

I crouch down next to my back left tire and locate the valve. I take off the cap and use my keys until I hear the hissing noise telling me air is coming out. I get into the driver's seat and send Stella a text telling her I'm here. She responds immediately, telling me that she's coming down. The only thing stopping me from full-blown thinking I'm a psychopath is the laugh Stella and I will probably have about this in five years when we are happy and living together.

"Why are you gripping the steering wheel so hard, psycho?" I glance down quickly to see that she's right, my knuckles are pretty much white. I loosen my grip, checking my side mirror to see if the tire is still working fine. It's starting to hit me that it may have been slightly idiotic and dangerous to damage my tire, knowing I don't have a spare.

"You know, calling someone a psycho is rude, right?" I ask, trying my best to match our usual banter.

"Yes, Lucas, I am aware; however, I like having no filter." I can feel the smile she is currently sporting, feeling pretty proud of herself. She's currently scrunched up in the chair, her feet on the seats. The ultimate passenger princess.

"Hopefully, Daniel the douche will like that," I say and immediately regret it based on the look on her face.

"You are acting so weird today, Luke."

My apology is cut off by the feeling of a drag behind us. Okay, breathe, Luke.

"Oh shit," I say and start pulling off to the side of the road. Stella sits up, putting her legs down, alarmed.

"What's wrong?"

"I think the tires burst or something." I stop the car and get out. "Stay here, I'm going to check it out." I walk to the back tire, seeing that it is, in fact, flat. I quickly put the cap on, hoping it's not obvious that it was drained manually.

"So the tire's flat?" Stella asks, standing over me, causing me to jump.

"Jesus Goldie, I told you to stay in the car." She hovers over me, crossing her hands over her chest. "I'm not going to make the date, am I?" She asks, clearly already resigning to that fact. I shake my head, but keep my face down – trying not to show my happiness.

I stand up facing her, "Maybe it's a good thing? The whole night has been a bit fucked." She slightly nods her head as I rub her shoulder. "Daniel seemed off anyway. You are probably way better without him." Stella backs up, walking towards the hood of my car at that. Her face scrunches up as she turns around.

"What?" I ask, confused, why her mood shifted.

She turns back towards me, "Why the hell are you being such a dick right now? It feels like this entire night you have been trying to convince me to not go out." True. But I stay silent. "What? What is it? You know something about Daniel that I don't?"

"Well, I know him, okay? He works at the Black Lantern." I'm tripping over my words trying to come up with an excuse. "He's not a good guy, okay? You could just do better."

Her eyes squint in disbelief.

"It's not that. If that was true, you would have just told me from the get-go." She pauses, waiting for me to say something. I stay silent. "Luke, I swear to god. What is it?!" She shouts. I take a deep breath.

"I don't want you going out with him because."

"Because?" She presses.

I sigh, resigned to what I'm about to say.

"Because I don't understand why you need them, when I am right here waiting for you."

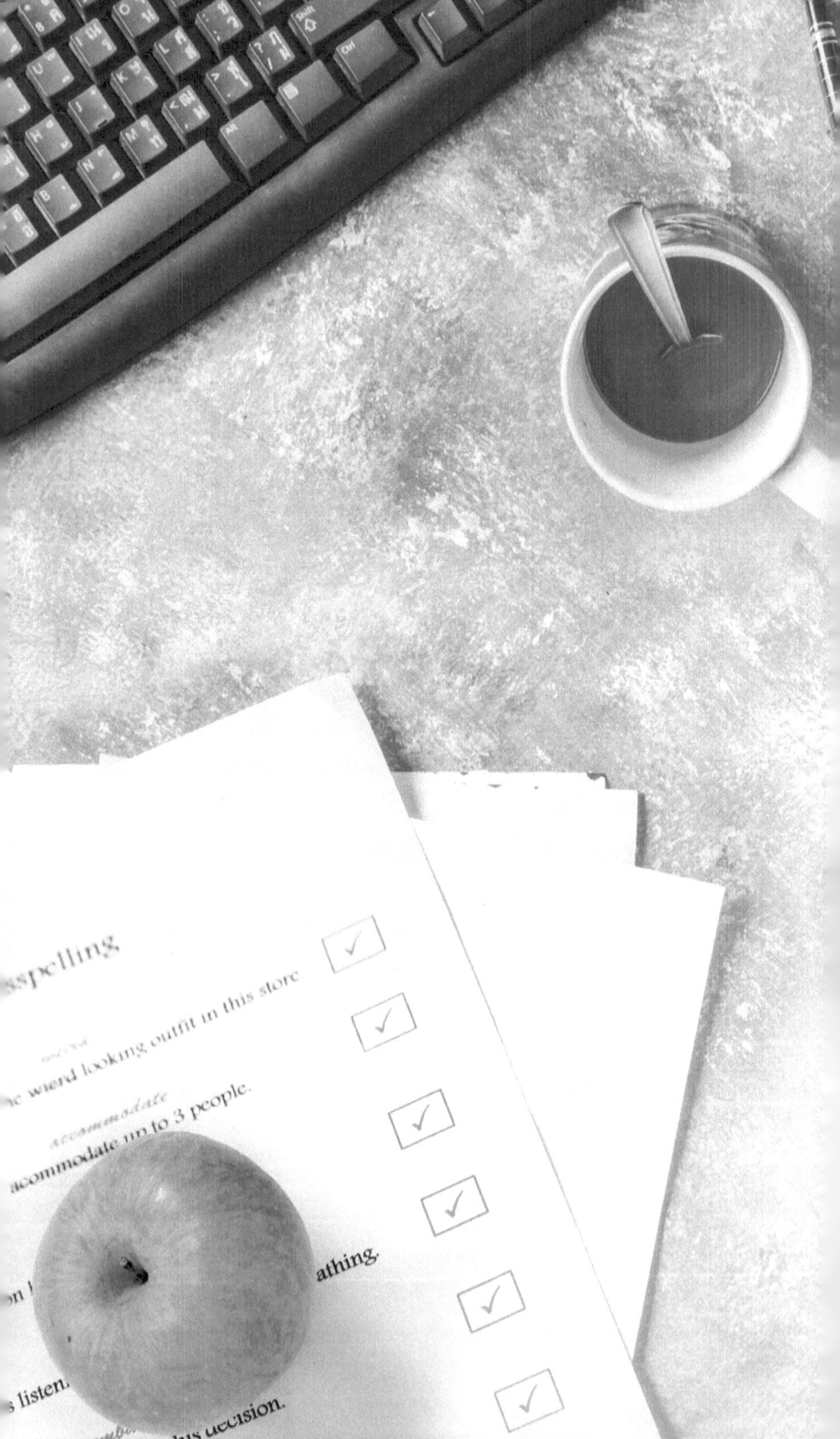
sspelling
wierd looking outfit in this store
acommodate
acommodate up to 3 people.
athing.
s listen
decision.

Chapter Thirty~Four

STELLA

I DON'T KNOW WHAT TO SAY TO THAT.

I look up at him, 99% sure I misunderstood him. I'm standing right in front of the hood of his trunk, and he's a few steps away from me. He stares at me, waiting for my response. I'm suddenly very aware of his presence. All I can smell is his cologne, and all I can see is him. It takes one simple sentence from him to make me forget we are stuck on an empty road. All I can hope is that the dim street lamps are dark enough to hide the blush I can feel creeping up my neck.

"What did you just say?" I ask, my voice quivering slightly. I'm trying my best to remain confident as I ask, but I know he can tell how I really feel by the way he smirks as I ask. He steps forward and places each hand on either side of me, boxing me in against the hood of his trunk. I instinctively tilt my head down, all of a sudden overwhelmed by him being this close. I feel one of his hands brush the underside of my jaw before reaching my chin. He tilts my head up, forcing me to look at him.

"I said, why do you need them?" He leans in closer, his breath hot next to my ear. I can feel heat starting to pool in my abdomen. "When you have me ready and waiting for you." As he says this, he pushes his hips towards me, and my legs separate involuntarily. I can feel him against me, causing the slightest amount of friction – but it's not enough. I push against him slightly and hear his groan. I can't hold back the whimper when I hear him say those words to me and move the way he is. I've never had such a visceral reaction to someone before, but something about him makes me want to beg for him to touch me.

Even if it was just this.

I take a deep breath and stare straight at him. "I didn't know you were waiting for me."

He laughs before looking me straight in the eye.

"I don't think there is a single man who wouldn't wait for you. Who wouldn't beg you to let them taste you, to let them know what you sound like when you come? I am certainly no exception, Stella.

He called me Stella. Hearing him admit that he wants me unlocks something in me. I don't want to pretend I'm not attracted to him anymore.

"Waiting for me how?"

"You know how."

"You'd beg for me, Luke?"

"I'd get on my knees and crawl to you if you asked me to."

"Do it," I say, the challenge clearly in my voice. He drops to his knees without any hesitation, looking up at me. I try to keep my face straight as I stare down at him. It becomes harder as he starts kissing his way up my leg. His hands are slowly roaming, slower than I want them to.

Grabbing him to come up to me, his face snaps up, his gaze is full of hunger, but he doesn't move.

"What are you waiting for?"

"For you to say yes."

His eyes search mine, looking for an answer.

I push my hips into his again, before I breathlessly say, "Yes."

He's on me quicker than I can blink. His hands grab my face, pulling me towards him, and he kisses me. There's nothing slow about the way Luke Astor kisses me. It's full of need, of want. He kisses me like he has something to prove, his hands getting tangled in my hair, pulling me as close to him as I can go. He picks me up without showing a second of struggle, placing me on the hood of his truck. My legs instinctively wrap around him, wanting to be closer.

He lets out a low groan before pulling away.

"Fuck if I knew how good this was, I wouldn't have waited so long."

I pull his head down towards mine, "I told you I was a good kisser."

He laughs, "Now who has the big ego?"

I cut him off before he could say anything else, wanting to feel him again. His hand reaches underneath my shirt, cupping my breasts.

"Do you know how mad you drive me walking around like this? Letting me see just enough so I'm so hard I can't even think straight." He uses two of his fingers to pinch my nipple.

I move my hands to the edge of my shirt and slowly lift it over my head. I see his eyes trailing every inch of my body, watching me put on a show for him. I've always liked being a tease, but right now I don't want to do this so slowly. Once my shirt is off, he stops and just stares at me.

On display for him.

Only for him.

"Jesus Goldie, you're even more beautiful than I thought you'd be."

He's back on me in an instant. I feel his hand start to drop lower, finally reaching where I need him to.

His hand reaches the edge of my skirt on my thigh and looks up at me, "Is this okay?"

I nod probably too enthusiastically, but I'm too turned on to be embarrassed.

"If you get uncomfortable, we stop. Got it." I nod again, but before I can process anything, his hand brushes over the lace in my underwear. He moves his hand down, teasing me.

"Fuck Goldie, you're wet."

"Please," I say, my hips lifting off the truck towards him involuntarily.

"Please, what? Use your words, Stella."

Fuck I hate him. I stare at him, my stubborn nature starting to come back. He matches my stare, smirking as he drags his hand lightly back across my underwear. I moan, half-hating my body for giving in, but mainly wanting him.

"Say the words, Stella."

My head snaps up, staring him dead in the eyes. The lust in his face is clear, and in that moment, I don't care to be in control. I just need him.

"Please touch me, Luke." He grins.

"Lift up for me, Stel." I lift myself up slightly, arms shaking with adrenaline. He pulls my skirt and my underwear off without any hesitation. He puts the skirt on the trunk but throws the underwear to the side. I look at him, confused.

"I don't want anything that you put on for him. Plus, it's

not like you'll be needing that when you're around me." He doesn't let me respond before he drags his finger between my pussy. Just brushing by the place I so badly want him to touch.

"Don't be a tease, Lucas."

"Like you were earlier?" I go to respond, but I am cut off by the feeling of his fingers circling my clit. My breath gets caught in my throat as he keeps moving while looking at me. He keeps his thumb on my clit as he pushes one finger inside of me.

I raise slightly, hoping he'll get deeper.

"Greedy girl," he keeps moving "Would you like a second?" I nod, unable to form the words. "I'm going to need you to say it, Goldie."

"Yes. Fuck." He pushes inside of me so suddenly I nearly scream. My head falls against his chest as he goes faster, my eyes closing. I feel his other hand lift my head up.

"I want you to watch. To see how good you look riding my fingers." Jesus Christ, who taught this man to talk like this? I look down and see him moving, and the image is too much.

"Luke," I say, breathlessly, as I come. I can hear his groan as I tighten around his fingers. He slowly pulls them out before licking one of his fingers.

"You taste just as good as I dreamed."

I look up at him, feeling as disheveled as I probably look. "You dream about me, Lucas?"

"You know I do." He brings his hand up and puts his fingers in front of me. "Taste them. See how good you taste when you come because of me." He pushes his fingers inside my mouth, and I suck on them like it's something else I'd like to try.

I slowly run my hand along his chest and down his

stomach. I can feel his abs that I've seen time and time again peeking through the shirt. I trace down the V that his body forms before cupping him through his jeans. I feel him twitch as I run my thumb along his length.

I look up at him, mustering the sweetest smile I can. "Can I suck your dick, Lucas?"

Chapter Thirty-Five

LUKE

FUCK. YOU DO NOT KNOW WHAT IT FEELS LIKE TO have the girl you've been fantasising about nonstop naked in front of you, asking to suck your dick. I genuinely think if I died right now, I'd die a happy man.

I grab her hand as she goes to reach for my dick. She looks up at me, confused.

"As much as I want to fuck your mouth, there's somewhere else I want to be first."

She smiles and sits back. Waiting for me to move.

She knows I'd do anything to hear my name come out of her mouth again. I like that she knows what she does to me. I walk around and grab a condom from the console of the car before coming back and standing in front of her.

I take my shirt off and start undoing my jeans. Taking it just as slow as she did earlier with her top. She starts squirming, clearly desperate for anything. When I'm down to just my boxers, I see her start to move towards me. She gets off the hood of the car and cups my dick again, moving her thumb over the head. I move her hands to the waistband to get her to take the boxers off me. It's embarrassing how fast this will be over if she keeps touching me like that. It's been a while since the last time I did this. She moves down with the boxers, pulling them off me, and she stays on her knees, staring.

"My eyes are up here, sweetheart."

She licks her lips as her eyes slowly move back to my face. I laugh and bend over to pick her back up.

I set her back on the truck, "Like what you see?" I ask, aware of how cocky I probably sound.

"Nope." She says, her tongue darting out again.

I tilt my head, rubbing my dick down her, getting it wet. The lights are just bright enough for me to see the glimmer of her juices on my dick. She whimpers, her body moving towards me. I love how she wants me, even when she tries to fight it.

"Sure you don't," I say right before I push the head in. She tilts her head back, her breathing getting heavy. I slowly push all the way in. I'm in heaven. That's the only word I can come up with to describe what it feels like being inside Stella. Heaven. Like we fit. Like we always will.

"Luke," she whimpers, and I nearly finish right there. I move in and out, slowly, not wanting this to be over too fast. She starts moving her hips back and forth, trying to match my thrusts, getting me to speed up. I'm enjoying seeing her so desperate for me. I pull her towards me and feel her tits smash against my chest. She's grabbing onto my hair and my back, trying to hold on.

After a while, I flip her over and bend her over the hood of my car. This time there's no teasing. I push inside of her grabbing a fistful of her hair and wrap it around my hand. Using it, I pull her head back so she can look at me.

"You are perfect, Stella. I know you can't see it, but you are taking me so well. It's like this pussy was fucking made for me." I push into her harder and hear her moan in response, especially as my free hand wraps around to rub her clit.

"I wasn't joking when I said I'd beg to feel this pussy again. You feel heavenly." Just as I say that, I hear her moan my name and feel her squeeze around me. It's impossible to keep myself together when that happens. I see stars and push inside of her one last time.

I stay inside of her as she comes down. We are silent for a second, our breathing slowing down. I pull out and sit her up.

"Stay here," I whisper in her ear. She nods tiredly, and I pull on my boxers as I walk back towards the console. I put music quietly in the car and clean her up, before pulling my shirt over her.

"There's dirt on this." I hear her whine as I'm picking up the rest of our clothes. I turn back in disbelief.

"I just fucked you on the hood of a truck on the side of the road, and you're complaining about some dirt on the outside of the shirt you're wearing."

She proudly nods, and I know I'm done for. I dump the clothes back on the ground and throw her over my shoulder. She's giggling and kicking her feet, but not fighting the carry. I open the back seat door of the car and drop her in before climbing in after her, positioning us in the most comfortable way possible in the back seat of the car.

"That was."

"Yeah." There isn't much else to say when something like that happens.

She goes quiet again for a second before sitting straight

up. I smile, knowing why she's doing this. She turns her head towards me, shock planted across her face.

"Is this the Taylor Swift playlist I made for you!?"

I smile and close my eyes, "I have no idea what you're talking about."

She smacks my chest, "You are totally a Swiftie. I knew it, I converted you."

She lies back down next to me, seemingly proud of herself. I kiss her on the head and whisper,

"I'll be anything you want me to be, Goldie."

I feel her push closer towards me, and I wrap my arms around her. Something I've done numerous times before this, but it feels different now. More.

"I don't want to ruin the moment." Shut up, Luke. Why are you speaking? "But, unless I have worse memory than I think, Fucking wasn't in our agreement."

"Actually, from memory, I'm pretty sure you said this would happen. You know you're a sex god and all." She says sex god in air quotes as if it's even slightly wrong.

"Do I need to remind you of what just took place outside the car?" I turned my head to look at her. "But seriously, we should talk about this right."

Her body stiffens just slightly. It's subtle, fleeting, but enough for me to notice.

"I don't think so. We were fake dating. Now we are fake dating, but we fuck. It's not that deep."

"But what about your dates?"

"Like you said, Luke. I don't need them, I have you. We are friends who are fake dating until New Year's Eve and exclusively fuck until then. Pretty easy definition if you ask me."

She turns on her side away from me, but still rests her

head on my arm and holds my hand. I hear her try to stifle her yawn as she settles in. I nod against her head because I know she's right. I ignore the sour taste in my mouth, trying to convince myself I can do casual.

spelling
wierd
he wierd looking outfit in this store
accommodate
acommodate up to 3 people.
athing.
s listen.
his decision.

Chapter Thirty-Six

STELLA

THE FIRST BEAMS OF SUN FILTERED THROUGH THE blinds, causing my eyes to open, taking a second to adjust to the sudden light. A heavy arm is draped around my waist, and my head is resting on his chest. I tilt my head up slightly to see Luke, still sleeping peacefully. He looks beautiful. The sunlight is hitting him perfectly, outlining every line and curve of his face. His hair is messy, half of it falling in front of his face. Somehow, he still looks put together even first thing in the morning. I think there needs to be a study on how this man is allowed to look this good.

I put my head back down on his chest, taking a deep breath. One that is necessary as I look down at his body. I didn't get an opportunity to fully take him in last night. Shockingly, street lamps weren't designed to see the details of someone's naked body.

He looks like he was sculpted by Michael Angelo. Every part of him is sharp – completely polar to the guy I've gotten to know over the past few months.

Memories from last night keep flooding into my brain, causing a pool of warmth to form in my abdomen.

It was good.

I have to stop myself from laughing, because honestly, good is the understatement of the century. I've never done anything like that. Every time I've had sex, it's been in a bed or at most in a bathroom. I know, scandalous. But I don't know if it was the openness of it all or if it was him, but I can easily say it was the best I'd ever had.

Not that I'd ever tell him that.

But honestly, it wasn't just the sex. Yes, that was probably the highlight, but it was everything that happened after. The way he played Taylor for me in the car and held me as I fell asleep. The way he called us a car – leaving his ute for the night, took me to get food, somehow finding a 24/7 sushi restaurant. And even though it might have been the most disgusting sushi I've ever had, it was the fact that he did it. Without me asking. He also asked if I just wanted to be dropped off at mine, making it clear he didn't want to put any pressure on me spending the night, but that he would love it if I did.

His place was closer to where we were, so I said I'd crash. That's the only reason.

Nothing else.

When we got back to his place, I was too tired to stay awake for long, despite my vagina's objections. I'm sure I look horrific, forgetting to fix my hair or take my makeup off last night. I'm probably the ghost of hookups past right now.

For some reason, though, I can't bring it in me to care – because I don't think he would.

Luke stirs softly beside me, still completely dead to the world despite the brightness that has now fully taken over the room. As he does, he pulls me in a bit tighter, and it seems to make me fully aware of the situation.

He's cuddling me.

After we had sex.

Luke is cuddling me. I start to feel my chest beat a bit faster, and his hold stops feeling comforting and nice the way it was ten minutes ago. What am I doing? I don't cuddle. I barely spend the night in most cases – stumbling into my room at three am.

I gently lift his arm off me and sit up, placing it down gently on the pillow I was just lying on. He shifts slightly, but doesn't wake up. Slowly, I slip off the bed, searching for my clothes.

Shit, what did he do with them? I seem to remember him throwing my underwear somewhere on the ground. Did he pick it up? I actually really liked that pair.

I frown slightly, thinking about my lost clothes, before pulling on some sweats and a shirt I see on the floor. They are way too big for me, but thank god for drawstrings. I am highly aware that the second I am witnessed by a single other human being, they will know damn well what I was doing last night. But I couldn't care less.

I grab my purse that's flung over his chair and go to leave, but I look back at him one last time. He still hasn't woken up.

My stomach twists thinking about him waking up to me just gone. Without any explanation. It feels wrong; he's not just some hookup.

He's Luke.

I quickly grab a pen and scribble a note on a piece of paper he has on his desk, laying it on the pillow next to him. When he turns over, I quickly run out the door – leaving his apartment behind me.

As I'm walking down the street, I come to two very obvious realisations. Firstly, I put on sweatpants in October. I can already feel the sweat starting to pool, making me regret not just staying in the boxers I was wearing when I woke up. And secondly, I actually have nowhere to go. And for the first time in a long time, I don't feel like I have to catch up on sleep.

Pulling out my phone, it's on 20%. I see one message from Keets, though, letting me know she's home at the apartment today and wants to hang out. Perfect. I shoot her a quick text telling her to come meet me at the Abernathy Dining Hall. I'm almost never up early enough for breakfast, but when I am, I take complete advantage of it. The waffle bar and hashbrowns have the ability to get me pregnant.

It's a short walk from Lukes to the dining hall, and yet somehow Keets has beaten me – and with her hair done and wearing a pink workout set. I think there needs to be a study on how much this girl gets done before the rest of the world is even awake.

I walk over to her, struggling not to laugh at the face she makes once she clocks my clothes.

Her eyebrows danced with mischief as I walked up. "Good night?" She asks, sounding almost like Matthew McConaughey.

The laugh I was holding slips out as I sit across from her. She's already made me up a plate of my favourites.

"You could say that." A suggestive tone in my voice as I take a bite of the hashbrown – moaning as I do so.

"Stella. Keep those noises for Luke." Keets teases, taking a sip of her coffee. "But no, seriously, I'm not joking. Give me the details. Now." Her tone switches to serious so fast it's slightly shocking.

I sadly put down my half-eaten brown, highly aware I'm not going to be allowed to eat until I finish it.

I lower my voice slightly, aware of all the people around us, "he may have fucked me on the hood of his truck on the side of the highway."

Her eyes just about bulge out of her head as she screams.

"Stella Quinn Faraday!"

Everyone around us turns to look, concern on their face clear. I reach over, placing a hand on her mouth, giving a small apologetic smile to the people sitting around us.

"Keets – shut it," I whisper-hiss. She takes a breath before nodding, and I move my hand.

Keets leans in, her voice dropping. "Was it good? Did you get caught? Jesus Stella, tell me everything – you slut."

I laugh at her excitement for something that didn't even happen to her. "Yes, it was good – It's Luke. And no, we didn't get caught, but considering we were butt naked underneath a street lamp, we were definitely tempting fate."

Keets' head shakes in disbelief, "Scandalous sex. I hate you. Why can't I have hot, scandalous sex?"

I pout my lips in slight pity as my head drops to the side. "How long has it been?"

"Way too long, Stella. I'm starting to understand why people can refer to their vaginas as Sahara deserts." Her voice stays the same level as she says, "My hairbrush is starting to look at me a certain way, Stel."

I laugh, not at her statement, but rather because of the movement of the people who were sitting next to us. Apparently, too traumatised by our conversation to remain sitting there.

"Oops." Keets shrugs her shoulders, completely

uncaring. And honestly, I feel the same. We are in our 20s, people; it's time to stop being prudes about this stuff. "So you were at his last night?" She takes a spoonful of her cereal.

I nod.

"Jesus, you must be tired."

"I'm actually not." I say, shaking my head, "Not quite sure why."

Her eyebrows furrow a bit, "No nightmare?"

My mouth drops slightly in realisation. "No nightmare."

Keets smiles, but I'm still surprised. The main reason I don't spend the night with guys is that I always have nightmares. When I'm on my own, they are less frequent, but throw a member of the opposite sex in the mix, and I might as well be in a Stephen King novel. But with Luke, nothing. The first time we spent the night together, I didn't have one either. It's weird as hell.

"Seems like a perfect romantic night." I try to stop the wince that comes on my face with the word romantic. It's hard to remember that Keets thinks I am a changed woman – a girlfriend. She seems to notice my reaction, because she backtracks slightly. "How is that going? The whole romance being in a relationship thing." Her voice is light, cautious.

I chuck a smile on my face. "It's good. He's so sweet to me, and I just enjoy my time with him. Beside you, of course." She smiles, framing her chin with her hands, "He's my favourite person to be with." As I'm talking, I realize that none of this is a lie. He really is good to me, and I do love spending time with him. The more I think about it, the more I find myself wanting him—more and more. But not in a relationship way. No. It's just... like friends who hang out all the time, have sex, sleep together.

It's normal.

It's casual.

It's nothing more than that.

I shake off the slightly strange sensation that settles in my chest, opening my mouth to ask Keets a question. "Enough about me, how are you?"

"I'm good, feeling happy and positive. Ready to kick the ass of anyone or anything who comes at me." I smile softly at her. I genuinely have no idea how she's able to stay positive about everything around her. It's contagious.

Chapter Thirty-Seven

LUKE

MY EYES OPENED SLIGHTLY, THE LIGHT BEAMING through the room, feeling like a personal attack. I close my eyes again, rolling over to wake up Stella, who I can only assume is still sleeping. Reaching my arm, I'm met with a cold, empty bed, the bedding having been thrown off towards me.

What the hell?

My eyes open quickly, and I sit up looking around the room, but she's nowhere to be found. And her shoes and bag are gone from where she threw them last night.

I guess she snuck out.

My jaw clenches slightly, upset that she left without saying goodbye. I pull the covers off, standing up, and throw on a hoodie. Beck always keeps the house freezing cold in the morning. I walk around to her side, to grab her clothes that I put underneath the bedside table, and notice a note on her pillow. I'm not sure how I missed it before.

I had to leave because I had a stupidly busy day, but you looked like Sleeping Beauty next to me, and I couldn't wake you.

I'll see you later xx.

Stel

A small smile shadows my lips as I read the note. Still would have preferred her to wake me up, but it makes me feel good that she didn't just forget about me.

But wait, are wake-up calls not a thing in Friends with Benefits? Are we meant to sneak out and leave notes? Is that how this works?

I groan, rubbing my face, trying to stop my brain from overthinking this. It's not like I've never done a casual thing; I'm no saint. But there are always lines, always boundaries with what we can do.

With Stella, it feels like we are constantly dancing between the lines. And it doesn't help that we are also fake-dating at the same time.

My head hurts.

Walking down the stairs, I am immediately greeted with Beck's naked ass.

"Dude!" I shout, using my hand to cover his ass. "Clothes?"

He grabs his boxers that were hanging over the chair and puts them on, "My bad, bro. I was just making sure the boys were all good. You know, testicular cancer is most common in 15 to 35-year-olds. We are right in the prime."

I walk over to the coffee machine, making myself a cup. "But in the kitchen, Beck?"

He shrugs, "Nothing you haven't seen before."

Rory chooses this moment to walk in, spared from the

torture my eyes just witnessed. "Morning." He grumbles, grabbing eggs from the fridge.

I nod at him as Beck speaks again. "Also, Luke, it's not like you can talk. Someone had a guest spend the night." That catches Rory's attention, causing him to spin around to look at me.

"Really?" He asks, drawing out the word.

"Mhm." Beck walks up and leans on the other end of the island. And I have on good authority, ie, seeing her leave this morning, that it was the one and only Stella Faraday."

Rory's hand snaps up to his mouth in shock. I can't tell if it's genuine or not. Knowing these fuckers, probably not.

"So having a sleepover is a crime now." I put my hands out in front of me, "Arrest me."

"Oh, it's not a crime. More just confusing, considering you and Stella aren't together. No romantic attraction, if I do remember. Rory, was that right?"

Rory nods, a smug look plastered on his face. I want to punch them.

"Okay, so maybe some romantic attraction has developed, but we still aren't together." They both look at me, confused. "What, it's just sex. We are still doing the whole fake dating thing, just getting some extra benefits."

"You and Stella? Are you having casual sex?" Rory asks, his eyes widening.

"Yes. Why is that so confusing?"

Beck straightens up, "Um, because it is so unbelievably obvious you both have feelings for each other and should just be together and get married and have lots of babies."

Rory throws a pillow that he grabbed at Beck's face, causing him to scream.

"Hey, what was that for?"

"They aren't ready for that, Beck. We have to remember

we are dealing with an idiot over here." His head tilts towards me. Rude.

"Oh, right, my bad. No casual sex is a great idea, Luke. Keep it up." He throws me two thumbs up to match his goofy grin.

"Guys, apparently, despite your beliefs, I'm not an idiot. I do know I have feelings for her." I take a sip of my coffee.

"Oh. Okay." Rory turns his body towards me. "Then why are you okay with being casual with her?"

I shrug, "because that's what she needs. I'm okay with going at her speed."

Beck straightens up slightly, hesitant. "But what if you get hurt in the process?"

"Then I get hurt." I move to grab an apple that's lying on the island, throwing it up and catching it. "I like her. A lot. I'm willing to risk it if there's a possibility I get her in the end."

They both look at each other, clearly apprehensive. But in the end, they both nod.

"If you think it's the right choice, we support you," Rory says, smiling at me. It's clear they are wary, but I know it's right. I don't want to rush her – she needs to open up to me at her speed.

"Okay, changing topic," Beck says, shifting on his feet. "Have you invited Stella to the Halloween party yet? We weren't sure if she and Keets knew about it."

"Oh shit. I completely forgot." I pull out my phone to text Stella, purposefully ignoring Beck's teasing.

> Me: Hey Goldie, what do you say about coming to a killer Halloween party on the 2nd?

She responds immediately.

Goldie: After Halloween? Rookie
behaviour.

Goldie: But yes, I'd love to. Keets and I
already have costumes planned.

Me: Oh god – you take Halloween very
seriously, don't you?

Goldie: I don't play around about
Halloween, Lucas. You should know this
about me.

Me: My bad, too busy learning other things
about you. Like the noise you make right
before you come.

The break in her fast texting makes me smile. For someone so confident, I seem to make her flustered a lot.

"Ooooo, Luke is smiling. I repeat, Luke Astor is smiling at his phone."

I flip off Beck, who's acting like a kid on a playground. My phone buzzes again.

Goldie: There's a lot more to learn, Lucas

Me: I can't wait

I want to see her.

Me: Speaking of – can I see you today?

She types. Then stops. Then types again.

Goldie: What for?

> Me: A guy can't just see the girl he's fake dating/fucking/friends with?

She repeats her typing routine before sending another message.

> Goldie: I have work, so I can't. I'm sorry :(

> Me: What did we say about saying sorry? But also, I'd love to come see you work. If you are okay with that? If not, tell me to fuck off, and I will.

She responds immediately.

> Goldie: Okay, yeah. That would be nice. Tell reception to call me when you get there. I start at 1.

I turn my phone off, "Alright, boys, I've got a hot date at the primary school, so I've got to go." I see Beck's mouth open and immediately realise my mistake. "Don't." I get out before running upstairs to have a shower.

The school from the outside is beautiful; it looks straight out of a movie. The building is made out of red bricks and has flowers and vines growing up the side of it. It must be another original building in the town.

I walk into reception, telling them I'm here for Stella, and they direct me to the class she's teaching today. They said she was covering first grade, and when I asked which class, they told me the only one. I'm surprised they only have one class for the kids – I know for a fact there are more kids than that.

I can hear her voice as I approach the room.

"He's a good friend of mine and will be helping us out with our activities, so I need you guys to be on your best behaviour, okay?" There's a pause. "Yes, Kyle, you can call him by his first name. In fact, do a favour for Ms Faraday and call him Lucas, okay?"

Shaking my head, laughing to myself, I knock on the door. It's immediately opened by Stella. She looks beautiful. She's wearing a long skirt with a loose blouse tucked in, and her hair is down and wild. Just the way I love it.

"Hi." She says quietly. I smile back at her, wanting to say many things I shouldn't in front of 7-year-olds. "Okay, everyone, this is Lucas."

I follow her to the front of the classroom and wave as a series of little hellos get thrown back at me. There must be at least 30 kids in this classroom.

She leans into me and whispers, "Can you go sit over there for a second. I just need to get them started on their projects." I nod, resisting the urge to kiss her, and go sit down.

"Can someone please tell me what it is we are doing today?" At least ten hands go up the second she finishes speaking. "Mandy?"

"We are working on our research projects on endangered animals."

Stella smiles sweetly at the little girl, "Very good. Why don't you guys get started?"

They all pull out their notebooks, listening to her without any hesitation. Once she's satisfied that they are all okay, she walks over to me.

I look up at her, visibly impressed, "Do you fully teach a

class?" I don't know what I thought it was she did here, but it wasn't this.

She laughs lightly, "No, I'm not a teacher. I just fill in wherever I'm needed. And recently, that's been used as a substitute. The school doesn't have enough money for all the staff it needs – so I'm here whenever they need me."

"Wait, you don't get paid?"

"I do, just not the salary of a teacher by any means. And if they wanted to pay me that, I'd turn them down. It's more important that the money cycles back around to the kids. To what they need."

I nod, about to speak, but am interrupted by a little boy coming up to us.

"Hi, Lucas." He says to me before turning to Stella. "Can I have some help, Ms. Faraday?"

Stella bends down, grabbing his hand, "Of course, Kyle, let's go back to your desk." Her head turns around, smiling at me, before sitting down with Kyle. She looks complete – I don't know how else to describe it.

My thoughts are interrupted by the feeling of someone poking my arm. I turn to see a little redheaded girl staring at me, her arms crossed. I know she's 7 and like a third of my height, but something about her is making me feel slightly uneasy.

"Hi, what can I do for you?" Is that the right thing to say to a child? Her finger curls as she gestures for me to come closer to her. I squat down so that we are face-to-face. She's still staring at me strongly.

"I'm Lily. And I like Ms. Faraday a lot."

I smile, nodding, "That's good. I like her a lot, too."

Lily's gaze doesn't soften even slightly. "Good for you." She says, sizing me up. "Lucas, listen to me. If you hurt Ms. faraday." She punches her left hand. I like this girl.

"I'm not going to hurt Stel- Ms. Faraday, Lily. I promise." She nods strongly.

"It's just sometimes friends are mean. And it's not nice when they are mean. I don't like it and I don't want Ms. Faraday to be sad." I go to say something, but am cut off by Lily talking. "I mean, she's already sad enough because you know – she doesn't have a boyfriend or girlfriend." My eyebrows raise in shock, and I have to swallow the laugh that is threatening to come out.

"I think she'll be okay." Lily nods, patting me on the head before walking away. I guess she decided not to beat the crap out of me in front of the entire class. I can understand now why Stella loves her so much; there are a few more similarities between them than she might notice.

I turn back to look at Stella, who's moved to helping another student. It's incredible how she's able to float from student to student, helping each one with a smile on her face. It's so clear this is her calling – what she's meant to do.

Without a second thought, I pull out my phone to text my dad. These kids deserve a school that's as incredible as Stella.

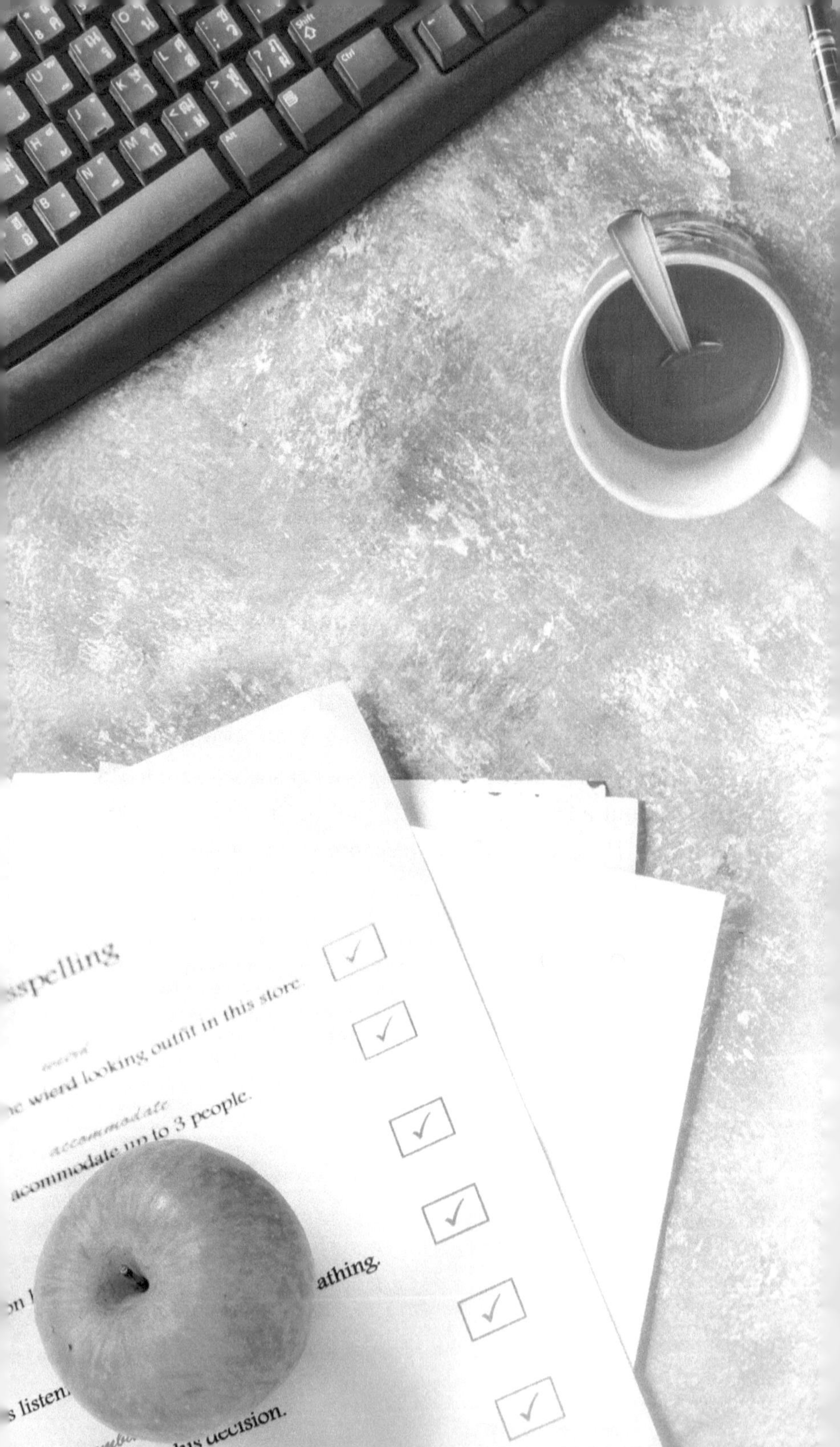
sspelling
he wierd looking outfit in this store.
acommodate up to 3 people.
athing.
s listen.
this decision.

Chapter Thirty-Eight

STELLA

HALLOWEEN HAS AND ALWAYS WILL BE MY favourite holiday of the year. There is something so exciting about dressing up as someone, or something, else. Just the fact that for one night, you can be whoever you want. It makes me feel free.

There is no surprise that I take the plans we have for Halloween very seriously. Most years, I go out both weekends and force Keets into a different costume each day. She pretends like she hates it, but we both know she doesn't.

Halloween has technically already passed this year – it was yesterday. Keets and I handed out lollies to some of the trick-or-treaters who walked around Brookstone. It's actually a really sweet tradition at our university. The kids from the primary school I work at, and some of the faculty's kids, go on a route that students who live on campus can sign up to be a part of. Naturally, Keets and I sign up and try to turn our door into a mini haunted house. I'm not sure how much the kids enjoy that part, but we love it.

Tonight is our last Halloween celebration, and I've saved my favourite costume for last. I'm dressed up as Puss in Boots tonight. I've got a brown corset and black skirt on, with matching boots and a hat. Keets helped me out with some cat makeup, and I've got the sword and holster to go along with it. It's not super complex by any means, but I think Puss in Boots deserves his moment. Keets opted for Alice from Alice in Wonderland, and is pulling off the blue dress beautifully.

Pulling up to Luke's, I am shockingly surprised by how full-out they've gone. He only told me about the party last week, so I kinda assumed it was a last-minute thing. But there are lights and cobwebs illuminating the outside. Looking at the front garden, I spot the skeletons posed in nefarious positions. I know exactly who did that.

"I'd be willing to bet big money that that was Beck's idea." Keets laughs, taking the words out of my mouth. The idea was definitely Becks, but in seeing the last skeleton's pose, I know Luke had a hand on it, considering the position the skeletons are in is on the hood of his truck. My cheeks flame thinking back to our first time sleeping together. Keets clocks the skeletons as we walk in and nudges me while winking. She kind of looks like she's having a stroke, but I react all the same.

"Oh my god!" Keets exclaims, grabbing two of the welcome shots set up in the entrance. "Who knew the guys liked Halloween so much?" Keet's hands me the little bottle and we down it together, moving further into the house. The inside of the house is just as decorated as the outside. The walls are covered in blood splatters, and you can't make a turn without running into some spider web covered in little critters. They've got animatronic Halloween decorations scattered around the place. Moving killer clowns are scary enough sober, put alcohol in the mix, and you've got a very common blood chilling scream. The house is about as packed as it could be, and everyone is dressed up in their various costumes.

I hear laughing right next to me and turn to see Keets crouched over, clutching her stomach. I follow her eye line, only to see what can only be described as the best costumes of the night.

Rory, Beck, and Luke are standing there, dressed as the Powerpuff Girls. And I don't mean some sort of gender bent Powerpuff Girls. No, I mean bows in the hair, skirt wearing, Powerpuff Girls. Rory's hair has been temporarily dyed black for Buttercup, and he's wearing a green corset that looks surprisingly good on him despite his lack of boobs. Beck has the biggest blue bow that I've ever seen for bubbles, somehow attached to his basically bald head. And Luke... Luke is wearing a tight red skirt that doesn't leave anything to the imagination and has bright orange dyed hair. They look incredible. As they spot us and walk up, I'm not sure I'm ever going to get this image out of my head.

"Meoow." Beck says, looking at me as he walks up, "and Ms. Alice, try not to fall down some creepy hole tonight, please? It wouldn't do well for the party vibe." Keets and I both laugh.

"Nice costume, guys. Although you're missing a Mojo Dojo and Professor Utonium." Keets says.

Beck groans, "Guys, we could have done a genderbent Powerpuff Girls costume altogether. We are idiots."

Rory laughs, "Stella would make a good Mojo Dojo," he says, pointing at me. I flip him off as Keets and Beck start laughing. I turn to look at Luke, and he's just staring at me. His gaze was burning. It felt like he was trying to memorise every inch of my body. I take a good look at him, truly noticing all the details. Including the knee-high socks I somehow missed earlier. My mouth is almost on the floor.

"Close your mouth before I put something else in there, Goldie," he says with his signature smirk. Any other day that would have me speechless, but today all I can do is snort.

"Blossom, you've lost all aspects of making me wet right now."

He shakes his head, looking down, "Are you trying to say it's not hot for guys to wear skirts. Wow, Stella. Just, wow." Sarcasm is thick in his voice. He walks up closer to me, grabbing my face to look up at him, "Plus, we both know I don't need to do much to make you wet for me."

My wide eyes are clearly the response he wants because he backs up slightly and grabs my hand.

"C'mon, gorgeous." He quips, dragging me towards everyone else who is now on the dance floor.

Somehow, five songs later, and I'm still on the dance floor. I say somehow, even though I know damn well I have made no efforts to leave. The guys ditched us two songs ago, claiming they had to go host. Both Keets and I coughed, boring into our arms, but were quickly shut up when we were handed more shots. Keets and I dancing looks a little something like birds trying to do a mating routine. She's the one person I can act like a complete fool around and not care in the slightest. I know she'll always match my energy, no matter how ridiculous – we're more than friends; she's my sister.

Despite looking like absolute maniacs, every time my gaze lifts, I spot Luke. And every time I find his eyes, they've already found mine. Something about knowing he's always there makes my chest feel tight. I'm so aware of his presence whenever he's near. I feel safe enjoying tonight. I feel safe with him.

I turn back to face Keets, but it's clear her energy has dropped a bit. I give her a questioning look, and she grabs my hand.

"Hey, Stel love, I think I'm gonna call it a night," Keets says, catching her breath.

"Are you okay?" I ask, concerned. I grab her hand and walk out of the dance area to somewhere quieter.

"Yeah." She nods softly, "just having a flare-up." I tilt my head in understanding.

"Okay, let's go," I say, walking towards the door.

"No, Stel, stay." I go to interject, but am cut off. "Stella, you are having fun. Go find your boyfriend. I'm gonna be upset if you come home with me."

"I'm not letting you get an Uber alone, Keets. You aren't sober."

"Neither are you. And Rory said he'd drive me home because he is. I'll be okay, I promise."

"Okay." I reluctantly agree, mainly because I know if I go home with her right now, she'll never let it go. "But if you need me, I'm there instantly. No hassle. I love you more than an orgasm."

She puckers her lips, "Aw, babes, you are gonna make me cry." I smile and kiss her on top of her head, which is alarmingly easy in my boots. I forgot how short she is.

"Bye, Keets." She mouths bye as she walks out the door. Rory nods to me as he follows. I know she's good with him.

Turning around, I look straight back into the main area

searching for Luke. He's been so easy to spot all night, but now it seems like he's disappeared into thin air. I walk through the living room and kitchen, but can't see him anywhere. I spot Beck in the garden, but he seems to be aggressively flirting with some guy, so I leave him be. Maybe he's in his bedroom? I walk up the stairs and turn down the hallway towards his room.

I stop in my tracks immediately.

I'd recognise the blue eyes staring back at me any day. They are still filled with the same hatred they always have been. His hair is slightly longer, but the curls and light blonde colour are all the same. It's the first time I've seen him in a year. He looks down at me, a look of disgust on his face. I freeze, not able to move. Why can't I move? Just turn around and walk downstairs, Stella. My eyes look behind him, hoping he's not alone, but feel my fear heighten when I see he isn't. Luke, I need Luke. Just walk past him and find Luke. It's fantastic that at this moment, I've learned I have an inability to fight or flee.

"What are you doing here, Stella?" He spits out every word dripping with venom.

"I-" I stutter, my breathing is getting shallower.

"You?" He asks, stepping closer. I instinctively flinch, moving back. When I step back, I feel something hard against my back. I look up to see Luke; he looks down at me, his face soft. He has a hint of a smile on his face, but it disappears immediately when he clocks mine.

"What's wrong?" I don't know how to respond. Speak, Stella, for fucks sake.

"Nothing is wrong, man. Just old friends catching up." Parker leans against the wall, trying to brush Luke off. It doesn't work.

"Doesn't seem that way." Luke looks back at me. I still

can't speak. I lean back slightly into his chest. Breathe. Just breathe. You are safe. "Who are you?" Luke asks, wrapping a hand around my waist. Breathe. It's okay. He won't touch you.

Chapter Thirty-Nine

LUKE

"I'M PARKER." HE HISSES. PARKER, THAT NAME seems weirdly familiar. He's shorter than me, but not by much. He has some muscles, but it's pretty obvious they are just for show. I don't think he could actually hold himself in something physical. His face is rough, scathing. I don't know how else to describe it.

"And who are you?" He's clearly angry for some reason.

"I'm Luke. This is my house. And from the looks of it, you are making my girl uncomfortable, so I'm going to ask you to leave." I don't miss the way Stella still hasn't said anything, or the fact that she's shaking slightly. I'm missing something here.

"Your girl?" He sneers, brimming with disdain. "Wow, Stella. So I'm not good enough for you, but he is? The bartender? Fucking hell, I always knew you were looking to trade up."

She pushes into me more, clearly trying to be as small as she can. The look on her face makes it clear she's terrified.

Her eyes quickly flash up at me, and I can see the tears pool. And then it clicks.

Parker. The guy she mentioned when we talked.

The one she could barely say his name without crying.

The guy I'm about to fucking kill for hurting her.

"Don't you dare say her name ever again," I growl, tightening my hold on Stella just slightly. I want to make sure she knows I've got her. "I'm only going to ask this one more time. Leave." He looks me up and down and scoffs. Clearly, he's not taking me fucking seriously.

"Everything okay up here?" Beck asks, standing on the stairs. The hallway is blocked from the rest of the house unless you come up the stairs. I'm not sure what made him come up, but I'm glad he did. He looks between me and Stella, and there's a visible shift in his demeanor as he does. "What do you need me to do?"

I look back at Stella, she needs out. I should have gotten her away as soon as I came up.

Leaning down, I whisper in her ear, "Beck is going to take you to the study. No one's in there." She nods against my chest. She feels so small, and it breaks my heart to see her like this.

"Beck, take her downstairs. I'll be there in a second." He moves to take her hand, but is stopped by Parker reaching out and grabbing her wrist. Harder than anyone should touch another person.

"She's not going anywhere. We were having a conversation." I push his hand off her.

"Beck, take her now." I don't want her to see any of this; she's scared enough. They both walk down the stairs, Stella leaning into him. Every part of me is aching to go with her, but I know I need to get this dickhead out of my house. "Parker, I am done playing nice with you. I can say with absolute certainty you were not invited here. I have asked you to leave twice, and you haven't. Not only have you not left, but you insulted and laid hands on my girl. I am not against resorting to violence to solve this issue. In fact, I think you need a good knock in the fucking head if you ever thought it was okay to hurt that girl. And looking at you, then at me, it's pretty clear you'd be bleeding on the floor before you got a swing in. Now for the last time, leave my fucking party." He chews on his lip, thinking before responding. For a split second, I think he's going to be smart.

Then he opens his mouth.

"You are really doing all of this for that whore?"

On instinct, hearing that, my fist shoots out, hitting him square in the jaw. His hand moves up, grabbing his chin, the force of the hit pushing his head to the side. Staggering back, he tries to regain his footing. He throws himself forward at me, hitting me back. I know it hurts, I can feel the blood trickle out of my nose, but I don't care. I hit him again before grabbing his shoulders and kneeing him in the balls. He bends over involuntarily, allowing me to shove him down on the floor. I lean down, fighting the gag that comes up as I get closer to him.

"If you ever touch her again, talk to her again, even look in her fucking direction again. I will kill you. Got it?" My voice mimicked the anger he displayed earlier. "Now get your sorry ass up and out of my house." He scrambles to his feet, and I follow him down the stairs as he runs out the door. It's almost funny how quick his tough guy act fell apart. The pain from my nose is starting to become more obvious, but there isn't anything more important than Stella right now. I beeline for the study off the entryway, ignoring anyone who tries to ask what's happened to my face. I open the door slightly and slip in, making sure no one sees me go in and get any ideas.

She's sitting on the chair, scrunched up, head in her lap. Beck is sitting on the floor watching her. His face is soft, but I know him. His eyes are filled with rage. I know what he would have done if he were left alone with Parker.

She lifts her head up slowly, as if it weighs more than usual, and makes eye contact with me. Tears have pooled in her eyes, and her lips are quivering.

"Baby," I say, running and crouching in front of her. Beck leaves, saying something about clearing out the house. I don't see or hear anything but her.

I don't know how long I'm crouching there before she speaks. "Is he gone?" She asks, her voice quieter than I've ever heard it before.

"Yes, Stella, he's gone." She nods, "he won't ever talk to you again." Her eyes are moving, looking everywhere except at me. Outside of this room has become dead silent.

"What do you want to do?" I ask, not wanting to touch her right now. I don't know if that would help or make it worse.

"Can you just," she chokes slightly on a sob. "Take me upstairs." I nod, using my thumb to brush under her eyes. I scoop her up, her arms wrapping around my neck. I can feel her tears cold on my neck, as she nestles closer. I've never seen her this resigned before. It's scary.

I carry her up the stairs to my room, she clings onto me tighter as we walk through the hallway, Parker just was. There's a stain of his blood on the carpet. I set her down on my bed, and go to unzip her boots. She's just staring ahead, not looking at anything in particular. I help her get out of her clothes, and she puts on one of my shirts before lying back in bed. Throwing on a shirt over my outfit, I go and lie next to her. Close enough that she knows I'm here, but not so close that she feels out of control.

She looks up at me, nodding, and I immediately move to her and pull her in next to me. She scrunches up next to my body, her breathing starting to slow. I rub my hand up and down her back.

"Do you want to talk about it?" I ask softly. She shakes her head. I lean up to turn the light off, but she stops me.

"I don't want to sleep." I grab my phone and check the time. It's 3 am.

"Stel, you need to get some sleep; it's been a long night."

She takes a deep breath and sits up.

"I don't want to have a nightmare." She confesses. I feel my heart crack slightly. How she is able to be how she is every day, carrying around this hurt, I can never understand.

"Okay." I nod, "then turn around for me." She tilts her head to the side, confused.

"Just trust me," I say, reaching into my bedside table for the pack of hair ties I bought a bit ago. She turns around, and I grab her hair, splitting it into three pieces. Desperately trying to remember what the video I watched said about how to do this. What do you do after you cross two pieces?

As I'm scrunching my face in thought, she pipes up.

"Are you plaiting my hair?" She sounds louder than she did before. That's good.

"I didn't want you to have knotted hair tomorrow. I know this is what you like to do before you sleep. And at some point tonight, you will be sleeping." I keep braiding her hair, finally getting the hang of it. Once I'm done, I take one of the hair ties and wrap it around her hair, struggling a bit. She feels the plait and turns back towards me. Her face was heavy with emotion.

"Thank you." She says, quietly. Her voice feels soft, like there is a sense of calm settling.

"Anything for you, Goldie," I murmur softly, pulling her back towards me. We lay there in silence before I started asking her questions.

About anything I can think of. The bookstore, her classes, and Reginald.

Slowly, but surely, I can see the light come back to her face.

And by the time the sun rose, My Stella was back.

Chapter Forty

LUKE

IT'S ALWAYS AN ODD FEELING WHEN SOMETHING IS simultaneously the best time of your life and the worst.

The beginning of November, all the way through to the end of term, has just been straight exams. And not just for me, but for every single student in Brookstone.

Already, Brookstone is a pretty small campus with only a couple of libraries, but throw in every student trying to cram for exams – I felt like I couldn't breathe. It wasn't just me; there were numerous times I had to stop Rory from physically throwing someone out of a seat because he was so stressed.

I think exams are getting the best of all of us.

The joys of the end of the academic year, right?

The worst part of November, though, was not seeing Stella at all. She's been cramming for her exams, trying to play catch-up on all the lectures she missed. It was hard to feel bad for her, though, especially because most of the ones she missed were in the afternoon, making her excuse of sleep hard to sell. I'd get texts from her every couple of hours that either contained jokes about her hanging herself or thank you's for the flowers and coffee I'd send her to prevent the former.

I saw her a couple of times after Halloween, but we barely left her apartment. While I have absolutely no complaints about spending a lazy day fucking and watching movies, I really wanted to take her out. Every time I saw her, I had to remind myself we weren't dating. That it wasn't casual to ask if I could take her to a gourmet meal where we both get dressed up in black tie and end the night in a fancy jazz bar.

I don't know, I'm starting to wonder if I can do this, if I can just be, what? Friends with benefits? I don't even know what to call what we are. The more time we spend together, the more lines blur. There are times I catch her staring at me, as if she's memorising every curve of my face. We talk and laugh. Moments where there's silence aren't uncomfortable. Rather, they are filled with something else. A sense of comfort. It makes me genuinely believe she's starting to play catch-up to the feelings I have.

Even if she's not quite there yet.

We've been on holiday for a couple of weeks now, but I haven't seen her. She went to stay with her mum for a week before going to her dad's place in Adelaide – she's spending Christmas with him and his wife. We've called a lot, though. Even if she won't admit it, I know she likes it.

I miss her.

Beck is off with his massive family for Christmas this year. They do a big family trip every year and spend Christmas week celebrating in some small town. It's incredibly fun to make fun of the matching PJs he wears every year to match the rest of his family.

I'm assuming my parents are enjoying Christmas at

their place with my brother. I don't really follow their holiday plans anymore – not when I haven't been back since I moved out. For some reason, their disdain for me kicks into overdrive this time of year. Something about the holiday season seems to ignite their worst behaviour.

Instead of dealing with that, I'm at Rory's. It's the third year I've spent with them, and the third time I've genuinely loved this time of year. When Steve found out I was planning on spending Christmas alone my freshman year, he wouldn't have it. He practically packed my bag for me to come stay at their place over the holiday season. I tried to object, but was shut up quickly when I saw Jessie and Evie's homemade gingerbread houses. No one was going to say no to those.

I think, to the surprise of no one, Rory's family goes crazy for Christmas each year. They decorate their house floor to ceiling with red and green decorations, and music fills your ears nearly everywhere you turn. It's impossible to deny the warmth radiating out of every corner of this house. This is the house I want to give my kids when I'm older.

One filled with warmth and love, not the cold one I grew up in.

"Coffee, son?" Steve asks, standing in the kitchen. It's 9 am, and Christmas morning has officially begun.

"Yeah, that'd be great. Thanks, Stevo." He nods his head towards the lounge room, letting me know he'll bring it in when it's ready.

Walking into the living room takes my breath away. Rory's family gets a fresh tree every year that fills the space with a scent of pine cones. The tree is meticulously decorated, something Evie barely lets us help her with.

Some would say she's a perfectionist. Not to her face, of course – not if you want to keep your head.

The part that I always love is seeing the presents surrounding the bottom of the tree. Despite both Rory and Jessie being well past Santa's age, the presents never show up until Christmas morning. Almost as if some fat man with a beard dropped them in the middle of the night.

"Merry Christmas, Luke," Rory says, giving me a hug as I walk into the room.

"Merry Christmas, Ror," I say, hugging him back. He pulls away, and I see Jessie impatiently sitting on the ground, almost shaking with anticipation for the presents. She smiles at me, and I count myself lucky getting any recognition from her this morning.

I walk over to Evie, sitting in her armchair next to the tree. Bending down, I kiss her on the cheek.

"Merry Christmas Eves."

She beams up at me, holding a cup of coffee. "Merry Christmas, sweetheart."

I pull back to go join Rory on the couch. Opening presents is always my favourite part of Christmas. It's not about the gifts – Rory's family is always thoughtful and gets me one or two. It's the love between them, so obvious and genuine, that makes it feel like something far more special. Every single gift is thought out fully, and they know each other better than anyone else in the world. It's beautiful.

"Okay, okay, I'm here. We can start opening presents!" Steve exclaims, hurrying into the room. He passes me my cup of coffee right before Jessie sets off, opening her presents. This girl is the most humble and sweet every other day of the year.

However, today, no one gets in the way of her and her presents.

I watch as she and Rory start opening theirs, sitting back, waiting to give my presents until the end.

"Aren't you going to open your presents, Luke?" Evie says. I look at her, confused. Normally, they give me a present at the end that I open. She sees my confusion and points towards a pile of presents next to the tree that all have my name written on them. There must be at least ten there, all meticulously wrapped.

I look back at them, my eyebrows furrowed and my mouth slightly open.

"Those are for me?" I ask quietly, not really believing any of it.

Evie nods as Steve pipes up. "You are part of the family, son. That means way too many presents around the holiday season."

I shake my head in disbelief but move to start opening them. My throat is tight. I have to keep blinking my eyes to stop the tears that are threatening to fall. Each gift feels like a tiny piece of their love for me, a love I didn't know I could ever receive. A feeling settles in my chest, unfamiliar and warm, but too much to fully absorb.

Two hours later, we finished opening all the presents. Jessie disappeared thirty minutes ago to go set up her new bookcase, which her parents got her. I can't help but think she'd get along insanely well with Stella.

Steve is wearing the bright pink jumper I got him proudly, as Rory is talking his ear off about the comic they bought him. It's nice getting the chance to see Ror as comfortable as he is around his parents. Only a handful of people get to see him like this.

I count myself lucky that I'm one of them.

"Hey, love." I turn my head to Evie, standing in front of me, holding one last present. It's got a different wrapping than the rest of them, though – it's dark green. "You've got one last one to open."

She hands me the present and walks away. I quickly open it to see an old leather book. The edges of the book are warped with time, and the cover is filled with raised designs that are cool to the touch. I turn it on its side, and my heart nearly stops reading the words that are embedded on the spine.

The Hidden Alibi

The name of my bar. Opening the book, I see that the pages are blank – bar the endpaper. There's a photo of Rory, Beck, Keets, Stella, and me in the Black Lantern stuck in the back with "we are always with you" written underneath.

I look back in the wrapping to find the note I hoped would be there. The front of the card has a drawing of Reginald, making me laugh.

> *I wanted to give you a place where you could keep all the memories of opening your bar when the dream becomes a reality. Don't let them fade away.*
> *Merry Christmas, Lucas.*
> *From,*
> *Goldie.*

My fingers trace over the indents of the pen, my chest tightening. "I'll be right back." I managed to get out, standing up and walking out of the room. I know the looks they were probably all giving me, but I don't care. I need to call her.

"Merry Christmas, Lucas." She says the moment she picks up. I can hear "Let it Snow" playing in the background, along with a silent buzz of people talking. I know Christmas is meant for families, and I should let her be, but I can't.

I need to hear her voice right now.

"Merry Christmas, Goldie. I got your gift." I can't see her, but I'd be willing to bet millions that a blush is creeping up her neck.

"Do you like it?" She asks softly, her confidence shaking slightly.

I don't miss a beat responding.

"I loved it, Stella. Thank you."

There's nothing more I want right now than to see the smile that I hope is covering her face as we talk. I want to hold her.

"I knew it. I am a fantastic gift giver."

I laugh into the phone, "Where did the shy, sweet girl from two seconds ago go?"

"Oh, she's long gone. Plus, you like this version of me better."

She's not wrong there. "I plead the fifth." I hear her giggle, and all I can think is how I want to record it and play it on repeat forever. "Did you get my gift?" I ask, hoping she somehow managed to find it.

"Gift?" Confusion laces her voice.

"Go open the bottom zipper inside your suitcase. If Keets did what she promised me she would, there should be a present there."

I hear her set the phone down, mumbling something

about Keets betraying her, before I hear the crinkle of wrapping paper.

She picks the phone up again. "Okay, I'm gonna open it."

"No, wait!" I shout, possibly a bit too loudly. "Turn your camera on."

She accepts my FaceTime request, and her beautiful face fills my screen. She's wearing reindeer ears and plaid pjs. My girl looks gorgeous.

"Okay, can I open it now, creep?" She says when I don't say anything. I got slightly distracted. I nod, too excited to speak.

She pulls the book out, and her face scrunches slightly. "Thanks, Luke, I love this series!" I can tell she's trying to cover the fact that she already owns the book.

A fact I know.

"Open the book, Goldie."

She opens to the first page and practically screams when she sees the autographed copy I got her. Keets told me the last book was her favourite, so I got it signed with character notes added in.

"How did you get this!!" She squeals, holding the book closer to her chest. "They don't do the character plates anymore!!"

"The elves are good at getting gifts, what can I say?" I shrug as she rolls her eyes, opening the book up to read the notes.

I don't tell her that I drove five hours with Beck to a tiny town right on the edge of New South Wales, where the author was doing a book signing. I also don't tell her how I had to practically bribe the Authors to do the character plates for her, even though they haven't done it for years. It was worth it.

Stella finishes reading the notes and looks back at me. Her smile spreads like sunshine, brightening the entire call.

"Thank you, Luke." She says quietly, putting the book back down. I just smile back at her.

"How's your Christmas going?"

"Good. Dad's really leaning into the family vibes today, as much as possible." She looks behind her back towards what I assume is the kitchen. "I probably have to go soon." I stay silent; she doesn't look like she's done talking yet. "Luke."

"Mhm."

"I hate how much I miss you when you aren't here." She says quietly, her face confused. I get the feeling.

"I miss you too, Stella." She smiles a little bit before whispering bye. I give her a wave right before she hangs up – her voice lingering in the air.

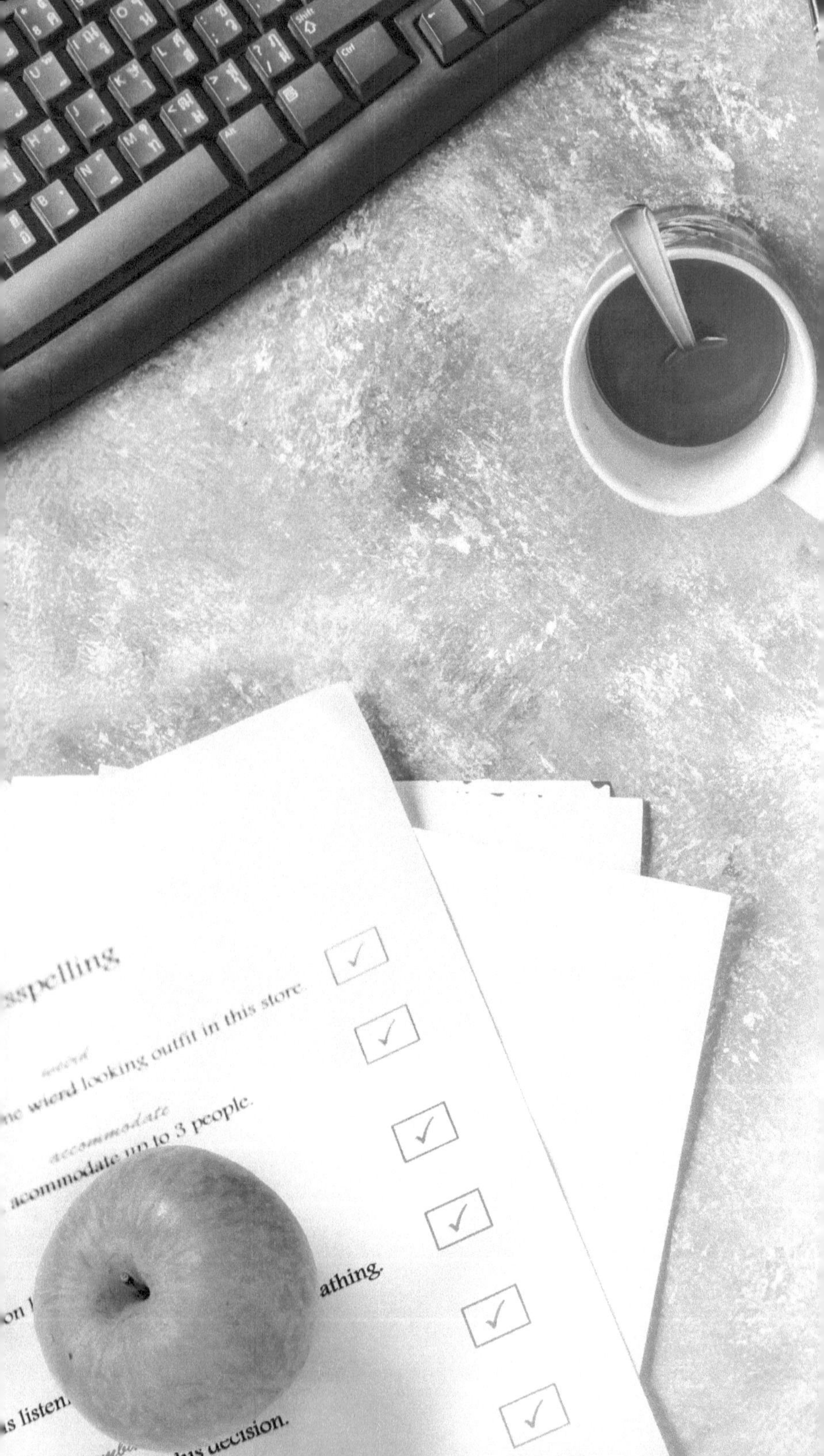
spelling
word
ne wierd looking outfit in this store.
accommodate
acommodate up to 3 people.
athing.
s listen
us decision.

Chapter Forty-One

STELLA

I'M BACK AT BROOKSTONE EARLIER THAN I EVER have been. The campus is completely empty because everyone is with their families for the holidays. It's weird being here right now. but it's nice in a way, the air feels lighter.

Luke and I are driving to Byron first thing tomorrow morning, but I wanted to come back today to give myself time to pack and get ready. He's been perfect these past few months, and it's all because of what he needs from me this weekend. I have to be perfect for him so he doesn't think everything he's done so far was a waste.

If I'm being completely honest, I'm kind of sad we've gotten to this point. I don't know how it's going to work once Luke and I "break up." Do we stay friends? Will Keets immediately go back to being worried about me? Will he still want me? I haven't let myself think about this because I know what will happen.

I need him, and I hate it.

Every second of every day, I want to be with him. If he's

not there, I ache for him. In a way, I haven't ached for anyone. I'm helpless and scared, and there is nothing worse to me. If I block it out, if I stop thinking about next year, it won't be real. I can shove whatever I'm feeling so deep inside of me that it never resurfaces.

I've done it before, I can do it again.

The second I walk into our apartment, I pull up my phone to order some dinner and dump my bag. Luke said I needed multiple black tie outfits. Which is insane because who the hell wears a black tie to a family reunion? I silently thank the packing list he sent me before starting to pull items from my closet.

Ten minutes into packing, I'm grateful for the call I hear from Keets, Emily, and Immy.

"No, it was crazy, mum and dad went psycho this year." Immy finishes, holding up what looks to be some car keys. She always has the best presents out of all of us.

"Hey, guys," I say, settling down onto the couch.

"Stella!" All three of them shout, a smile creeping across my face.

"So how's the packing going?" Keets asks, "That doesn't look like your room, Stella."

"Shut up. There's too much to pack. I'm just going to give up. Not to mention, I have to pack black tie dresses. What 21-year-old owns multiple black tie dresses?" I groan, grabbing one of Keets' stuffies to shove in my face. Packing is my worst nightmare – how am I meant to anticipate what I'll need for three whole days? "I hate Luke. I hate having a boyfriend. I hate-"

"Stella!" Emily yells, cutting me off, "There's someone at your door, idiot. They've been knocking."

I lift my head up, just registering the noise. Must be my food.

"One sec, guys, I think it's my Indian takeaway. Keep talking – try not to miss me too much."

"Ooo hard," Immy says, dripping with sarcasm as I put my phone down and walk to the door. Opening it, I'm expecting a delivery guy, but instead it's someone holding garment bags.

"Stella Faraday?" He asks in a gruff voice. He's wearing a suit and has one of those Bluetooth earpieces in his ear.

"Yes?" I'm extremely confused. He pushes the bags towards me.

"This is for you." I grab them quickly, trying not to drop them. I don't get a chance to ask any questions because he just walks away. Closing the door behind me, I examine the bags I've been given.

"What the hell?" I mumble

"Stella?" I hear from my phone, "What's happening?" Sitting back on the couch, I set my phone up on the coffee table so they can see the garment bags.

"I have no idea, this random James Bond-looking dude just dropped these off."

"Well, open it!?" Emily practically screams, making the rest of us laugh.

I unzip the first bag and am met with the most beautiful dresses I have ever laid my eyes on. The first one is a complete black lace, with a nude slip dress attached underneath. The back is corseted, threaded with a matching black satin ribbon. The second one is exactly like the yellow dress from How to Lose a Guy in Ten Days – low back and everything. But the last one catches my eye the most. It's a dark green satin dress covered with floral appliqué. There's a long slit coming up almost to the hip, and the bust is boned. It's beautiful.

"Stel, those are gorgeous." Keets chimes in, cutting

through the quiet that had blanketed the call. We were all too focused. "Who sent those to you?"

I shake my head, "I have no idea."

"Is there a card?" Immy asks. I go to search in the bags, finding a note in the garment bag that held the dark green dress.

I thought you needed some dresses that are half as beautiful as you. I can't wait to see them on you this weekend.

- Lucas

A small smile creeps onto my face as I read the note. I can't believe he sent these to me, and not only that, but they're exactly the dresses I would pick out myself.

He knows me that well.

The feeling of warmth, however, is quickly replaced with an anxious feeling in my stomach.

"Well?" Emily pushes. I hold up the note to show them, causing them all to swoon and freak out.

"Oh my god, Stella. That's crazy, those dresses must have cost him a fortune." I look back down at the label. I don't recognise the brand, but I can tell it's Italian.

"Yeah, but his family is rich. It's probably nothing." I shake off the feeling of unease. He probably just knew I wouldn't have dresses and didn't want me to embarrass him or something.

"I wouldn't say it's nothing." Emily pipes up, talking in a schoolgirl voice. I give them a tight smile, unable to ignore the pit in my stomach. They must notice because Immy starts speaking, "uh oh. Stella doesn't look too happy about this."

I shake my head quickly, trying to force a smile.

"No, it's fine, it's sweet. It's just – I wasn't expecting it, that's all." It's kind of a lot, no?

There's a small laugh that comes from my phone. "Oh, I see. It's bolting time." Emily says, shaking her head.

"Bolting time?" I ask, confused.

"It's getting properly serious, so you want to run. It's classic Stella." Immy laughs, clearly seeing the joke. I muster up a laugh, not wanting to get defensive. But I don't bolt, right? It's not like I run because it gets serious. I just don't want to be serious. That's all. A text notification from Keets pulls me out of my thoughts.

> Keets: I'm sure it's nothing, like you said, he's loaded. Don't let this ruin your weekend, my love.

I look up to see her reassuring smile and decide that she's right. This is going to be a good weekend, I'm not going to let my head ruin that.

A loud, relentless pounding on my door yanked me out of my sleep. What the hell? Groaning, I roll over, checking the time.

6:00 am.

Shit, I was meant to be meeting Luke downstairs fifteen minutes ago. Quickly rolling out of bed, I throw on the clothes hanging on the back of my chair and run out of the room. Last night I planned out my road trip outfit. Based on the vibe Luke had given about his parents, I thought showing up in sweats probably wouldn't go over well. I opted for a white sundress with cap sleeves and some sneakers. It's the most normal outfit ever; no one could have an issue with it. My hair is braided, so no need to worry about that. I need my bags and my phone.

Shit, where's my phone?

I walk back towards my room, but it's not plugged in beside my bed.

What?

"Looking for this?" Luke's voice carries through the apartment, causing me to run back into the living room. He's sitting on the couch, my suitcase next to his legs, holding my phone. "Who charges their phone in the living room?"

I walk up and snatch my phone from him, "I do. Or at least I do when I don't want to be late. Usually, my alarm being that far away makes me get up."

He shrugs lightly, "Clearly didn't work today." I slightly wince, feeling really bad for running late. He had been so specific about the time to meet so that we would make it on time. I know it's just 15 minutes, but I've never seen him this stressed about something. I really don't want to add to that.

"I'm really sorry, Luke. I'm ready now and organised. Stella has finally shown up." He raises an eyebrow, seemingly unconvinced. "I swear," I say, placing one hand on my chest and the other in the sky, trying to mimic how people pledge.

"Mhm," He murmurs, grabbing my bags that were by his feet – wheeling them out. I grab my purse off the counter, double-checking that I have everything I need. Once I feel confident that I'm ready, I gesture to Luke that we can go. He's standing by the door very impatiently. If he wasn't so stressed, I'd probably fuck around for a bit more just to annoy him, but I'm feeling nice this morning.

I check my phone, 6:10 am. Not so bad.

Holding up my phone to show him, I say, "See, not horrible."

"True." He says, tilting his head. "Good thing we don't have to leave for another 20 minutes." He sets off, practically running after saying that last part. That fucker.

Four hours later, and we are just under halfway through our drive. I don't know why his family chose a place that was an eight-hour drive away from Sydney and a 10-hour drive from Brookstone, but here we are. I've spent the last three hours fast asleep after being dead silent for the first hour. I don't think Luke minds, though; he's barely uttered a single word this entire time. I didn't want to push him. It's like he used all his talking ability during those ten minutes in my apartment. I sat up straighter, adjusting my dress that wasn't designed for sleeping in the car. Turning to look at Luke, I see his white knuckles gripping the steering wheel. He looks like he's about to crush it.

"Hey Luke, you know suffocating the steering wheel doesn't actually make you a better driver, right?" I joke. He quickly loosens his grip on the wheel, shaking out his hands.

"Sorry." He murmurs under his breath, not unlocking his gaze from the road ahead of us.

Shit, he's really stressed.

"You good there, buddy?" I ask, my voice coming out slightly higher than I intended. He quips some sort of yes, nodding his head. It's shockingly unbelievable.

"Okay, pull over the car." When he keeps driving, I repeat myself louder this time. "Luke, I do not want to crash because you are on the verge of a panic attack, pull over this damn car." He seems to fully register what I'm saying and pulls over the car. His hands drop from the steering wheel as if it were made of lava the second the car stops.

"Dude, what is going on with you?" I ask, feigning confusion. I know he is stressed about his parents and how this weekend is going to go down, but he didn't seem like he wanted to talk. But he looks like he's about to walk the plank, I can't just leave it.

"Nothing. I'm fine, just tired maybe. We can eat and then I'll be all better." He goes to reach for the steering wheel again; however, this time, I can see the shakiness in his hand up close. I wrap my hand around his, grabbing it to stop the shaking.

"Yeah, no. We aren't going to do that. Explain what's going on, Luke." When he stays silent, I turn towards him – staring directly at him. "Luke, I'm worried about you, c'mon. You can talk to me about anything."

This seems to finally crack him, and he turns to look towards me. He's pale, his face completely devoid of colour. "I'm scared." He says under his breath, almost as if he's scared to admit it.

My face softens slightly, "Of what?"

"Everything." He shifts in his seat. "I'm scared to see my parents and my brother. I'm scared this thing we are doing isn't going to convince them. But honestly, most of all, I'm scared they are going to scare you off." His shoulders slump, eyes clouded with worry. I had a feeling this was impacting him more than he was letting on, but I knew I had to wait for him to bring it up himself.

"Okay, well, firstly, I get it with your parents and brother. After the shit they've put you through, it's normal to be nervous. But you aren't doing this alone. I'll be there ready with daggers if they say anything to hurt you. I've been told I'm very scary." A quick burst of laughter escapes his mouth, and his eyebrow lifts in unconvinced. "Shut it," I say in response, unable to contain the smile spreading from seeing a second of my Luke flash through. "Secondly, I'm a good actress. I've got this. But because I understand the stress, and I am too, we will spend the next six hours of this car ride having an excruciatingly long conversation about every second of this weekend and every little thing I need to know about you. Plus, I'm pretty sure considering how we've been the last few weeks, the chemistry won't be an issue." I shoot him my best wink, purposefully looking like a forty-year-old man hitting on a twenty-year-old. He smirks slightly at that. "And lastly," I shift closer to him, my hand resting on his thigh for balance as I reach up toward his face. "I'm kind of enjoying being around you. It'll take a lot more than your dickish family to scare me off." He pulls his face closer to me,

"You enjoy being around me?" He asks, his face shifts into a lazy smile.

"Just a tad," I whisper before meeting his lips, kissing him. His hand reaches behind me, cupping my face, matching my speed. My hand moves up slightly, grazing over his jeans. His hardness is obvious, causing heat to pool in my abdomen. I can feel my body wanting more, but also know that we are on a tight schedule. Pulling back, I smile at him before sitting back in my seat. I pull out my phone, opening a new document in notes, ready for our invigorating conversation.

"Okay, so your mother. What do I need to know?" I shift back to him, my brows lifted expectantly. His shocked gaze is on me, matching his open mouth. The urge to make a dirty joke is strong, but I don't want to fuel the fire. "What?" I ask innocently, knowing exactly what's wrong.

"You are an evil woman." He says, running his hands

through his hair, creating a shadow over his eyes. I love how effortlessly captivating he looks. Even in moments like this. He puts his hand back on the wheel, starting to drive. "Okay, so my mother might be the world's best backhanded compliment giver." He begins to say.

This weekend might be harder than I thought.

Chapter Forty-Two

LUKE

"YOU KNOW EVENTUALLY WE'LL HAVE TO GO IN," Stella states the obvious. We've been parked outside the hotel for ten minutes now, but I haven't found it in me to get out. The hotel mum and dad have chosen this year is massive. The main building is white, with trees spotted around the entrance. There isn't a main door, but rather an open reception area with staff waiting in matching white uniforms. The hotel is a little bit out of town, but it has everything you could need for a weekend. There's a spa five minutes' drive by golf buggies where you can get almost anything done – not included in the cost of course.

Nothing sounds better than spending every waking moment with the Astors. Truly.

I let out a heavy breath. No turning back now. I unbuckle my seatbelt and open my door. The second I get out, the employees spot me and come over to grab the bags. They are speaking to us about the room we are in and what we can do this weekend, but I'm not processing anything they are saying.

Deep breaths and smile, Luke.

You've got a part to play.

I feel Stella's hand slip into mine as if it were the easiest movement in the world. Every ounce of anxiety leaves my body when I look at her, when I feel her hand in mine. I think she knows that.

She looks up at me and smiles softly, "Just remember, picturing beating people up is always helpful. Luckily, no one can see inside your head." She gives me a look of complete innocence before following behind our bags that are being taken to our room.

This girl.

"Here we are, room 208." The guy carrying our bags said as he opened the door. "Dinner is in an hour in the main restaurant downstairs. Your mother asked me to remind you that dinner is formal dress." He gives us a solid hospitality worker smile before excusing himself, leaving us alone in the room.

"Oh my god, Luke," Stella exclaims, her mouth falling open. "I swear to god this hotel room is bigger than my entire apartment!! Is this just your life?" She looks back at me. Honestly, even by my parents' standards, this hotel is massive. They must be going all out for my brother's engagement announcement.

Walking into the room, we're met with a living room. There's a sofa big enough for three people to sleep on, opposite the biggest flat screen I've ever seen. Straight across from the door are floor-to-ceiling glass sliding doors that open to a wrap-around balcony surrounding the entire room.

I follow Stella to the left, seeing the massive king-size bed, which I know we'll put to good use later. Stella squeals as she finds the bathroom, fit with two sinks and a tub.

When I walk in, I see her clutching a robe as if it's her lifeline.

"Luke. Feel this robe." She holds it out to me, almost shaking with anticipation as I walk up. I feel the robe is pretty standard. However, I don't think I've ever seen her this excited.

"Whoa, that's soft." I put on my best excited voice I can, happy when she smiles in response.

"Do you think we can keep it?" She asks, putting it on over the adorable dress she was wearing in the car. The drive was harder than it should have been, especially because the dress kept falling – revealing parts of her I couldn't see. Not when I was trying not to crash the car. It should be illegal for her to wear a sundress when I can't do anything about it.

I walk towards her, pulling the robe together and tying it around her. It's way too big on her, which makes me laugh.

"I'm sure they'd let you keep it, Goldie." She does a twirl, showing off her new clothing item. I'm sure there is some ridiculous fee I'm going to have to pay for that, but I don't care right now.

She pushes past me, heading back towards the living room. I immediately turn and follow her, curious to see where she's heading. When I walk in behind her, I notice the tray of fruits and champagne they've laid out for us. There's a folded note placed neatly in the middle of the tray. Picking it up, channeling my best posh accent, I read it out loud.

"Welcome, Mr. and Mrs. Astor. If there is anything we can do to make your stay more pleasurable, do not hesitate to ask." Mr. and Mrs. Astor – that sounds good. I look up to see a small blush creeping up on Stella's neck, and I laugh a little before noticing her face flinch for a second. It's only a split second, and then she's back to smiling. I want to ask, but the way she's looking at me right now makes me think she won't talk to me if I do. So I drop it.

"Okay, Mr. Astor, what is the game plan tonight?" She picks up a piece of watermelon from the plate, taking a massive bite. I pick up a napkin and hand it to her before the juice dribbles down her chin. "Thanks." She murmurs, her face contorted in slight surprise. She does that a lot. I nod before sitting myself on the floor opposite her.

"Tonight is the welcome dinner. They are announcing Leon's engagement tonight, so mum and dad are going to be on edge to make everything perfect."

Stella nods, "So they're just automatically going to hate me?"

"No, you are perfect. I'm saying this more to prepare you for how they are going to act around me. Surprisingly, even the present company won't stop them from projecting their lack of parenting skills." I smile softly, but it barely reaches my cheeks. Stella's hand reaches out, passing me some blueberries that were on the plate.

"Good thing I'm really scary then." Grabbing the blueberries from her, I join her in devouring the fruit platter and the champagne. There is no doubt that a buzz is needed to deal with tonight.

Once we finish the food, Stella stands up.

"Okay, I have to go get pretty." She says as if she doesn't already look perfect. She stares at me for a beat before following up with, "This is where you tell me I'm always beautiful."

I stand up quickly, walking towards her. "I'm sorry, Goldie, you are always beautiful. You could go downstairs right now, in this robe, and everyone would still be in awe."

She nods in approval, and I bend down to place a light kiss on her forehead. The way her face lights up fills me with a comfort I can't describe. A feeling I never thought I'd feel this weekend.

My heart is racing faster and faster as we walk up to the restaurant. The reality of what we are doing is starting to sink in. Who brings a fake date to a family reunion? Stella was right, no one does this in real life. What is wrong with me? Genuinely, why did I listen to Beck?

I feel a small hand creep into my hand, her fingers intertwining with mine. Looking down, I see Stella holding onto my arm. She's wearing the black dress I gave her and looks incredible. Her hair is natural, and half of it is held up with a matching black bow. The dress isn't full-length, so her long legs are sticking out from beneath the dress, finishing in black heels. My girl looks gorgeous.

"We've got this." That's all she says. She doesn't need to say more.

I don't miss how she doesn't offer for us to leave, she knows what I need. Sometimes I think she knows it better than I do.

Stella keeps me beside her and pushes the door to the restaurant open. As we walk in, I feel her squeeze my hand a few times – and I know she's not going anywhere.

The first thing I see in the restaurant is the wooden bar straight across the room. There are backlit shelves filled with bottles of alcohol, making it look like stained glass. The bartenders and servers are all wearing three-piece suits, fit with matching bow ties. It looks like something out of the 20s. The restaurant itself is more modern, with tables draped with white tablecloths and too much cutlery than one could use. It still keeps some of the vintage feel, however, with red velvet chairs set up, it reminds me of the black lantern.

Looking around, I can see that it is completely packed with my family. There is not a single seat that is empty. The noise is palpable. People talking to each other, tight smiles on their faces, nodding as if there was nowhere else they'd rather be.

I know that couldn't be further from the truth.

I've always felt like this whole thing was very Gatsby-esque.

"Should we find your parents?" Stella says, pulling me out of thought. She looks completely poised and put together. I have no idea how she isn't freaking out right now. I nod, unable to speak properly. It doesn't take long to spot my parents standing near the bar, talking to some suits. There is no doubt in my mind that there are some business associates of my dad who scored a ticket to this shit show through sucking up to him. It's the mantra of most of their supposed friends.

I take a deep breath before walking over to them, keeping Stella at my side. She doesn't let go of my hand for one second.

Even as we walk up, neither of my parents turns their head – apparently, the conversation they are currently having is too invigorating. I let out a small, deliberate cough, letting them know their son is here. They both turn towards me, finally giving me a small acknowledgement.

"Hello mum and dad. How are you?"

I get a curt nod from Dad as Mum speaks. "We are good, just enjoying the beautiful festivities of tonight." She turns back towards the men they were just talking to, giving them a smile with a double meaning. They seem to get the message, because they offer a small goodbye and walk off.

Mum's face drops, her true character slowly seeping out once she knows the important people are gone. She turns slightly towards Stella.

"And who might this be?"

I go to open my mouth, but Stella jumps in, placing her hand out to shake my mother's. "I'm Stella, Luke's girlfriend." She moves on to my dad, "It is such a pleasure to meet you both. Luke talks about you both all the time." The smile that is decorating her face almost makes me laugh. I'm sure to them she looks like a sweet, caring girl, but to me – she looks downright possessed.

My mother looks slightly shocked as Stella pulls her hand back, settling in next to me. I wrap an arm around her, pulling her in towards me. The feeling of her slows my heart.

"Oh wow, it's incredible to meet you, Stella." My mum smiles. "You are even prettier in person."

Usually, a compliment like that would have my girl blushing, but her demeanour doesn't change.

"Thank you, Mrs. Astor. Had to look the best to meet Luke's family." My mother nods, seemingly impressed with her answer. Stella is saying all the right things, and my mum is clearly picking up on it.

Stella turns towards my dad slightly, "Luke tells me you are a lawyer? That's very impressive."

My dad smiles, clearly happy with the acknowledgement. "Yes, I am, it's hard work, but luckily I'm good at it." He lets out a hearty laugh, signaling to the rest of us that we are meant to laugh as well. Stella forces up a giggle, one that to the trained ear is clearly fake.

She's doing well.

My mum turns to Stella, asking something about her dress. There's a part of me that wants to hide her from this life, from my mother. But I know I can't – that's not why we are doing this.

"You kept up your end, so I'll make the donation tonight." My dad says, pulling my attention back to him. A weight is lifted off my chest hearing that. I had called him once I had dropped Stella off after her day at school. Those kids deserved a better chance to learn than they were being given. He told me he'd help out with the school, as long as I kept up my end of representing our family well tonight. I hate the warmth I feel knowing that he's happy with how I've behaved. I feel like a dog with the way they've trained me to respond.

My dad chimes in again, "You must really love this girl, Luke."

Love? I don't love her, right?

My eyes find her as she's talking to my mother. They are deep in some conversation that I can't hear properly, but I can see the flashes of disgust whenever my mother looks away. It makes me smile seeing how bad she is at controlling her face.

I've never thought about loving Stella – I've never really loved anyone before. How are you meant to know? I'm happy when I'm around her, I'm safe,

I can't picture my life without her.

I can't picture my life without her.

That thought echoes in my head, getting louder with each passing second. When I look at her again, I see her smile, the way she speaks, captivating everyone around her, and it becomes clear.

I'm not just happy around Stella, I'm whole. There's no

me without her. She's in every single future I can imagine. I don't just like her – I love her.

The realization hits me like a freight train. And all of a sudden, every moment I spend not telling her feels like a lie.

Just as I go to speak, my brother walks up with Camilla. She's wearing a white dress with sleeves and matching heels. My brother's tie matches her dress. They look like they are meant to be together. Perfect for tonight.

"Leon!" My mother exclaims, going up to hug him the second he walks up. Both Stella and I have to take a step back when she does. Nothing can get in her way.

"Hello mum. Hey, dad."

"Hi, son." My dad says, smiling at him. "You look absolutely beautiful, Camilla." He steps up, kissing Camilla on each cheek. She accepts his kisses before moving back next to my brother. Rory and Beck always joke that in another life, she would have been royalty. I'm not sure that I disagree with them.

"Hi Luke," Leon says, looking towards me. His face quickly changes from stoic to smiling when he clocks Stella standing next to me. "And you must be Stella. Luke has told me a lot about you."

I feel Stella straighten up slightly. Technically, he's not lying. Over the past few months, Stella has become my favourite topic of conversation, even if not necessarily with him.

"Luke has also mentioned you quite a bit," Stella adds. Leon's face brightens up just slightly at that. It's small, but I can tell. Seeing my kid brother light up about something so little twists something inside of me. My head dips slightly, swallowing my guilt.

My brother goes to say something else, but he is cut off by my mother.

"It's time for the announcement!" She moves and grabs Camilla's hand, pulling her towards the front of the restaurant. My father grabs Stella's hand, asking her some questions about her degree, leaving Leon and me to follow behind. His face is clouded with an emotion I can't quite place. Before I get a chance to think about it too much, I pat him on the shoulder. He turns and looks at me, his eyes wide. I smile at him before catching up to our parents. His shock every time I do something even remotely brotherly guts me.

The more time I spend with him, the more I realise how much better he deserves as a brother.

How much better we both did.

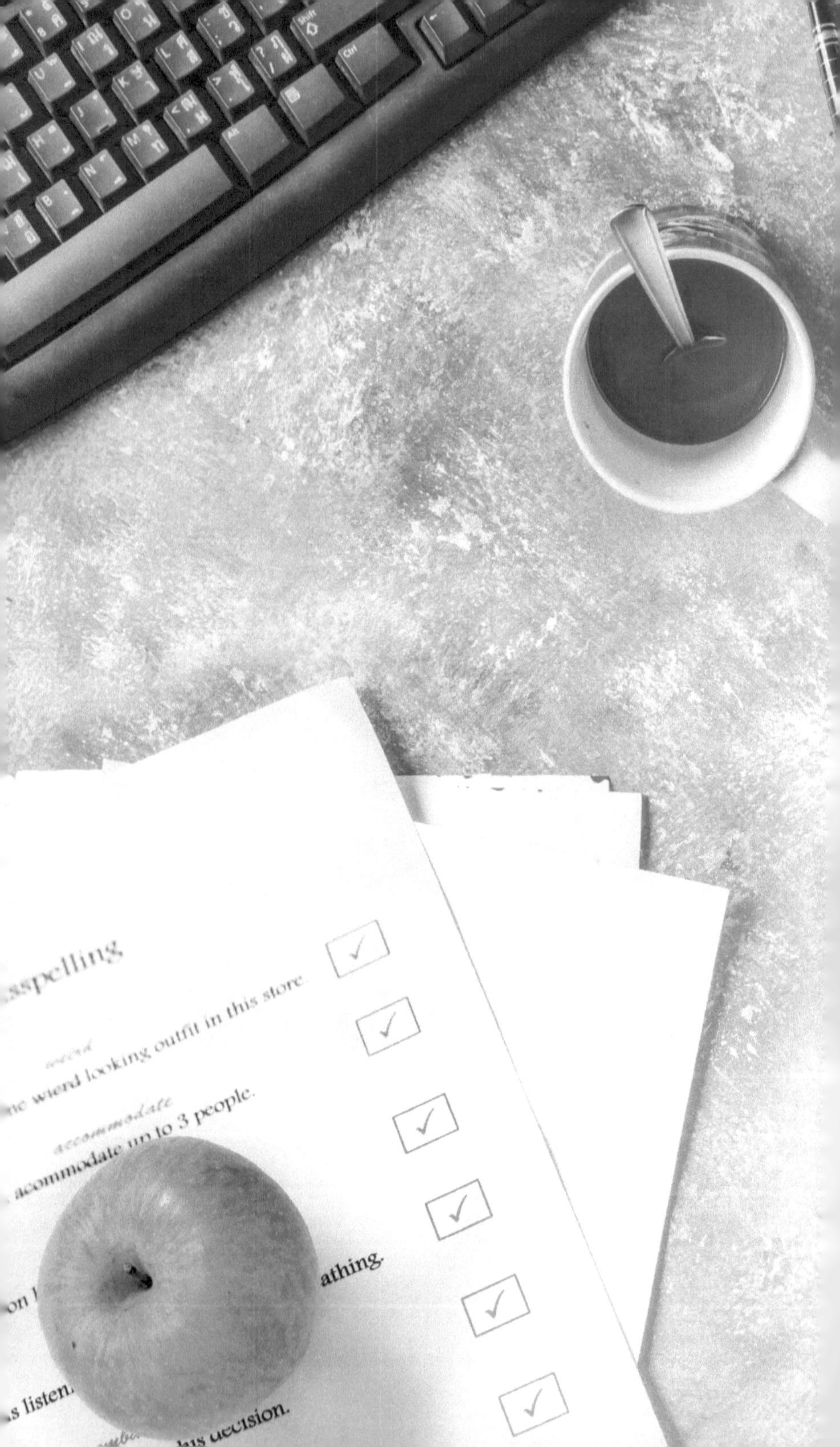
sspelling
no wierd looking outfit in this store.
acommodate
acommodate up to 3 people.
athing.
s listen.
s decision.

Chapter Forty-Three

STELLA

I CAN'T COUNT ON ONE HAND THE AMOUNT OF times I've had to swallow vomit when talking to this man. I've only had to interact with his parents for ten minutes, and I already want out. I don't know how Luke does it. I take another breath, trying to keep myself steady. I am so anxious I don't even know how to think, but I've been trying to keep it together for him. He needs me to be solid, not an emotional wreck.

Quickly glancing behind me, I see Luke and Leon standing together. Both of their faces are thick with emotion.

I wasn't lying earlier when I said Luke mentions Leon a lot. Luke might not be aware of it, but he does. It's clear to anyone looking in that those two have so much love for each other, they just don't know how to show it.

I'm standing next to Luke's dad in front of the restaurant, half-listening to him drone on about his current client. Luckily, I'm saved by the feeling of Luke's arms snaking around my waist, pulling me into him. He's always been touchy, but these past few hours here – it feels like he's scared to let me go.

And honestly, I don't want him too. I feel safe in his arms.

The clinking of Luke's mum's fork on a glass silences the room immediately. I would be impressed by her ability to shut everyone up if she weren't such a horrible human being.

"I am so sorry to interrupt the festivities this evening. This welcome dinner has already been one for the books, and we are just on the drinks!" Her voice is higher than it was when she was talking to me.

"Maybe that's why!" Luke's dad jokes, pulling a small laugh out of everyone in the restaurant. I struggle to force a laugh, my ability to be fake wavering.

"Oh, you!" His mum exclaims, lightly slapping Luke's dad on the chest. "We would like to let you all know that we have a very exciting announcement to make." She puts her hand out, pulling Camilla and Leon in the middle of her and her husband. My face scrunches up slightly, seeing the picturesque family they are creating, with Luke standing on the outside.

I feel a slight tap as Luke bends down to whisper in my ear, "As sexy as you look right now, your face of disgust should probably be hidden." I laugh, surprised by how he could tell without even looking at me.

"Our son Leon has made us extremely proud by asking Camilla, here, to be his wife!" His mum exclaims, causing a round of applause amongst the group as if this is some prized achievement. It's weird the way they've removed the love from engagement, stripped of all the beautiful emotion that should come along with it. It's a contract for them. I would never want that life. His mother starts to speak up again, cutting off the applause.

"Camilla has been a part of our family for a few years now, and she's made it better in every way. She's like the daughter we were never blessed with, and now that she will officially be a part of the family, we have never been happier." Camilla smiles sweetly, and it seems genuine. I go to look at Leon and see his face falter slightly. Something about his demeanour makes me think he doesn't want to be here. Although I don't know why that would be the case, I thought Luke said Camilla and he were genuinely in love.

It's now his dad's turn to speak. "And Leon, we must say how proud we are of you." I feel Luke tense behind me. I rub my hand up and down his arm that's around my waist. He needs to know I'm here, and at least right now, I'm not going anywhere. "You are at the top of your law class, en route to join my firm when you graduate. You are engaged to a beautiful young woman, following in the footsteps of your old man. It is incredible to see a reminder of what our family is capable of when they put their mind to it."

I'm going to kill them. I'm not even kidding, I am going to kill them. And make it slow and painful. They might as well have been telling Luke that he is the failure in the family. I cannot believe they would say something like that, not just in front of him, but in front of 50 other people.

How dare they?

I want to scream, but Luke stops me. Holding onto me tighter. I tilt my head up to look at him, not giving a damn who might see. He is still smiling, standing up tall, but I can see sadness in his eyes. Luke shakes his head slightly, telling me to leave it. I look back towards the front, desperately trying to keep the front that he needs me to have right now, but every part of me is screaming to go full Karate Kid on his dad. I don't know who the fuck he thinks he is, hurting Luke.

My Luke.

Or at least mine for now.

There's more applause as Leon hugs both of his parents, and Camilla follows suit. Neither of his parents acknowledged Luke, leaving him standing there applauding. I feel my jaw tense as I bite my lip to stop myself from speaking. I know it won't help to yell, but right now that's all I want to do.

The only thing that calms me down is when Leon lifts his head, finding his brother's eyes. Leon mouths, 'I'm sorry,' before getting pulled into the masses. My eyes find Luke's face, heavy with emotion. He shakes it off quickly before turning me around to face him.

"I'm going to kill them, Luke. And I'm going to fucking enjoy it." I snarl. He starts to laugh slightly. "I'm serious, Luke. How dare they say those things? And about you? Do they not realise how fucking lucky they are to have you in their life?" He stops laughing and cups my face.

"I love that you want to kill them, but it's okay."

I shake my head, my eyebrows knitting together in disapproval.

"It's not okay, Luke. Nothing about this is okay."

He smiles softly, "I know, but this is my life. It's been my life. I don't have it in me anymore to defend myself. To fight with them. I can't do it." His voice is dripping with exhaustion. It breaks my heart to see him like this. To see the Luke I know pushed to the side, for them. He may not have it in him to defend himself, but I sure as hell do.

I nod and place a chaste kiss on his lips. He sighs as he kisses me back, not caring where we are.

I pull back, staring him directly in the eyes. "The second this dinner is over, we are running away, okay? The night is still young."

He nods before pulling me towards the table. Dinner is served.

It's two hours later before I finally find a moment to excuse myself to go freshen up. The past couple of hours have been filled with conversation that can only be described as an interrogation. We are seated with Luke's parents, his brother, Camilla, and his grandparents and aunt on his mother's side. I genuinely didn't believe that that many bitchy people could exist in one room without it imploding, and yet here we are, still in one piece.

I really didn't want to leave Luke alone, but after I clenched my fist so hard I cut my skin, he told me to take a breather. The entire night, every piece of conversation directed to Luke was some sort of criticism. Some backhanded compliment that was clearly about how he wasn't good enough or how he wasn't doing what the "Astors" do. The need to give it a fucking break.

The bathroom is just down the hallway from the restaurant and is exactly as fancy as the rest of this hotel. I've never felt more out of place in my life. The wall is covered in white brick and is decked out with floor-to-ceiling mirrors. The lighting is just bright enough to show every single insecurity you've ever had about yourself.

I walk up to the sink and splash some water on myself. My cheeks have gone red with how angry I'm getting sitting in that room. I have to get my shit together – for him.

Taking a few deep breaths, I think I'm ready to go back

out. I go to leave, but I stop once I see Luke's mother walking in.

"Mrs. Astor," I say, mustering the biggest smile I can right now. She walks fully into the bathroom, closing the door behind her. I step back slightly, not wanting her to get too close.

"Stella, darling. I was hoping we'd get a chance to speak tonight. Just us girls." Her words seem sincere, but each syllable is a poison dart.

I keep up the girl next door voice. "What can I do for you?"

"Why are you here with my son?" She asks bluntly. I stumble a little bit, caught off guard by her question.

"Excuse me?"

"Why are you here? We both know you could do a lot better than my son, and I really do care for him." I struggle to hold back my scoff as she says that. "I want to make sure you are here for the right reasons. Is he paying you? Does he have something on you? What is it?"

I can't control my face as it drops in complete shock. I have never met someone who is so quick to assume the worst of someone they are meant to have unconditional love for. Granted, Luke and I aren't technically together the way they think. But that doesn't change the fact that any girl would be lucky to have him. Including me.

"I'm going to leave before either of us says something we might regret." I try to walk past her, but she stops me. Not letting me pass. My patience is running thin.

"I don't regret anything I say, Stella. I am complimenting you. You are gorgeous and very conversable. There is no doubt in my mind that you could do a lot better than my son. Sure, he's got some of his father's looks, but his future is practically non-existent. He lacks ambition. I love him, of course I do, but I don't want to see him get hurt by someone who is clearly not here out of love."

The sweet girl I've been pretending to be this whole night disappears about halfway through her idiotic statement. All I can see is red. "You are an idiot," I say simply, a short laugh coming out. She steps back and gasps.

"What did you just say to me?"

"You heard me. You are an idiot. You are an idiot for not seeing the incredible person your son is. Luke is kind, caring, beautiful, and he is the type of person I want to be. I have never felt safer than when I'm with him, never felt more seen. Your son is the best fucking thing that's ever happened to me, and I know his friends at university would agree with that. And normally, I'd say congratulations on raising such an incredible child, but it's clear to me you didn't raise him. Which makes Luke even more impressive because he became the person he is today on his own." I step closer to her, my words mimicking the same poison she's been spitting all evening. "And as for his ambition. You clearly don't know your son at all if you think he has no ambition. He has a plan for his life, a plan that he's done on his own. I can say with 100% certainty he'd be in the same place if you never existed, probably further."

The shock on her face hasn't dropped. "How dare you speak to me like this! I am going to tell Luke you've attacked his mother, you'll be gone like that." She snaps in my face.

I laugh at that. "Go ahead. Tell him. He can throw me out and never speak to me again, and I won't regret saying this to you." I brush past her, turning around before I open the door. "It's up to you whether he knows about this conversation. I didn't do this for brownie points from him or to make him angry – so I won't tell him. The only reason I didn't stay silent is because someone needs to tell you that you are a horrible mother who never deserved Luke in the first place." She stares at me, her frown becoming deeper. "Nice girl talk, Mrs. Astor. I'll see you at the table."

And with that, I walk out of the bathroom and back to the table. Never in a million years did I think I would hear a mother talk about her son that way. When I sit down, I make a point to kiss Luke and grab his cheek. The shock on his father's face when I came back is apparent, and tells me he knew exactly what his wife was going to say to me in that bathroom. But as I said to Luke earlier, I'm not easy to scare off.

Chapter Forty-Four

LUKE

STELLA'S PLAN FOR US TO RUN AWAY DID NOT happen, considering that by the time dinner finished, it was already midnight. I don't think I've ever been as exhausted as I was when I finally stumbled back into the room. After Stella came back from the bathroom, it was clear something had shifted in the air. I knew when I saw my mother stand up to follow her that it wouldn't end well – but I also knew my girl could hold her own. And based on the look my mother had stuck on her face the rest of the night – she did.

When I asked Stella what had happened, she said that she just did what I didn't have the energy to do anymore and left it at that. There was a part of me that wanted to know exactly what was said, but I knew it would just hurt me more. So I left it, and Stella was happy to let it drop.

I had a better time last night than I thought I was going to have. It was impossible to ignore the fact that I felt like I was glowing knowing that Stella had defended me. And even more so, knowing that she wasn't going to tell me. She truly acted for me.

The rest of the night was filled with light touches and stolen glances. There were moments where it felt like it was just the two of us. She makes even the worst times feel good.

"Ugh, why did you have to buy me a corseted dress, Lucas. Do you hate me?" Stella groans, rolling over towards me. She's still wearing her dress from last night, claiming she was too tired to take it off.

I chuckle, pulling her towards me. "I do seem to remember offering to help you take it off. If you had taken me up on that offer, you'd be feeling much more comfortable right now."

Her head swings up as she gives me a cold stare. I braided her hair last night before she fell asleep, but missed a few pieces. Her face is surrounded by little curls, making it hard to not smile when looking at her.

"If you had done that, we both know where that would have gone. And then I'd be even more sore and even more sleep deprived. Sex is great, but neither of those is ideal for the shit we have to do today."

"Goldie, you are really good at boosting a guy's ego."

She drops her head face-first into a pillow, throwing up her arm to flip me off. No matter how many times I've woken up next to her, I'll never get tired of it. I lean over to grab my phone, conscious not to move Stella. It's 9:30, meaning we have exactly 30 minutes before we have to be downstairs.

"Baby." I duck my head, whispering.

"Mhm," she says, her face still smushed in the pillow.

"We have to go in 30 minutes." I'm trying to keep my voice as light and sweet as possible. Trying not to poke the beast too much.

Her head flings up, and she gets out of bed, huffing.

"Okay, you can have the first shower, gorgeous!" I shout as she closes the bathroom door. I hear a distinct "I hate you" before I hear the water start.

How could you not love this girl?

By the time we practically stumble downstairs, it's 10:05, honestly, not too bad. I wish I could blame our lateness on Stella, but today it was 100% me. Rory and Beck were texting me about a disagreement they had had. Well, I use the word disagreement lightly. Beck had been planning a New Year's Eve party for the past month with the intention of having a New Year's kiss with the guy he's been seeing on and off for a couple of months. However, when the guy cancelled on him, Beck said he had to find a replacement for a New Year's kiss. Which naturally was Rory. When Rory said no, Beck took personal offence, stating that it was ridiculous that Rory wouldn't want to kiss him. Honestly, there wasn't much I could say in this situation, and I just enjoyed reading the messages.

We walk into the reception smiling, and I immediately spot a big group of people standing in the reception. I'm actually excited about where we're heading today. It's a beach about thirty minutes away, but it's a special place for me. There's a spot I've been visiting since I was a kid, tucked away at the far end of the shore. The rocks there line the edge of the beach, and one in particular sits almost in the ocean. It's high enough that you don't get wet when the waves crash, but you still feel the spray. It's a bit tricky to reach, but once you're there, it's worth every step. You are surrounded by water and by nature; not a single person can hear you. And while it's still visible, it feels like not a single person can see you. Other than Leon, I've never taken anyone there.

"It's nice of you to finally join us, Luke." My dad says, anger lacing his tone. He looks down at his watch. "Are you aware of how time works?" I feel Stella shift next to me. I know how hard she's currently trying to stay quiet. I check my phone, it's 10:06 now. I'm 6 minutes late, not to mention the group looks about half full. We aren't the only ones who are late.

"It's only 6 minutes, dad," I mumble, shocking even myself.

"Excuse me?" My dad says, his voice low but loud.

"Nothing, just that 6 minutes isn't that bad. I could have been an hour late." I try to make the last bit into a joke, but it doesn't land. "My bad, dad, won't happen again."

He seems to accept that, walking back towards the group. I feel invigorated for some reason. I don't think I've ever been that short with him. I feel Stella go on the balls of her feet, standing up taller to whisper in my ear.

"I'm so proud of you." I turn back and kiss her on the head. I'm proud of myself, too.

"Okay, everyone, gather around so we can talk about today's plans." My mother's voice cuts through the conversation, causing immediate silence. "So, as you might know, we've had a change of plans. We are going on a wildlife tour today. There are cars outside to take us to the start of the track, so please head out there and have fun!!"

Wildlife tour? That's not what the schedule said. I pull my phone out to check. It definitely said we were going to the beach today.

"Everything okay?" Stella asks, clearly noticing my shift in behaviour.

"Yeah, just one sec." I walk towards my mum, who is standing with my dad and brother.

"I thought we were going to the beach today?" I ask, not bothering to say hello. It's not like one more formal introduction is going to make them love me more.

"It was, but we changed the plans. We aren't going to the beach."

"But-"

"There's a pool right there if you want to swim, Luke."

"It's not about swimming," I say, looking back at Stella. She hasn't moved, but her face is twisted, clearly worried. "Is it okay if we go to the beach anyway? We can meet up with you later for dinner."

My mother's eyes look like they are going to fall out of her head. My dad cuts in, "Son, it is New Year's Eve, you are going to be with the family. Don't be ungrateful and get in the car." He turns around immediately, dismissing me. I know I have free will, but right now it doesn't feel like it. I'm about to gesture for Stella to come over when Leon intervenes.

"Let him go," Leon says, conviction in his tone.

My mother's eyebrows raise, "Excuse me? You heard your father, Leon."

His face scrunches slightly, but he straightens up before anyone notices.

"Think about it. He's difficult when we are all together. It'll be easier if he isn't there." Ouch. That feels like a dagger to the heart.

My parents think about it for a second, a silent conversation passing between the two of them. After a minute, my mum speaks.

"Okay, fine. Luke, we will see you later." Her palm

brushes by Leon's face as she walks outside, my dad hot on her trail.

Leon turns to me. "Make sure she doesn't hurt herself on the rock. I hope you have a good day, Luke." He walks away before I get a chance to say anything.

He knew why I wanted to go to the beach today.

He knew.

Stella is immediately beside me once they have left.

"What's happening?"

A smile takes over my face, thinking about what just happened. "I have something to show you." That's all I say, before pulling her behind her out the door.

"I genuinely think you are trying to kill me sometimes, Lucas." I laugh, looking back at Stella. She looks like she's walking on a tightrope with how unbalanced she is. We are only a couple of steps away. I already offered to carry her, but she told me she was a strong, independent woman and didn't need help from me. I can't help but think she's second-guessing that right now.

"Almost there, Goldie. You can do it, I have so much faith in you."

As expected, I'm met with a death stare at that one. I truly think if she could reach me, I'd be dead on the floor.

I reach the rock and hold out my hand for her to grab onto, and after thinking about it for a second, she lets me help her. I sit down and pull her down, sitting in front of me. She settles into my lap, lying down on my chest, taking in the view. My arm wraps around her, pulling her as close to me as I can.

"Wow." She lets out, staring at the waves.

It's exactly how it's always been. The waves are loud and crashing against the edge of the rock. It's a beautiful sunny day, but the wind from the ocean is keeping us cool.

She tilts her head up, looking at me, "How did you find this place?"

I smile, thinking back to when Leon and I were younger. "My family was having dinner at a restaurant on the other end of the beach. Leon and I did something to get us in trouble, so naturally, we ran away. We came down to the end of the beach and saw the rocks. I think we liked the fact that we were completely alone – just the two of us." I pause, looking out at the water. "It's the only place in the world where all I feel is peace."

She smiles, turning back around, looking out at the waves. "Can I ask you something?"

"Anything."

"What happened to you and your brother?" I blink. "Every story you tell me from when you were younger, it seems like you were best friends. And I can still see the love you have for each other. I just– I don't understand how you got to how you are now."

I think for a second. That exact question has been on my mind for years now.

"Honestly, I don't think there is one answer. I think as we started getting older, we took such different directions in life. I was always independent from my parents, and he wasn't. And then the life choices he made started aligning more and more with what my parents wanted him to do. So I started getting pushed to the side more and more. And as a kid, when that started happening, I blamed him. I was too young to see that it was my parents' fault. So when I turned 18 and moved out, I never reached out. I was still so angry and so broken from growing up in that house that I took it out on him." I take a deep breath, rubbing my hand up and down her waist. "I hate that it took me so long to realise that my parents weaponised us against each other. And now I'm scared it's too late to go back to how we were."

I feel her head shake against my chest.

"I don't think it is. He cares about you, too, Luke. It's so clear in how he's acted this weekend."

"Maybe. I wouldn't blame him if he doesn't want to fix it. An older sibling is meant to be there, meant to be someone you can lean on. I've never been that to him. Why would he want that now?"

Stella sits up and turns around to look at me. Her face is serious. "Luke, it's not your fault either that you had a bad relationship with your brother. In the same way, it isn't his. You care so much, Luke, and it's one of the things I lo-" she stops talking and backtracks slightly. "It's one of my favourite things about you. But you need to stop carrying everyone's burdens. You were a kid, too. They were the adults." I nod, it's not the first time someone has said this to me, but it feels like I'm finally hearing what she's saying. She turns back around and nestles into my lap. I want to bring up what she nearly said, the word that nearly came out of her mouth. But I'm scared. At this moment, my entire body is aching to tell her how I feel, but it doesn't feel right. Not right now. Not when we still have another day left of doing whatever this is. It's a battle to keep it in, especially knowing that once this weekend ends, so does our agreement.

I can't help but wonder if what we've built in this short time is strong enough to push through the fear we both hold inside.

Instead of saying anything, I let us fall into a comfortable silence. Quiet with her never feels empty; I never feel the urge to fill the space like I do with others. It just feels calm. I let my hand move to stroke her hair, leaning my head down on hers. There is no doubt in my mind that there is nowhere else I'd rather be right now.

"Parker and I dated for the whole of my first year at Brookstone." She cuts through the silence. I don't say anything, not wanting to scare her off from talking to me about this. "I thought he was the love of my life, but I was wrong. Clearly." She lets out a dry laugh. "I'm sorry I can't tell you what happened the way you have with your family. But I need you to know that I know you aren't him. I'm scared of everything, but slowly it feels like I'm not scared of you."

I don't know what to say to that. How to respond to her being so vulnerable. So open with me in a way she hasn't been before.

Deciding words aren't enough, I grab her chin and tilt it up to me. I press my lips to hers slowly, trying to tell her I love her through my kiss.

Every kiss with Stella is magic, but today it's different. There's something unspoken. The way our mouths melt together, the way I can feel her heart beat faster. It's saying everything we are both too scared to say out loud. Every part of me wants to stay here at this moment with her.

Forever.

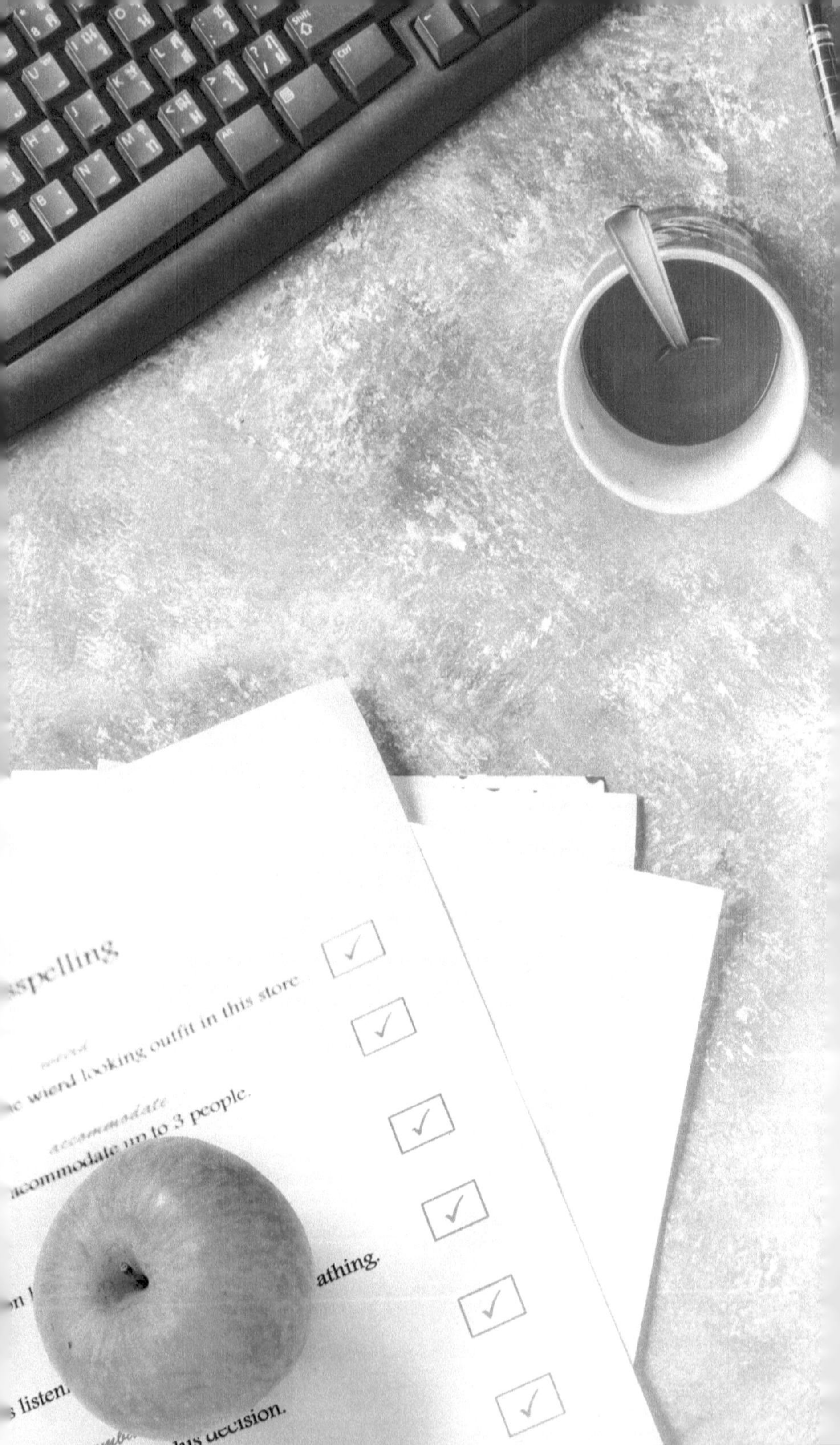
spelling
wierd looking outfit in this store
accommodate
acommodate up to 3 people.
athing.
s listen.
his decision.

Chapter Forty-Five

STELLA

"HOW LONG DO WE HAVE UNTIL DINNER tonight?" I ask through the bathroom door. I took a shower once we had come back from the beach today, and my skin was covered in a layer of salt. Normally, I hate that feeling, but today I didn't care. Luke and I spent the entire day talking on that rock. The conversation never died down; it never felt awkward. And I know neither of us wanted to be anywhere else.

"A little bit over an hour, maybe? We probably came back sooner than we had to." He shouts back from the bedroom. I nod to myself in the mirror, wrapping the smallest towel I've ever seen around my body, barely covering my ass. Hopefully, my hair would dry before we had to go to dinner. I tuck the towel into itself so it will stay up, and I open the door to the bathroom. Luke is lying on the bed, without his shirt on, scrolling through his phone. It's unfair how sexy he looks, even when he's not trying.

The second the door closes behind me, he looks up, barely keeping eye contact for a second. His eyes roam my entire body, covering every single inch. Memorising every curve. There is hunger in his gaze that made my legs squeeze together involuntarily.

There's something in the way he looks at me that makes me want to be on display for him every day. My confidence is never higher than when I'm with him. I like that he isn't scared to show me exactly what I do to him.

He gulps, standing up, and lazily walking towards me. He's in no rush, keeping his eyes roaming as he walks closer to me.

Luke stops once he is right in front of me, his eyes making their way back to my face.

"Fucking hell, Goldie." That's all he says, his voice strained. As if he can't say anything else.

"Are you doing okay there, Lucas?" I say, trying to stop my voice from quivering. His right hand shoots out, grabbing my waist, pulling me towards him slowly. It starts roaming up and down the side of the towel. My legs squeeze tighter, desperately searching for something. He tilts his head down, nodding.

A small smile takes over my mouth, "Okay, then I'm just going to go back into the bathroom now. Get dressed and all." I go to turn out his grasp, but he stops me. My smile grows wider. I look back at him, my eyebrows raised. I push myself into him slightly – feeling how hard he already is. He groans, just from that small contact.

"What's wrong?" I ask, feigning innocence. It's fun teasing him, I like knowing I do to him what he does to me.

"Stella." He growls, "I'm trying to control myself here and you're not helping."

I am highly aware that in a little over an hour, we need to be down for the New Year's Eve party, and that I should be good.

But I don't want to be good right now.

I push out of his hold, just enough space for my hands to move. I undo my towel, dropping to the floor, standing in front of him – not wearing a single thing. His tongue darts out and licks his lips.

"Who says I want you to control yourself?"

My simple statement seems to break him, because one second I am standing in front of him, waiting for him to move, and the next I am pushed up against the wall. Every part of him is close to me. His hand grips the underside of my chin as he kisses me. It's rushed, fast. He bites my lip, causing me to moan into his mouth.

"Fuck you are perfect." He says, staring at me. I'm fidgeting, searching for some friction. He notices and smirks, kissing my neck. His hand roams down, flicking my nipple as he passes my breast. He keeps moving his hand down lower and lower, excruciatingly slowly. One thing about Luke that I've learned is that he likes me begging for him. He stops right as he reaches the place I desperately want him to be.

"You okay there, Stel?" He asks, repeating the same words I just said to him. I nod. He chuckles before I see him get down on his knees.

The way he looks at me makes me think he's worshipping me. He kisses the inside of my thigh as his fingers finally touch the place where I'm aching for him.

"Luke," I say breathlessly.

"What do you want, Stella?" He asks, moving his fingers around my clit, slowly. Too slow.

I take a deep breath, confident as I speak, "I want you to go down on me."

He smiles, his free hand still roaming up and down my thigh.

"Atta girl." He whispers before bringing his mouth down, doing exactly what I asked for. My hand instinctively shoots out to his head, holding onto him as I ride his face. It becomes too much when he puts two of his fingers inside me, the sensation overwhelming me.

He doesn't stop for a second once I come down, immediately coming up and kissing me. I'm grabbing onto him, desperately trying to hold myself up.

"Do you like the taste of yourself, Stella?" He asks, his face glistening. I nod, telling the truth. Before I can even react, he's lifting me effortlessly, his hands firm around my waist. The air thickens as he carries me to the bed, each step making my heart race faster. He places me down with a carefulness that only makes everything feel more intense. He stands up and takes off his shorts, his dick ready and waiting. He grabs a condom and puts it on before positioning himself in front of me.

"I wish you could see what I could right now." That's all he says before pushing into me. I gasp as he thrusts in and out. There's nothing gentle about how he's fucking me right now, and I love every moment of it.

My eyes open, and I can see the mirror behind us. I can see him thrusting, him fucking me. I can't tear my eyes away from us. From how good we look.

He notices I'm looking away from him and turns around, seeing the mirror. Luke stops moving and pulls out, a mischievous smirk on his face.

Leaning down, he whispers in my ear, "You like watching as I fuck you, Stella?" I smile, expecting embarrassment to take over, but it never does.

"We look good," I say simply, sitting up slightly to see where we are connected.

"It's my favourite thing to watch. Do you want to see it

from a better angle?" I nod again, curious to see what he's about to do. He picks me up effortlessly and lays me down on the bed, his hands gentle as they lower me into place, facing the mirror. I am turned away from him, but we both can see in the mirror. The reflection shows the distance and closeness between us, all in one. He sits up, his hands gripping my waist.

"Show me how much you like it, Stella." He growls.

I sit myself up, lowering myself onto him. We both groan as he enters me, going deeper than he was before.

I start to move, my eyes closing instinctively.

"Open your eyes, baby. Look at us." My eyes snap open, and I look into the mirror. I can see his hand sneaking around my body, starting to rub my clit. I move faster, getting more and more excited seeing us together. "That's it. Fuck, Stella, you look so beautiful."

I start to get more confident, taking exactly what I want from him. His breathing starts getting heavier. I've never been this full in my life, or this turned on.

"Luke." I moan breathlessly, "I'm going to-"

I feel him nod against my back, "I'm right there with you, Goldie." He says right before I let go. Riding through the high.

Chapter Forty-Six

LUKE

HER BODY SLUMPS SLIGHTLY AS SHE COMES DOWN from her orgasm. My breathing is heavy. The second I felt her squeeze around me, I was a goner. The way she was taking exactly what she wanted from me while watching herself ride me. I'm surprised I lasted as long as I did. Every time I am inside this girl, it feels like heaven.

That's the only way to explain it.

I pick her up, turning her around to face me. She slumps onto me, clearly tired. Her head lifts up to look at me, and I lean in and kiss her.

"You did so well." She smiles at me, nodding. I stand up, still holding her in my arms, taking her with me to the bathroom. I set her down on the counter as I cleaned myself up. Handing her a cup of water, I look over to the clock to see we only have 20 minutes until we need to leave. Leaning down, I kiss her on her forehead, groaning that we have to get ready. I don't want to be anywhere but here with her.

"We have to go in 20 minutes, Goldie." The sluggish, slow Stella who had been here just moments ago disappears, and she sits up straighter.

"Oh shit." She hops off the counter, her legs a bit shaky as she stands. She holds onto the sink top to stabilize herself.

I smirk, going to say something, but am cut off.

"Don't you dare." I swallow my laugh. "Go get my dress. I'm wearing the dark green one tonight." I nod, not daring to say anything else. I walk up behind her, giving her a kiss on her shoulder, reeling in how her body leans back into me the second I touch her.

"Leave now, Lucas. Or we won't make it to the party." She whispers, pushing back into me just slightly. As much as I want to stay with her, I know we need to go. That is the only reason I leave her in the bathroom.

15 minutes later, I'm ready, sitting on the couch. I'm wearing a tux, and despite the slight discomfort, I fucking love it. I love the way my tattoos creep out onto my left hand and the way they fit.

It would be a lie to say I'm not feeling anxious for tonight. Every time I have to see my parents, a massive pit in my stomach forms. And it doesn't go away until I get to go home. The only thing that's keeping me calm right now is the fact that I know Stella will be on my arm, by my side, the entire night. I can't think of a better way to ring in the new year.

The sound of Stella's heels on the floor causes my head to snap up to look at her. She's wearing my favourite of the dresses I gave her – the one I hoped she would wear tonight. The corset fits her flawlessly, accentuating her figure in all the right ways. The emerald green shines as she moves, pooling at the floor – only slightly covering her black heels. My favourite part of the dress, though, is the slit that shows off her entire right leg. I have to take a breath to stop myself from fucking her against the wall she's currently standing next to.

"Wow." That's all I can think to say as she stands there. She brushes one of her curls behind her ears, and I see the stacks of jewelry she has on. I love the way Stel wears an entire jewelry store every time she goes out. I can't wait to add to her collection – a necklace, a bracelet.

A ring.

My girl does a little twirl, the dark green fabric flowing perfectly.

"You like?" She smiles sweetly. I stand up and walk towards her. I grab her waist, pulling her closer to me. Something about Stella makes me want to constantly feel her. She turns me into a caveman. I nudge her chin upward, directing her gaze at me.

"You are the most incredible girl I have ever seen, Stella." Her breath hitches, and her eyes look thick with emotion. I lean down and give her a kiss on the cheek. She looks at me with a face I can't quite place. "What are you thinking?" I ask, still holding her close to me.

Her gaze drops slightly. "I'm thinking –" Her voice is low, almost a whisper. "I'm thinking that you are the only one who makes it feel like I can breathe."

My chest tightens as she looks up at me. There's no trace of hesitation, no nervousness in her eyes. Instead, she looks at me with a quiet certainty, as if her confession is not only true but something to be proud of, something she's finally at peace with.

I lean down and give her a light kiss, knowing that she wouldn't want me to say anything right now.

"We should go, Goldie." She nods and walks towards the door, holding it open for me.

As I look at her, something shifts inside me. For the first time since I admitted to myself that I loved her, I knew – really knew – that she might love me back, and more importantly, that she was ready to hear me say it.

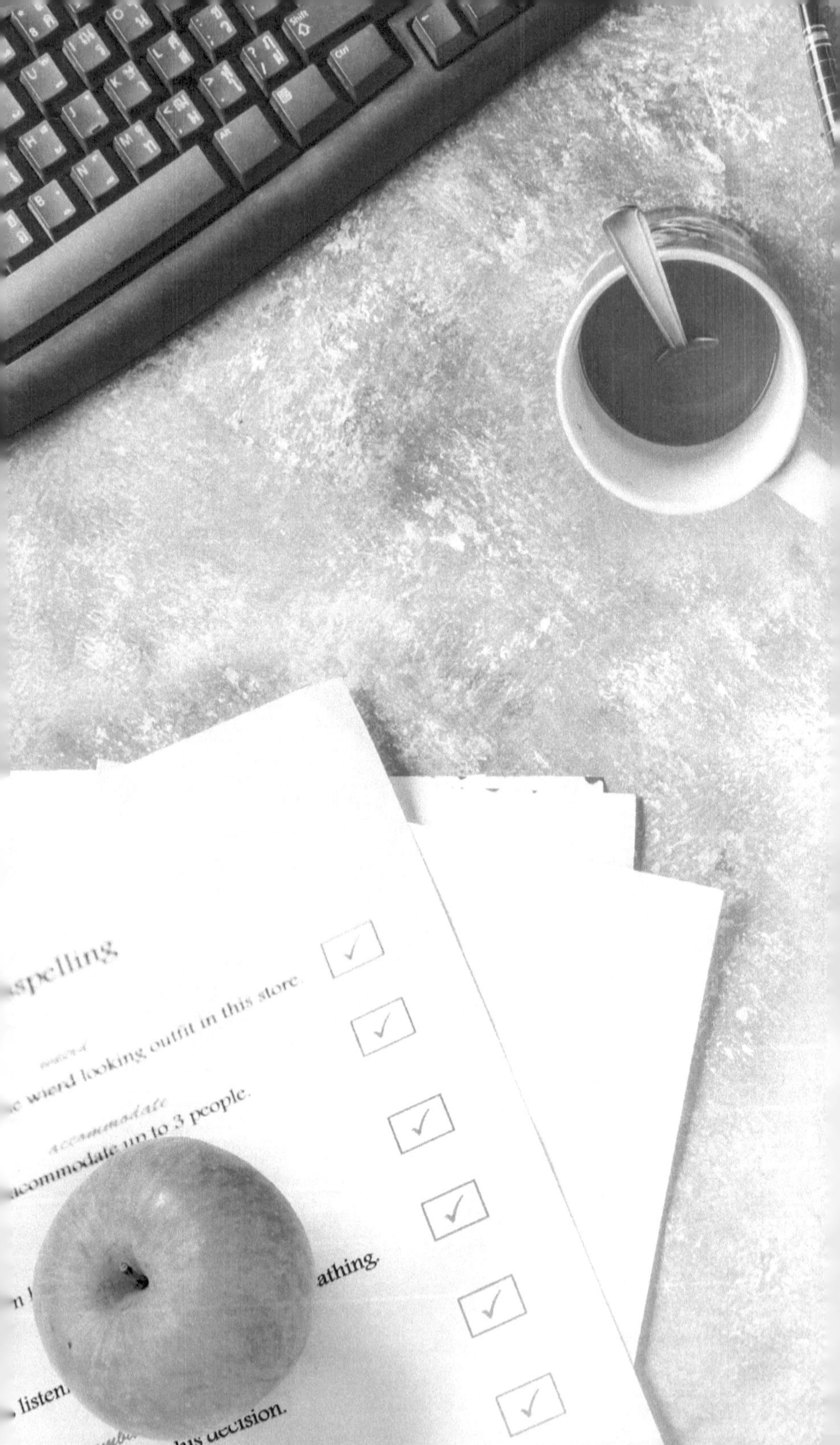

spelling
e wierd looking outfit in this store.
accommodate
commodate up to 3 people.
athing.
listen.
decision.

Chapter Forty-Seven

STELLA

HIS FAMILY IS HORRIBLE IN EVERY SINGLE WAY; there is no argument from me, however, they know how to put on a party. The room we are in is nothing short of a ballroom. Moulding covers every part of the marble walls, surrounding the mirror and candles sticking out from the sconces. Tables are set up, but no one is sitting. People are floating around the hall, noses pointed slightly up as they convene with each other. Everyone in attendance is dressed to the nines and is sparkling with the jewels adorning their body. It's almost funny to see the physical shift in demeanour as someone walks away from a conversation. I truly have learnt this weekend that Mean Girls doesn't just apply to teenagers.

There is some sort of quartet at the end of the room, playing a fast-paced classical arrangement reflecting the movement of all the people.

The area is lit up with a warm glow from the candles and chandeliers decorating the ceiling. It's clear the lighting is trying to convey a feeling of welcome, but there is a cold sensation flooding every inch of this party.

As we walk further into the party, Luke's grasp on my hand gets stronger. He hasn't said anything since we walked in. I can feel his breathing as he tries to get back to himself. There is a massive part of me that's silently wishing he would walk over to his parents and tell them to fuck off, but I know he won't. It's not him. He sees the best in everyone and would sacrifice himself time and time again for others. It's one of my favourite parts of him, but also the part of him I want to protect the most.

"Hey," I say, pulling him in front of me. I reach up to cup his face, forcing him to stop looking around the room and look at me instead. "Tonight is going to suck."

He lets out a dry laugh, clearly not expecting me to say that. "You suck at pep talks, Goldie." He shakes his head.

"This isn't a pep talk, Lucas. Tonight is going to suck. We are about to spend the next three hours surrounded by people who have somehow mastered the art of complimenting you while also making you feel like a failure. But that's all it is – three hours. Then we are going to go get some food, because all of this," I gesture to the trays of food tuxedoed waiters are carrying around. "Looks gross, then we are going to go to the hotel and just be you and me."

He smirks, "Just you and me, huh?" I try to hold back the blush I can feel forming. I hate how this man can do that to me with barely any words.

"Shut up and let me finish my pep talk."

"I thought this wasn't a pep talk," He grins.

"Lucas," I growl, and his mouth snaps shut. I continue. "And then tomorrow we'll leave, and you don't need to deal with any of this anymore. It'll be over." I take a breath. "Everything will be over."

His eyes widen a little bit, making a look I can't quite place. The grin that was plastered on his face disappears, and he just stares at me. Nothing I said wasn't true. Tomorrow, this is all over. We had two goals with our arrangement: to give me an alibi and reason for my actions and give him a ruse with his family. Keets is convinced, and once we break up, she'll understand me returning to how I was before. Even if it's just for a bit. The weekend with his parents is nearly done. There's nothing left for us to fake. I keep trying to convince myself it can be more, but I know it can't. I know I can't.

We both need to accept that.

"What if I don't want it to be over?" His words carry despite barely speaking them. It's clear that he's not talking about his family, but I can't deal with any other conversation right now. Or ever.

"Then it won't be. They are your family, Lucas. It's up to you." He swallows and goes to say something else, but I cut him off by leaning up and kissing him. It feels slower than normal; the usual dance we do is missing. It's almost like he's searching, clinging onto something we both know I can't give him. Even if I wanted to.

This can't become real.

"Do you want to get some champagne?" I ask, tilting my head towards the champagne tower sitting on the far corner of the room.

"No." He says, "I want to dance."

The music the band is playing slows down, and I feel Luke's fingers intertwining with my hand. His hands are soft like feathers, and with a quiet pull, I go with him to the dance floor. My left hand wraps around his shoulders, and my right hand rests on his chest. I can feel his heartbeat, steady and warm beneath my hands, as his hand covers mine. I lean into the curve of his neck, closing my eyes for a moment, letting the feeling of him surround me. We are swaying, and his free hand is running up and down my back. It's soft, a comforting feeling. As if he's reminding me he's there, that he's not going anywhere. Even as the song finishes, neither of us moves – waiting for the next song to start up. I'm sure his parents are lurking around somewhere waiting for us, but that thought feels distant. I don't want to let go.

Once I do, I know it's done.

I think, deep down, he does too.

Two more songs have passed without us saying a word. The end of the final song signals the start of the dinner service in the room next door. I lift my head up from his neck and look at him. He drops his head, resting his forehead on mine. Every other couple has left the floor, leaving us completely alone in the room. The musicians start to pack up their instruments, the sharp clang of metal echoing in the silence, the only sound that fills the air. A speech starts in the other room, and I can't make out what they are saying.

We should probably be in there, but still, he doesn't move. Unwavering. I want to speak, but I don't know what to say.

"I wasn't talking about my family." He lifts his head up, his eyes are full of a tenderness that makes my heart ache. I dip my head, looking at the floor, wishing he'd stop.

"I know," I say, barely getting the words out. His hand reaches out and cups the side of my face, forcing me to look at him. I can feel tears start to swell in my eyes. I don't know why they do.

"Stel, I don't want this to be done. You and I. It's not fake and it hasn't been for a long time. You know I'm right."

"Stop, Luke," I whisper, my throat getting tight.

He takes a step closer, his voice low. "You're scared, I get it. I am too. It feels like you have become a part of me; you are woven into the very core of my being. Losing you will unwind every piece of me that matters. The idea of never seeing you again, never holding you again, it shatters me. I don't know when it happened, when the moment we shifted, but it did. Every part of you is perfect to me. The way you chew on your lips when you're thinking. The way you desperately try to replace your caffeine addiction with tea but fail every time. The way you did all of this, just because your best friend said she was worried. Every single part of you, Stella." Staring up at him, I can't say anything. He can't mean these things. "Whenever I touch you, it feels like the world stops. Like everything that has ever happened, happened just to lead us to this moment. To the moment where you and I were together. Each moment we've spent together has shown me a love I didn't know I deserved; you've shown me that love."

I know what comes next. I know what words are on the tip of his tongue. I know the words I'll never be able to say to him. I drop his hand harshly and step back.

He can't say this, I can't hear it.

"Stella?" He asks. I step back.

"You can't do this, Luke. This wasn't a part of the deal." He steps forward, towards me. He's too close.

"Life doesn't work like that, Stella. You can't just stop yourself from falling. The whole point is you do it without thought, without abandon. You let yourself fall."

"Please don't say it," I say, wrapping my arms around

myself. It's okay, he's not Parker. This isn't that. It's okay. I can't tell if he can hear me. I don't know how loud I'm speaking. My head won't be quiet. All I can think is that he's only saying this to trap me. To tell me he loves me, just so when he hurts me, there's a fallback. So that I won't truly believe how bad it is, because how can someone who loves you do that?

I don't want to lose the control I have left.

"I lo-" He starts to say.

"Stop!" I shout, shutting him up. "Luke, Stop. Please don't say anything else. Please." My voice is dripping with distress.

He needs to stop.

Luke's arms drop in desperation and confusion. "Why won't you let me love you, Stella?"

I take another step back, feeling like the walls are closing in on me.

That fucking word.

"Because I don't know how." There are tears welling up in his eyes, and every part of me is saying to run to him. To kiss him and tell him I know it's not fake. But I can't.

Instead of running towards him, I turn and run away – leaving the life I could have had behind me.

Chapter Forty-Eight

LUKE

I WATCH AS SHE LEAVES THE ROOM. AS SHE RUNS away from me – from us. I want to run after her, but I know I can't. She made it pretty clear where she stands, and I can't pretend like she didn't. I know she feels the same, but she's scared. And I knew she would be scared, and I pushed it anyway. Why did I push her? Why was I so desperate for her to tell me she felt the same? I knew how she felt. I could have waited. I should have waited. I just thought, maybe she was there. At the same place I was. But clearly I was wrong, and now instead of walking out of this room with the love of my life – I'm left standing alone. I ruined everything.

Who can I turn to now? My parents haven't even noticed I'm not in the next room. And even if they did, they wouldn't care. All they'd see here is that I failed at yet another thing in their eyes. I couldn't even keep the girl. Leon isn't here either, but he shouldn't be. I may not be the best older brother, but I know it isn't his job to look after me. I can't turn to Rory and Beck; they don't deserve to have me unload on them. Already, they have to deal with too much; I can't have them leave me, too.

I'm alone.

The weight of everything that's happened these past 48 hours crashes into me. My breath catches in my throat, the air struggling to make it down. Tears burn my eyes, threatening to fall. I couldn't do it. I couldn't help her. I couldn't make her love me. And now I'm left in this empty room, with people next door who would prefer it if I disappeared. Whose life do I make harder by being here? The strength in my legs starts to fade, as a tremor runs through them. Sobs escape my mouth. I can't hold it back anymore. There's no point in hiding; no one can see me break.

Just as I crash towards the floor, I feel a pair of arms come around me. Catching me before I hit the ground.

"I've got you, Luke. It's okay." I hear my little brother's voice whisper as he holds me.

"Leon?" I manage to say between the sobs. My voice is tired, and I can barely hear myself speak.

"I'm here."

"She's gone." A sob escapes me, and I feel Leon's grasp get tighter. "She's gone." I don't know if he was here, but I don't care. In no world would I be able to explain what just happened if he didn't see. If he did, he'll know we were faking, he'll know she didn't choose me.

No one chooses me.

"I know." He says quietly, dipping his head to rest on mine. He keeps rubbing my back, telling me it's okay.

"Why wasn't I enough?" My voice cracks, and I hate how it sounds. I feel helpless.

I don't know how long we stay like that, but he doesn't move.

He doesn't leave.

"What the hell are you two doing?" My mother hisses in a whisper as she enters the room. I shake Leon off immediately; he shouldn't have to face the backlash I'm about to receive. I take a deep breath and stand up. Leon slowly rises next to me, his back becoming stiffer as he does so.

"Sorry, mum, just having a brother bonding moment." I try to muster up a smile, but it barely reaches my cheeks. She looks between us, shaking her head.

"Luke, you should know better than dragging your brother into your troubles." Leon shifts on his feet, and I hear his mouth open. I tap his hand, signaling for him to shut up. "Clearly something has happened here. Give me an explanation before I have to call your father in."

"Stella left." I offer up simply. There's nothing more to it. Nothing else to tell her. I see my mother falter, and for a split second, it seems like she might use the single maternal bone in her body for me. But the second fleet, and she goes stiff again.

"Well, she did always seem a little out of your league, Luke. It's better you know now." My eyes flutter slowly, closing. I'm tired of this hurt. Of what she does to me. She starts walking towards Leon and me, the sound of her heels clacking on the lacquered floor. I see her hand reach out towards Leon. Her features soften as she looks up at my brother, reaching her hand out slowly to cup his cheek. Affection I've never been exposed to. "Sweetie, let's go back to your father. Some of his law school friends want to meet you." Leon's head looks back towards me, but I have nothing to give him. He should go. He doesn't need to be miserable with me. I've been a shit brother, but at least he can have our parents.

"No, I'm okay." Leon barely musters, stepping back from our mum slightly. The shock on her face is apparent.

"Excuse me?" She asks, her voice high. She snaps her hand back, her head moving, confused.

"I said I'm okay. I'm going to stay with Luke." This time, there's more conviction behind his statement. My throat starts to get tight again. I've never seen him act this way, never sided with me over them.

"Leon, I understand that your brother may seem like he's struggling right now, but there are more important things at stake here." Her head tilts to the side, and a short smile replaces the scowl that was just there. It's almost frightening how fast my mother can put on a mask. I guess I learned from the best. "You need to think about your future. Not your brothers. Trust me, you don't want to end up like him." She turns her head at me, making an emphasis on that last point. Normally, I'd sit here and take it. I'd let her make an example of me and let my brother go. I wouldn't tell him how it hurts me; I'd just accept that I don't get a family. That I don't get people, and I don't know if it's because I'm so damn tired of them, or because Stella left. Or even because my brother decided to take another step towards us when he stood by my side. But today I'm not taking this shit right now.

"Mother, please, for the love of god, shut up." Her mouth falls open, some sort of tortured gasp leaving her throat. "I am so done with the way you and Dad talk about me, talk to me. Your son just lost the love of his life, just fell to the ground sobbing in his little brother's arms. And you couldn't care less. It's like I'm not your child. What kind of mother acts like that?"

I see her jaw tick, but she stays silent. Of course, because why would she fight back against anything I just said? I scoff.

"You know, for years, I thought if I just did one more thing to make you or dad happy, that I would somehow earn your love. I'd somehow become deserving of it. But you know what?" I walk closer to her, keeping Leon behind me. "A child shouldn't have to earn their parents' love. It's meant to be unconditional." A sound from the corner of the room alerts me to my father standing there. He's still not speaking either. Cowards. "A parent's love is meant to be the purest thing in the world, but instead, for me, it's filled with venom and poison. It's filled with every ounce of self-doubt I've ever had. It's filled with a need to be perfect to those around me so they won't find a reason to leave me, and it's filled with the desire to push others to show me how they feel, so I don't spend my days panicking about being alone. About believing I have no one to turn to, believing that there isn't anyone who wants me in their lives." I think back to Stella, to what I did. "You two did that." I point at both my mother and father, anger radiating in my voice. I can feel my hand starting to shake. "And you know what's worst of all?" I turn back to look at Leon, whose eyes are starting to well up slightly. "You ruined us. You made me hate him for the love you gave, for the praise you gave to him, but never found it in you to give me." I take a step back away from them, suddenly disgusted to be in their presence. I see my father's mouth open, but I cut him off. "No, you don't get to defend yourself. Maybe five years ago you could have, but not today. This is the last time I will do anything for you. I want nothing to do with you – and if that means you take away my house, my tuition, the future of my bar, I don't care. I don't care what my life looks like from today forward, as long as it doesn't have you in it." I take a breath, inhaling all the air I missed when I was talking to them. The walls in the room start to feel smaller, closing in on me. I turn away from them and leave the room.

As I pass my brother, I touch his shoulder, "I'll do better by you from now on. I swear." He doesn't react, so I leave.

I don't blame him if it's too late for us.

There's a cool breeze from the ocean outside. It's a perfect evening for a party. I can see people falling out of bars along the street, laughing, drinking champagne out of the bottle. They pile into cars, refusing to take midnight at the end of the night. Confetti of different colours scatters the streets. The stars light up the night sky, fireworks popping left and right.

I guess it's the new year now.

I take a seat on the stairs leading up to the building, taking off my tie. It's dark green. I wanted to have a piece of her with me, even when she physically wasn't there. She noticed it. She always noticed me, in a way no one else ever has. I let my eyes close, wondering how things got so messed up.

"Do I need an invitation to join this party?" I hear from behind me. I turn around to see Leon looking down at me, holding his jacket. He shouldn't be here; he shouldn't be ruining what he has. I pat down the space next to me, not having the energy to fight anymore tonight.

"Do you remember Christmas, when you were 8 and I was 6? Mum and Dad had accidentally wrapped your Christmas present in my wrapping." I tilt my head to look at him, smiling at the memory of us as kids.

"Yeah, it was a Lego set I had been asking for for years. 5000 pieces." I truly went batshit crazy over Lego when I was younger.

"When I opened it, I was so excited, I felt like an adult. That I was finally old enough to build the big kid Lego." He shakes his head, laughing softly. "Then I looked over at you, because all I wanted to do was show you my Lego. And I saw your face and I knew that something was wrong, but you didn't let it show. One second, it seemed tears were pooling in your eyes, and the next you came over and were telling me how cool I was for being able to build the set."

I nod. I remember that day clearly. It wasn't an accident that they gave it to Leon. Before we left for Christmas break, I had gone with Dad to a work meeting. I got sick halfway through and had to throw up in a plastic bag in his office. And I was told that if I didn't shape up, they would take the Lego away. I cried and apologised, but it wasn't enough. There was a part of me that didn't think they would do it, but when I came down that morning and saw the tree, I knew they weren't bluffing. It was the last time I thought they were lying when they'd threaten me.

"You looked so happy, I wasn't going to take that away from you."

"That's the last memory I have of us being normal. Being the brothers I wanted us to be. Want us to be." I drop my head, playing with my sleeves. I don't know how to do this, but I have to try.

"I'm sorry, Leon." I choke out. "I hated you. Every time I was around you, all I saw was the love I'd never get. And it made me want to scream, so I left. I left and didn't look back because I knew they wouldn't do to you what they did to me. Not as long as you kept the way that you were going. But I know it's not your fault they loved you more.

They made me hate you, and I let them." I turn to face him. "I swear to you I will spend the rest of my life trying to be the brother you deserve, Leon." He lets out a puff, and I notice the tears that are falling down his cheek.

"I'm sorry too, Luke." He uses his sleeve to wipe a tear off his cheek. "Every time I saw you, I was reminded of the life you got to have, and I didn't. I saw you at Brookstone with friendships that looked like family, dreams that you came up with, and a life you chose. And I was jealous. Because I had spent my entire life doing what they wanted, because I thought it would make them happy, make me happy. I went to the school they wanted, did the degree dad did, and dated the girl mum approved. And with every praise they gave me, the worse I felt. Because nothing about who I pretend I am today is who I actually am. But that isn't your fault either." He turns to face me, so we are looking face to face. "And I'm sorry I didn't notice how they were treating you. I don't know if I saw it and blocked it out or what – but I didn't stand up for you. And I should have."

I reach my hand up and grab his shoulder, "Hey, now, that's the older sibling's job. You just get to sit there and be a damsel in distress." I say lightly, causing him to let out a laugh. His hand comes up and covers mine.

"I don't know where we go from here." He admits.

"I don't either. But." I stand up, putting my hand out to pull him up with me. I don't know if we'll ever be able to get back to how we were. "We'll figure it out. Together."

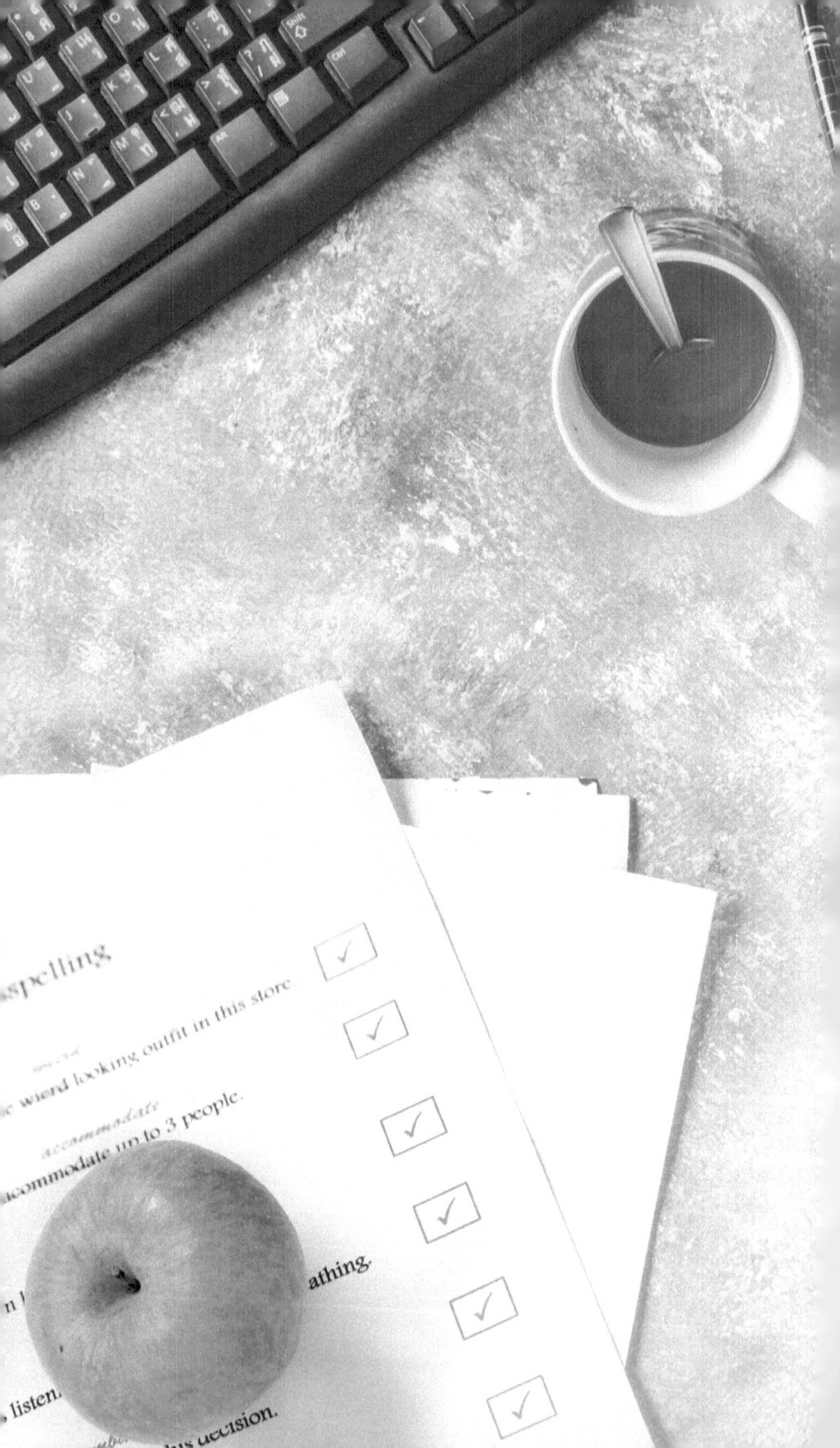
spelling
wierd looking outfit in this store.
accommodate
accommodate up to 3 people.
athing.
listen.
decision.

Chapter Forty-Nine

STELLA

THE SUNLIGHT STREAMS THROUGH THE CRACKS OF my curtains, creating pools of light on the wooden floor. On a normal day, this would have woken me up, but I've been up for hours. Honestly, I'm not sure I ever went to sleep. I sit up in my bed slightly, looking around the room. Mum has changed nothing from when I was in high school. I still have the same posters covering the walls and the extremely expired makeup pouring out of my dresser drawers. There are photos of my high school friends and my family sprawled around the room, cards from birthdays. So many memories of when I was happy.

Being in this room feels like a time capsule. Back to when I felt safe.

When I showed up last night, it was nearly one in the morning. I'm lucky that my mum's place is pretty close to Byron, so it wasn't hard to get here. I didn't know where else to go. Going back to Brookstone couldn't happen. Not when I didn't know where he was.

A buzz from my phone pulls me back to reality. I check it to see two messages come in from Keets.

> Keets: Hey, I just saw Luke on campus – where are you?

> Keets: He didn't look good.

He's back. Why did he come back? I guess to see Rory and Beck. I hate that he doesn't look good. I hate that I was the one to cause it. It's not fair. It's not fair that I had to hurt him. But he knew. He knew I couldn't give him more than what we had. It doesn't matter what I might have felt or what it could have been in another world. In this world, the one we are in, it couldn't happen.

I type out a quick response telling her I'm fine, but can't talk and swipe out of my messages. There was a part of me that thought I'd have something from Luke, but there's not a single message. Why would there be? I left him alone the one time he needed me. The whole reason he agreed to our stupid arrangement was for that weekend – and I just left. He probably hates me. Good, he should. It'll make it easier.

My phone chimes again, and I see a notification from the Photos app. Tapping on the notification, I'm taken to a slideshow. 'Memories from Byron' it's called. There are photos of the beach, of me in beautiful dresses, and it finally stops on a photo of Luke and me. Right before the New Year's Eve party.

I was trying to take a photo of my dress, and he came up behind me. His hands wrapped around my waist, and he dipped his head into my neck. I remember him whispering how beautiful I looked, even though he had already told me ten times that night. My smile was small, but it lit up my face. I haven't seen myself that happy in a long time. I forgot this photo existed – immediately after I took it, he grabbed my phone and threw it on the bed before kissing me.

How was that yesterday?

I'm about to turn my phone off, but it starts ringing. Rory. I immediately answer, knowing that even though I can't talk to Luke. This is pretty damn close.

"Stella?" He says the second I pick up, his voice is laced with concern.

"Hi." My voice comes out barely a whisper, rough from crying. He doesn't respond, taking a deep breath instead. I shouldn't have picked up on the fact that he's upset with me. I just left his best friend at the moment he needed me most. If someone did that to Keets, I would kill them. With zero hesitation.

"Are you okay?" He finally says. What? When I don't respond, he pushes. "Stella, I need to know if you are okay."

Finally taking a breath, I respond, "No, I hate myself for what I did to him. I miss him, and it's only been a few days. I don't know how I'm meant to do this."

"I know. You take it day by day. You need to figure out what is best for you. As much as I know this is killing him, I also know that you need time." It's hard to hide the look of shock that's taking over my face. I knew we had gotten closer – but this. I don't think I'll ever be able to tell him what this means to me.

We are both silent for a minute, while I work up the courage to ask him what I really want to know.

"Is he okay?" I can practically see the face Rory would make at this moment, the softness that would take over his features. Trying to soften the inevitable blow.

"He loves you, Stella, and he lost you. But he will be,

especially if he knows you are." I nod, tears starting to pool in my eyes. "Also, Stella?"

"Mhm?"

"We all love you, and it hurts to see you in pain. You're one of my best friends, Stel. I'm here for you, too."

I smile softly before hanging up, throwing my phone back on my bed.

I can still see the look on his face when I asked him to stop. Begged him to stop. The way his eyes softened, how his voice cracked when he said my name. I couldn't even let him say the words before I ran. I wanted to believe what he was saying, but everything about the words falling out of his mouth screamed danger.

I know it's not fair, it's not fair for me to run because of him. That's not Luke. Luke is kind and patient and has made me feel things that I've never felt before. Luke says he loves me now, but what happens when that changes? What happens when he realises that I'm not good enough for him, when the love fades, and he's left with just me?

What happens when that love turns to hatred?

It's not like I feel the same way that he does. I can't. Love isn't something I can feel anymore, not purely at least. I love Keets, I love my parents. But this type of love – I can't. When I'm with him, the world stops. Nothing else matters except him and me. And he makes me feel safer than any other person in this world has. But loving him would mean giving him pieces of myself that I don't know, pieces that aren't healed. Loving him is like handing him a weapon and praying he doesn't use it against me.

I can't give him that power. I can't lose it again.

Luke

"You don't have to go in there if you don't want to," Leon says as we pull up outside our place. I can see Rory and Beck's car in the driveway. They were both meant to be with their families this week, not home. I don't know how to tell them what happened.

"I know, it's fine – I want to see them. I just don't know how to." I close my eyes slowly, taking a breath. "I don't want to be too much for them, I don't want them to leave." I can't break down in front of them like this.

"They are your friends, Luke. No, I'm sorry, that's wrong, they are your family. Those two guys see you as their brother." There's a hint of sadness on his face as he speaks, but he doesn't stop. "They love you unconditionally. I love you unconditionally. Stop hiding." He turns back towards the house, hiding his face. I can't remember the last time he told me he loved me.

I know he's right. I need to stop thinking I'm some heavyweight to everyone who knows me. There is not a single world where I wouldn't stand by those guys.

Where I wouldn't stand by Leon.

I deserve that too.

"I love you too," I say quietly, smiling slightly when his shoulders relax.

"Plus, I'm sure they know," Leon says, Shrugging and walking forward. How would they know? My face scrunches in confusion as I follow behind Leon, who lets himself in.

He's staying; he didn't even need to ask.

I walk in and see Rory and Beck sitting on the island stools. They both get up as they see me, their faces covered with sadness. I don't want them to be sad; I know they were friends with her. I wonder if they think I'm going to make them stop talking to her. I would never do that.

"Hey, guys." Rory goes to open his mouth, but I hold my hand out. I need to say this now, or I won't be able to.

"Just listen, okay. Stella and I broke up after I told her I loved her. She wasn't ready." They both shift slightly but stay quiet. "After, I cut my parents off, because instead of being a mother, my mum wanted to leave me broken and crying. She's been like this basically my entire life, my dad too. And I've been scared to tell you because I've always felt hard to love. Maybe it's because of them, I don't know." I take a breath, trying to fight the tears that are starting to form. Leon holds my shoulder from behind. "I was scared to say anything because I really didn't want to give you guys any reason to leave me." My head drops slightly, my lips quivering. I feel pathetic.

Beck is the first one to move, walking over and pulling me into a hug. His hands wrap around my shoulders, and he holds me tight. Tears start to form in my eyes in shock; he's never hugged me like this before. I wrap my arms around his waist and let myself fall into him.

"You are not a burden, Luke. We are here for you, idiot." Beck whispers as he holds me. A sob escapes my mouth, and I let myself fall apart.

A few hours later, I'm lying down on the couch. We didn't talk more about what happened in the kitchen, because I couldn't. But for the first time in a really long time, I wasn't scared they were going to run. Every time I cried, every time I couldn't keep it together – they were there. They didn't move, they didn't seem like they were angry.

They were just there.

I let myself settle more into our couch, too tired to move upstairs. The early morning light is flooding in through the glass doors, lighting up the room. The sky looked like a painting – orange and pink streaks were covering every corner. Stella would love it. Beck fell asleep about an hour ago, curled up on the chair next to me, snoring slightly. Leon is sitting on the bean bag right below my head, silently watching the show on the TV. Rory's on the other end of the couch, turning his head to check on me every few minutes.

My eyelids are heavy, and every part of me wants to sleep. But I don't want to miss something from her, and I don't want to see what my head has in store once I give in to it. I try to set myself up higher, but am stopped by Rory's soft voice.

"Go to sleep, Luke, we've got you." Leon holds up my phone, showing me he's got it. If she calls, they'll wake me up. "Let us look after you for a change." I nod softly and settle back down, pulling the blanket over my head.

I feel myself drift off quickly, but right before sleep takes me, I swear I hear Rory say, "Thank you for calling us, Leon."

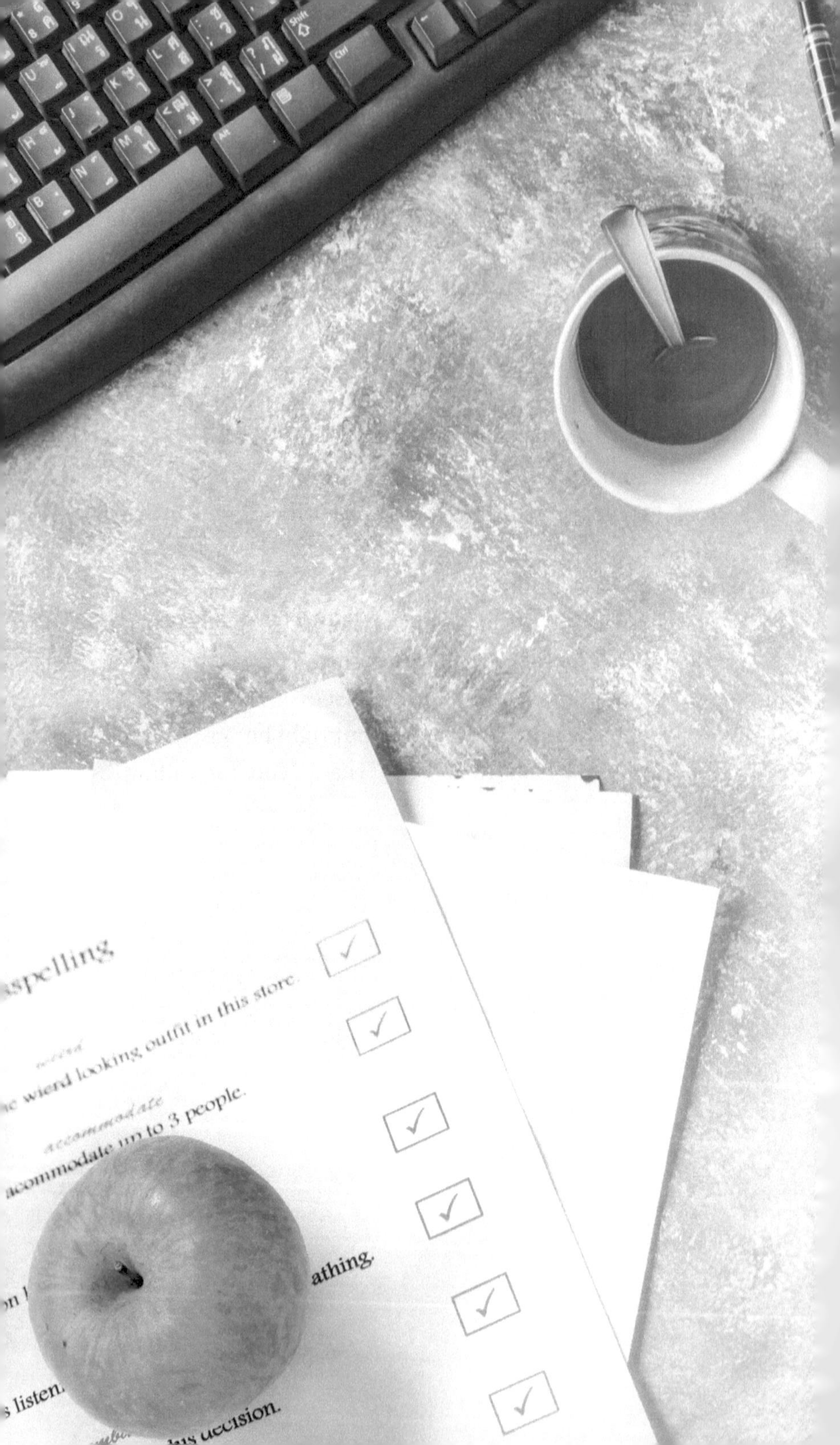
spelling
weird
e wierd looking outfit in this store.
accommodate
acommodate up to 3 people.
athing.
s listen.
decision.

Chapter Fifty

STELLA

THE APARTMENT IS DEAD QUIET AS I WALK IN. I CAN smell the faint scent of coffee floating through the air as I drop my bag in the entryway. For a second I think I'm home alone, but that thought disappears as I see Keets sitting on the couch, waiting for me.

"Hey." I say tiredly, "I'm just gonna head to bed for a bit." I start walking towards my room, wanting to hide for a bit longer.

"No." Keets says, stopping me in my tracks. "Sit down. We need to talk, Stel." Her voice is serious. She sounds almost angry. She should be. I've been a dick for disappearing these past few days, I can't do that to her again.

I sit down on the couch across from her. Her gaze lingers on me and the silence is heavy. I adjusted how I was sitting, fidgeting with the sleeve of my shirt.

"I'm sorry, Keets. I didn't mean to just disappear. I just didn't know how to come back." My voice waivers, hoping for some kind of reaction. She doesn't move, staring at me. I can't seem to utter the words that Luke and I broke up. That would mean I would have to explain everything between us – I can't do that while she's angry. I lift my head up from the low hung position it was in when she doesn't respond.

She's so quiet.

The silence stretches until it feels unbearable. Just when I'm about to get up, she moves. She stands up and walks towards me, sitting down right next to where I am. I feel her arms wrap around me as she pulls me in. It feels warm and steady, she feels safe. For the first time in days I let myself lean into someone, grateful for the silent support she's giving me.

"Stella." She says, her voice soft, as she pulls back slightly. "What happened?"

I take a deep breath, knowing that I need to tell her. Even if it kills me. "Umm." I chew on my lip, trying to stop myself from starting to cry again. "Luke and I broke up."

I see her facial expression change slightly in realisation, and almost understanding. "Oh, Stella. I am so sorry."

I shake my head, sniffling. "No, it's okay. I was the one that ended it." I muster up the best smile I can. It's not like that's a lie. I was the one who walked away. Her brow furrows slightly, clearly seeing through everything I'm saying.

"Okay, what happened exactly?"

"He told me he loved me and I wasn't ready to love him back. We agreed it wouldn't get that serious and he broke that agreement. It's simple." I can barely get the words out. I shrug my shoulders and start to stand up. I need to get away from this – I can't pretend with her right now. Not anymore.

"Stella Faraday, sit your ass down right now." She spoke

steadily, each word lacing with conviction. I sit back down. "What do you mean it isn't serious? You guys were dating, he was your boyfriend. That's pretty damn serious."

I shake my head. She doesn't understand. Of course she doesn't, she thinks we were actually together.

"Stella?" She asks, "I'm sure if you two just talk you can work it out. He doesn't seem like the person to just give up. Especially if he love-"

"Stop Keets! We weren't actually together!" I scream, tired of hearing that fucking word. There's no point in hiding it anymore. Keets just stares at me, her expression unchanging. "It wasn't real. None of it was real. Okay?"

"Of course it was." Jesus Christ is she not hearing me.

"Keets it wasn't. Listen to me. We were fake dating okay? I was worried about stressing you out and he had shit with his family so, we thought faking it would help us figure out our shit okay? It was fake from the beginning." I stop talking, expecting her face to change. For shock to take over. For her to yell at me for lying to her. Anything to show that she's understanding what I'm saying.

"Yeah, Stella, no shit. But just because you were faking it at first, doesn't mean it didn't become real."

"What?" I manage to ask, though my confusion is obvious.

"I'm your best friend Stella. You haven't dated anyone in years, and then all of a sudden this random guy you've never mentioned before changes your very dead set mind like a week after I tell you my concern? I knew you were faking it, but I also knew that you were doing it for me. So I wasn't about to say anything. And then the more time you spent with him the happier you seemed. I just didn't realise you were so unaware of how you felt."

I stand up, backing away from the couch slightly. "What is that supposed to mean?"

She tilts her head back, rolling her eyes in frustration. "Stella, I'm sorry, but clearly you need someone to wake you up. You love Luke, you've loved Luke for a really long time. But you are so fucked up from that dickhead that you can't seem to let yourself love."

My jaw clicks, "don't talk about him."

"That's what I mean Stella. You can't even say his name. And I get it, trust me. Everyday I wake up wanting to kill Parker for what he did to you. But even more, I wake up terrified of the day you finally piece it all together and I have no idea how you'll react. It's been two years and you haven't even begun to process what happened to you. And I've sat here and stayed silent while you've ignored it. While you've done everything to pretend like it didn't happen. But I refuse to do that anymore. Not when you are about to lose the best fucking thing that's happened to you."

"Keets stop it." I snap.

"Luke is the best thing to happen to you Stella. I have never seen you this out of your shell, this excited. And you are messing it up."

"You don't have a right to say this to me." I say, pointing my finger at her. My hand shakes as I feel anger flush through my body.

"Maybe I don't." She says simply, her voice no longer raised. "But I'm going to say it anyway. And I don't care if you kick me out and never speak to me again because someone needs to say this to you. How do you feel when you are around Luke?" I stay silent, not wanting to respond. Or acknowledge the warmth that spreads through my body at hearing his name. "Stella. Answer my question."

"I feel happy okay?" I cry out, my voice cracking with frustration. "I feel like everything that's wrong in the world is right. Like there is some quiet unspoken silence and peace in the chaos. I look forward to the simplest things now, mundane stuff I used to overlook. To cleaning my room, to studying for class, to washing dishes, all because I know he's there with me. Whenever I'm with him that tiny voice in my head telling me I'm broken goes dead. It goes silent. Is that what you want to fucking hear Keets? That I love him? I know I do – I'm not stupid. But that doesn't change the fact that I can't be with him. Every single bone in my body is aching to be back with him, but my limbs won't move. No matter how much I plead, my head won't shut up. So it's great that you've spent the last two years waiting for the other shoe to drop, but try living in my head for ten fucking seconds. Try feeling the disgust I feel everytime I see myself in the mirror knowing Parker touched me, try feeling the complete terror I feel when thinking about letting myself fall again. You wouldn't last a day. And honestly, I barely do." I sigh heavily, falling silent, my chest rising and dropping with effort. I can't keep trying to convince myself I don't feel the way I do for him. It won't change anything, but I'm so tired trying to shove it down. Trying to keep it in that box where I keep every other hard part about myself.

"I'm sorry Stella. You're right, I have no idea what you are going through. And I know you've tried and I know you are just trying to get through each day. But don't you want to get to a point where you aren't living day by day – but for your life?" She looks up at me questioning.

I stay silent, not sure how to respond. She reaches up

and takes my hand pulling me back down to the couch. I let her, exhausted from fighting.

"Stella, it's okay to admit that you are different because of what he did to you. It doesn't make you weak. It doesn't mean he still has power over you. No one should have to go through that, but you did."

Tears start to fall down my cheek slowly.

"I don't know how to get better." I whisper, my voice quivering as I speak. "How to stop being scared of what I could have with Luke. How to stop being scared of the fact that I'm..." I take a deep breath, my voice dropping lower. "In love with him." Tears stream down my face, faster now. I can't stop it. The floodgate has been opened and I don't know if I can ever close it again.

"It's okay." Keets pulls me back into her as I cry on her shoulders. Sobs falling out of me. My throat feels tight, like I'm choking. Each sob is me gasping for breath. "We'll figure it out. I'm here for you. Always." She holds me, unwavering, a silent promise in her arms as I finally let myself fall apart.

Chapter Fifty-One

LUKE

Goldie: ARE YOU FREE TO TALK TODAY?

My heart hasn't stopped racing since I received that message this morning. I don't think I've responded to a single message faster than I responded to Stella's. That message was the first thing I've heard from her in two weeks.

Two weeks without her.

I wish I could say I'm doing better, but I'm not. Sure, I've gotten back into my routine, but I'm not okay. Beck and Leon have been coming with me to the gym every single morning – sometimes dragging me out of bed. Rory's been helping me plan out my next year. I had to pick up a lot of extra shifts to cover the rent that my parents stopped paying for. Cutting them off has set a pretty big dent in the Hidden Alibi, but I don't care. Even though my heart is more broken than I thought possible, I also have never felt freer. And that feeling has nothing to do with Stella and everything to do with the fact that I don't have the crippling weight of my parents' expectations weighing me down anymore.

The only bright spot in these two weeks, aside from the freedom from my parents, has been Leon.

He has been here every single day.

I honestly don't know how he has been able to swing it with school and with Camilla, but he won't answer me when I ask. He always tells me it doesn't matter and he's not going anywhere. At first, he'd ask if he could stay the night each day, but now he just does. There's a silent agreement with everyone in the house that until I'm okay, he's there.

I've never felt the type of support those three are giving me right now, and I don't think there are words that can even begin to explain how grateful I am for them. There have still been moments where I've been scared that one day they will wake up and realise this is all too much – but that day hasn't come. And they each keep telling me it won't.

I think slowly, but surely, I'm starting to believe that.

They have also been stopping me from going to Stella. I can't count the number of times I've wanted to text her, call her, show up at her apartment, and beg for her to talk to me. But I haven't. It took a while, but I realised I had to let her process on her own. I'm the type of person who needs the immediate conversation, the constant communication when there's a fight – but that's not her. She needs space, she needs time. Right now, it doesn't matter what I need. It's her.

So when I got that text this morning, I immediately texted Rory, cancelling our lunch date, and showed up to the diner two hours too early, just in case she did too. The fact that she chose the place where this whole thing started makes me feel better. It makes me think she's still thinking about us.

The sound of the bell causes my head to snap up, and I see her. She's wearing denim shorts and an oversized t-shirt with the collar cut off. The shirt is for some sort of sports team, but I know her well enough to know that's one from her books. It almost makes me laugh thinking about how many of her casual clothes are probably merchandise for fictional worlds. Her hair is tied up in a ponytail.

She looks breathtaking.

She spots me immediately and slides in across from me. She looks down at the iced chocolate sitting in front of her and deeply swallows. Should I not have done that?

Maybe that was too far.

I want to open my mouth and apologize for pushing it now like I did on New Year's Eve, but she speaks first.

"Hi, Lucas."

Every anxious feeling leaves my body the second I hear her call me Lucas. She has a shy smile on her face, like she's not sure how to do this either. I let out the smile that I've been holding back since I saw her standing in the doorway.

"Hi Goldie." She smiles a little wider, looking at me. I can see the gears turning in her head as she thinks of what to say. I don't jump in like I desperately want to; I let her think.

"How have you been?" My eyebrows raise involuntarily when she speaks. How am I meant to answer that?

"Honestly?"

She nods.

"Not good." Her mouth falls open slightly, but she closes it. I don't know what the right thing to say now is. "You?" I throw it out lightly.

"Bad." She laughs dryly. "I did officially swap to a

teaching degree, though." A small smile grows on her face as her eyes search mine.

"Stella. Oh my god, congratulations." I say with genuine pride, there is no doubt in my mind that that was the right choice. I want to say more, but she cuts me off. "I'm sorry, Luke," she says sincerely. I'm shocked when she says that, because honestly, I didn't think she had anything to apologise for. I fucked up, I pushed her. I go to tell her that, but she cuts me off. "Let me finish. I'm sorry for running out, for not explaining what was going on. You deserve more than that. You deserve everything, Lucas, and I'm sorry I couldn't give that to you." She chews her lips, wavering slightly.

"Thank you for saying that," I say, unsure of how else to accept her apology. "I'm sorry too." I see her open her mouth, but now it's my turn to cut her off. "Stella, listen to me. You made it clear from the beginning that you didn't do relationships. Then you made it clear you wanted what was going on between us to be casual. I pushed you when I told you how I felt on New Year's Eve. It wasn't the right place to tell you how I felt, and it wasn't the right way." I drop my head slightly, "I have a hard time believing that people care for me in the way they might say they do. I'm trying to get better, but it doesn't excuse it. So if you're sorry, then I am too." I lift my head in time to see her nodding, unable to argue with me. I continue speaking, spewing out the words that have been running through my head since the moment she ran away from me. "I understand if you don't want this to continue. I'm not going to force you to feel things for me that you don't. But I want to say I'm okay with slowing down if that's what you need. Doing this again with no expectations." I look up at her. I had been staring at the table as I said that.

She's shaking her head, her eyebrows furrowed in disbelief.

I guess she doesn't want to try.

"Or we can just go back to being friends. That's also okay." I need to get out of here. I can't go through this right now. Not here. I go to stand up, but her hand grabs mine, holding me in place.

"Luke, if you think I don't feel the same way you do, then you don't know me as well as I thought you did." My heart stops as she speaks. She loves me.

She loves me.

She actually loves me back. I sit back down, confused.

"If you feel the same way, I don't understand then."

"I know. I promise I'm going to explain everything to you." She starts fidgeting with her sleeve; she's anxious. There's a part of me that wants to go over to her side and pull her into my arms. Tell her I don't need to know and that I can keep on going how we were. But I can't. I need to hear what she's about to say.

"I need you to hear me out, okay. I need you to listen right now, because every part of me is screaming to run. To leave this diner and never come back, but I'm trying to be better. Promise me you'll listen."

I nod, staying silent like she asked.

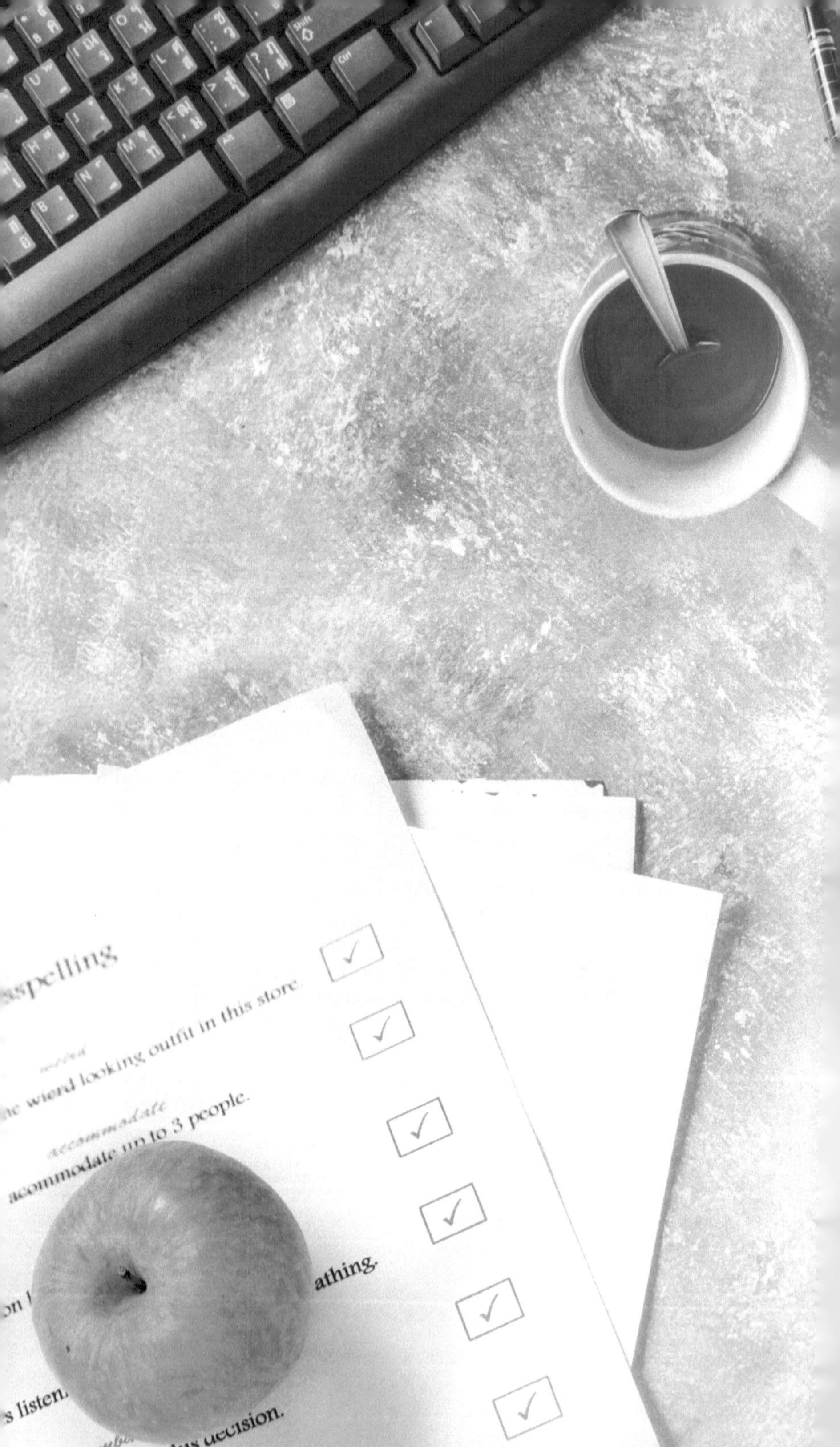
spelling
he wierd looking outfit in this store
accommodate
acommodate up to 3 people
athing
s listen.
us decision.

Chapter Fifty-Two

STELLA

HE NODS IN FRONT OF ME, BARELY MOVING. I TRY to remember what I was meant to say to him. Just before this, I was with my new therapist, talking through how I was going to have this conversation with him.

I take a deep breath, pulling out a piece of paper from my pocket. I had written down everything I wanted to say. I didn't think I could do this without it.

"I know I've always made it clear that I can't do relationships, that I don't do serious. Everyone who knows me knows that. But I've never told you why. Only one person really knows why, and that's Keets. And honestly, the only reason she knows is because she was there when it was happening. She saw it. I never had to tell her."

His gaze is heavy; I can feel his eyes on me like weights. I keep going. "I know you probably figured out my last relationship wasn't good. You saw what happened when I saw him again." My voice waivers, and I stop for a second. Counting down from ten in my head. I can tell he wants to do something to help; it's who he is. It's one of the things I love most about him. But I also know he's going to respect what I asked of him, even if it kills him to do so. "He's the reason I can't be who you need me to be, Luke. Because of what he did. And I promised I'd explain everything to you, and I will. I just need you to promise that when I finish, you won't look at me with pity, you won't judge me. I will still be the same person."

He nods, smiling softly, giving me reassurance that he can't say.

So I start speaking.

The first time I ever laid eyes on him, I think a part of me knew he would change me in some way. I don't know how to explain the feeling, but it just felt like he would always be a part of me and who I would become. I just didn't think it would be in the way it was.

I think the only reason I genuinely felt an attraction to him was because of how carefree and open he was. It caught me off guard completely; it was different from every other person I had encountered. He walked into class and sat at the table with two new girls and didn't think twice about starting a conversation. He was so open, telling us about his life and joking with me about the books we read. I was so scared of starting university, but he made me feel comfortable at school after only being there for two hours.

I messaged him that night after the first day, saying I'd never met someone so social before. He responded immediately. We messaged back and forth for basically that entire night, and by morning, I knew I was long gone. We had more in common than I thought I had with anyone else in my life, and he made me laugh, and I made him laugh.

I had started my friendship with Keets and I remember at lunch that day mentioning his name and being told to stay away from him. That they didn't know him, but they heard things, and that he wasn't the type of person you wanted in your life. I should have listened, I should have un-added him, stopped sitting with him in math, and moved on, but I didn't. I didn't think it was fair to hold him accountable for something people I had just met thought, or to not give a second chance for a mistake he may have made in the past.

I was always a big advocate for second chances.

I don't think I am anymore.

We texted more, we sent videos, we joked, we flirted. For the first time, I was genuinely developing a crush that I wanted to go somewhere with. When he asked me out, I didn't tell anyone – not thinking they would understand.

The day rolled around for the date, and I was a nervous wreck. I was terrified. I had had crushes before and been on dates, but this felt different. It was more official in a way, I guess? I spent two hours in the morning picking out the perfect outfit, painting the perfect face on, and curling my hair just right. I felt beautiful. My friends asked me where I was going after class, and I finally told them. They said that if I saw a different side of him, I should trust my gut.

So I did.

I was terrified that we would have nothing to talk about and that all the texting had just been a fluke, and in real life, we didn't work. But it was the complete opposite. The conversation flowed; it didn't stop. I don't remember exactly what happened after the date, but it was just good.

We went on more and more dates.

He seemed like the perfect guy who was sweeping me off my feet. He left notes in my bag telling me I was beautiful and joking about the show we were watching together, he called me love, and he made me feel safe.

Over the next month or two, everything seemed perfect. We were spending practically every free moment together, happy and blissful. I was settling into the school, making friends, and getting closer to my best friends. I missed home, but I was happy. For the first time in years, I felt like nothing was too much for me.

And then we hit our first roadblock. The first night he spent at my house was right at the beginning of April. He came over and we spent the evening eating food and talking. And then we went upstairs and started kissing. We moved to my bed and he kept kissing me, wanting more. I wasn't enjoying myself and tried getting out underneath him for a second, but he didn't really stop. I don't want to say he kept going when I explicitly said no this time, but I wasn't in a position where I was comfortable, and that feeling wasn't something I hid. I pushed him off and ran to the bathroom, because the idea of doing anything more than a peck made me physically ill. I told him I was overwhelmed with school and with people, but really, it was he who made me feel like that. I don't know why I didn't end it right there, but by the next day, I had forgotten all about it.

His birthday rolled around, and I was so excited. I planned the entire day, bought presents personalised to him. And wrote a long letter where, at the end, I told him I loved him. He said he loved me back.

I will never be able to describe the feeling of showing your love to someone and having that person take that love and give you back as much. To stand in front of the person you love and know that they love you back. I had never felt this type of emotion before, and I knew I was going to hold onto it with everything I had in me.

The next little bit is kind of blurry in my memory. It was just good.

It's crazy how quickly things can go from being good to not.

How something can seem so perfect and then be burned to ashes in the blink of an eye. A month after his birthday, we slept together for the first time. It was my first time, and he was nice.

He didn't make me feel unsafe, and at that moment, I thought it was perfect. Something shifted that night, though. He changed.

Our relationship went from being sweet and romantic to only being about sex. When he would see me, it was all he wanted. And at first, I was happy, I was excited about exploring this part of life that I hadn't before.

But then it started getting too much. I wanted to stop, but he didn't.

It didn't matter if I wanted it or not.

He was going to do what he wanted.

But every time he would, I would get a necklace or a love letter written in his neat handwriting. Sent to my door apologising for what he had done, and every time, I believed him.

I wanted to believe him.

I distinctly remember at university, once he texted me asking for a quickie in the bathroom. I told him no. He threatened to break up with me. The way he said it was cold, like he didn't care about me at all, only about getting his way. And for a moment, I was paralysed by the thought of losing him. It wasn't love anymore, but I couldn't see that at the time. I couldn't see how toxic it had become.

Let's just say, he wore me down.

I often felt that once he started something, it had to be finished because I didn't think I could stop him. And so I let him. I let him push me into saying yes, into giving in, even though I didn't want to. I couldn't find the words to stop it, and I didn't know how to make it end. I would let him wear me down to saying yes because I just didn't have the fight left in me.

It didn't even surprise me when he went all the way, but at this point, I didn't know how to get out.

I felt broken, I felt disgusting. Every time I would look at myself in the mirror, all I could see was him. All the things he did and the things he said. I didn't see the girl I used to be, the one who laughed freely or spoke her mind without fear. I only saw the aftermath of his touch, his words echoing in my head like a never-ending loop.

I hated myself.

I hated myself even more when I would finish with him.

When my body would betray my brain, that was screaming to fight. It moved in ways that made me feel like it had forgotten that I could say no.

He would tell me it was my fault. That I wasn't good enough, that a good girlfriend would give him what he wanted.

And the icing on the cake was how he would use the word love.

How he would tell me how much he loved me when he was inside of me, how he loved me when I would let him use me how he wanted, how he loved me every time I'd come to him apologising for something that wasn't my fault.

How it was all okay because this was love.

There was a lot going on socially at this time, and I was trying to balance everything. Be a good friend to Keets and Emily and Immy, be a good daughter to my parents, be a good girlfriend to Parker. It was hard.

He would get upset with me about this, and when we were apart, he would become mean. Making comments about me and, in general, that made me hurt. He would always apologise and say he didn't mean it, but I could start to feel like I was losing myself a little bit. Keets noticed it and asked if I was okay, but I didn't tell. I didn't tell anyone. I retreated into myself so much that I started to believe that he was the only one I had.

One night, right before our six-month anniversary, I went out with Keets. We got drunk, really drunk. The type of drunk where you have no filter, where there is nothing to stop things from coming out of your mouth. I told her everything he had done to me, every single time. I was crying to her on the floor of the club bathroom, unable to pretend I was okay with any of it anymore.

She later told me that she felt her heart crack hearing me, that she had never seen me that small before.

She asked me why I hadn't left, and I told her I didn't know. I think a part of me felt like if I didn't have him, I'd have no one. That even if he was hurting me and pulling me apart, at least he loved me. I had convinced myself he just had an off way of showing that love. She told me I had to break up with him. I said I was scared, but that I would. She hugged me.

He broke up with me a week before our six-month anniversary, the night after I went out with Keets. He was saying he had fallen out of love, that he wanted a fresh start. I didn't even get to break up with him; I was too shattered to do anything.

After that, I made it my mission to never put myself in that position again. Never let myself be manipulated and worn down like he did to me. I built myself back up, refusing to talk to anyone about what happened. I made Keets swear that she would never bring it up to me ever again, and I avoided every place I knew he would go to.

Just like that, I had erased the first 6 months of my university experience like it was nothing. I started enjoying casual sex, enjoying the power it gave me.

It shut up the voice in my head that kept saying all the things Parker said to me.

I was okay.

Well, I was okay enough.

Chapter Fifty-Three

LUKE

ONCE SHE FINISHES TALKING, SHE LOOKS UP AT ME. While she was talking, she'd cry at times, but wouldn't move to wipe away the tears. It was like she couldn't even bear the thought of touching her own face, as if she couldn't stand the evidence of her own pain. Every part of me would ache to move to hold her, but I held tight. I listened and watched as she broke apart, telling me everything he did to her.

I feel anger radiating through my body, like hot burning coals searing every part of my inside. I wanted to kill him for what he did to her, for the way he made her see herself.

These past few months, I've gotten to know Stella, I've seen her cry, I've seen her laugh, and I've seen her strength. I've seen every part of her – the real her, the woman who is so much more than she knows, who has been hidden away for too long. And there is not a single part of me that can comprehend why someone would want to break that. Why would someone want to take every part of her apart, piece by piece, and leave her with nothing but doubt and shame?

I want to reach inside of her and take away all the pain. To erase every moment of fear and hurt she'd felt, to give her that freedom. But I couldn't. I had to sit here helpless, feeling my heart shatter for her, thinking about what she's endured.

But looking at the woman in front of me, the one who is stronger than I've ever known, the one who has built herself up and found herself again, I also feel pride. Pride over the fact that despite it all, she still is the beautiful woman I fell in love with, the fact that she wakes up every day and lives her life the best she can.

That's fucking impressive.

I sit up, wiping the tears that have fallen past my eyeline. She is sitting there, not speaking. The expression on her face was a storm of emotions I couldn't quite place. I don't know if she can either.

I take a deep breath, wanting to think before I speak.

"You are so strong, Stella." Her head picks up slightly, a flash of shock passing her face. The fact that she's surprised that I said that cracks my heart more. "You have to know that. You aren't disgusting, you aren't weak, you aren't stupid – you are strong. You are strong for getting through that and coming out the other end." She starts to cry silently, again not acknowledging the tears. I'm not sure even she knows they are there. I reach out and cover her hand that's resting on the table. Being close to her is what I want, but I'm unsure if being in her space will offer any comfort right now. Looking at her, I feel helpless, unsure of how to help. "Every second you are alive, every minute you fight, you are proving to him that he doesn't own you. That you are so much more than he could even comprehend. Don't think for a second that he defines who you are, Stella."

She nods, staring directly into my eyes. As if she's searching for a hint of a lie in my words. When I look at her, every moment of the last few months clicks into place. Why was she so against anything serious? Why did she run when she heard the word love.

I hear her take a deep breath, closing her eyes for a second. "I want you, Luke. I know that, there's no doubt in my mind about it." I smile at her, happy to hear those words. But I can feel anticipation of what's coming. "But I can't be with you. Not in the way you need me to be."

"Stella, I don't need anything from you. I need you to be okay."

"I know. And what I need to be okay is to focus on myself. To get help, to actually get better." She forces the words out, her voice quivering with each one. The tears I am trying to hold back start falling, knowing that this was the end. "I've been seeing a therapist, and she's been helping. A lot. But I'm not naive enough to think I'm going to get better in a week. I know it'll take time, and I need to do this. I need to give it the time it needs. It's not fair for me to drag you down with this."

"You haven't dragged me down, Stel," I say, my voice barely above a whisper. She reaches her hand out, grabbing mine.

"Luke, I have, but more importantly, I've dragged myself down. Staying with you, hurting you like how I have, is a disservice to both of us, and I can't do it anymore." She squeezed my hands, hesitating before speaking again. "I don't expect you to wait for me. Honestly, I don't want you to. I want you to live your life and find someone who can love you the way you deserve to be loved." She sniffles, finally wiping her tears. She's smiling at me, trying to reassure me that it's okay.

"I'll wait for you, Stella." She tries to speak, but I cut her off by standing up. I pull her with me, tilting her head up to look at me like I've done time and time again. "I would wait my entire life if it meant spending my last minute on this earth with you, Goldie. You take as much time as you need, and when you are ready, I will still feel the same. You are worth it." I brush a piece of hair out of her face, smiling softly. "I'm not that easy to scare off," I say, mimicking what she told me just weeks ago in Byron. She laughs through her sniffles, smiling up at me.

She looks beautiful; she always looks beautiful.

"I hope one day I can tell you about the love I feel for you, Lucas."

"I can't wait, Goldie," I say. She stands on the tips of her toes, lifting her lips to mine. She kisses me slowly, searching, savouring every moment. I can feel her tremble slightly in my arms, as if she were scared to let go. I deepened the kiss, my thumb brushing against her jaw, memorising the curve of her face. Hoping she can feel the unvoiced promise in my kiss.

She pulls back, her face contorts with emotion. Mine probably looks the same. I close my eyes and lower my head, resting it gently against hers, my hands enveloping hers in a quiet, steady hold.

"I need you to walk away, Stella. I can't leave. Not when I know you aren't leaving with me."

I feel her head nod slowly, before she lets go of my hand. She says nothing as she walks out of the restaurant, leaving me there.

I watch her go, knowing I'd wait for her forever if I had to, but something about this moment – her silence, the distance growing between us – feels like a goodbye, a closing chapter I never thought would come.

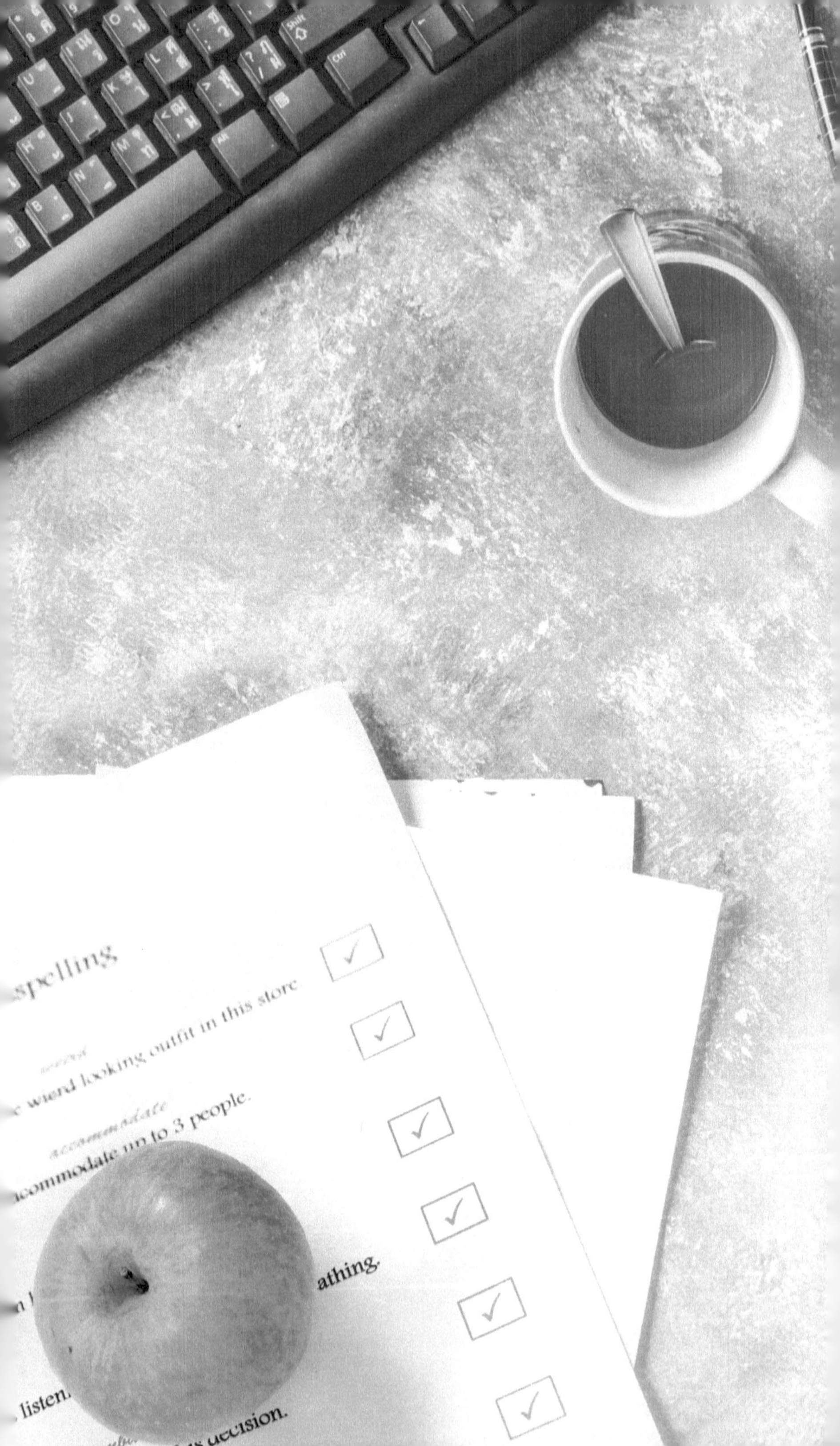
spelling
e wierd looking outfit in this store
accommodate
ccommodate up to 3 people.
athing.
listen.
decision.

Chapter Fifty-Four

STELLA

6 MONTHS LATER

I LIKE DR. BENNET'S OFFICE. IT DOESN'T FEEL LIKE you are talking to a therapist. There's no red leather couch to lie down on, the walls aren't covered with motivational posters, and the bookshelves aren't filled with psychology textbooks. Instead, all of her furniture is some variation of pastel colours. She has plants on every windowsill, funky clocks, and posters on the walls. The bookshelves are filled with books that look normal, but if you look closer, the titles are insane. Other than the books, Dr. Bennet loves knick-knacks – collecting really eclectic vintage decorations. I think it also helps that she's in her 30s, so I don't feel like I'm talking to someone who wouldn't understand.

I can't quite explain it, but I feel safe here.

Keets found her the day after I came back from my mum's. She called around and somehow got me an appointment that day – without a referral. I'm not entirely sure how she made that work, but I am forever grateful that she did.

Keets has been so insanely supportive these last few months. She sits and listens after every appointment, and squeals with me every time I make a step in the right direction. She's had a tough last month or so, but she never let up. Our friendship has become stronger than it was before, both leaning on each other in a way we didn't fully before.

I've been seeing Dr. Bennet for nearly six months now, and I've never felt this okay in my life. I'm able to talk about what happened to me without breaking down. I no longer see Parker in the mirror every time I look at myself. I feel like my brain has finally understood that what Parker showed me wasn't love. The word no longer scares me like it used to.

I also started journaling again. When Parker and I were together, I loved it, but as things started getting worse between the two of us, my journal started getting dark. Eventually, I avoided writing in it because I couldn't even bring myself to be honest there. Once we broke up, I threw it out – not wanting to be reminded of anything from back then.

"So, how are you feeling today, Stella?" Dr Bennet asks, pulling me out of my thoughts. She's wearing a baby blue blazer that reminds me of Rory's hair. I haven't seen him as much these last few months as I would have wanted to. I just needed to disappear from everything for a bit.

"Really good, actually." I frown for a second, trying to search for something else to say, but nothing comes to mind. I didn't have an awesome week last week, but since then, nothing has happened. "Yeah. I mean, just good. Literally nothing bad has happened this week."

Dr. Bennet smiles, "That's really good news, Stella. I'm remarkably proud of you."

A blush creeps on my cheek, a feeling of pride filling my core. Validation from your therapist is the best form of validation. I take a deep breath, ready to ask her a question I was talking with Keets about last night.

"Do you think I'm ready to reduce the number of sessions I'm having?" She closes her notebook, smiling as she sits up.

"Yes, Stella, I do. I think the progress you've made is tremendous. I don't think we need to continue the weekly sessions. Not anymore."

There's a part of me that wonders if I'm meant to be sad when she says that. I've been seeing her once a week for two hours every single week. She knows the deepest parts of me. But when those words come out of her mouth, all I feel is excitement. Excitement that not only do I feel okay, but someone else has noticed the work I've put in.

The progress I've made.

"I think a session every two weeks is still a good idea, just for now." I nod, agreeing, I'm not 100% yet. "But I want you to know two things. The first being, if you ever need me, I'm always here. You can call me for extra sessions whenever you need to. It's okay if you go through a rough patch and need to move backwards a little bit." I smiled, nodding again. We talked a lot about how healing wasn't linear. "And second, I am so proud of you and your accomplishments. I know I already said it, but I need to reiterate it. You have been through more than anyone your age should have to and have come out on the other end one of the strongest people I know."

I have to fight the tears that are brimming in my eyes. "Thank you, Dr. Bennet."

"Of course." She says, beaming with happiness, "If you have nothing else to talk about, then we might as well end early today."

I nod, standing up. She walks over towards me and gives me a quick hug. Hugging her back, all I can think about is how happy I am at this moment.

"I'll see you in two weeks, Stella."

I grab my bag and walk out the door, letting her know I'll be there. As I step outside, the air is crisp, the cold nipping at my skin. The warm weather went nearly as fast as it came, but I don't mind it.

When I walk home from Dr. Bennet's office, I always deviate slightly to walk past the Black Lantern. It adds an extra five minutes to my walk, but I can't seem to stop myself from doing it. I haven't spoken to him since we said goodbye in that diner. It's what I needed, and I stand by the decision. But I couldn't just never see him, not after he had been a constant in my life for the entirety of last semester.

Each time I'd walk past, I would let my gaze scan the room – trying to see if he was there. He never was. I guess that's what happens when you walk past a bar in the daytime.

For the first few months of seeing Dr. Bennet, I'd always ask her when she thought I'd be ready to be with someone again. To be with Luke. Every time she said that wasn't a question she could answer, the only one who would know that is me. I never understood what she meant, because how was I meant to know – I thought it was her job. She said there would be a moment where the thought of us being together, the thought of loving him, didn't just feel like a dream – but something that I wanted. After some time, I stopped asking and stopped bringing him up. Not because I didn't want to, but because I knew that I needed to do this for myself. He promised he'd wait for me, but I needed to know that if he didn't, I'd still be okay.

Just when I'm about to turn onto the road that leads me to the black lantern, my name echoes in a scream.

"Stella!" I whip my head around quickly, recognising the voice immediately. Parker stands across the road, staring at me. Clearly waiting for me to walk over.

I know Dr. Bennet would probably tell me to ignore him, to walk the other way. That being the bigger person is the best revenge.

But fuck that.

For the first time since he touched me, I'm not scared to be around him. I'm not anxious. All I feel is rage.

A smile grazes my face as I see him shift on his feet. He clearly notices that the small scared girl he was expecting to talk to isn't here anymore.

"Hello, Parker. Did you need something?" I say, smiling sweetly once I reach him, but there is nothing sweet about the way I'm looking at him. His eyes dart around my face, clearly looking for a trace of something he can cling to. He finds nothing.

"We never got to talk after your dickhead of a boyfriend kicked me out of his house."

I nod, "true. What was it you wanted to say?" His brows furrowed a bit, but he started talking – apparently trusting the front I'm putting up.

"I still love you, Stella." My eyebrows raise involuntarily. That's not what I thought he'd say. "I know we had our ups and downs, baby, but you know we are meant to be together. Don't you remember the fun we had?" He steps towards me, his hand reaching out to my waist. I step backwards just in time, causing him to slip slightly. A small giggle escapes me at seeing him fall. His attitude shifts immediately as he sees my face, clearly realising I'm not going to fall for his shit again.

"You think that's funny? What's funny is that you thought I'd ever take someone like you back. Someone who's used property like you."

I feel the anxiety start to rise slightly, but I push it down by breathing. There is nothing he can say that will take me back to who I was. Taking a step forward, I get close to him. Holding my ground, even as he doesn't move back.

"You know what I think, Parker," I say, my words as sharp as a dagger. "I think that you are a pathetic excuse of a man. I think that every day you walk on this planet is a complete and utter waste. I think that you hurt other people because you are trying to cover up the fact that you are just an insecure little boy who can barely get it up." I see his jaw clench, but I don't stop. Stepping forward more. "You are the worst of the worst, Parker. And for so long, I let you dictate my life, let you have a voice in every single thing I did. But you know what – I'm done. I'm done giving someone as disgusting as you a single second in my head. If you disappeared off the earth tomorrow, there is not a single person who would come looking for you." He steps back slightly, faltering.

"And you know what, even though every part of me hates you, I just feel sorry for you. Sorry that you will never experience love or kindness because all you have is poison running through your veins. I am better off without, and I cannot wait to live my life, never seeing you again." I step back, running my hands through my hair. My heart is running a million miles per hour. I want to say more, but I know I should just leave it. Just as I turn around, I'm cut off by him opening his mouth.

"You are never going to find anyone better than me, Stella. You don't fucking deserve anything."

Rage takes over my brain, and I don't think as I turn around and punch him straight in the face. He falls back a little bit, his hand coming up to clutch his very bleeding nose. Before he gets a chance to say anything else, I turn back around and start walking away.

"Have a shitty life, Parker." I throw over my shoulders before I practically run home, shaking the entire time.

"KEETS," I shout the second I fling the door open. My heart hasn't stopped racing this entire time.

"Stella?" She questions jumping up immediately. She was sitting on the couch, probably didn't need to scream as loud as I did.

"Are you okay?' I'm pacing around, unable to stay still.

"I just ran into Parker." Her face pales. "No, it was so good. I yelled at him, Keets. I told him he was pathetic and that I was done wasting any time thinking about him anymore."

The smile that graces Keets' face looks like it went up to her ears. "Fuck yeah, Stella." She says, putting her hand up for a high five. I high-five her, but don't stop.

"That's not even the best part." I take a deep breath, having to calm myself down to tell her. "I punched him. Right in the face." She stays silent for a second, and then screams, running up to me and hugging me.

I laugh, and she picks me up, spinning me around.

She puts me down, and I stumble slightly.

"Oh my god, Stella. The amount of money I would have paid to be there at that moment."

I smile at her, "It was incredible. I've never felt so alive. I want to run and jump, and I want..." And it hits me. I need to see Luke, I missed walking past the bar today because I was so wired I went the normal way home. All I can think about is seeing him. I'm ready. That moment Dr. Bennet was talking about, it's now. I know. "I want to see Luke."

A small smile flashes across Keets' face, "Go Stella. Go find him." She starts ushering me towards the door.

"Okay, okay." My pulse was still pounding, frantic and out of control. Just as I open the door, I turn back towards her. I can see tears welling in her eyes. Leaving the door, I run back and give her a hug.

"I love you, Keets. Thank you for everything."

She gives me a squeeze back and whispers in my ear, "I'm so proud of you. Go get him."

Letting go, I start running and I don't stop. For some reason, I went to the Black Lantern, not to his apartment. My body was telling me to go there. On the run over, I couldn't stop thinking about what I'd say when I finally saw him, what he'd look like. If his hair was the same. If he still loved me.

Even though I was scared, I didn't stop running. I had to see him.

The second I reach the door of the bar, I push it, relief flooding me when it opens. Running inside, my gaze trails the entire bar. Looking for a single sign of him.

But I can't see anything. He's not here. I let myself catch my breath, my heart sinking into my chest slightly. Maybe it isn't time to see him again, maybe this is the universe's way of telling me I'm not ready or something.

I brush my hair over my shoulder and open the door to walk out, feeling defeated. Just as I was about to turn and leave it all behind, I hear it – a sharp clang, the sound of bottles hitting each other, shattering the silence of the moment. My body reacts before my mind can even process it, spinning around on instinct.

And there he is.

It feels like time stops when I see him, everything disappearing except me and him. His eyes meet mine, and my heart stops. Not from shock, but from the relief of seeing him again. Of seeing those beautiful eyes.

He looks the same as the boy I knew 6 months ago. His hair is a bit shorter, but it still has that messy look that I love. The smile that spreads on my face is uncontrollable. I take a step forward towards him, wanting to close the space.

"Hi." Is all that comes out of my mouth.

Chapter Fifty-Five

LUKE

STELLA IS STANDING IN FRONT OF ME. SHE'S NOT A figment of my imagination, not some other girl who looks like her. It's Stella.

My Stella.

She looks beautiful, almost stronger. There's a new aura surrounding her, one of confidence. Her hair is down and loose with little braids scattered throughout it. She's wearing jeans and a dark green sweater. It's still my favourite colour.

"Hi." She says, her voice quiet. The smile on her face lights up the street. I drop the bottles, not giving a single shit about them anymore, and run up to her. She runs, meeting me in the middle as I pick her up, holding her in an embrace. I know I should wait for her to tell me why she's here, but I can't. She giggles as I swing her around, and I want to bottle it up and keep it forever. Keep hearing that noise for the rest of my life.

Setting her back down, I look down at her, my hands

finding the curve of her jaw. Still disbelieving that after 6 months, she's in front of me.

"Hi Goldie." She blushes, her hands reaching up to cup mine. I see tears start to swell in her eyes, mimicking the ones I can already feel falling.

"Hi, Lucas." She says again, making me laugh. She has absolutely no idea what to say.

She's nervous again.

Cute.

I tilt my head, looking at her closely, taking in the features I didn't notice before. My brows furrow as I see her right hand; it's bruised.

All excitement disappears, replaced with anxiety as I run my thumb over her knuckles.

"Why are they bruised?" I ask, concern lacing my voice.

She smiles shyly, "I punched Parker 20 minutes ago." Pride fills my chest hearing that she finally gave that fucker what he deserved.

"Atta Girl," I say, letting her hand drop. Every part of me is aching to kiss her, to hold her tight and never let her go again, but I don't. I still don't know why she was here. Not for certain.

"Stella, why were you just inside the bar?" I ask, having seen her walk out five minutes ago.

She takes a deep breath, closing her eyes, before settling on mine. "Because I came here to tell you I love you, Luke." There are no words to describe what happened inside of me when she said that. My heart stopped, my stomach dropped, and I couldn't believe that she said it. The tears are free-falling now, and I'm unable to stop them.

"What?" My voice is small, quiet, shrouded in disbelief.

"I love you, Luke. I love everything you are and everything you make me. There is not a single part of you that isn't perfect for me. These last six months have been some of the hardest of my life, but I would go through it again just to make my way back to you." She moves forward, stepping up on the balls of her feet, cupping my cheeks. "I used to think love was a tool that was used – a means to manipulate. That love, the type of love I feel for you, only existed to control someone, to cover hurt and anger. But you have taught me it's everything but that. It's every small moment that happens in between the lines. It's knowing each other's favourite foods and getting them without telling the other person, it's knowing what the other person is thinking without needing to speak a single word, it's knowing with complete and utter confidence that the other person is your lifeline, and without them, you aren't complete. I know that I can live on my own, I know I can survive. But I don't want to. Not when you make everything feel better."

My smile grows bigger. "Say it again," I say quietly, needing to hear it one more time.

"I love you, Luke, I love you so much. And I want to be with you, for real. And I'm sorry that I hurt you and that it took so long-" I cut her off, leaning down and kissing her. No more apologies. I kiss her deeply, trying to make up for the time we missed. She kisses me back, her hands threading through my hair, pulling me closer, deeper, as though she's trying to fuse herself into me. Time stops. There's no past, no future – just the feel of her lips against mine, the heat of her touch, the undeniable certainty that I need her in ways I never thought possible.

When she finally pulls away, her breath mingling with mine, I can't let her go. I can't. I hold her there, my hands firm around her, unwilling to release the one thing that makes everything else in the world fade to nothing.

I look into her eyes, searching for the words to encapsulate how I feel in this moment, but for the first time, words fail me. There is nothing I can say. All I do is keep holding her. She is my every breath, my every reason for living. And I am never losing her again.

Not even with my dying breath.

Epilogue

LUKE

10 YEARS LATER

"JACK, I WON'T ASK AGAIN, DOWNSTAIRS NOW!" Stella yells, standing at the bottom of the stairs. Our three-year-old son, Jack, comes stumbling down, enjoying his newfound ability to run. Something Stella and I sincerely regret letting him learn.

"Sorry, Mumma." He shouts, running straight past her out into the back yard where everyone else is. I walk up to her, pulling her into my arms.

"I love him so much, but I think he's aged me by ten years." I laugh, looking down at her. She's being ridiculous; she looks just as beautiful as the day I met her.

"Yeah, I think that might be the Astor genes. Sorry, Goldie." She scowls at me. "Hey." I point at her face, "Don't want those aging lines, right?" She smacks me, but laughs as she does so. I lean down to give her a kiss, but I'm interrupted by the screaming child outside.

"DADDD!"

I pull back from Stella, grabbing her hand, "The princess is calling."

We walk outside into our garden where Lily is sitting with Beck, Leon, and Rory – all intently listening to her speak. As soon as she hears Stel and me, she runs up and jumps into my arms. She's Jack's twin, and they are pretty much polar opposites. Where Jack is active and quiet, Lily is calm but strong. I guess that's how some twins turn out.

"How are you, pumpkin?" I ask, running my hands over her curls. She's got her mother's hair.

"Uncle Leon and Beck want to take me to Movie World over the summer. Please say they can, please please please." I look up at Beck and Leon, who are standing there with their hands in their pockets, making matching puppy dog eyes to my daughter. I sigh, placing her down, knowing that even if I wanted to, there was no getting out of this one. But honestly, there's no saying no to her.

"Yes, you can go. But only if Uncle Rory is coming with you, I don't trust you alone with those two."

Leon gasps. "What, us?"

"Yeah, that's insanely rude, especially considering the fact that you still owe me 100 dollars."

"100 dollars?" Rory asks from where he is standing with Jack.

"Yeah, don't you remember. The bet that Luke wouldn't fall in love with Stella?"

Stella's face drops, and she turns towards me, "You made a bet that we wouldn't fall in love?" She grabs her chest, "How could you?"

"I'm sorry, Goldie, it was before I realised what a smokeshow you were." Lily makes a gagging noise in front of me, causing Stella to laugh.

"Gross, daddy."

"Sorry, baby." I look up at Beck. "I will pay you $100 right now to leave and never come back."

He tilts his head, acting like he's thinking about it for a bit. "Yeah, no, I'm good right here."

Lily nods before clearing her throat, pulling my attention back to her. "Uncle Rory is coming too. And Jack, of course."

"Well, that sounds perfect." I give her a kiss on the head before she runs to join her brother, who's talking to Rory in the corner.

"I'm late, I know, I know. There were too many people at the store today," Keets says, walking out into the garden, holding bags of groceries. Okay, we are off."

"Auntie Keets!" Both of our kids scream, running to give her a hug, slightly knocking her off balance.

"Hey, kiddos." She turns to Stella. "You and I need to talk about the new episode of 'Too Hot to Handle' that just came out."

"Oh my god, yes, Luke refuses to listen to me talk about it anymore." She turns back towards me, smirking, knowing damn well my entire night was spent listening to her talk about just that. I'll never quite understand how that show is still on, and how Stella, even after a full day of teaching, still finds time to watch every single episode.

"Well, no shit, that's what I'm here for. Best friend over husbands any day." She grabs my wife's hand, dragging her over towards the table, Lily following quickly behind them. I can hear Stella's laughs float through the air, light and unfiltered, pulling an even bigger smile from me. She's fully immersed in our life – working hard, doing what she loves, and being true to herself and everything she has fought through. I have never been prouder of a single person in my entire life. Watching her become exactly who she was always meant to be – it undoes me in the best way.

Grabbing a beer, I turn back to face Rory, Leon, and Beck, who are now standing with Jack, intently conversing about something. I see Beck bend over, throwing Jack over his shoulder and running straight for the pool, as Leon and Rory laugh, watching them. Hearing my kids laughing, seeing them so free, so safe – it warms my heart in more ways than I can say. Seeing them get the family that I didn't have growing up, seeing them surrounded by love, by these five people who would do absolutely anything for them, makes me feel like I did something right. Like maybe this messy, loud, beautiful home we've built is proof that healing is possible. That home isn't a place, but it's the people, it's a feeling. One that's all around me.

"The kids are both in the car on the verge of passing out. We'll bring them around lunch tomorrow." Keets grabs the last of the kids' things, heading towards the door. I see Reginald resting under her arms, despite it technically being Stella's; the kids have become obsessed. Neither of them goes anywhere without him. "Enjoy the time alone." Her eyebrows waggle as she turns back to wink at me.

"Thanks, guys," I say, smiling at them as all of them filter out of the house, the sun setting behind them. Stella and I haven't had an anniversary alone since the kids were born. They all decided that for our ten years we deserved some time alone, so Keets and Rory are taking the kids for the night, and Beck is looking after the Hidden Alibi.

"Remember the condom, Lucas. Unless you want a third

one of those running around." I flip him off as he walks out laughing.

A third kid does not sound bad at all. I love those kids to bits, and more Stella in my life is a good thing.

The second the door slams shut, I walk up to Stella, kissing her on the forehead.

"Happy tenth anniversary, Goldie." She looks up at me, a playful glint in her eyes, and her lips curl into that smile – the smile that has stolen my heart for a decade

"Happy tenth anniversary, Lucas." Even after all these years, I still feel that pull in my heart when I look at her. The same rush of excitement I felt the first time I laid eyes on her. Every single day, I wake up grateful that I get to wake up next to her. There has never been a part of me that wasn't wholly in love and obsessed with this girl.

"So." Drawing the word out teasingly, mischief dancing in her eyes. "Nap time?" She asks, her tone light and playful.

I can't help but let out a dry laugh – half from amusement, half from the way she always knows how to push my buttons. "Ha ha, funny."

"Oh, right, my bad, we should probably do some work, right? I know I have lesson plans up the wazoo, and I'm sure you have some planning to do for the bar, no?"

Without saying a single word in response, I roll my eyes and scoop her up, throwing her over my shoulders. She yelps in surprise and starts hitting my back in protest, but I don't let go.

"Lucas, let me go right now!" She squeals, her voice muffled slightly by my back as she keeps hitting me. Despite her actions, I can hear the laughter in her voice.

"Don't you remember Stella?" I say, bringing her down, so I'm holding her in front of me. Her chest heaves up and down with each breath she takes. "I'm never letting you go again."

I see her facial expression soften, the way she takes in every word I say to her. She smiles again, a smile that covers her face, one that I can't look away from.

"Good." She whispers, her voice low but filled with the love I know she has for me. "Because neither am I."

Authors Note

Each character and story I write has a part of me or people I love in it. Stella's story throughout this book holds personal significance to me, and similar to her, I made it out. To every person out there who was treated how Parker treated Stella, and to every person whose first love was ruined by a dickhead – never forget your strength. Never feel ashamed for what they did to you. You are strong, you are brave, you are loved.

You will be okay.

For people who need to talk to someone for support (Australia):

Beyond Blue Counsellors
1300 22 4636

1800RESPECT
1800 737 732

Acknowledgements

I honestly don't even know where to begin. The fact that I wrote a book still hasn't quite hit me, so writing this feels somewhat like a haze. This is going to be a long one and I can say with 100% certainty that I could not have done this without all the people I am going to mention.

Not to sound full of myself, starting this off with me, but I want to thank myself. Thank you for pushing through the imposter syndrome and the fear, thank you for writing this story even when it was hard for you to do. I am so grateful you did.

To my family, your endless support and cheering will never go unnoticed by me. The only reason I believed I could do this was because of you raising me and teaching me to chase my dreams. Even when they seem unreachable. There is not a single day I don't wake up grateful that I get to call you my mum, dad, and brother.

To my beta readers – this book would not be where it is today without you. Your advice and feedback on this book are what shaped it to be the book it is today. I genuinely believe people aren't aware enough of how much teamwork goes into writing a book. I may have written it, but each of you shaped it into being a book that I love and that I hope readers love, too.

To my best friends, Himara, Serina, and Fatima, people

without whom this book would not be where it is today. I will never know how to say thank you for everything you did for me these past few months. Spending time listening to my anxieties, helping me write, reading endless drafts, and listening to my character rants. I promise there is an endless amount of gratitude and love for each and every one of you. And trust me, if it doesn't take the pages, I would thank all of you individually one more time in the book, but I'll have to settle for in person and over numerous texts and calls.

To every single incredible person who read this book and enjoyed Stella and Luke's story, or followed my TikTok, or just listened to me rant about where I was in the story. Thank you forever and ever.

To my editors, Tori and Meredith, and to Ellie at LoveNotesPR thank you for your endless expertise and for answering every single question under the sun, none of it went unnoticed.

Thank you to Meera and Melina for your in-depth feedback on my book. And thank you to Lara for your endless support on my TikTok and hyping me up – even when I wanted nothing more to do than to quit. I love you guys so much.

To my friends I made at university after this book was written, thank you for every ounce of support you gave me from day one. Releasing this book made me terrified but each and every one of you supported me and helped me keep going and for that I won't ever be able to repay.

Finally, I have to give a special thank you to my best friend, Mireia. Without you, this book would not even exist. The first scene was written because you told me I should do it, and the rest of the story continued because you encouraged me and supported me every step of the way. I get to live my dream because of you. I love you like Chewie loves Han.